Honor's Paradox

BAEN BOOKS by P.C. HODGELL

CHRONICLES OF THE KENCYRATH

The God Stalker Chronicles
(omnibus containing *God Stalk*
and *Dark of the Moon*)

Seeker's Bane
(omnibus containing *Seeker's Mask*
and *To Ride a Rathorn*)

Bound in Blood

Honor's Paradox

Honor's Paradox

P.C. Hodgell

HONOR'S PARADOX

This is a work of fiction. All the characters and events portrayed in this book are fictional, and any resemblance to real people or incidents is purely coincidental.

A Baen Books Original

Baen Publishing Enterprises
P.O. Box 1403
Riverdale, NY 10471
www.baen.com

ISBN 13: 978-1-4516-3762-5

Cover art by Clyde Caldwell

Maps by P.C. Hodgell

First Baen printing, December 2011

Distributed by Simon & Schuster
1230 Avenue of the Americas
New York, NY 10020

Library of Congress Cataloging-in-Publication Data

Hodgell, P. C. (Patricia C.)
   Honor's paradox / P.C. Hodgell.
      p. cm.
   ISBN 978-1-4516-3762-5 (trade pb)
   I. Title.
   PS3558.O3424H66 2011
   813'.54—dc23

                                        2011036884

10 9 8 7 6 5 4 3 2 1

Pages by Joy Freeman (www.pagesbyjoy.com)
Printed in the United States of America

I would like to thank all the fine folk
who have responded to my LiveJournal entries at
http://tagmeth.livejournal.com with everything
from literary criticism to encouragement
to information on parasitical fish.

A special thanks to those who have given me
permission to use their poetry in the current work:

Tiel Aisha Ansari—"Massacre at Gothregor"
Cindy Duckert—"Shwupp"
Ry Herman—"What the Dead Know"
Paul Howat—"Ashe's Limerick"
Paula Lieberman—"The Three Lordan"
Scott Life—"The Highlord Calls"

CONTENTS

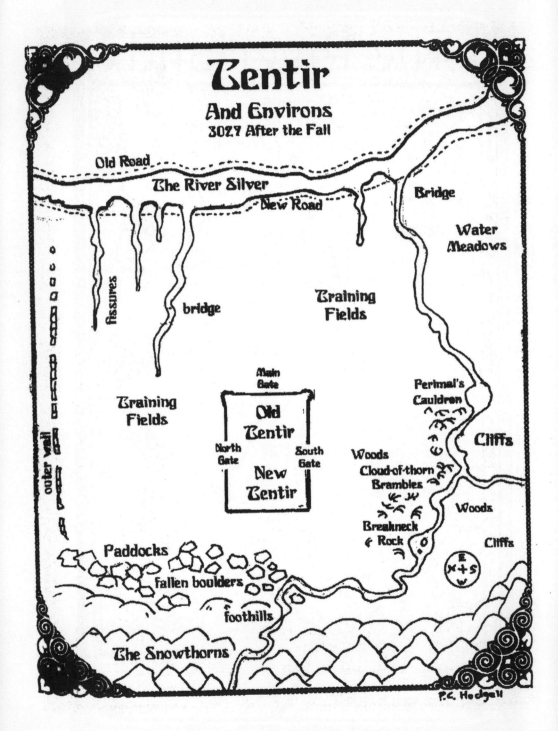

CHAPTER I
Songs in the Night

Winter 64

I

"GERRIDON HIGHLORD, MASTER OF KNORTH, *a proud man was he. The Three People held he in his hand—Arrin-ken, Highborn, and Kendar—by right of birth and might.*"

The Tentir cadets listened intently as the haunt singer Ashe limped back and forth before the great hall's fireplace. Flames outlined her black-robed form. A hood overshadowed her face, but they caught glimpses of its haggard lines as she turned. She chanted hoarsely rather than sang and accompanied herself with a small lyre on which she struck chords apparently at random.

The song itself was as old as the Fall, three thousand years ago. Some believed every word of it. Others thought that the Singers' cherished prerogative of the Lawful Lie had played a role in its composition or at least in its transformation over the millennia. So much had been lost in the flight to this world, Rathillien, that much of the past had become garbled. So, at least, many claimed, the Caineron loudest of all.

"*Wealth and power had he, and knowledge deeper than the Sea of Stars.*"

This too was old news: so had their lords. The self-styled Highborn had ruled over the lowly Kendar almost without restraint since the withdrawal of the catlike Arrin-ken who had served as their judges and mediators. Some lords were good, others . . . demanding. "The gentle brush of our lord's whim," as another old song put it; "The crack of his displeasure."

1

"But he feared death."

Eyes jerked up at a discordant note and a sudden squawk from Higbert. The tip of Ashe's little finger had broken off as she struck her lyre and had flipped into the Caineron's mug of cider. He threw both vessel and contents aside, perhaps by accident into the lap of Gorbel, his lord's heir. Gorbel retrieved the partial digit and returned it to the singer without comment.

"My thanks, Lordan," said Ashe, pocketing it. "I will sew it back on later."

The cadets watched this transfer intently, reminded, as if any need be, that the haunt singer was herself neither alive nor quite dead.

As would-be randon, death was to become a way of life for them, both their own and that of anyone under their command. Would they be strong enough to make such mortal decisions? An honorable death bought freedom—from their lords' dominion, from their hated Three-Faced God who had set them such an impossible task as to stop the Shadows' spread down the Chain of Creation. Singer Ashe must be very strong not to have chosen the oblivion that she had earned from her wounds taken even before the battle at the Cataracts. As for the Master, the mere fear of death was no excuse for anything.

Ashe cleared her throat, spat out a loose tooth, and continued.

"'Dread lord,' he said to the Shadow that Crawls, even to Perimal Darkling, ancient of enemies, 'my god regards me not. If I serve thee, wilt thou preserve me, even to the end of time?' Night bowed over him. Words they spoke."

At the far end of the hall, the outer door ground open a crack. Through it squeezed an ice-crusted figure accompanied by whips of freezing snow and blades of wind. The cadets huddled closer together. Some glared. Others looked wide-eyed with surprise. Who traveled so late at night, in such weather?

Rue of the Knorth jumped up and went quickly to help the new arrival shed her outer garments. The hood slid back from black hair intricately braided and from silver-gray eyes set in a thin face pinched with the cold. Beneath the coat, the newcomer wore a cadet's jacket, fur-lined boots, and heavy mittens. These last she stripped off to reveal black gloves.

"Lady, what are you doing here?" Rue demanded over her armload of winter gear. "You should still be snug with your lord brother at Gothregor."

The other laughed wryly. "Tori and I are seldom 'snug.' Anyway, you know that I have to ride north tomorrow to be with the Merikit on the solstice."

Rue made an unhappy sound. None of her people welcomed their lady's bond with the wild hill folk nor understood it. Wasn't it enough that the Highlord's sister was a cadet here at the college where no Highborn girl had ever been before? Why did she have to complicate matters with heathen connections?

She patted Rue on the shoulder. "Never mind. I'm here now and so, I see, is most of the student body. Didn't anyone go home during the break after the Winter War?"

"A few. The weather kept most of us here. Ashe was benighted on her way south to Falkirr and the Commandant asked her to sing for us. But come to the fire, lady. God's claws, you're all but fringed in icicles."

Across the room, the Ardeth Lordan Timmon smiled at her and Gorbel grunted something that might have been a welcome.

"*Then went my lord Gerridon to his sister and consort, the priestess Jamethiel Dream-weaver, and said, 'Dance out the souls of the faithful that darkness may enter in.' And she danced.*

"Greetings, my lady." Ashe broke off to incline her head to the young woman known as Jameth, who bowed in return and settled down among her ten-command.

Pretty Mint hurried to bring her a mug of warm cider which she cupped in chilled, gloved hands. Dar said something that made Quill laugh and the new cadet, Damson, glower. Erim, Killy, and Niall bobbed their heads. Leaning against the wall, wooden faced Brier Iron-thorn gave her a brief nod.

"*Two-thirds of the People fell that night, Highborn and Kendar. 'Rise up, Highlord of the Kencyrath,' said the Arrin-ken to Glendar. 'Your brother has forfeited all. Flee, man, flee, and we will follow.' And so he fled, Cloak, Knife and Book abandoning, into the new world. Barriers he raised, and his people consecrated them. 'A watch we will keep,' they said, 'and our honor someday avenge. Alas for the greed of a man and the deceit of a woman, that we should come to this!'*"

The last words fell like the blow of an axe on dead flesh, not quite sundering it from the living present.

The cadets clapped, as if to draw some warmth back into their hands. As old as the song was, it still struck cold. Moreover, there sat Glendar's heir, the Knorth Lordan, last (save her brother) of that ancient, fabulously pure bloodline. It was enough to give pause even to those who believed in the Lawful Lie.

"The Master I understand—somewhat," Rue said, "but nothing else in the old songs explains the Dream-weaver. How could she do something so wicked?"

Jameth moved as if to comment, but bit back whatever she had been about to say.

"You just heard the story," said Killy. "She followed her lord's command."

"And so became entangled in Honor's Paradox," added Quill, so named because his parents had wanted him to become a scrollsman. "Where does one's honor lie, in following orders or in oneself?"

No one answered, although many stirred uneasily. Honor might have held the Kencyrath together since its creation, but in these latter days it had become a complicated thing as some lords pushed hard to bend it to their own use.

"Sing something funny!" called a voice from the safety of the crowd.

Straight-faced, the singer responded:

> "There was a young randon named Ashe
> Renowned for her battlefield dash
> Struck down only once
> By some Central Land runt
> She limped evermore with panache."

This drew genuine cheers which the singer acknowledged, but then she struck a chord and continued with barely a pause.

> "Ganth Gray Lord, Gerraint's heir
> Grim he went riding from Gothregor.
> High in the White Hills harm awaited
> The hard-handed lord and the host he summoned.
> Trace now the tangled cause of this trouble:
> If I tell this tale, tears will follow."

The hall quieted. If the Master had been the first to fall, this was the prologue to the second cataclysm, triggered by the massacre of the Knorth ladies by Bashtiri shadow assassins. No one knew who had sent them, but they had surely come and slain all but the child Tieri whom Aerulan had hidden. Ganth's misplaced revenge had led to his exile and, seemingly, to the end of the Knorth highlords. However, first Torisen and then his sister Jameth had appeared to reestablish the line. As the song ended, some cadets glanced uncertainly at the latter. Her father might well have been Ganth, but no one could name her mother, nor had she been willing to do so. The lords made more of that than the Kendar did. The latter, more practical, dealt with what they found, and the Highlord's sister had so far proven to be a formidable if unnervingly unpredictable young woman.

Ashe sang again, this time about the second, more recent battle in those infamous hills, some thirty years after Ganth's fall:

> "The White Hills have drunk my blood,
> Red, red, the flowers
> Oh, when will I breathe free again?
> Red, the flowers, red.
> My face is pale, my hands are cold.
> Red, red the flowers.
> My day is done, my night has come.
> Red, the flowers, red."

The ballad continued, shading into "The Cataracts," both told from the viewpoint of the dead and the dying. In the first battle, Ashe had been savaged by a haunt and had let the wound go untreated. During the second, she had fought at Harn Grip-hard's back although she had been three days dead at the time.

The Knorth cadet Niall began to shiver. He had slipped away from Gothregor and had seen that latter dread battlefield when the Kencyr Host had clashed with the Waster Horde, led by darkling changers in rebellion against the Master himself. Some nights, he still woke screaming.

Ashe changed the theme once again:

> "Came the Highborn to Tentir
> Randon training beckoned,
> Came the Highborn to Tentir
> Three lordan to the Keep."

The cadets' eyes darted from Timmon to Gorbel to Jameth—Ardeth, Caineron, and Knorth. To have even one lord's heir at the college was unusual; three, unheard of, much more so in that one of them was the Highlord's newfound sister.

> "Long long away,
>   No Knorth Heir neither Highlord
>   Abandoned by the Arrin-ken
>   And our God silent so long
>   Long long away
>   In the White Hills where is our honor?
>   Now three lordan enter Tentir
>   And we fear that all shall change."

Ashe finished and turned to Jameth. "Lordan, will you add a coda to my song?"

Jameth hesitated, looking blank. Clearly, nothing came to mind. Then, as if despite herself, she began softly to sing:

> "Lully lully lullaby.
>   Dream of meadows, free of flies,
>   Dream of friends who never lie,
>   And of love that never dies.
>   But all life must end in sighs,
>   So lully lully lullaby.

> "Lully lully lullaby.
>   Remember that all men do lie,
>   If not in words, then deeds belie
>   And they will hunt you till you die
>   And then your mouth will fill with flies,
>   So lully lully lullaby."

The last note faded into plaintive silence. Some cadets clapped but hesitantly, as if not quite sure what to do with their hands.

"Well," said the Commandant, detaching himself from the opposite wall, sardonic hawk face and white scarf of office moving into the firelight. "I think that's enough for one night. To bed, children, and pleasant dreams to you all."

II

SOME TIME LATER, Jame paced her quarters. Rue had stoked the fire under the bronze basin until the apartment was warm enough for shirt-sleeves and light danced on the brightly mura-led walls. These chambers had belonged to her uncle Greshan's servants, and a darker, more dismal suite of rooms would have been hard to imagine. Truly, her cadets had worked hard to make them appealing to their eccentric mistress, although she still missed the airy freedom of the attic above.

Why, oh why had she sung them the Whinno-hir Bel-tairi's sad little song? Now she couldn't get it out of her mind:

Lully, lully, lullaby.
Dream of meadows, free of flies...

Her bones ached and her head still buzzed with the day-long winter silence through which she had ridden. Even traveling by the folds in the land, Tentir was a long way from Gothregor, and nightfall a long time since morning. Before dawn she must journey on if she hoped to make the northern hills in time. What she needed was a few hours of *dwar* sleep, but not yet.

She thought about Ashe's songs, which amounted to what most Kencyr knew about their history. How strange to hear her ances-tors' deeds described and to know that she lay in their direct line of descent. Not so long ago, she hadn't even known that she was Highborn, much less the Highlord's sister. After all, who would guess such a thing when he, her twin, was a good ten years older than she thanks to her time in Perimal Darkling?

That, Ancestors be praised, was something about which her fellow cadets knew nothing, much less that the Master himself was her uncle and the Dream-weaver her mother. Whatever the songs said, Gerridon had gotten some good out of his dire bargain in the form of prolonged life, at the cost of his followers' souls reaped for him by his sister-consort. What he hadn't gotten was her, Jame, whom he had bred to replace the faltering Dream-weaver. Thus, in the end, he might yet lose all.

The cadets didn't know her in many other ways as well, some for the better, some for the worse.

Oh, they had all heard those doggerel verses that Ashe could have sung but hadn't—one supposed, through good manners or good taste—about the Knorth Lordan's career as a randon cadet:

> Rider Jameth ne'er will be
> Until the land o'erwhelms the sea.

Or

> Swords are flying, better duck.
> Lady Jameth's run amuck.

Trinity, but she hated being called "Jameth." Whatever other secrets she kept, it irked that she couldn't tell them her true name. After her winter in the Women's Halls at Gothregor, she had sworn never to wear a mask again. Her old friend the Kendar Marc might well ask, "Is this confusion of names any different?" Wise Marc. How she missed him, but he had his own work repairing the stained glass windows at Gothregor that she had shattered.

Someone knocked softly on the door.

"Come in," Jame called, wondering if Rue had found another tiresome way to make her comfortable.

Ashe entered, closing the door behind her.

Jame fought an instinctive surge of revulsion. The scar on her arm where a haunt had once savaged her twinged, but at least she had found help soon enough to avoid becoming a haunt herself.

"Singer." Jame gave a jerky half salute. Before she had retired to Mount Alban, Ashe had been a senior, highly respected randon, and she had saved Harn's life at the Cataracts. "How may I serve you?"

The haunt singer shuffled forward, leaning on her staff. "With some information . . . if you please, lady." When not in performance, her voice roughened into a hoarse, halting thing, mere air pushed through dried cords by shriveled lungs. She drew a deep, whistling breath and declaimed:

> "The dead know only what concerns the dead
> And what concerns the dead is more than death

Unsettled crimes and unrequited passions
All matters left unfinished in their fashions
Are whispered among those who lack for breath.

"What I know, lady...is that fewer of us walk the Grayland...than we did a day ago. I would know...why."

The Gray Lands was the border between life and death where some Kencyr found themselves trapped if their remains were not given to the pyre. To Jame, from her glimpses of it, it looked much like the accursed Haunted Lands surrounding the keep where she and her brother had been born during their father's bitter exile.

"It came to my attention," she said carefully, circling the fire to keep it between herself and the haunt, "that those death banners woven from the blood-stained clothes of their subjects had snared their souls in the weave. Not all Knorth wished to remain so trapped. I offered them freedom."

"Oblivion, you mean...with a torch's flame."

"They chose to embrace it. I forced no one. By the way, if I might point out, you yourself stand in imminent danger of immolation."

"Ah." Ashe looked down at the hem of her robe, which was beginning to smolder where cinders from the fire had fallen on it. She paused to consider, then thumped out the sparks with the iron-shod foot of her staff. "Someday, perhaps...but not just yet. Life is still...too interesting."

Jame was suddenly enlightened. "You hope to see it through to the coming of the Tyr-ridan and the Master's second fall."

"If fall...he does. What singer willingly...leaves a song unfinished?"

"And I already know that you think I may become Nemesis, the Third Face of our God."

Ashe spread her hands. Several fingertips were missing. "Who else...is there?"

Indeed, there were only three pure-blooded Knorth left—herself, her brother, and their first cousin Kindrie, who had only recently discovered that he was legitimate. However, each had to recognize and accept his or her role for the Tyr-ridan to be complete. Torisen had no idea that he might become That-Which-Creates. Given how he felt about the Shanir, that was bound to come as a shock. Kindrie guessed that as a healer he was destined to become Argentiel, Preservation, and the thought horrified him. She was closest to fulfilling the position for which thirty millennia of her people's history had sought to prepare her, but—Ancestors, please!—not just yet.

She looked sharply at the singer. "You're here to try to talk me into staying away from the hills."

"Think . . . what you may someday mean to your people. Should you risk yourself . . . for such foolishness?"

"Ashe, last Summer's Eve you witnessed the Merikits' rites. You know that they deal with real power, however alien it is to us. And we need this world's good will in order to live here. I didn't choose to become the Earth Wife's Favorite, you know. It was literally thrust upon me. Now every time I miss a ritual, something goes wrong. Besides, didn't you once say that only a Kencyr can kill a Tyr-ridan?"

"So an old song claims. But at present . . . you are only *a* nemesis . . . not the definite article."

"So I should be wrapped in cotton until fate decides? Ashe, I can't live that way. There's too much to do."

Ashe sighed. "Can you at least . . . try to use . . . a little common sense?"

Jame smiled, her thin lips tugged further awry by the scar across one cheek bone, a present of the Women's World. "I can try, but you know me: if I knew what I was doing, I probably wouldn't be doing it."

A muffled cry full of terror rose from the barracks below.

Jame cursed. "I *knew* we were going to give Niall nightmares. I've a cadet to comfort, then a few hours of *dwar* to catch before I leave for Kithorn. Ashe, please go away and do whatever it is you do instead of sleeping."

She left the apartment as the frightened cry sounded again and other voices rose in drowsy protest.

Ashe grounded her staff and shook her grizzled head. "Some nemesis," she muttered.

CHAPTER II
Winter Solstice

Winter 65

I

FOUR FANTASTIC FIGURES gamboled by torchlight in the snowy courtyard of ruined Kithorn.

One, short and stocky, wore a gaudy skirt and goat udders that slapped against his bare, sweating chest as he pirouetted about the square.

Another fluttered around him with black feathers sewn to every inch of his clothing, ruffled by the cold wind into cat's-paw waves.

A third figure smeared all over in charcoal stalked them both on tiptoe with exaggerated caution.

Under their feet crawled the fourth, shrouded in the head-and-skin cape of a huge catfish.

The Burnt Man popped up in front of the Earth Wife (who shrieked) and shoved "her" backward over the Eaten One's scaly form while the Falling Man flapped in protest. Then they were all up again, panting smoky clouds, circling each other like carnival clowns.

Earth, Air, Fire, and Water.

Why are they playing the fool? wondered Jame from the snowy hollow outside the gatehouse where she crouched. Didn't they know how dangerous it could be to mock the Four?

They weren't drunk, she decided, watching their lurching, desperate sport. They were exhausted. It must be nearly dawn, the solstice night almost past. How long had they been cavorting, and for what audience?

Jame lowered herself in the depression and peered upward through the gatehouse. Something sat on the shattered tower of Kithorn, as if on a throne, something huge, defined against the moonless night sky only by the glowing fissures in his skin. Jame's own skin crawled. The Burnt Man himself brooded over the shambling shamans below.

Well, whatever their game, she knew better than to disturb it.

She was about to push herself up to leave when a burnt, sizzling stick was thrust into the snow inches from her face. No, not a stick. A bone—more specifically the knobby end of a human humerus. Clumps of charred flesh clung to it near the shoulder, and to the half-skeletal body to which it was attached.

A blunt, blind head swung inches over her head as if questing. Fire had burned away its nose and sheared off its lips from yellow, snaggle teeth. The remaining flesh crackled and split as it moved, expelling waves of heat and a pyric stench. Other forms shuffled around the hollow in various stages of combustion.

The Burning Ones, thought Jame, trying not to breathe, holding very still. *The Burnt Man's hunting pack.*

Their usual prey were kin-slayers. While they could neither see nor smell, they could track guilt.

Vant, she thought, and the ravaged head swung toward her.

"Huh!" it said, snorting out chunks of its own charred lungs.

The cadet's death in the fire pit of Tentir still haunted her. As unpleasant as he had been, he hadn't deserved such an end, nor should it interest the Burnt Man's servants in her. Yes, Vant had been bone-kin, the grandson of her wretched uncle Greshan, but she hadn't been there when he died. It wasn't her fault... or was it? Vant would never have tackled her brother Torisen if he hadn't thought that he was striking at her. She was the one whose very existence had driven him to such behavior, even though it was Tori whom he had nearly killed. For that matter, why had he been so clumsy? Rue had told her that it almost looked as if he had been pushed.

The Burning One cocked his head as if testing her thoughts. It doubted her innocence. She almost agreed.

Then a yelp in the square drew its attention. The creature swung about and shambled toward the gatehouse on the knobs of its truncated limbs, followed by the others.

Between their contorted, smoldering bodies, Jame saw that

the shaman playing the Burnt Man had appropriated one of the torches that defined sacred space and had set it to the Earth Wife's flaring skirt. Fire bloomed. The Earth Wife squealed and ran about the square trailing flames until the Falling Man tripped him. As he floundered on the ground, the Eaten One lumbered over on all fours and doused the flames with more watery vomit than seemed humanly possible.

Much more of this and none of them would survive.

Jame rose and backed away. When she was clear, she turned and ran.

Away from the torches, the night was very dark indeed, lit only by such stars as shone through a shifting overcast, and they were further dimmed by a gentle fall of snow. Shadows shifted from ink black to dusky blue, then back again. Faintly glimmering snow crunched and squeaked underfoot. Where was the damn village? Jame had counted on its lights to navigate, but not a candle illuminated the benighted landscape. She slipped and fell. The ground under her was unnaturally flat for hill country. No, not ground at all but rock-hard ice. She had strayed onto the frozen Silver. At least it would lead her upstream, so she followed it, if with some trepidation: the river was treacherous. Those who fell in seldom emerged nor could any boat sail on it for long.

River Snake, River Snake, sleep deep.

I tread as softly as I can.

To her left, starlight shone briefly on snow-pillowed heights. Ah. The hill upon which the Merikit village was built.

Jame left the river and nearly fell into the pit that was the ruins of the maidens' lodge. The previous Winter's Eve, part of the yackcarn stampede had shattered its low roof and plunged into it, wreaking havoc. Apparently the Merikit were waiting for spring to begin repairs. However, that didn't explain the sharp tang of pitch rising out of it.

Skirting the gaping cavity, Jame climbed. She knew she had reached the hilltop palisade when she ran into it nose first. Following its curve, she found the gate by touch. Inside, wooden walks echoed under her feet. Like the girls' dwelling, most of the lodges were half sunken into the ground, marked only by long barrows of snow and smoke holes. Their entrances opened into the passageway under the boardwalk that connected the entire village.

Where was everyone?

Then soft voices reached her, and ahead she saw a large clot of shadows standing, their breath a halo around them. One turned.

"There you are at last," it said in Merikit. "Hurry. Gran Cyd is waiting for you."

Hands tugged at her sleeves, guiding her forward. She felt as much as saw that all were women, and here was their queen, recognizable by her regal height and by the faint glimmer of golden torques twisted around her wrists and neck.

"Sorry I'm late," she said as they descended into Gran Cyd's lodge. Without even starlight, one might as well have been stricken blind. "We started out before dawn, but I swear the colt lost his way more than once."

"Huh."

It could have been one of the Burning Ones passing judgment but softer, forgiving now that she had finally arrived.

"Stay there."

Jame stopped. She could hear breathing all around her, from great, gusty snores to piping whistles, and she smelled rank fur. All breathed in unison, in and out, in and out. The rhythm of it tugged at her, catching her own breath. She swayed. It was a long time since her few snatched hours of *dwar* sleep the night before.

In and out, in and out...

A spark caught at a candle's wick. Even such feeble light struck the eyes like a blow. Jame had the dazzled impression of Cyd's strong, white arm encircling the flame and one of her dark red braids swinging perilously close to it.

They seemed to have descended into a cave, full of hibernating beasts. At her feet lay a pair of hedgehogs curled up together, whistling softly in their sleep. The ceiling was hung with stalactites and the crumpled forms of sleeping bats. To one side, a mountain of fur that, surely, was a cave bear snorted and briefly stirred. It didn't greatly surprise Jame to see a familiar fireplace at the far side of the rocky chamber nor the untidy figure sprawled on its hearth, her toothless mouth loudly agape. The Earth Wife's lodge turned up wherever it was needed and so did Mother Ragga, the Earth Wife herself.

Jame started toward the sleeper, picking her way, but Gran Cyd turned and stopped her with a gesture.

"She won't wake until the dawn. Rouse her now and she might die."

The earth, die?

"Who makes up these rules?" she had once asked Mother Ragga.

"They just are," had come the implacable reply.

Something apparently governed even the Four, as haphazard as their actions seemed to be. Jame wondered what.

The candle flame danced. Cyd shielded it as a girl with long, tawny hair slipped down the stairs.

"They said that you had come!"

"Prid, the light."

"Oh." Prid shut the door quickly behind her.

"Why is everyone else standing in the dark?" asked Jame.

"Because it isn't dawn yet, nor may it ever be."

Jame considered this. It was still the solstice, the year's longest night. That it fell during the dark of the moon helped her to understand. The Kencyrath went through something similar nine times a year, according to the lunar cycle—five nights with little or no light, made darker by the fear that the moon had been swallowed by the Shadows and would never return, heralding the end of their last sanctuary.

The Merikit girl shivered, hugging herself. "Suppose the sun never rises? Suppose we stay buried in the dark, in winter, forever?"

On this world, faith sometimes shaped reality. What if she was right? Winter forever . . .

Then Jame remembered something that the scrollsman Index had once told her. "Wait a minute. Aren't you supposed to burn a log representing the Burnt Man to prevent that and to help the season turn? Index called it 'burying winter' or 'burning the Burnt Man.'"

"We are supposed to, yes. You aren't the only one who has kept us waiting."

"Let me guess. The log is Chingetai's responsibility."

Once again, it seemed that the Merikit chief had thrown the rituals out of joint. The previous Summer's Eve he had neglected his own borders in a bid to claim the entire Riverland. Jame had accidentally thwarted that by pocketing a Burnt Man's bone. Then he had named her the Earth Wife's Favorite and his own annual heir to try to save face. Despite that, he had attempted to cut her out of every ceremony since, often with calamitous results.

Mother Ragga found the whole situation funny; the Burnt Man, however, was not amused.

Think you can fool me? Not again. Never again.

Not that he was a friend—to anyone, as far as Jame could make out, except perhaps to the blind Arrin-ken known as the Dark Judge. Now there was a link between Rathillien and the Kencyrath that boded well for neither.

Meanwhile, the shamans were working themselves half to death to keep his smoldering attention diverted. How long could they last? Where in Perimal's name was Chingetai?

Gran Cyd raised the candle, illuminating an expanse of furry sleepers.

"Gently, gently," she said to her granddaughter, adding, to distract her, "One way or another, life goes on, yes, even into endless winter. Have you thought about what I said earlier? You are almost of an age to choose. Your mother was a master weaver, as the hangings in my lodge show. You loved working on the hand loom as a child. Now her lodge and great loom wait for you to become a woman."

The girl tossed her head. "'What want I with hearth or house-bond? What is a lodge but an earthbound trap?'"

"Prid! I know that you watch the sacred mummeries even though they are forbidden to all womankind, but don't quote them, especially not that one. Consider what happens in it."

"Sorry, Gran, but you know that I only want to run free as a war maid."

"But you don't like to fight or to shed blood, even on the hunt. Moreover, ask your great-aunt Anku what she and the other so-called free women do day by day. Theirs is a job like any other, not an excuse never to grow up."

Prid muttered something.

"What, child?"

"I said, grown-ups die."

"So do we all, eventually; yes, like your mother."

The door opened a crack.

"We see him!" someone hissed through it.

The animals stirred, then subsided. On the hearth the Earth Wife groaned and tossed.

Gran Cyd swept from the room with her candle, followed by Jame and Prid.

Outside, everyone was pointing uphill, toward the sparkle of torches that seemed to hover just above the tree line. The queen raised her light, a solitary beacon. One torch above waved in response. The others formed an inverted "V" that swayed back and forth. The clouds cleared. By starlight, Jame saw two lines of men tugging on thick ropes. Between them, a raw spire rose, dipped, and fell.

"Ah," breathed the women.

"They've been a fortnight cutting and trimming that tree," Prid whispered to Jame. "I hear that this year's is three feet across and fifty feet long. Chingetai has made something special to make it go faster than usual."

Upslope, the lines disintegrated and re-formed on either side of the tree trunk. Down the mountainside it came, bucking, gathering speed, to the sound of distant cheers.

"They're riding it?" Jame asked.

"Yes! Isn't it exciting?"

The word for it was stupid, Jame thought, but oddly stirring.

The log picked up speed. Flecks of light began to tumble off of it. The women fell silent.

"Should it be coming straight toward the village?" Jame asked.

"No." Gran Cyd peered uphill, shading her eyes from her candle's light. "It looks as if they've lost the pilot rope to the skid."

"And that's not good."

"Thirteen tons of lumber aimed straight down our throats? No."

The erstwhile riders had grabbed the trailing lead ropes and were trying to slow the monstrous log's descent, without success.

"Maybe the hill will turn it," said Prid, beginning to sound nervous.

"You want to bet?" Jame stirred restlessly. It wasn't in her nature to watch disasters unfold without lending a hand, yet what could she do?

"Damn," she said, and took off at a run down through the village, calling for the rathorn colt as she went.

He answered her outside the gate, below the hill. Starlight shone on the cold white of his ivory, on his cresting mane and flowing tail. The ride north had been long and he was out of temper, not eager to be ridden again. Twin horns slashed at her, daring her to step into them. He wouldn't hurt her on purpose, but accidents didn't count. She lunged, caught the saddle horn, and pulled herself half onto his back. He took off at a gallop with her clinging to his side.

"You damn fool," she hissed at him as she pulled herself upright. His ears flicked derisively and he bounded over a snowdrift, nearly dislodging her.

By now, the log was halfway down the mountain, a batter-ing ram aimed straight for the front gate, with Merikit chasing it and Chingetai still grimly astride. It dipped and plowed up sheets of snow. As they came alongside, Jame saw that the butt was mounted on a metal skid with an attachment not unlike the prow of a boat but hinged to allow it to swing back and forth. Chingetai hadn't lost the pilot rope after all, but neither could he lean out far enough to turn the log. That flaw apparently hadn't occurred to him before.

"Throw it to me!" Jame shouted to him.

He snarled back at her through a mass of flying braids, right side for children sired, left for men killed. She would have to ask what a braided beard meant.

"Everything is under control. Go away!"

The colt would have liked nothing better. Flying snow hit him in the face, and the log yawed ominously. The stumps of lopped off branches glistened with an effusion of resin and perhaps with blood. How many hillmen had it crushed? Death's-head squealed and bucked in protest. Jame scrambled back from his neck where he had tossed her.

"Throw it, now!"

The Merikit chief darted a chagrined glance at the rapidly approaching village.

"Here, dammit!"

Jame grabbed the rope as it whipped past, wrapped it around the saddle horn, and let Death's-head plunge away to the left. Hooves skidded and the saddle girth groaned. It was like trying to shift the foundations of the world. The prow creaked over. It was turning, not much but hopefully enough. The hill loomed, then the ruins of the maidens' lodge yawned before them. Jame cast off the rope. The log shot into the cavity headfirst and rammed into the far wall with an earth-shaking boom. Chingetai flew off and tumbled end over end into the adjacent ruins of the boys' lodge.

Jame and the colt hurtled past. Now they were sliding on ice. The rathorn sat down, clearing a great swathe of snow with his rump. Jame fell off. Beneath her, something huge moved under the ice, dimly seen as giant scales sliding past. It bumped its fro-zen roof. Cracks radiated out under Jame's hands. River Snake or Eaten One? Not waiting to find out, she scrambled to one shore, the colt to the other.

Before her was the log, jutting out of the pit but mostly in it. Again she smelled pitch. A moment later it ignited, wrapping the log in flames. Dazzled by the light, Jame thought she saw a gigantic form loom over it, over her.

"You," it said, in a voice seared clean of all emotion except recognition.

Then it lowered itself limb by limb into the blazing trench, the Burnt Man reluctantly joining his effigy in the earth

The Burning Ones lined the far side of the pit, baying flame-mouthed after their master.

One stood among them, taller than they, silent. His gaze met Jame's across the fiery abyss, and he smiled.

Vant.

They never found his body, Jame thought, trying to catch her breath.

He looked as she remembered him, except for the red light reflected in his eyes. Surely, though, he was dead. Well, so were his companions. But a Kencyr in such company? How could that be?

The Burnt Man and the Dark Judge.

The Earth Wife and her unlikely Favorite.

Rathillien and the Kencyrath.

It could happen, as it had before. Bonds were being forged, despite both. But Sweet Trinity...!

He raised his hands. The blunt, charred faces of the Burning Ones rose with the gesture, their cry cut short. All stared at her, crimson-eyed, as if taking note as they had been bidden. Then the fire flared and they were gone. With their lord in the ground, did they now follow a new master?

Voices called to her, making her start, and dark figures rushed out of the night to throw their arms around her. One was Prid, another Gran Cyd, and half a dozen other women besides.

"Well done," said the queen, helping her to her feet. "We could do without our chief, but not without the father of our unborn children."

Jame gazed in dismay at the assembled throng, who smiled back at her. Gran Cyd had promised that as the Earth Wife's supposedly male Favorite, she would be credited with any babies conceived on Winter's Eve, and here was the proof.

"Oh no," she said. "Oh, Cyd, not you too."

❦ CHAPTER III ❦
Pyres and the Pit

Winter 70

I

JAME HALF WOKE, tangled in sleeping furs.

Where am I? she thought.

The white-washed wall beside her danced with murals given life by the low fire sulking beneath the great bronze basin while rain tapped on the copper smoke hood above. Rue snored softly in her own mound of blankets by the door. Of course. She was back in her quarters at Tentir, almost too tired from the long ride south from the Merikit village to sleep.

But she had slept, and dreamed of dark things. Fire and ash, furious blue eyes in a charred face, a seared finger encircled by a ring, jutting out of a pile of corpses...

Some images she recognized, but to whom had the other ones belonged? Over the past year she had sometimes shared the dreamscape with both Timmon, set on seduction, and her twin brother Torisen, pulled in against his will. Neither showed her anything she wanted to see. To sleep again was to risk falling back into nightmare, but oh, she ached for rest.

A branch snapped and the flames leaped. Her eyelids flickered, then fell again. Through them she still saw fire....

Such pulsing heat, such an incandescent glow! Beads of sweat burst on her brow and trickled down, stinging, into her eyes. It hurt to breathe. Tentir's fire timbers loomed around her like a forest perpetually eaten by sullen, internal flame.

The vents far above sucked in a breath of hot air: "Aaaah..."

Embers glowed, above, below, while black flakes of combustion fluttered against ironwood trunks like infernal butterflies.

At her feet, the floor fell away into a wide-mouthed pit where once a fire timber had stood. "Haahh..." breathed the searing air again, and coals glowed in the pit's deep bed.

"Afraid, little man?"

The creature who spoke looked like Caldane's son Nusair, but its hair was white under its ruddy fire-tint. It was a Shanir—worse, a darkling changer, once one of the Master's most loyal servants, now turned against him in a desperate bid for freedom.

"Afraid? Of you? Moderately."

That wasn't her voice, nor her hand creeping to the collar of her dress coat where (since when?) she carried a set of throwing knives.

"Now, what would really frighten you? Shall we find out? Beauty, now!"

Something gray near her foot, something that sank fangs into her leg even as her hand whipped down to bury a blade in its head, and her senses reeled.

But the darkling wyrm is cocooned in a trunk in Greshan's chambers, she thought, bewildered. It had bitten her brother two years ago when he had visited Tentir on the way south to battle at the Cataracts, and now she was protecting it while it meta-morphosed into... what?

Then wyrm and changer were gone and again she circled the pit. This time Vant moved opposite her, his handsome face underlit by glowing coals, twisted with hate.

"Does honor mean nothing to you?" he snarled at her. "Do the rules? Then again, why should they when the Commandant lets you break them over and over? Quite his little pet, aren't you? You think you're so clever that you can get away with anything. Well, not this time."

"What are you talking about?"

"Your scarf. Someone has already scalped you, but here you are, still in play."

It was the Winter War, and Timmon had seized her scarf before the contest had even begun, officially removing her from competition.

"You think I'm Jame," said the voice that she now recognized as her brother's.

Vant spoke to him, not to me. I wasn't there. Rue told me.

Vant spat on the stones. His saliva skipped among them, sizzling, going, gone. "The spoiled brat. The Highborn little lady. What did your brother think, that Tentir needed a mascot? It was an honest mistake!"

"What was?" asked both siblings in one voice, and that his.

"How could anyone seriously believe that hillmen were attacking on Tentir's doorstep? What logic was there in that? What sense is there in anything that you do or that happens around you?"

"You didn't send help. You laughed. A cadet died."

The steel in Torisen's voice pierced her. Beneath it she felt his barely suppressed rage that one of the precious young Kendar entrusted to him had been lost. The other lords mistook his mild ways for weakness, but for thirty millennia his ancestors had been Highlord of the Kencyrath, just as he was now, and their power ran in his veins. As such, he was responsible for the well-being of all his people, in life, in death.

Anise with a Noyat arrow jutting out of her stomach, so scared, then so cold. And I nearly flayed you alive for it, Vant, Ancestors forgive me. Now here you are, with fire at your feet.

"I was master-ten of my barracks. I still should be." Before his lord, the cadet's outrage thinned to a self-justifying whine. "Am I to pay for one misjudgment forever?"

"That depends on you." Trinity, but Tori sounded cold, no less than an Arrin-ken passing judgment. Despite the heat, the words half froze on his lips, issuing forth in a plume of frost. "In Sheth's place, I would have thrown you out of Tentir altogether."

"You misbegotten bitch!"

Suddenly Vant was upon him, grappling, trying to throw him onto the coals. They wrestled back and forth on the pit's rim. Then Vant lurched free, shaking his head. He looked startled and dazed, as if dealt an unexpected blow.

"You..." His eyes wildly searched the shadows. "Don't!"

And he reeled again, over the edge, onto the coals, rolling to his feet. For the first time he clearly saw and recognized his adversary as the Highlord.

"Oh."

"Now that that's settled, get out of that damn firebox." In life, in death...

Do it, you fool! Jame thought behind the mask of her brother's face. *Don't haggle!*

But even now Vant didn't believe that such a terrible thing could happen to him.

"Not until you make me master-ten of my barracks again and withdraw that bitch sister of yours. You must see that her presence here isn't right!"

Get out, get out, get out...

"I suppose you know that your boots are smoking. I can't be blackmailed, Vant. It would be a betrayal of my position."

The cadet beat at his smoldering clothes with a kind of exasperated irritation.

"You're Highlord, dammit!" The furnace breath of the pit made him increasingly hoarse as his throat closed. "You can do...what you please!"

"Not so," came the pitiless answer. "To lead is also to serve... something that you never seem to have grasped. What you ask would be a betrayal of responsibility. Come out, Vant. Now."

Fire flared under Vant's hands.

"I don't believe this. I don't accept it. It isn't fair!"

"Is the truth? Come out. Here, take my hand."

The flames rose, licking from pants to jacket, with a sudden rush to the hair. At last Vant believed the unthinkable.

"I *will*...have justice," he panted as the smoke gnawed at his throat, "or I will...have revenge."

Torisen/I/we reach for him, but Brier stops us.

"He would have pulled you in, lord."

Tori didn't deserve that. Did I? Did Vant?

Pyre succeeded pyre, as if all the flames in the world roiled through her dreams:

At the Haunted Lands keep, where her father Ganth presumably had burned.

But I wasn't there either. Kindrie told me.

In Wilden's forecourt.

Ah, Rawneth. How much will your people endure when you put their children to the torch?

At the Cataracts.

Oh, Tirandys, Senethari, I will never forget.

At the Cataracts again.

This was confusing. Who had told her about the common pyre and why did she remember it now? A ring, a blackened finger, broken off, pocketed.

I took both from my father to give to my brother, but who else would do such a thing, and why?

She couldn't see the faces of the living or of the dead. What she did see, abruptly, was a fair-haired young man with a swollen nose.

"I think you've broken it," he said in a nasal, petulant whine.

He looked like Timmon. His eyes were Timmon's, wide with surprise to hear his father's voice issuing from his lips. Once again the Ardeth Lordan had invaded her dreams, damn him.

"Why did you do it, Pereden?"

That was her brother again, speaking to Timmon's father. They were in the Highlord's tent at the Cataracts. Torisen sounded exhausted, as well he might be, having fought and won such a battle. Worse, he had just come from culling the bloody field where he had granted so many of the fatally wounded the White Knife. The least they had deserved was an honorable death at the hands of their lord. In death as in life, they were his responsibility, at whatever cost to him. Yes, he was exhausted, but there was hurt in his voice too, and a desperate need to understand.

"Why, Peri?"

"What else had you left me to do? Damn." His nose had started to bleed. Torisen gave him a handkerchief. Pereden began to pace, he and a bewildered Timmon both, overlapping, caught in the same dream of a memory that was Torisen's. "Taking my rightful place as commander of the Southern Host, turning my father against me... You lied to him!"

Behind Pereden's fury, his son's bafflement and interest grew. Jame knew from a previous dream where this conversation would end, if not what went before. Timmon mustn't know, even if to stop now was to thwart her own curiosity. Why had Torisen broken not just Pereden's nose but his neck, then sent his body to burn on the common pyre?

No more of this. No more. Wake up, wake up, wake up—

And she did, to find Rue hovering anxiously over her.

"You were having a nightmare, lady."

"You're telling me."

Jame threw back the furs. Her slim, naked body steamed with sweat while the cold air raised goosebumps down her arms.

"Damn and blast that Timmon," she said thickly, rubbing her face. "He's gotten into my dreams again and between us we've ensnared Tori. But who else's dream was I in? That finger, that ring...ah, never mind," she added, seeing Rue's confused, concerned expression. "Fetch me something to drink, please."

The Ardeth Lordan was a charmer, a dream-stalker, and a would-be seducer, except every time he tried to entangle her in one of his erotic fantasies, between them they seemed to open the door to her brother's sleeping mind which, while fascinating, was hardly fair to Tori.

As for that last dream...

Timmon had adored his father and still tried to imitate him. Jame suspected that therein lay the source of half the Ardeth Lordan's personality flaws, not that Timmon saw them as such.

"Damn him," she muttered again, accepting a cup of cold water from Rue. In so many other ways, he was almost worthwhile.

II

AS IT HAPPENED, their first class was together.

Timmon arrived with his ten-command, looking aggrieved, with dark smudges under his eyes.

"What's the matter with you?" he demanded. "I try to arrange some harmless fun on a fur rug in front of a cheerful fireplace, and you drag me from one immolation to another."

"Good morning to you too. Sorry about that, but I did warn you to keep out of my dreams."

"If I were Torisen, you wouldn't fight me so hard," he muttered. It was a sore point that, despite herself, Jame found her brother more interesting than she did him. "And what about that last bit? My father called your brother a liar!"

"I have no more idea than you do what that was about. Of all people, you should know that dreams don't always make sense."

Seeing that he was about to argue, she abruptly changed the topic.

"For that matter, I've a bone to pick with you. Why did you tackle me in Greshan's quarters before the Winter War even started?"

"I didn't think you'd let me do it afterward."

"Let you? Huh. And how did Torisen get my scarf back from you?"

At this, Timmon looked distinctly sheepish. "If he hasn't told you, I'm not going to."

"Could it be...oh no!" She burst out laughing. "You tackled him in the Knorth kitchen thinking he was me. He took the scarf and locked you in!"

With that, Jame stifling mirth and Timmon very red in the face, they reached their destination: a room in Old Tentir with rush mats strewn about the floor. Timmon stopped on the threshold.

"Oh no. Not the Senethar this early in the morning. I'm for my bed again."

"Not so fast." The randon instructor entered behind them.

Timmon smiled, all dimples with the trace of a pout. "I didn't sleep well last night, Ran. Really, I'd rather not."

The randon, an Ardeth, smiled back with more teeth than humor. "Like it or not, young Lordan, you'll learn your lesson. Everyone, coats off and take your places for the fire-leaping kantirs."

"Losing your charm, Timmon?" Jame asked.

"I don't understand. Usually the only one who denies me is you. What's gotten into the randon of my house lately?"

Still grumbling, he and Jame dutifully squared up as their ten-commands followed suit. Fire-leaping Senethar consisted of a series of kicks and blows. Its kantirs could be practiced alone but when in class two opponents mirrored each other, starting slow, getting faster, not seeking to connect. Jame's fist brushed past Timmon's ear, and his past hers. Simultaneous kicks pivoted them away from each other, then back. So far, properly speaking, they were engaged in the Senetha, the Senethar's dance form. The pace quickened. Each focused on a point just short of the other. Timmon's booted foot stopped close enough for her to smell its fine leather and to see, cross-eyed, the dirt engrained in its sole. Hers brushed the tip of his nose.

"Sorry," she murmured.

You broke my nose, Pereden had said to Torisen. When and why?

...two figures in the Heart of the Wood at the Cataracts, fighting. The one in black drove the other's nasal guard back into his face with the hilt of his sword. The one in dusty blue dropped. Then the changers came...

Turn, back kick. A thud as two other opponents misjudged and fouled each other. The randon's measured rebuke. Closer now, one arm scooping around the other's neck. An extended foot sweep that would have brought both of them down if it had connected.

Tori broke Pereden's neck.

"Why did you do it, Peri?"

Do what? If that had been Pereden in blue armor, why had he and Torisen been fighting at all while the greater battle with the Waster Horde raged around them?

Someone came to the door and spoke to the instructor.

"Your lucky day," he said, turning to Timmon. "There's a lady to see you. I think it's your mother."

"You call that luck? Now can I leave?"

"Go. But you still owe me three kantirs. The rest of you, mind your manners: Ran Aden is with her."

"Who?" Jame asked the cadet next to her.

"Lord Ardeth's war-leader, also his younger brother, also a former commandant of Tentir…"

"And therefore a member of the Randon Council," Jame concluded.

So that was the name of the Ardeth who had watched her with such cold disapproval during the last cull and then voted against her. Around him she would certainly watch her step.

The lesson continued, with Drie as Jame's new partner. At their first move, he slid past her in water-flowing, nearly causing her to fall as she anticipated a different maneuver.

"Drie, that's the wrong kantir," she hissed at him. "Wake up!"

Timmon's servant smiled at her dreamily and continued to drift through the forms. Water-flowing was often used to counter fire-leaping as it channeled aside any attack. They were moving fast now, Jame on the offense, Drie on the defense, and others were making room for them. The instructor watched without comment. Drie moved beautifully, fully poised as little as he seemed to be paying attention, tempting Jame to step up her assault. Spin, kick, strike—except for the whisper of contact she might have faced wind-blowing, that most difficult of forms. He slid backward, water over stones, tempting her into an unwisely extended move. In the moment that she wavered, off balance, the Kendar calmly tapped her on the forehead and landed her flat on her back on a rush mat in a billow of dust. Rue looked startled; Brier raised an eyebrow: Jame rarely lost at the Senethar. The class, both Ardeth and Knorth, applauded. So did Jame after a moment of surprise, slapping the floor with an appreciative hand.

"There you see a perfect example of fire-leaping's weakness," said the instructor. "What should you have done, cadet?"

Besides disobeying instructions to respond?

"Not over-extended to begin with, Ran, then countered with earth-moving," said Jame, rising and dusting herself off.

Who but Drie, she thought, could do things his own way and get away with it? Come to think of it, whatever the lesson, she had never seen him do anything except water flowing, and no one had ever called him on it. After his own fashion, he was as much a charmer as his master Timmon.

⚜ III ⚜

THE MORNING'S SECOND CLASS was for those Shanir with special links to animals, conducted in the Falconer's second-story mews.

A gust of welcome warm air greeted Jame and her blind hunting ounce Jorin as they entered. With the onset of winter, the windows had been sealed with oiled linen and fires burned at both ends of the long room, more for the comfort of its avian inhabitants than for the cadets.

The Danior Tarn was already there with his Molocar pup Torvi; the Edirr Mouse with her twin albino mice perched one behind each ear; the Caineron Dure with his secret in his pocket; the Coman Gari, thankfully without any insect horde; the Randir Shade with her gilded swamp adder Addy; and the Ardeth Drie, whom no one could explain.

Jame stripped off her coat and joined Shade by the back wall, away from the others. In general, she wished that all of Tentir could act as much in fellowship as the Falconer's class, regardless of their house affiliations, but she had a special reason for seeking out the Randir.

Shade looked even more attenuated than she had during the Winter War, as if her very bones had lengthened or perhaps multiplied. Long, white fingers played restlessly with Addy's gleaming coils.

"How are you?" Jame asked in a whisper as the Falconer turned his attention to another cadet.

Shade gave her a hooded look. "How do you think?"

Jame remembered that strange scene in the Caineron barracks when Shade had held off Fash with Addy twined around her arm—and vice versa. No normal limb bent in such a sinuous fashion. The Randir master-ten Reef had also been there. Jame wondered if Reef or anyone else had been at the right angle to witness the phenomenon.

"I'd be shaken," Jame admitted. "It's not something one would expect. I always thought that changers were made in the depths of Perimal Darkling"—*like Keral,* she thought—"not born free here on Rathillien."

"Is that what I'm becoming, a darkling changer?"

"I think so, although again how and why baffle me."

"Born, not made. Is that any better?"

"It is if it makes you an unfallen darkling"—she glanced around; no one was listening—"like me. I grew up under shadows' eaves, in the Master's House itself. A lot of it I don't remember clearly, but I do know that I never submitted to his will. We can't help what we are."

"You, a Knorth, tell me this?"

"Not as a Randir. As a member of the Falconer's class. As a fellow randon cadet. Honor is hard for us, but not impossible."

"Blood will tell," said the Randir morosely. She tugged an earlobe and grimaced as it stretched.

Jame was suddenly reminded of Prince Odalian of Karkinaroth pulling his fingers like taffy and laughing hysterically. Another innocent victim, forced into a changer's role. She put a quick hand over Shade's.

"Don't. Not until you're sure you can return to normal."

The other gave a crack of laughter that turned curious heads. "Normal. Will I ever be that again? Was I ever, to begin with?"

Jame's answering grin was lopsided. "First, define 'normal.' We are more than blood, Shade, more than our heredity or our past." *One has to believe that,* she thought. Oh, but sometimes it was hard. "You haven't fallen."

"Sometimes I think that my entire house has, except for the Randir Heir."

That was harder to answer. Given the pernicious influence of the Witch of Wilden, Shade's grandmother, how many remained untainted? Jame thought of the silent Randir Kendar standing by the pyre of their young, of Randiroc and of Sargent Corvine who had carved the name of her dead son into her flesh, lest she forget. Then too, there was Quill's guess that not all Randir were bound to the same lord, or lady. Rawneth had her share of followers, but not all embraced her power. Some clearly looked elsewhere, and not necessarily to her son. It was a confusing situation, especially hard on the innocent.

"There's honor in your house yet," she insisted, "however endangered."

"If you say so."

"I do. Listen, Shade, what you are becoming is complicated, but no disgrace unless you make it one."

Shade grunted. Jame didn't think that the Randir believed her, not that it was an easy thing to accept. The only changers she had previously known, except for Odalian, were the Master's servants, corrupted by their own will—yes, even Tirandys, however much he had regretted his action and tried to rebel against it. But how had Shade gotten the darkling taint into her blood, and how strong was it?

"Whatever you do," she told the Randir, "don't let the rest of your house know."

"Why?"

"I think your granddam Rawneth has been spying on you through Addy, perhaps to see if you begin to change. You may have broken that bond when Addy bit you, if you're a blood-binder too, but I don't know for sure. Does your bond to her feel any different now?"

The Falconer's merlin had been staring hard at them. Now it gave a jeering cry. Its master's sealed eyes followed the raptor's gaze.

"You," he said, jabbing his sharp chin at Jame. "Repeat the purpose of this class."

Jame started like the guilty schoolgirl that she was. "T-to learn how to enhance the bond with our bound-creatures, Ran."

"And are you satisfied with your progress?"

Jame sighed and rubbed the creamy fur of Jorin's belly as the ounce stretched out beside her, purring. "No." When upset or frightened, the ounce still tended to withdraw into himself, not that he ever seemed to lose the use of her senses.

"Then pay attention. All of you, focus on your partners."

Jame closed her eyes and tried. What she felt mostly was hunger, having had little appetite for breakfast, but was that her, or Jorin, or both of them? Smell: the sharp scent of raptor droppings, leather from their tack, a dead mouse in the wall. Touch: the hard floor, warmth to one side where the fire burned, the sudden butt of Jorin's head demanding more attention. Hearing: the others' breaths, the dry rustle of Addy's scales, the Molocar Torvi's gaping yawn.

"Oh, wake up," snapped the Falconer. "What's wrong with all of you today? You, Dure, show us what you keep in your pocket."

Reluctantly, the Caineron drew out his right hand, holding what appeared to be a gray rock. When he tickled its underside, however, it extruded tiny bright eyes and clawed feet. Those who hadn't seen it before leaned forward to look.

"Why," said Mouse, "it's a trock. A scavenger. We had an infestation of them once in the outhouse. Father couldn't sit down for a week."

Dure glowered. "Well, this one is my trock. I've had it since it was a pebble. Generally, it isn't very useful unless I want it to gnaw through something. Eating is what it does, and it can digest anything."

Gari nudged Mouse. "Can you send your mind after it into the gutter?" he asked innocently.

"Now, children." That was Tarn, speaking from the lofty, highly functional link that he shared with the huge Molocar pup sprawling at his side. "Not every bond is equal. For that matter, to whom or what is Drie bound?"

They all looked at the Ardeth cadet, who as usual was staring dreamily into space.

"Wake up!" the Falconer shouted at him.

Drie blinked but didn't answer.

The randon snarled and launched his bird. The merlin dived straight for the delinquent cadet's face, shearing off at the last moment with a near squawk. Drie scrambled to his feet, suddenly wide awake, and fled, closely pursued. Behind him he left a trail of wet footprints.

"Damn," said Tarn. "Now we'll probably never find out."

"Maybe, maybe not," Jame said. "Now I'm curious."

"Huh-oh." Gari shivered. "Why do I smell disaster?"

In exiting the door, Drie nearly collided with Gorbel as he entered, pook under his arm.

"You said I should ask," he growled at Jame. "Falconer, am I bound to this thing?"

The "thing" wriggled and produced a pair of button eyes

amidst all of its shaggy fur. "Woof," it said, and produced a red, panting tongue.

Pooks were odd, native creatures. Technically canine, despite diminished smell and sight, they could track prey across the folds in the land, which made them invaluable to those Kencyr who admitted that said folds actually existed. Gorbel had sent to Restormir, his father's keep, for this particular specimen when he had set out to hunt the cave bear that was preying on Tentir's herd. Arguably, the pook had saved his life by guiding Jame to him.

Master and dog scratched their ears simultaneously. The infestation of fleas that Gari had set loose during the Winter War in the Caineron barracks still seemed to be rampant. Gorbel glared at Gari.

"Sorry about that. I'll clear them out if you like," Gari offered.

"You do that."

Torvi the Molocar rose and ambled over to inspect the new dog. His paws on Gorbel's shoulders, he presented the lordan with jaws capable of removing the front of his head, skull and all. Gorbel held the squirming pook out of reach. "Down," he said with the authority of a hunt master. Torvi licked his face apologetically and retreated.

"There's definitely some link there," said the Falconer, "but undeveloped. You'd better start attending my classes."

The Caineron sat down with a grunt next to Jame and wiped the dog slather off his face with a sleeve. "Is this going to help?"

"I'm not sure. The skill seems to be something that can be learned, but not necessarily taught." She scratched what she thought was the pook's head, only to have a short tail wave in her face.

Soon after, the class ended.

"Who was that cadet who nearly ran me over?" Gorbel asked as they left the mews together.

"Drie, one of Timmon's ten-command. No one has figured out yet what creature he's bound to."

"Humph. Well, it may mean nothing, but last fall, hearing that he didn't like to swim, Fash and Higbert threw him into the Silver. Don't look at me like that; it wasn't my idea. Most people don't come out alive. He did, with a smile."

"So Drie may be bound to something aquatic. Well, that's no surprise, if definitely weird."

On the boardwalk that ran around the training square they encountered Fash, one of Gorbel's ten-command but never noticeably subservient to him. To Fash, everything seemed to be a private, not very pleasant joke. Jorin growled at his scent. During the Winter War, the Caineron had only been stopped from skinning the ounce alive by Shade's intervention. He grinned at the furry bundle under Gorbel's arm.

"Good old One Eye. No, wait. I think you're carrying him backward."

Gorbel hoisted the pook and examined him, one end, then the other. "You're right. I swear this pup can turn around inside his own skin."

He trudged off, bright eyes peering back at them from under his arm.

Fash transferred his toothy grin to Jame. "Good old Gorbelly. Don't they make a sweet couple? Of course, the question is 'A couple of what?'"

"Half of it is the lordan of your house."

"For a while. Until his father gets tired of his failures."

"Which are?"

His smile broadened. "Well, you're still here, aren't you? At least until this afternoon."

"And then?"

"You'll see, beastie girl. You'll see."

With that he turned on his heel and strolled off, laughing softly.

IV

BRIER IRON-THORN spent the lesson period after lunch in the barracks, overseeing the ongoing renovations to her lady's chambers and setting the garrison's affairs in order for the coming week.

She preferred to do the latter in the privacy of the empty dining hall, having only learned how to read and write since she had come to Tentir and feeling that her efforts still halted badly.

There. The wretched quill had sputtered and blotched again as she leaned too heavily on it. Incompetence fretted Brier almost as much as cowardice; certainly, one saw the first more often than the second in the Kencyrath, where neither should exist at all. Grumbling, she started afresh, a swath of hair like fresh-cut mahogany swinging into her jade-green eyes.

Like most traditional Kendar, Brier trusted her memory more than words on paper. Paper could be destroyed. Well, then, so could people. That had been an added tragedy to the Fall: so much knowledge had been left behind that now fact and the singers' cherished Lawful Lie were often hard to tell apart. There was something to be said, however, for a notice that could be nailed to the wall rather than repeated nine times to the other house commanders. Certainly, the posted, official lesson schedule made planning easier, even when subject to last-minute alterations.

It still struck her as odd that, following Vant's demotion and subsequent death, she had become the barracks' acting master-ten while remaining the Knorth Lordan's five-commander, a backward situation if ever there was one. The former never would have worked in her early days at the college when most Knorth had seen her only as a Caineron turn-collar inexplicably accepted by the Highlord into his service. She supposed that she had won their trust, although how remained a mystery to her when she still didn't trust herself. Maybe being competent was its own reward, assuming that she was.

Her own feelings about her change of allegiance remained confused. Yes, she would serve her new lord with body, soul, and honor, yet behind her stood generations of Caineron yondri-gon. Did one ever successfully change houses or lords?

Scullery, stable, laundry, latrine, trock duty...

With their lord's newfound wealth from selling Aerulan's death banner in perpetuity to the Brandan, he could have afforded to assign some of his Kendar to act as servants for his cadets as was done in other houses such as the Caineron and Ardeth. However, Jameth hadn't asked for them. Brier approved. They had done well enough so far without such help, sharing the least favorite duties. Being a randon wasn't all glory—far from it. Lessons in discipline and endurance learned at the college would be invaluable later.

She paused to consider what to assign her own ten-command with its lordan leader. Vant had thought he could drive Jameth out by heaping unpleasant chores on her, not that her ten had let her accompany them on the worst of these. To have their lordan up to her knees in sewage hadn't pleased any of them, as willing as she had been to serve. But she was also considerate and honored their feelings.

Usually.

All in all, thought Brier, dripping the pen again, *what a long way they both have come.*

In the early days at the college, no one had been able to look the Highborn in her bare face, so used were they to females of her sequestered caste wearing masks. And that scar across her cheekbone—could it really have come from some squabble in the Women's Halls? Who would have dared to cut her? Moreover, how had they survived her backlash? People didn't affront Jameth without cost. That much Brier had learned in her short time under Knorth rule. Once the thought of a lady striking back would have horrified her house. Now most of its Kendar showed an odd pride in Jameth's eccentricities and knack for absurd situations.

Brier herself reserved judgment. Nothing in her past as a Caineron yondri inclined her to trust any Highborn, not that the Knorth hadn't treated her well. That more than anything else kept her off balance, waiting for them to show their true colors. Still, there was something about this odd lordan that, against her will, compelled her attention.

"Fallen for the Knorth, have you?" jeered the Caineron lover whom she had left behind. "And you really think that you can trust them?"

Brier didn't know, but she would try. What else, after all, could she do?

Voices sounded in the outer hall. Someone laughed. Brier gratefully put down the again sputtering quill and went to investigate.

Her ten-command were shedding their winter coats and shaking snow off of them. Smallest and slightest among them, the lordan was easy to spot. But what had happened to her face? Brier stalked over and caught Jameth by the chin, turning her head to see. The Highborn gave her a rueful smile. One of her eyes had swollen almost shut and her lip was split.

"I got run over by a cow," she said.

It was calving season for the black, bad-tempered herd, whose expectant mothers liked to wander off to bear their young in private. Cadets were duly sent to bring them back. That had been the ten's charge instead of their usual third-period class.

Dar grinned. "We came on her just after she'd dropped, with the calf steaming in the snow, barely on its feet. Of course she charged us. M'lady's horse threw her, getting out of the way, and both beasts trampled her."

"Actually," said Killy, "I think it was the calf scrambling to catch up who did the worst damage."

Brier let go of the lordan's chin. *I sent her on that duty,* she thought, then chided herself: *Am I to blame that the chit can't stay out of trouble? And who am I, anyway, to touch her?*

"You could have been gored," she said gruffly.

Jameth shrugged it off, as unnervingly dismissive of risk as always. "So could any one of us."

"There was a funny smell, too," said stolid Erim, obviously following his own line of thought. "Like burning fur. And we saw prints in the snow."

"Cave bear?" Brier asked sharply. Any large predator on the prowl was cause for concern with the herd willfully astray.

"Bigger than that, and melted, then frozen again, around the edges."

"I think it was the Dark Judge," said Mint, for once without the trace of a smile. "Haven't you heard him howling in the night?"

They had all heard something.

"The wind," said Killy, uncertainly.

"Wolves," suggested Quill.

"*'All things end, light, hope, and life. Come to judgment. Come!'*"

A shiver ran though the assembled cadets as the lordan murmured the blind Arrin-ken's terrible cry. The third of the Three People had disappeared into the wilds of Rathillien so long ago that they had come to seem like legends of another age. It was hardly fair that the Riverland itself should be haunted by the most dire of their ranks, a great cat blinded by the changer Keral with burning coals on the Master's own hearth, now as bent on justice as a lesser creature might be on revenge. Indeed, could he still tell one from the other? Either way, who was he hunting now?

Brier clapped her hands, making them all jump.

"Enough shivering at shadows. Time for your fourth-period class."

As the cadets dispersed, Brier touched the Highborn's sleeve.

"They go to study the Senetha," she said. "The Commandant has sent word that he expects you in the Bear Pit."

One eyebrow raised while the other twitched over its swollen socket. "So that was what Fash meant," the lordan murmured to herself. "Thank you, Brier. I'll see you at dinner. I hope."

And with that she was gone, leaving her coat a muddy, forgotten mound on the floor.

V

THE PIT WAS AS JAME REMEMBERED IT—a windowless
thirty-foot-square room deep in Old Tentir, its walls serrated
with splinters, its floor gouged here, stained there. A round hole
in the ceiling surrounded by a waist-high wall opened into the
room above, forming a balcony. Torches flared there, casting a
wavering circle of light on the floor below. No sound penetrated
this far into the old fortress. One might have been stricken deaf.
This was the dark, bloody heart of the Shanir, where their god's
chosen monsters battled with claw and tooth, where those such
as Jame—gifted (or cursed)—learned how to fight.

The arena was empty, the balcony deserted, but a heavily
padded coat and leather helmet with a metal face grid hung
from the wall. Jame put them on.

As she waited, her thoughts returned to the Dark Judge. If
he was nosing around, someone was guilty of something, or
so he at least believed. His prey were Shanir linked to That-
Which-Destroys, and she knew that he ached for the excuse
to judge her.

By association, she considered the Burnt Man, now safely in
the ground until Summer's Eve. He and the blind Arrin-ken
had made a lethal pair, the most dangerous aspects of Rathillien
and the Kencyrath combined. She had noticed before how this
world responded to such correspondences.

What would the Burning Ones do in their master's absence?
If she had guessed right at the solstice, Vant now led them in
another cross between the two worlds. So, whom did the Dark
Judge and the Burning Ones hunt, assuming they both followed
the same trail? Vant was the crux, and Ancestors knew he had
no love for her. At least like the Burnt Man, the Burning Ones
tended to stay far to the north, on Merikit land. It wasn't their
footsteps that she had seen melted into the snow.

Ah, enough of that, she thought, shaking herself. Back to the
matter at hand.

It was a long time since her last lesson here, before her brain-
damaged Senethari had been judged too dangerous to impart
such potentially lethal instruction. She had worried about him,

but denied entrance to his hot, close apartment, she had been unable to visit him, much less to see to his needs.

No one else understands, she thought. *He's trapped. Buried alive. His brother should know better.*

As if in answer to her thought, she heard a whisper of cloth above and looked up to see a dark silhouette behind the balcony wall. The face was invisible, but firelight turned the Commandant's white scarf red as if dipped in blood.

Jame saluted him in silence. In silence, he inclined his head.

The opposite door opened. Through it came a shuffling, snuffling sound, and then a dark, hunched form that filled the frame from side to side.

Jame hadn't seen Bear since the night when renegade Randir cadets had tried to assassinate their natural lord in Tentir's stable. As Bear emerged blinking into the light, she was appalled at his filthy condition, even more so by his enormous ivory claws, far too large to retract. Those on his fingers were bad enough; those on his toes, however, had again grown to curve back on themselves, piercing the soles of his feet. He entered, shambling, on all fours. Firelight defined the fearful cleft in his skull left by an enemy's axe, seared by the pyre that had failed to consume him. No one so grievously wounded should still be alive, but Kencyr are hard to kill. So he had been for the past thirty-some years.

Jame stared. It had been some time since she had last seen him, admittedly, but wasn't the chasm in his skull marginally shallower than it had been? She remembered it as nearly splitting an eyebrow. Now the stub of a white scar rose to disappear into the wild tangle of his gray hair.

He sat back on his haunches and surveyed the room. Her heart ached for him; this wreckage had been one of the Kencyrath's greatest war-leaders, victor of a hundred battles. No one, great or small, should come to such a state.

His nostrils flared and he grunted.

The next moment, he was upon her.

Jame ducked as lethal claws swept over her head, raking splinters off the wall. Their return stroke rasped against the metal mesh protecting her face. She dived sideways, but he followed, teeth bared. His bite tore away half of her sleeve. She blocked with the other one, desperately wishing for her knife-fighter's d'hen with its reinforced fabric. Mere padding was slight protection here.

Rolling out of his reach, she set herself on guard with claws out. Sweet Trinity, did she really want to use them on him, against no armor at all? On the other hand, he seemed set to disembowel her if he could.

The Commandant had discontinued their lessons because he had deemed them too dangerous. Why had he changed his mind?

Here Bear came again. As she threw herself under the arc of his blow, she felt his claws rip open the lacing of her helmet and tangle in her hair. Now he was lifting her. Her feet left the floor.

With a swirl of black, the Commandant vaulted the railing and landed behind his brother. Jame pulled off her mask, keeping her eyes on Bear.

"S-senethari..."

"Huh." He lifted her further still and held her inches from his face. "You." He touched her blackening eye, the split lip. A tremor wracked him. He dropped her and retreated, shaking his head as if it hurt. "Ca...ca...can't!"

The Commandant put a hand on his shoulder and escorted him from the room. Jame, left alone, thoughtfully stripped off what was left of her armor.

VI

ON THE WAY BACK TO HER QUARTERS, crossing the great hall, she encountered Timmon, his mother, and Ran Aden.

Lady Distan wore a damask travel cloak trimmed with pink fur over a rippling peach gown. Head to foot, she seemed all the hues and fragrances of a walking rose garden, yet so proud and sleek as to put that lovely flower to shame. Under her mask, no doubt she strongly resembled both her handsome son and his father, her consort and half-brother Pereden.

"So," she said, regarding Jame down her exquisite nose, "this is your little friend."

Jame raised an eyebrow. If the lady was taller than she, that was due to undoubtedly lovely hair piled up under her riding hood. In all her elegant assurance, though, she did make one feel small, especially with a bruised face and torn clothes.

So did Ran Aden, standing back and regarding her with cool, critical disdain.

"Mother, Granduncle Aden, this is Jameth, the Knorth Lordan."

Jame sketched a salute, thinking, *Trinity, I hate that name*; but she was in no mood to make the Ardeth a gift of her true identity.

For all that, she was acutely aware of how these two nobles must see her—a disheveled hoyden playing at soldier. Highborn girls sometimes went through such a phase, Brenwyr had told her, never mind that Brenwyr herself had never fully outgrown it. Mock berserker states sometimes accompanied it. Timmon knew that there was nothing feigned about Jame's occasional flares.

"One can see the Knorth in her—barely," said his mother, pulling on a pair of pale pink gloves. "How old are you, child?"

That was a good query. To say "as old as my brother" was to raise more questions than it answered, given that her twin was a good ten years older than she was. For that matter, she had no idea who had been born first.

"About Timmon's age, lady."

With a clatter of hooves, Distan's mare was brought up from the subterranean stable. Jame felt that only by an oversight was the horse white rather than rose-tinted, until she saw the glow of pink, albino eyes.

"And who was your mother?"

To ask directly was a gross impertinence. Clearly, Lady Distan saw no reason to be polite with such a snippet as Jame.

Receiving no answer, she sniffed delicately and turned to her son. "Has she told you?"

"No, Mother." Poor Timmon looked embarrassed and uncomfortable up to the red tips of his ears. Clearly, he didn't feel that his dam knew whom she was talking about, which was quite true. "We aren't on those terms."

"Then try harder. Adiraina swears that her bloodlines are pure, appearances notwithstanding. Someone has to bed her. It might as well be you."

"Yes, Mother." His whole face was burning now.

Curious. In the past, he might have laughed. Jame wondered if, despite his attempt last night at a cozy fire, he was finally beginning to take her seriously.

Lady Distan patted Timmon's cheek. "Take care of yourself, my dear boy. Remember what I told you, also what you owe both to your blood and to your dear father's memory."

Other hooves resounded on the ramp: m'lady's escort. She kissed Timmon, accepted Ran Aden's assistance to mount, and rode out of the hall in stately grandeur, followed by her uncle.

Timmon deflated with a long, pent-up sigh. "If it's any help," he said, "I apologize. To her mind and Granduncle Aden's, no blood is finer than their own, and you do look like a proper hobbledehoy. What happened to your face?"

"First a horse, then a cow, then her calf, and finally Bear. I feel as if I've been trampled by an entire menagerie."

"The Commandant threw you back into the Pit? Why?"

"Be damned if I know, unless Lord Caineron is riding him again to have me torn to pieces, which nearly happened. Timmon, how long does it take a Kendar Shanir to heal?"

"You're asking me? Eventually, I suppose most do, if they aren't killed outright. Why?"

She told him.

"You're dreaming," he said. "Why now, after so long?"

"Maybe," said Jame, "because he finally has someone to teach. A vacant mind rots. But as long as he's locked up in that hellhole, how can he get better?"

Timmon shook his head. "More wishful thinking. Focus on the present, and the future. Did you know, by the way, that your lips are turning blue? Here. Take my coat." He shrugged it over her shoulders.

"Following mother's advice?"

"Mother knows best. Sometimes. You know that I want to bed you—I've certainly been trying hard enough—but not for Mother's sake or for her precious bloodlines. Although mind you," he added thoughtfully, "it couldn't hurt right now."

"Why? What's happened?"

They had walked out onto the snowy boardwalk, where Timmon's coat was indeed welcome. Now it was his turn to shiver, although not necessarily from the cold.

"You know that my grandfather Lord Ardeth has been in the Southern Wastes since last winter looking for my father's bones. Well, in his absence Cousin Dari has been managing the house."

"He with the breath of a rotten eel."

"Well, yes, but that's not entirely his fault. The poor man is allergic to his own teeth. They keep rotting, falling out, and growing back. Anyway, now he's applied to the Highlord to be made lordan regent."

"He can override you and dethrone his lord that easily?"

"Only if the entire house and the Highlord agree. So far, Dari doesn't have enough support. Mother fears, though, that Grandfather is going soft. He's certainly old enough and with this obsession of his..."

That, Jame could understand. Highborn lived a long time, but their ends tended to be abrupt, as if their brains suddenly crumbled under the weight of years. The strain of Adric's grief might well hasten that decline, especially as his search continued to be futile.

...a ring, a blackened finger, broken off, pocketed...whose, and by whom?

"Wait a minute. These Ardeth randon who've been so hard on you recently—are they by any chance bound to Dari?"

He gaped at her for a moment, looking very young indeed. "I think you're right. Nice to know that the change is in them, not in me. So now all I need to worry about is the Lordan's Presentation."

"The what?"

His face broke into a grin. "No one told you? Again?"

"Timmon, you know that I'm new to all of this."

"It's nothing all that frightful this time—usually. Toward the end of winter, the High Council meets to determine who's hiring out mercenaries to whom, so that we don't end up meeting each other in the field. The lords use the occasion to introduce their current heirs to each other."

"What, all of them?"

"Well, as many as are free to come. Some are with the Southern Host or off on diplomatic missions. With Dari on the prowl, I have to go to uphold my status as lordan. Gorbel probably will too, unless that fickle father of his pulls a sudden switch on him. As for you, out of sight, out of mind—or will your brother force the Council to gaze on your naked if battered splendor?"

He meant her refusal to wear a mask like a proper Highborn lady. Be damned if she would, thought Jame, fingering her split lip. Anyway, there would be time to heal, barring any further stampedes.

But Timmon had also reminded her of that old, nagging

question: would Tori really let her finish her training at Tentir, much less let her go on (assuming she passed) to join the Southern Host? She knew that he had doubts. Like Chingetai, he had been trapped by his own impulsive choice to make her his heir. The other lords would prey on that uncertainty if he let them.

"I think I'll go too," she said, "invited or not."

Supper followed, an evening of going over Brier's arrangements for the coming week, and finally bed.

On the edge of sleep, Jame mulled over Timmon's words and came wide awake with a jolt. All the lordan...Kirien!

CHAPTER IV
Relics

Winter 80

TORISEN BLACK LORD SQUINTED at the parchment on the desk before him and damned its wriggly lettering. Why couldn't the Edirr find a scribe who could write? Perhaps, though, it was just his own tired eyes. After all, he had been working at the foot-high stack of correspondence for days on end.

Stop whining, he told himself. *This is what you get for letting things pile up.*

Other Highborn had scrollsmen to help them. He could too, easily. Unlike the priests at Wilden, the scholars of Mount Alban didn't have to be Shanir, and there were Knorth among them. As the commander of the Southern Host he had learned how to delegate responsibility. Why, as Highlord, was he finding it so hard?

Perhaps because some things are meant for your eyes alone.

That, no doubt, was true, but still he wished he had the support of his former commander and present war-leader, Harn Grip-hard.

Torisen wondered if Harn had yet reached Kothifir. After the randon's rough time at Tentir that fall, it had seemed best to post him as far away from the college as possible for the time being, even though the one at fault had been his sister's Southron servant Graykin, apparently possessed by Greshan in the form of the Lordan's Coat. How in Perimal's name did Jame get into such scrapes, much less attract such followers? Of all foul tricks, to drug someone with black forget-me-not...Torisen wasn't sure exactly what had happened, except that the potion had forced Harn to relive his father's suicide after Greshan's death...or was that because of Greshan's death? The Commandant had been

45

vague about that, another reminder that Tentir held some secrets which he, never having been a cadet there, would never share.

Unlike your sister, whispered his father's hoarse, mocking voice at the back of his soul image, behind the locked door. *The randon may have raised you, boy, but she is their darling now.*

Parchment crumpled in his grip. *Only if she passes Tentir.*

Ungenerous, unkind, unjust. After all, he had sent her to the college in the first place.

Trinity, look at all the papers left. He had let them pile up in the first place because he had been afraid that one of them would report that Jame had flayed that wretched cadet Vant alive. Of course, she hadn't. Instead he had fallen into a pit in the fire timber hall, tried to drag Torisen in after him, and then burned to death.

Should he read another petition, or give up for the day?

Torisen rubbed a hand across his face. It felt strange to encounter a beard there; however, he was determined never to be mistaken for his sister again as he had been by both Timmon and Vant during the Winter War. Timmon had wanted to seduce Jame, which made some sort of sense. True, she wasn't to every man's taste, but he had glimpsed her in dreams that made him stir uneasily even now. Why, though, had Vant wanted to kill her?

"You think you're so clever that you can get away with anything."

Well, so far, she had.

As he hesitated, his mind on other things, his hand reached out as if with a life of its own to pick up the next paper.

Where had this sudden compulsion to finish come from? What was he looking for in this stubborn stack mostly of foolishness? The answer came as soon as the question framed itself: news. Information. A warning meant for him alone. About what? Torisen pinched the bridge of his nose, feeling the start of a headache. He could even date the beginning of this obsession, some ten days ago, after that foul dream.

He had stopped staying awake for days, even weeks, trying to forestall certain nightmares. Even now, he told himself, when they came they meant nothing. He was no Shanir, dammit, to far-see. But the image of fire haunted him, pyre after pyre. Then a charred hand had reached out of the flames. Someone had snapped off one of its beringed fingers. Who, and whose? Ah, it made no sense, like all dreams, no more than did this futile quest for a clue.

It would come as writing on a page.

He should be focusing on reports less than ten days old, not pigheadedly working his way from back to front.

A knock on the door heralded the appearance of his servant Burr, with an armload of fresh logs for the fireplace behind him. The wolver pup Yce, who had been curled up asleep on the hearth, growled at being disturbed. However, it was about time: the tower room was growing chill, and dark. How dark, Torisen hadn't realized until Burr lit the branched candles at his elbow. The sun had set. Shadows were seeping into the valley below like dark waters rising and cold air flowed over the windowsill.

"You didn't come down at noon," said Burr, glowering.

"I was busy. Just look at this." He held up the document he had been straining to read. "The Edirr suggest that there be a special award at the Lordan's Presentation for the best dressed heir."

"For stuff like this you forget meals?"

There, Burr had a point: the petition was clearly just Lords Essien and Essiar teasing the Coman and Caineron, who tended to dress for every occasion as if for their coronation.

He let the paper drop, then grabbed as the entire stack began to slide. "I promise I'll eat something for dinner. Just stop pestering me."

Burr grunted and turned to leave. "Oh," he said on the threshold, "I almost forgot. Steward Rowan says that a messenger from Lord Danior has arrived."

Torisen scrabbled for falling papers. Dammit, now they would all be out of order. What could Cousin Holly have to say, anyway, that was too important to wait until the High Council meeting?

"Tell Rowan that I'll meet Holly's messenger below."

Burr left.

On the stair down, following him, Torisen paused to watch Marc work at the eastern end of the High Council chamber.

The furnace built into the northeast turret glowed as the big Kendar reached into it and loaded his blowpipe with a gather of molten glass. Then he began to swing it slowly, blowing, careful not to inhale the searing fumes. A lambent cylinder formed. This he detached, cut open with a hot knife, spread out on a pallet, and inserted into the annealing oven in the opposite southeastern tower.

"D'you think this system will work better than your old one?" Torisen asked, descending the rest of the way into the warm hall.

Yce ghosted around his legs and made a dart at the leather apron that Marc was untying. For a moment Kendar and wolver played tug-o'-war with the braided cord that had secured it. Then Marc let the belt go. The pup dragged it under the ebony council table and set about "killing" it with noisy, slobbering glee. Marc removed his smoked glass goggles and wiped a forearm across his sweaty face, smearing it black.

"It's all an experiment, lad, like everything else I do."

He had done remarkably well, thought Torisen, given only a handful of clues from a Tai-tastigon glass-master who had made the common mistake of underestimating the big man's intelligence. Marc had always wanted to be a craftsman, an ambition thwarted by his size and general usefulness as a warrior despite his dislike for bloodshed. Now that late middle age had crept up on him, it seemed only just that he should be free to explore his other talents.

"It looks good," Torisen said, picking up a palm-sized bit of pale rose glass shot with gold filigree and holding it to the fading light, "if nothing like a map."

"Yet you can read it, lad."

"Only because you've told me what to look for."

"Ah." Marc surveyed the abstract swirl of hues, each determined by the native materials that had gone into its making—carbon and sulfur for amber, nickel for rich purple, copper for deep green and brick red. Fragments of glass from the original, shattered window made up much of each piece but somehow failed to dominate its hue. Most of the glass for the Riverland keeps was also mixed with drops of the Highlord's own blood, making those portions potential scrying portals, or so Marc believed. The Kendar had convinced Torisen to try, but all the glass had given him so far were bad dreams.

Like the one of the pyres. Where had he been staring then? At Tentir? At Shadow Rock?

"I've a strong desire to see how the whole looks against the light," Marc said. "Ebony as a backing gives a poor feeling for color. Then too, starting at the top wasn't the brightest idea, even if local materials are the easiest to come by."

"When you're ready with a section, we'll get it into place somehow. As a favor, though, can you start next with Kothifir and as much of the Southern Wastes as you can manage?"

He could have ordered it as the Highlord, but Marc had declined to be bound to him even as Lord Knorth. That still rankled, although it did make conversation easier between them.

Waiting for you, lass.

Where had he heard that? Most likely in one of his accursed dreams, not that he believed any of them.

"I've unearthed a report from the randon I sent to guard the priests on their way to Tai-tastigon," he said, changing the topic. "All arrived safely, but they report that the temple is a mess and the city is in turmoil. It apparently never settled down after the last Thieves' Guild election. Moreover, some say that the dead are coming back, both divine and human, whatever that means."

"Ah." Marc looked thoughtful. "Now, that's a city full to the rafters with power. Some of it comes from our own temple, but there's more to it than that. Our god and the native forces of Rathillien have become intertwined. After all, we've never been on any world this long before or become more involved with it. As Tai-tastigon goes, so I suspect does Rathillien. Eventually."

Torisen remembered his brief, nightmarish time there. Ancestors preserve them all if Marc was right. He knew that his sister and the Kendar shared a past in that city, but he hadn't yet brought himself to ask about it.

Sooner or later you have to.

Then too, the thought of Jame thrust into those dire southern realms continued to haunt him. If only he could scry what she was likely to face...!

Weakling, jeered his father's voice behind the bolted door in his mind. *Afraid to look, afraid to ask, and you call yourself Highlord?*

Think of something else.

"Have you had time for that other project I requested?" he asked.

"Oh, aye." Marc picked up a leather sack which he handed to Torisen. "Here they are: the lordan's tokens for the presentation ceremony."

Torisen drew out one, a chunky disc of glass with a house emblem embossed on it—by chance, his own. With this, he would acknowledge for all to see that Jame was indeed his chosen heir.

"Have you had any word of the lass?"

"Only that the college hasn't yet burned up or fallen down."

Marc chuckled. "Well, yes, she does have an unfortunate effect on architecture, our young lady."

"She would spit if she heard you call her that, and the Women's World would have a collective seizure."

Among the stack of neglected paperwork through which he was laboring was a request from the Ardeth Matriarch Adiraina that he allow the ladies to return to his halls in the spring. How had they ever come to establish their finishing school at Gothregor anyway? Some former highlord must have agreed in a weak moment. Now, when in residence, they and their guards almost outnumbered his garrison. Over the winter, he had enjoyed prowling that part of his fortress normally out of bounds to male visitors. If there was ever a disturbance there again, he wanted to know where, what, and why.

Still, it would be nice to have the Jaran Matriarch Trishien back. She, at least, he could talk to, even if their discussions sometimes left him feeling that more had been said than he had heard.

Jame's token was still in his hand.

"I keep thinking of her as the wild-haired child whom our father drove out of the Haunted Lands keep where we were both born. We were inseparable before that . . . most of the time."

He drew a small, wooden figurine out of his pocket—a cat, perhaps an Arrin-ken judging by the power of its head and shoulders, caught in mid-leap. Like most Kendar work, it had astonishing vitality. However, one of its hind legs had been snapped off.

"Our nurse Winter carved this for us, or rather for one of us, I forget which. We were very young at the time. Of course, we fought over it . . ."

Two young savages wrenching the carving back and forth between them, as if it embodied the love that each of them craved.

Mine, mine!

No, mine!

". . . and it broke."

"Yet you kept it."

"Yes, all this time, tucked away in my gear. I only came across it again the other day." He looked from the damaged carving to the glass token and back, holding one in each hand as if weighing them against each other, the past versus the future. "And now she is to be confirmed as my lordan. Can we share such power without breaking everything?"

"You've grown, lad. So has she."

"True enough." He returned the token to Marc and dropped the cat back into his pocket.

Marc drained a scooper of water through heat-chapped lips and shot a sideways look at Torisen. "By the way," he said, carefully offhanded, "I've heard a bit of news from my Ardeth friends. Lord Adric's grandson Dari wants to be made lordan regent. That would effectively make him Lord Ardeth, wouldn't it?"

"In all but name, yes."

"And you can do that?"

"Under certain conditions, if the health of his house demands it. As I confirm lords, so I can unseat them. Damned if I want to, though."

Everyone knew how much he owed to Adric. If the Ardeth lord hadn't hidden him in the Southern Host, he would never have survived to claim the Highlord's seat. The current breach between them made things doubly awkward, but what could Torisen do? The Highlord must not be an Ardeth puppet as the commander of the Southern Host had felt himself to be. Still, he had promised to look after his former mentor's interests.

"I also hear," said Marc, emboldened, "that Lord Ardeth is on his way north to attend the High Council meeting."

"Is he, by Trinity?"

He should have known that, Torisen thought, chagrinned. Ironically, it was because Ardeth had used Torisen's friends to spy on him in those early days that he had such an aversion to spying on anyone now. As a result, the Knorth possessed the poorest intelligence network in the Kencyrath, and Marc knew it. No wonder the Kendar was trying to impart his information so diplomatically. Torisen glanced at the stained glass map. Somehow, the thought of using it didn't agitate him the way using human agents did. How valuable it could be, if only it worked properly. Instead, he was reduced to allies casually passing on news.

"I thought Adric was going to wander the Wastes forever," he said.

"Not now that he believes at least one of Pereden's bones is in the Riverland."

Torisen stared at him. "Why in Perimal's name would he think that?"

Harn had put the boy's body on the common pyre at the Cataracts, he thought. It should be ashes on the wind. He had felt guilty about Ardeth's futile search of the Wastes and wondered how to end it. Now, however, he remembered his dream and was chilled. This was an ending unlike any he had ever envisioned.

"Well," Marc was saying, "the thing is that Lord Ardeth found the site where the central column led by Pereden clashed with the Waster Horde. Where else should he look for his son's bones? But they weren't there. At the same time, his Shanir sense told him that at least one still existed. Frustration was like to drive him mad, and his people with him. So he took one of his strongest potions to enhance his powers. They thought it was going to kill him. But after spinning around like a mad dowser until everyone with him was falling-down dizzy and fit to die, he ended up pointing north toward the Riverland."

"And now Adric is coming here to find it? Sweet Trinity."

The mere suspicion that Pereden had joined the Waster Horde had nearly given his father a fatal heart attack. If Adric did find a bone in the Riverland, now, how in Perimal's name could Torisen explain it when he didn't know himself?

Somebody cleared his throat near the southwest circular stair. Torisen lowered his hand from the collar of his coat where he had instinctively reached for one of his throwing knives.

Don't kill the messenger.

It was, of course, Cousin Holly's courier, whom he had told to meet him here.

The Kendar approached looking uneasy, handed Torisen a pouch, and backed away.

"Highlord, my lord asks that you treat this as urgent, not to go on your to-do pile."

Trinity, did everyone know that he was behind in his paperwork? Of course they did.

He flicked a knife out of his collar and sliced open the lumpy packet. Something black fell out. Yce snapped it out of midair and retreated with her prize, growling. Marc went after her under the table, like a large bumblebee in a small bottle. The table rocked. Glass slid.

Torisen shook out the rest of the packet's contents, consisting of a note and a heat-cracked moon opal signet ring in a tarnished silver setting.

For a moment he stared at the paper. It reeked faintly of burning. Writing on a page . . . This was the message that he had been looking for all along, in the wrong place.

Dear Tori, he read. *I took this at the Cataracts, just in case we ever had to prove that Pereden actually was there. I didn't mean to cause trouble. Now I don't know what to do with it, so here it is. Sorry. Love, Holly.*

Marc emerged from under the table with something in his big hand. He held it out to Torisen—a finger shriveled by the pyre, half its flesh seared away.

"Your family does make a practice of carrying around bones, I've noticed. First your sister with your father's finger and then you with my sister Willow's remains. So what's this?"

Torisen slid the ring over the bone and stared at the resulting combination. The former bore the Ardeth crest.

"Now my head really hurts."

CHAPTER V
The High Council

Winter 90–100

I

NOW CAME THE HARSHEST DAYS of winter.

Everyone huddled close to the fires at night under mounds of fur, and still an exposed finger or nose might turn ominously white by morning. Bare bodies threw on clothes in a hopping frenzy. Sheets of ice sealed wash basins. Food arrived at the breakfast table already cold. After the morning rally in the square, cadets hustled back indoors to make their way to classes by the interior hallway. Lessons proceeded as normally as possible if rather fast to generate heat for chilled limbs. Weapons, strategy, history, the Senethar, the dread (and freezing) writing class...

Nonetheless, everyone worked hard, all too aware that with spring would come the final tests that would determine not only if they passed Tentir but where their posting would be the coming year.

"Oh, let it be the Southern Wastes!" groaned many a miserable cadet. "No more winter, ever!"

At first, horses plunged about outside in drifts up to their shaggy bellies, muzzles clumped with ice, while cadets floundered out to them dragging sleds full of hay and ice-mantled water.

Soon, however, they had to be moved inside. The subterranean stable filled to overflowing; the extras were quartered in the great hall under the banners of the major houses. The air thickened with their steaming breath and droppings while the horse-master moved among them checking for strangles or any other deadly, communicable complaint. In passing, he patted the dappled flank of the Whinno-hir Bel-tairi and wondered how her companion was doing out in the snow. The last time he had seen Death's-head, the rathorn had grown a pelt as shaggy as a wolf's, but still, all that cold, cold ivory...!

Jame missed working with the colt and felt his aching cold through the bond between them enough to deepen her own shudders.

However, she was also glad not to go outside Tentir more than necessary.

For one thing, she had proved to be more susceptible to frost-bite than most Kendar, not surprisingly given her slighter build. Bits of her froze almost casually, over and over, and each time had to be reawakened to throbbing life.

For another thing, she didn't want to encounter the Dark Judge, if he really was haunting the college's environs. The colt's senses gave fleeting suggestions of this, but in general, rathorn and giant cat kept their distance from each other. Some nights Jame thought she heard that terrible voice pleaded with the wind, wailing word-lessly. Such hunger, such desolation! Was he only lashing out in his eternal pain, or did he think that judging her would make him whole again? Certainly, he longed to pass judgment on such a nemesis as she had proven to be, however innocent. What really drove him mad, however, was that he couldn't strike at the root of evil itself, Gerridon. In an agony of self-revelation, the great cat had told her that no Arrin-ken could enter the halls of the Master's monstrous house swallowed by Perimal Darkling until the coming of the Tyr-ridan.

Another memory, another voice, this one harsh and halting: Ashe had said that, according to legend, only a Kencyr could kill one of the Three. Jame feared that she was becoming the incarnation of That-Which-Destroys, the Third Face of God. It would be ironic if the Judge were to blast his last chance at revenge by destroying her, and it would indeed be the last: once there had been many potential Knorth nemeses—now there was only her.

But time passed and the howling on the heights abated, if it had ever been there at all. Jame began to doubt what she had seen and heard, both with the Dark Judge and with Vant among the Burning Ones. How likely was the latter, after all? A trick of the firelight, a shard of free-floating guilt.

As for the blind Arrin-ken, let him mind his own business. Be damned if she was going to run scared of a phantom bully, however bloodthirsty.

Meanwhile, she continued to work with Bear, after badgering the Commandant into letting her into the randon's cell to deal with his overgrown toenails and claws. She found that since she had last seen him, he had virtually destroyed his lodgings. Had he finally grown aware of how squalid they were, or simply succumbed to an extreme case of cabin fever? She thought that she saw improvement in him now if only in that he no longer tried to kill her during lessons and began to teach again. Once in a while, he actually spoke a word or two. Was it only wishful thinking, or had the scar on his forehead lengthened as his cleft skull finally began to close? Still, how could he really improve while tightly mewed in and isolated as he was most of the time?

Timmon continued to court her, if a bit absent-mindedly. Now that his instructors were holding him to schedule, he had less time and energy for amorous pursuits. As the easiest course, he had again taken Narsa into his bed. Jame worried about that. Surely the Kendar knew that he was only using her, but he had woven his charms so well that she probably didn't care. Whenever Jame saw her she looked happy, though with a certain uneasy, feverish gleam in her eyes.

Gorbel grumbled through his days, making up for his clumsiness with dogged determination, often with the pook Twizzle in the corner regarding him button-eyed and panting, occasionally shifting within his skin the better to deal with one arcane itch or another.

Fash watched everyone with his wide, white smile and his cold eyes.

At last came a day when the wind changed from the north to the south. Although snow still lay thick on the ground, something hinted at stealthy growth in the dark and at awakenings. Water dripped. Snow slid from boughs in miniature avalanches, echoed by massive ones from the heights. Cadets shoved back their hoods, sniffed, and grinned at each other. They had to endure one last blizzard, but after that the sun shone bright and the snow began to creep back into the shadows. A bird sang tentatively, then another.

Soon it would be time for the High Council meeting.

❦ II ❧

TORISEN SLID INTO THE DRESS COAT that Burr held for him and ran his scarred hands down its sleek panels. His Kendar servant had talked him into ordering new clothes from Kothifir for himself as well as for his garrison—the former a luxury about which he still felt uneasy. Black satin, richly embroidered with silver thread by his own people...they wanted to show him off. A pity that he didn't fill such extravagance better.

"I can still count your ribs," muttered Burr, mirroring his thoughts.

"So? No one else can, under all of this finery. Come summer, shall I try to pork up like Lord Caineron?"

"Huh."

Torisen's hand slid over his pocket and the slight bulge there. Pereden's ring and finger. How meaningless everything seemed compared to those, the dull sparks that might overthrow his entire world. If he gave them to Adric, how was he going to explain where they had come from and why they were here? He couldn't lie without the death of honor, without which there was nothing.

If he hid them, though, Adric's search would tear the River-land apart.

Burn them? His study fire wasn't hot enough, but Marc's would be. He should have thought of that before. However, what would *that* do to Adric?

Damn Holly anyway—a good idea at the wrong time. What if his cousin were to confess what he knew? That, after all, wasn't much. He shouldn't have recognized Peri in the first place. Much less did he know how Adric's heir had come to be on the common pyre. Would Adric recognize his innocence, though? A blood feud between the Ardeth and the Danior would destroy the latter and only benefit the Randir, who would love to take over tiny Shadow Rock so temptingly placed just across the river from them.

But Torisen couldn't permit that either...could he?

Wouldn't that be better than admitting his role in that wretched boy's death? Because that would lead to total civil war, the prob-able extinction of his own house, and quite possibly the end of the Kencyrath as he knew it.

One tried and tried to do the right thing.

Damn you, Pereden. I will not let you destroy everything that I've worked so hard to build. I will not.

Burr produced an iron box and opened it. They both regarded the Kenthiar, that mysterious, narrow, silver collar set with a gem of shifting hue. Only the true Highlord could wear it; anyone else hazarded his neck, not to mention his head. Torisen picked it up, gingerly, wary of its inner surfaces. Was he still fit to be the leader of his people? Had he ever been? Well, the accursed thing had accepted him before. He put it around his neck and snapped shut the hinges. Both he and Burr let out their breaths, which neither had realized he was holding.

Voices drifted up the stairs from the Council Chamber below. The lords were beginning to gather.

"Now," he said to Burr, "we go down."

A cloth had been spread over the ebony table to protect the glass beneath and both furnace doors were shut, leaving the chamber pleasantly warm on this cool, late winter day. Only one lord had arrived so far with his retinue in attendance. He turned. It was Adric, his skin darkened by the Southern Wastes in sharp contrast to his white hair and blue eyes.

"Ganth!" he exclaimed.

A chill went down Torisen's spine. So too the old Jaran lord, Jedrak, had greeted him out of the depths of his sudden senility before the Host had marched out for the Cataracts. He finished his own descent to the floor and crossed it to his old mentor. As he did so, a middle-aged man bent to whisper in Lord Ardeth's ear.

Adric drew back, waving a thin, fastidious hand. "Dari, please. Your breath would stun a horse."

So this was Adric's grandson and would-be lordan regent. He might have been handsome if not for his prissy expression, half disapproval, half an effort to move his lips as little as possible when he spoke. His teeth, briefly glimpsed, ranged from newborn white nubs to rotting black stumps, the rest a gray all the more distressing set against red, swollen gums. Trinity, what could cause a man's own body to turn against him so painfully? The healer's use of soul-images suggested that the body reflected the spirit. Was Dari really so ambitious that he would even devour himself? So far in his grandfather's absence, however, he had run his house well. Prune-faced or not, he was a competent man.

"Not Ganth. Torisen."

He took the old man's hand and kissed it. "How are you, Adric?"

The blue eyes blinked, then refocused. "Torisen. Of course. I am well, but will be so much better when I find Pereden. You aren't a father. You don't know what it's like, to lose a son."

Torisen almost asked, "To lose in what sense?"

How d'you think my father will react when he hears what I've done, and why? Pereden's voice jeered in his memory.

A little boy lost, long before Adric had realized that he was gone, now to be found again in what sense?

Torisen sat down beside the Ardeth lord, all too aware of the lump in his pocket.

"It won't be long now, though. I haven't felt so close to him since the Cataracts."

"Really, Grandfather, I keep telling you that Pereden is dead."

The old fire snapped into the Highborn's eyes. "Of course he is. D'you take me for a senile fool?"

His followers shifted uneasily. Torisen noted that some stood behind Dari, but more behind the old lord.

A scrap of sound near the stairwell, and there was Timmon, looking profoundly uneasy.

"Pardon, my lords, but I thought I heard someone call me," he said.

Adric saw him, and his face lit up. "Pereden, there you are at last!"

The cadet blanched and his gaze darted among the other Ardeth, looking for help. No one but Dari would meet his eyes, and that with a glower. To be fair, he did strongly resemble his father, from his golden hair to the trim fit of his garnet and red dress coat.

Peri should have attended Tentir, Torisen thought. In Timmon he saw a much less insouciant, feckless boy than he had first met when delivering Jame to the randon college the previous summer. Had Jame also changed as much?

Timmon gulped. "Here I am, my lord," he said.

❧ **III** ❧

THE LORDAN AND THEIR ATTENDANTS had gathered in Gothregor's outer ward, awaiting their lords' summons. The keep towered over them, but they stayed in the warm sunlight, avoiding its cold shadow. Some talked warily. Others stood haughtily aloof. All wore dazzling dress coats in shades from claret wine to cloud-flecked blue, from autumn gold to spring green freckled with flowers.

As Jame and Brier entered the ward, Rue made an unhappy sound behind them when she saw the others' brave display. Clearly, she thought that her own lordan could have outshone them all with the Lordan's Coat, but Jame had burned that haunted garment, relic of her detested uncle Greshan, earlier that winter—a necessary deed considering that his soul had been trapped in it, ready to possess whoever wore it. Nothing else in Greshan's adopted wardrobe matched its splendor, nor had there been a chance yet to spend any of Jame's new allowance on suitable finery. Jame had said that she didn't care as long as her cadet jacket was clean and not too obviously patched. Now, however, she felt plain and out of place, a crow among peacocks.

Speaking of peacocks, there was Gorbel in a bright blue coat trimmed with lumps of coral and silver filigree, flanked by his five-commander Obidin and Fash.

"I had to bring him," he had told Jame earlier, speaking of the latter. "Father ordered it."

Jame wondered, not for the first time, what Lord Caineron was planning. He had made it clear that he wasn't happy with Gorbel's progress in discrediting her—enough to replace him? Now would be a suitably dramatic time.

To one side, two identical boys dressed in sunlit wheat gold were teasing a sullen third in storm gray flecked with opal lightning.

"The Edirr and Coman Lordan," Rue whispered in Jame's ear. Although a border brat, the cadet liked to show off her second-hand knowledge of Riverland politics, which might or might not be accurate.

"Do the Edirr always do everything in twos?" asked Jame, thinking of the Lords Essien and Essiar who shared power in their house.

"More often than not. The Edirr produce so many twins that it saves trouble."

A little boy, perhaps four years old, pelted shrieking between them, pursued by a harried Kendar.

"Danior's son and heir," said Rue wisely.

Meanwhile Jame had spotted a familiar face across the ward and went to greet Kirien. White-haired Kindrie was with her.

"I came to see the show," he told his cousin, smiling.

Jame thought that she had never seen him look better, a long way from the tattered scarecrow he had been when they had first met. Perhaps Kirien was to thank for that. The Jaran Lordan smiled, as tranquil and handsome as ever. She too wore a dress coat, dove-gray with silver trim. With her dark, cropped hair and slender build, it wasn't at all obvious that she was female, not that she dressed so as to disguise the fact; these were simply a more elegant version of her working clothes as a scrollswoman of Mount Alban, who hadn't been overly pleased to be chosen lordan by the rest of her house. Few of the lords had guessed her sex. What they would say when they found out didn't bear thinking about.

"You've sent us an avid scholar," she said.

"Who?"

"Your servant Graykin. He's been reading everything he can find and questioning every scrollsman or singer he can catch about the history of the Southern Wastes."

Jame was taken aback. After the trauma inflicted on him by Greshan's coat, she had only hoped to keep Gray busy until the weather made travel to Kothifir safe, always assuming that she graduated to follow him.

"How is he getting them to cooperate?" she asked, remembering that most scrollsmen operated on a barter system when it came to sharing information.

"I've been able to help a bit there," said Kindrie. "Y'see, Index has been plagued with joint pains recently, beyond the help of his herb shed to cure."

Index, who had gotten his nickname because he knew where every arcane scrap of information was stored, be it in scroll, scholar, or singer. Index, whose knowledge had allowed him to amass a fabulous store of barter points.

"So you've been trading him points for your help as a healer. I appreciate that."

Kindrie's ears turned faintly pink. "Consider it recompense for helping me to escape from the Priests' College."

Jame felt like blushing herself when she remembered how harshly she had treated him on the journey to Restormir to rescue Gray, all because she hadn't been able to stomach his hieratic background, never mind that it had been involuntary. That prejudice at least seemed to have faded, at least where Kindrie was concerned. Would that Tori could say as much about his feelings toward the Shanir.

Timmon emerged from the keep, looking shaken.

"This is awful," he said to Jame, hardly seeming to care who else heard. "Grandfather is convinced that I'm Pereden. Dari keeps trying to tell him differently, and he keeps insisting that 'blood and bone, a father knows.' You should have seen Dari glare. He spat a rotten tooth at me."

Fash had drifted within earshot. "Gone soft, has he? Poor old man. Now everyone will feel free to take advantage of him."

Timmon bridled. "If you mean me..."

"Fash," said Gorbel. "Shut up."

Holly's small son rushed past again, this time in pursuit of Gorbel's pook, shrieking, "Doggie!"

"Here now, stop that," snapped the Caineron Lordan, and hurried off to his pet's rescue.

Fash and Obidin stayed.

"Oh," the former said to Timmon with his wide, white grin, "I didn't mean you, Lordan. Your cousin Dari, now..."

Timmon drew himself up, projecting more strength than Jame had yet seen in him.

"That is house business, Caineron. Butt out."

Fash actually recoiled a step, but no more. His grin, having flickered, came back. "And you, M'lady Kirien. Don't you think that the High Council deserves the truth?"

Kirien answered, still serene. "D'you think I've hidden anything from any of them? They see what they expect to see. Unlike you, I hide little."

Fash flushed, but his retort stuck in his throat. He knew better than to challenge a Shanir like Kirien whose power lay in being able to compel the truth. What was his game anyway, trying to pick one fight after another with his superiors? Gorbel would have stopped him, but Obidin just stood there, radiating mild interest. She wondered if, like a certain late, unlamented Randir, Fash's own talent lay in temptation.

Would you tempt the destroyer in me, Caineron?

As if he had heard her thought, he turned his white teeth on her.

"I see that you shun the flatteries of fashion, Lordan. How... modest of you. But that's not quite correct: you may wear your cadet jacket—very dashingly, I might add—but you dress your hair

Merikit style. Let's see: smooth on the right but, oh my, twenty
braids on the left, all twisted into one down the back. Have you
really killed twenty hillmen?"

The simple answer to that was "no." Jame had no idea how many
Noyat she had personally slain during their raid on the Merikit
village, but the Merikit women had credited her with all of their
kills as well and Gran Cyd herself had first braided the record
of the enemy dead into Jame's hair, slathered with their blood.
Why had she worn it into Gothregor? Perhaps to compensate
for her plain coat, or perhaps in defiance because other cadets
had started to gossip about her adventures among the so-called
savages. Only now did it occur to her that those rumors might
have been started by Fash, one of the few at Tentir who would
know what those braids signified.

"What happens in the hills is no business of yours," she told
him coldly.

Satisfaction glinted in his eyes. He knew that he had drawn
blood.

"Ah, but then hillmen die so easily," he said, "like the dumb
brutes that they are."

"That's all they are to you, isn't it? Mere animals."

Kirien touched her arm. "Gently, gently..."

The pook dashed past again, followed by Danior's son shrieking,
"Doggie, doggie, doggie!" followed by a panting Gorbel.

"That's right," said Fash, answering Jame, flashing an even wider
smile at her that was more like the bearing of teeth. "Pilfering
vermin, to be exact. A waste of skin."

Jame remembered the tattooed Merikit hides strewn like rugs
about Lord Caineron's quarters. Fash and his ilk had supplied
those. She thought of Prid's tawny mane or Gran Cyd's auburn
braids spread across the floor under Caldane's slippered feet. Dark
anger stirred in her.

"Half hill and half hall," mused Fash, eyeing her slyly askance.
"How many classes d'you reckon you've missed, playing savage
in the wilds?"

"Do you think me ill-learned? Yet I am still at the college,
after two culls."

"As am I. The randon, Trinity bless them, who are they to
deny a lord's heir?"

"Now listen here..." began Timmon ominously.

"Oh, no one questions you, m'lord."

"But you imply that they do me." Jame was too angry now for caution, although part of her mind noted the Caineron's manipulations and urged her back. But this...this beast had put his knife to decent Merikit skin and had lived to laugh about it.

"Challenge me," she heard herself say, "anytime, anywhere, and we will see."

Fash bowed himself away. "Oh yes. We undoubtedly will."

"That," said Kirien, "was not wise."

Jame sighed, letting the rage flow out of her taut limbs and her nails resheathe. "No, it wasn't. But one has to take a stand somewhere."

IV

AT LAST THE SUMMONS CAME and the lordan trooped up to the Council Chamber. There the lords sat around the table in coats of brocade, silk, and embroidery heavy with gold, far more resplendent even than their heirs.

Torisen stood framed by the empty window with his hands clasped behind him, a figure of slim, simple elegance in black and silver.

His beard startled Jame, who hadn't seen him since the Winter Wars. She wondered if he had grown it to disguise the hollows of his cheeks. Nothing dire that she knew about was going on. The job of Highlord was apparently wearing enough in itself when taken seriously as, of course, Torisen would. She wished that she could make him laugh. Even more, she wished that they could simply meet as the equals that they first had been. After all, they were twins even if Tori was a good ten years older than she.

But she was also a Highborn female, less than any lord, more and yet somehow simultaneously less than just about everyone else. Then too, she was also a randon cadet and her brother's heir, an anomaly anyway anyone cared to look at it.

She could feel the lords' eyes seek her out, some disapproving, some speculative. Caldane, Lord Caineron, glowered, but with a hint of eagerness in his stance, like a cat that has spotted its prey. His pudgy, beringed fingers drummed the table, stilled, and drummed again. Only Brandan and Cousin Holly looked at all friendly, the former nodding to her as she entered the room, the latter raising a finger in greeting.

"Before we start the business for which we are gathered," said the Highlord, "it is customary for us to present our heirs to the full Council and for me to give a token of approval to each. Lord Brandan, I understand that your nephew is absent on official business."

"Yes." Torisen's closest neighbor leaned forward, his face nearly as dark as Adric's and more seamed, although he was a much younger man. Not for Brant, the well-kept smoothness of the Ardeth lord; summer and winter, he worked beside his Kendar in the fields and in the Southern Wastes. "I left Boden in Kothifir, ready to finalize our troop contracts according to the decisions made here today."

"Lord Randir…"

Kenan, Lord Randir, leaned back nonchalantly in his chair. As usual, his haughty features reminded Jame of something, or someone, but she couldn't quite pin it down. Could she be thinking of Shade, his only child? "I have decades yet to rule my house. Ask for my choice of lordan fifty years from now."

"Very well." Torisen dipped his long, scar-laced fingers into a leather sack, drew out a chunky piece of glass, and glanced at the emblem stamped on it.

"Coman."

The Coman Lordan came forward, with a slight air of truculence: his house hadn't yet decided if it supported the Knorth or the Caineron. The Edirr twins came trying to look serious but failing. Danior's little son made almost everyone smile as he dashed up in his red coat crying, "Cousin Tori! Cousin Tori!" Timmon approached to soft applause from his beaming grandfather and a murderous look from his cousin Dari.

Torisen paused, looking troubled.

"Do you swear to uphold the honor of your house, to put its interests always before your own?"

Timmon blinked. No one else had been asked such a question. He glanced at Adric who was mouthing, "Go on, Pereden!" then back at the Highlord.

"Honor break me, darkness take me, I do."

"Then I entrust you with this. After all, it's primarily the business of your house. Do with it as you will." Instead of a glass token, he reached into a pocket, drew out something wrapped in linen, and handed it to the Ardeth Lordan.

Timmon retreated, looking confused. His bewilderment only grew when he examined the contents of the packet. Jame wanted to see too, but then Torisen called out, "Knorth."

A restive stir passed among the lords. Caldane gave it voice:

"Do you really mean to uphold this travesty? She may be your sister, but what kind of a fool picks a lady for his lordan?"

"As for her right to wear that coat," added the Randir, lazily fingering his wine glass, "what lord sends a lady to become a randon cadet?"

They've planned this, Jame thought as a murmur rose from the table, *and most of the Council agree.*

"It's not even as if she can properly defend herself," Caldane continued, leaning forward like a bulldog on a short leash, lower jaw thrust forward. "Put it to the test if you doubt me."

Torisen's troubled gaze sought her out. *Can you deal with this challenge?* his eyes asked her.

She met his worried look steadily and gave a brief nod. *If I can't, both of us are wasting our time.*

"So be it."

"Will I do as a challenger?" Fash ambled forward. "You did say 'anytime, anyplace,'" he reminded her with an amiable smirk.

So this was why he had taunted her in the outer ward, doubtless with Caldane's approval. She glanced at Gorbel, who had regained his errant pook and was holding it apparently upside down. If she failed, who would Lord Caineron present as his heir?

"I said it, I meant it," she said to Fash. "Choose your weapon."

"Swords, then."

Oh, schist. Fash knew perfectly well that swordcraft was her weakest discipline. Still, she accepted the blade thrown to her, and found it poorly balanced.

Before she could complain, Fash was on her with a vicious down cut. She blocked it, and felt the weight of the blow up to her shoulder. He slashed; she ducked.

This was hopeless. Attack.

He easily foiled her advance and, with a twist of his wrist, disarmed her.

A sigh arose from the onlookers, half satisfaction, half relief, but it changed to exclamations of protest as Fash lunged for her throat.

She turned her evasion into a backward somersault, kicking him in the face as she went over. He staggered with a bloody nose, cursing. Another backflip put her temporarily out of his reach. There had to be some way to defend herself. Under a nearby bench, neatly stowed, was Marc's glassmaking gear. She snatched out the leather apron and wrapped it around her left arm, just in time to baffle another thrust. Whatever his original intentions, to pink or merely to humiliate her, that kick to the face had infuriated the man. Now he was out for blood. Well, so was she.

Jame snapped the apron's braided belt like a whip, slashing his forehead. It wasn't much of a cut but it bled profusely, hindering his sight. He swung wildly. She evaded with water-flowing, channeling his blow aside. As he staggered, momentarily off balance, she stepped in and slammed the heel of her palm into his nose, this time breaking it with an audible crunch. He couldn't see, nor could he breathe except through his mouth, and blood was streaming into that fit to choke him. Jame circled warily. Out of the corner of her eye she saw Torisen watching with tightly folded arms, as if restraining himself. Fash swung again, this time clipping her shoulder. Cloth and skin ripped. The cut wasn't much, but Rue was in for more darning. She glimpsed the straw-headed cadet to one side, fast in Brier's grip as if struggling to intervene.

Time to end this.

She snaked the belt around Fash's sword hand and jerked. The blade flew free. Lords ducked. It crashed down on the table and skidded to a stop, its point facing Caldane. The Caineron lord recoiled.

"Hic!"

A look of panic turned his florid face blotchy. He grabbed the arms of his heavy chair and hung on like a drowning man.

"*Hic!*"

The chair started to rise, with him in it.

"*HIC!*"

Gorbel dropped the pook and quickly rounded the table to stand behind his father. With his hands on Caldane's shoulders, he brought his weight to bear and forced him down. Brandan (who didn't like wine) offered his cup of cider. Gorbel took it and poured it down his father's throat.

"...hic..."

The chair settled.

Meanwhile Fash angrily tried to wipe the blood off his face, although both forehead and nose continued to bleed. Jame stood ready with her leather shield and the belt, which she continued to twitch experimentally, trying to master its ungainly length and balance.

"Yield?"

He sputtered, fighting to regain control of himself.

"An...interesting demonstration, to make use of whatever crude means one finds at hand. And we all thought that your fighting style was so pure."

"Never assume. What works, works."

Torisen unfolded his arms and took a deep breath.

"I believe that my lordan has proved her point. Now, if we may proceed..."

Jame put aside Marc's apron and belt. The cut on her shoulder stung. Would these petty tests never end? Then again, she thought, glancing at Gorbel, not so petty after all, for either of them. As for Fash, an old friend had said it long ago: To such a man, she would always be a lure and a trap, because he would never take her seriously.

But her brother was holding out the emblem of his acceptance. She stepped forward to receive it.

"Doggie!"

The pook hurtled between them, pursued by a miniature whirlwind in red. The latter knocked the glass token out of Torisen's hand and Jame, recoiling, stepped on it. Crunch. Both regarded the shattered remains.

"Can we share anything without breaking it?" murmured Torisen. Then he sighed. "So be it." Reaching into a pocket he drew out a small, feline carving, and gave it to Jame.

She stared at it. "Oh. I'd forgotten all about this."

"I didn't."

Jame retreated with her prize, bemused.

Torisen dipped into the sack and drew out the next-to-last piece of glass.

"Caineron."

Caldane still clutched the arms of his chair but had stopped hiccupping. He glared at the gory, snuffling spectacle that was Fash, then turned to Gorbel. "Well, go on. It seems, after all, that you're the best of a poor lot."

Gorbel approached the Highlord and stolidly received his token. "Jaran."

Kirien had been standing thoughtfully to one side. Now she shrugged as if making up her mind, slipped off her gray coat, and approached Torisen in a discreet but still revealing white shirt.

Exclamations of surprise and horror rose from some (but not all) of the lords. "It can't be." "It is!" "Another damned female!"

"So what if it is?" Kedan, acting lord of the Jaran, waved off the outraged faces turned toward him. "Jedrak made his choice and the rest of his house supports it. If the Highlord does too, what right do any of you have to protest against it?"

Torisen handed Kirien the token. "You picked a fine time to unveil," he said, under cover of a growing storm of outrage.

"Unnatural, perverse..." "...bad enough that the Knorth have run mad, but the Jaran...!" "...rathorns and Whinno-hir, living together..."

Kirien smiled. "They had to find out sooner or later, for those who hadn't already guessed. Not that it was ever meant to be a secret. 'Observe, describe, learn,' we Jaran say. As it is, your sister diverts attention from me as I do from her. Let them fight us both, or neither."

Torisen considered this.

"I expect, when I have time to think, that I'll be grateful."

V

LATER, JAME SHOWED THE STATUETTE to Timmon and Gorbel. "We fought over it as children until it broke. I kept the hind leg..."

Until the changer Keral had taken it from her and dropped it into the fire over her furious protests.

"No mementos for you, brat. This is your home now."

"...until I lost it. What did you get, Timmon?"

The Ardeth opened the linen packet and showed them.

Gorbel peered at the contents. "A fire-cured finger and a cracked ring? I don't understand."

"Neither do I except—I think—this is my father's ring."

"And his finger? If so, how did the Highlord get it?"

"I don't know. I can't guess. He said that it was my house's business. 'Do with it what you will.'"

Jame wasn't sure that her brother had done a wise thing. She remembered her dream of Tori breaking Pereden's neck and of the pyre at the Cataracts from which someone had taken what were surely these relics. Since Adric believed that he had found his living son in Timmon, he would presumably no longer continue his bone hunt and would hopefully resume control of his house. She heard again the Ardeth lord's clear voice rising above the uproar over Kirien's "unmasking": "Be that as it may, we still have business to discuss."

In everything not touching on Pereden, he seemed to be all right, although no doubt Dari would continue to press for his replacement. But if Adric or Timmon were ever to learn the truth...

"Huh," said Gorbel. "You two have all the luck. All I got was this dumb chunk of glass."

CHAPTER VI

History Lessons

Winter 110

I

BARS OF LIGHT STREAMED through cracks in the shed's walls, piercing the jars shelved from floor to ceiling. The air was thick with motes and the scent of crushed herbs. Half a dozen jars had fallen and smashed on the floor, mixing their contents with shards of glass.

What a mess, thought Kindrie.

He gingerly stepped through the debris and picked up a fragment of dried root, trying to guess what it was. His job at Mount Alban was to memorize the order of the containers. However, curiosity as a healer had also led him to learn as much as he could about the herbs themselves. Grayish brown and wrinkled outside, inside white and spongy...but it was the fragrance that gave him his clue: angelica.

And this straight, dark brown root with its bitter smell—black snake root, surely.

Alfalfa, feverfew, ginger...

There was a pattern, of course: all were good for rheumatism.

He collected every bit he could find, carefully picking out the glass, wincing as splinters pricked his fingers, and laid them out on the table. Now the jars. Some large pieces fit together easily but others had been reduced to a powder that had joined the dancing dust motes. It was impossible to do a complete job, however long he took, and the day was already waning toward dusk.

There. Five partial jars held together by his will, filled with as much of their contents as had survived. Now to return them to their rightful places on the shelves.

Oh, bother. None of the containers were labeled and all had moved to fill any gap. Push some aside here, more there...

"Well?" said a sharp voice. "Are you done yet?"

His hand jerked. The shelves trembled, ripe for another disaster, and grew transparent. Kindrie hastily slotted the last jar into place. As he withdrew from the soul-image, its real life counterpart took shape around him, complete with his elderly patient glowering at him across the table. He released Index's claw of a hand.

"How do you feel?"

The old scrollsman flexed arthritic fingers.

"Better," he said, almost with reluctance. "Not perfect, mind you, but better."

"I'm glad." Kindrie rolled his shoulders to release the tension in them and ruefully regarded his own stinging fingertips. Metaphoric splinters were worse than real ones; the nerves remembered them far longer. "It's hard to replace what the years have taken away."

"No cure for old age, eh? There should be. And for death."

Kindrie sighed. If he had completed his training as a healer at the Priests' College, would he be better now or warped beyond redemption? Had it been selfish of him to flee? No. Lady Rawneth would have destroyed him even if her hieratic minions hadn't.

Index rose and started to putter around his shed, gathering the ingredients for alfalfa tea.

"Not perfect," he repeated over his shoulder, "but fair is fair. The scrollsman with the information that you want, Moyden by name, has gone on an ambassadorial mission to the Poison Courts. We may never see him again."

"Oh."

"However, I know something about the history of the Southern Wastes. Before we arrived on Rathillien, the natives say that in their place was a huge inland sea surrounded by rich civilizations. Then the climate changed from temperate to a desert, don't ask me why or how. They say that even the stars shifted in the sky. Anyway, the sea was cut off from its freshwater sources, turned to salt, and dried up. The cities that clustered around it disappeared into the sand and their people fled. Only their outposts remained—Kothifir, Hurlen, and Urakarn, for example. All of this was some three thousand years ago, during the Fifth Age. By most accounts, Rathillien has had seven."

Kindrie blinked, trying to comprehend the scope of such vast changes, so baldly presented. If Index had been a singer, and more poetic, he would have suspected that the old man was taking advantage of the Lawful Lie.

"I think," he said, "that I should talk to Moyden when..."

"If."

"If he returns."

"You do that. Tell him that you bartered with me and that I will repay him." Index poured boiling water over his herbs and cradled the cup in gnarled fingers. "Ah," he said, inhaling the fragrance. "Soul-images are all very well, but give me a fistful of dried leaves every time. You're doing this for that gray sneak, aren't you? Take my advice, boy: make sure that he pays you."

Kindrie stood up and executed a courteous if awkward bow. "All information, ultimately, is for my cousin. I don't barter with her."

"Ah." Index impatiently waved him away. "Beware that one: honorable as she seems, she has the darkling glamour."

As Kindrie climbed the shed's stair and crossed Mount Alban's cavernous entry hall, he dismissed Index's warning and savored that word: cousin. Bastards had no kin. He was not a bastard. He had a family, small though it was, and moreover not one cousin but two. The thought warmed him as much as his blue woolen robe, a gift from Kirien and finer than he had ever owned before. Kin, and friends.

Here was the central wooden stair rising in its square well up though the layers of the Scrollsmen's College. Within the cliff face itself was a maze of apartments honeycombing the rock. Bits of conversation reached him as he climbed, scrollsmen and singers at their eternal bickering:

"Facts are for small minds. You couldn't find yours with both hands and a torch."

"How could I search with both hands and still hold a...wait a minute."

"Who borrowed my concordance to the law scrolls?"

"I needed to look up a word that rhymes with 'splendiferous.' Why?"

"Has anyone seen my experiment?"

"D'you mean the purple thing with black spots? It went that way."

The voices faded behind him as he reached the three levels on top of the cliff, devoted to public spaces and the Director's quarters. Over these was the observation deck. The level rays of the setting sun met Kindrie as he emerged from the stairwell and half blinded him. Two figures stood silhouetted against the glare.

"Kindrie," said one warmly, in Kirien's voice.

"My lady."

She laughed. "Such formality."

The other figure by contrast radiated the cold of the unburnt dead. Kindrie braced himself.

"Singer Ashe," he said, with an awkward bob of the head.

"I was about to send for you," said the Jaran Lordan. "I have news."

She indicated a seat on the ledge between herself and Ashe. Kindrie self-consciously perched on her far side, putting her between himself and the haunt singer. Beyond Kirien's clean-cut profile, a wry smile quirked Ashe's thin lips away from yellow teeth within the shadow of her hood.

Kirien held up a fragile piece of linen dotted with knot stitches. "Getting this translated—and you were right: the stitches do constitute a code—has proved surprisingly hard. We have several former Jaran ladies turned scrollswomen at Mount Alban, but none wanted to violate an apparent secret of the Women's World. Finally I sent a transcript to my great-great-aunt Trishien."

"The Jaran Matriarch."

"Yes. She wasn't eager to translate it either, until she read it for herself. She asks where you got it."

Kirien's writing pad was out, her hand moving across it in her spiky script as she recorded their conversation for the matriarch's benefit. Kindrie imagined Trishien's own ink-stained fingers jerking across a page as she received Kirien's message.

"Where is she now?"

"Aunt Trishien? Back in the Women's Halls at Gothregor. Torisen has let all the ladies return, to my surprise. They haven't been exactly tactful in their past dealings with him. I hear that Adiraina even tried to slip him an aphrodisiac."

"What?"

Kirien laughed at his startled expression. "Oh, not for herself. But I repeat: where did you get this?"

"It was in the bottom of a knapsack that Jame gave me to carry...something else."

Kindrie hadn't yet mentioned the contract to anyone, fearing the next question: Who was your father? He himself hadn't gotten used to the idea of Gerridon as his sire—Trinity, who could? He, Jame, and Torisen were all children born of legend and nightmare. What others would say about their lineage hardly bore thinking about.

"I don't believe my cousin remembered that the cloth was there," he added. "Where she got it, I don't know."

Kirien scrawled Kindrie's answer, then paused, waiting for a reply. It was several minutes in coming. Then her hand moved again in even, rounded letters.

"'The knot code is a close-kept secret of the Women's World,'" she read. "'We use it to communicate, sisterkin to kin. I wouldn't betray it, except that the Knorth girl should know what this note says. This appears to be a fragment of a letter from Kinzi Keen-eyed to Adiraina stitched on the night of the Massacre.'"

Ashe began, harsh-tongued, to chant:

> "Down in a dark hall desperate footsteps
> Seek out the safety of shadows and silence.
> Beautiful Aerulan, Brenwyr's beloved
> Clutches a child's hand, white-cheeked with fear.
> Above, at the doorway already cold
> Kinzi lies killed among cascades of crimson.
>
> "Sweet pale blooms promise protection
> Concealment and comfort for cold Tieri.
> A woven hanging hides her behind it,
> Moon-garden entrance guarded by grace.
> Aerulan invites assassins to her arms:
> Her death distracts them from Tieri's trail.
>
> "Cut down like corn the women of Knorth.
> Ashes blew black from blazing pyres.
> Knorth's men, maddened, made for the hills
> Drinking full deep of destruction's draught.
> Under her home's halls Tieri lay hidden
> Last Knorth woman left all alone."

Kindrie shivered.

The sun had set, leaving the sky on fire—streaks of orange, smoldering red, yellow like a throttled shriek, a silent holocaust on high. Ever since the volcanic eruption the previous year, the evening sky had been ominously spectacular.

Kindrie became aware that Ashe was regarding him closely. The sunset gave the exposed quadrant of the singer's face almost a rosy glow, but cast into deeper relief the ravages of death. He bit back an instinctive response to use the pyric rune. Where Ashe walked, among the living or among the dead, was her choice. Whether the Jaran were wise to condone it was another matter.

"You saw her...didn't you? Your mother. In the Moon Garden."

Her harsh, halting voice scraped on his nerves, as did the memory. That thing of woven death banner cords, animated by hunger, swaying toward him—

"...*come*...*mine*..."

—mouthing that awful, mindless summons back to the thread-bare womb, to fill the aching void within.

Did I create that with my birth? Am I to blame?

So many years wondering what his mother had looked like, at last to see her like that.

"What...did you feel?"

Horror, pity, grief. And then the flood had come, washing her poor fragments away.

"Could I have saved her? Was there anything left to save?"

"Very little. Even with a name...the neglected soul wears thin. I have seen her pass...in the Grayland...no more than a flaw on the wind. Let her go."

Kirien's hand continued to move as Trishien translated the note for her. "'Can it really be twelve years since Gerraint died? You...' that would be Adiraina...'have been impatient with me for not having told..' The note is full of holes. This is one of them. And part of it has been ripped off. '...virtually nothing of what happened in the death banner hall before so much of it burned.'"

Kindrie scrambled to catch up. "She's referring to the night that Gerraint died and Ganth became Highlord?"

"Yes, twelve years before the Massacre, as Kinzi says. We've had so many disasters that it does get confusing. Trinity, listen to this:

"'You have laughed at rumors that Greshan was seen walking the halls of Gothregor when he was five days dead.

"'Well, I saw him too. In my precious Moon Garden. With that bitch of Wilden, Rawneth. She led him in by the secret door behind the tapestry and there, under my very window, made love to him.

"'Except it wasn't Greshan.

"'I knew that the moment I saw him, and I didn't warn her. Oh, Adiraina...I let her damn herself. Then he changed—into whom, I don't know. I couldn't see his face, but Rawneth did. She gaped like a trout, then burst out laughing, half in hysteria, half, I swear, in triumph. What face could he have shown her to cause that?'"

The three looked at each other.

"Rawneth made love to someone in the Moon Garden who at first appeared to be Greshan," Kirien repeated.

"But that was the price of Tieri's contract," Kindrie blurted out. "That Gerraint should get his precious son back." Then he felt the blood that had rushed from his face flood back. Oh, his wretched tongue.

"What contract?" asked Kirien. "With whom? For what?"

Her expression softened. She could have demanded the truth from him, that being her Shanir trait, but she took pity. "Never mind. Tell us when you're ready. The point is, Rawneth's lover altered his appearance. Only darkling changers do that, as far as I know, unless we include the Whinno-hir, the wolvers, and half a dozen other oddities. But we don't know whom he changed into. Kinzi says that she didn't know either, but that Rawneth was at first surprised, then pleased. How very strange."

Her hand moved again in Trishien's smooth script.

"Another break. Then, 'It has been three months since Lord Randir died and four since the Randir Lordan disappeared. My spies tell me that Rawneth contracted the Shadow Guild to assassinate him.' Another break. 'Now she insists that Ganth confirm her own son, Kenan, as the new lord of Wilden.

"'And here we come to the heart of the matter.

"'Rawneth went back to Wilden that same night, contracted with a Highborn of her own house, and some nine months later gave birth to Kenan. But who is Kenan's father—the Randir noble or the thing in the garden? Without knowing, how can I advise Ganth to accept or reject his claim? And so I have summoned Rawneth and her son to Gothregor while you are also here, since your Shanir talent lies in determining bloodlines at a touch. You will tell me, dear heart, and then I will know how to act. I must admit, I do hope our dear Rawneth has mated with a monster.

"'But if so, why did she laugh so triumphantly?

"'How the wind howls! Now something has fallen over below. I hear many feet on the stair. Perhaps it is Ganth, come home at last...'"

Kirien lowered her pad and picked up the fragile linen square with both hands, delicately, as if it might disintegrate at her touch.

"There this letter ends, I suppose, with the arrival of the shadow assassins and Kinzi's death. The breaks in the note appear to come where her blood has eaten through the fabric. Look."

They regarded the discolored cloth, dotted with stitches, fretted with holes, perhaps the last thing that the Knorth Matriarch Kinzi Keen-eyed had ever touched.

"Well." Kirien looked up. "Do you make of that what I do? Adiraina was going to establish Kenan's bloodlines, but before she could, the Knorth women were slaughtered. Ganth returned to find them all dead—except for Tieri, who was still in hiding—and stormed off after the wrong enemy. Adiraina never received this letter. The question of Kenan's parentage, therefore, has never been established except that, if Kinzi is right, his father was some kind of a changer. And we are left to imply...what?"

"That Lady Rawneth sent the assassins...to forestall her son's testing."

Kindrie was appalled. "For that, she would kill all the Knorth ladies?"

"There was bad blood...between Kinzi and Rawneth...long before the Massacre."

"That," said Kirien, ever the scrollswoman, "is one interpretation of the evidence before us. There may be others. Certainly, this raises questions, but it doesn't establish the whole truth. Kindrie, will you tell your cousins? They need to know this, for what it's worth."

"Yes, of course," said Kindrie. The blunder over the contract still rattled him, but even more so this sudden window into events that had shaped his life even before his birth. He thought of his mother, only a child, finding herself in a house of death and then being left behind to become a virtual prisoner, alone, in the Ghost Walks. It wasn't only his birth that had left her an empty shell.

Kirien rose and slipped her notepad into a pocket. The cloth letter she returned to Kindrie. "I have some research to do." She kissed the healer lightly on the lips. "Don't fret." And she left.

"She is fond of you," said Ashe. "Don't hurt her."

Kindrie fumbled with the alien idea that he could hurt anyone, much less the young woman whom he had come to think of as his patron, and his friend.

"You could hurt...you know. Badly." The haunt singer regarded him steadily from the shadows of her hood. More than ever, he felt the unnatural cold radiating off of her and ached to cure it with fire. "You have access to the soulscape...on our most vulnerable level. It is in your mind even now...to burn me where I stand."

"I wouldn't. Not without cause."

"It isn't enough...that I am dead? And if I told you...that I have guessed your secret? Tieri had a contract. That could only have been...for you...therefore you are legitimate. As for your father...the dead whisper each to each. Tieri spoke...to your great-grandmother Kinzi and to Aerulan...before her banner wore to rags with decades of exposure...and neglect. I could name the man...who sired you."

"Don't!"

"Would you stop me? You can...with one searing word."

Kindrie struggled with the thought. Until recently, he had been as alone in his way as his mother had been in hers. What would Kirien think if she knew that his father was the greatest archtraitor in the history of the Kencyrath? He could hardly blame her if she threw him out. But to hurt instead of to heal...

Yet he had spoken the pyric rune before the Haunted Lands keep to prevent the dead from rising. One of them, he gathered, had been his uncle Ganth himself, not that that had apparently stopped the Gray Lord from haunting his son.

There is a locked door in Torisen's soul, and behind that, a mad, muttering voice.

But those darklings had risen consumed with mindless hunger, not as Ashe had done, her intellect still held intact by her will alone, suspended between life and death.

"You're testing me."

"So I am. You are...potentially one of the Tyr-ridan. Are you worthy...that we should rest one third of our hopes...on you?"

"Trinity knows, I don't feel it, but then the idea is new to me.

And it may not come to pass. Are you testing Jame and Torisen as well?"

"Jame, yes . . ."

Despite himself, Kindrie was impressed; he would never have had the nerve.

". . . until Tentir took over that duty. The Highlord tests himself . . . so far with limited success . . . but at least he recognizes the need."

Somewhere nearby, someone stifled a sneeze. Ashe stepped into the shadows and out again hauling Graykin by the scuff of his neck, over his furious protests.

"So . . . the gray sneak."

The Southron bared his teeth at them both and jerked his robe out of the singer's grasp. "My lady's sneak, if you please."

"And what will you tell her . . . this time?"

"Everything, or at least as much as I could hear, which wasn't much. She doesn't need either one of you. She has me."

"She also needs whatever I can discover for her," said Kindrie mildly.

"Not if I find it out first."

"You were listening outside the herb shed."

"Of course I was, not that Index made much sense. Seas turning from fresh to salt to sand—bah."

"Listen . . . little rat. Your mistress does need to know . . . but the whole truth, not just such crumbs . . . as you manage to gather."

Graykin drew himself up. "Then tell me, if it's so important. I'm likely to see her before you do."

"Ashe?" Kindrie looked at the singer for guidance.

Thinking, Ashe chewed her lip. Part of it ripped off and was absently spat over the wall. "No," she said at last. "This is a story . . . for the three of you. You . . . will see your cousin soon enough. And you, little man . . . consider the danger of passing along incomplete information."

"Graykin." Kindrie touched his shoulder, and looked into the raging eyes of the scruffy cur that was the Southron's soul-image. For a moment, he thought that the beast would lunge for his throat. However, he also recognized the dazed emptiness behind that fury. "You must leave some things to others. Jame has taken you into her service, but the harder you clutch at her, the more she will push you away."

The shoulder under his hand stiffened, then slumped. "Yes.

All right. I know that she never wanted to bind me in the first place. It just happened."

With that, he turned and shuffled off.

Ashe regarded Kindrie with death-glazed eyes in which something yet glimmered. "I see ... that you can convince ... without hurting. Such is not ... my talent."

The healer sighed. "I saw myself in his eyes. We Knorth seem to be lonely perforce, with no home but each other. Have you finished testing me?"

"For the moment."

"Good," said Kindrie, and left.

CHAPTER VII

The Day of Misrule

Between Winter 120 and Spring 1

I

JAME WOKE TO A FAMILIAR SENSE of heaviness on her chest. The blanket there stirred with more than her own breath. Lifting up a corner of it, she found herself nose to nose with a triangular head and a flickering, black, forked tongue. Golden coils shifted sleepily between her bare breasts. At least the swamp adder's eyes were their normal fiery orange; when they turned black, Jame suspected that the Witch of Wilden was peering through them.

"Rue," she called, keeping her voice calm and low. "Is this a practical joke?"

Her towheaded servant came to an abrupt, wary stop in the doorway.

"It's no joke of mine, lady. Hadn't you, er, better get rid of it?"

"Not until I find out why Addy is here."

Either Timmon's jealous Narsa was getting repetitive, or Shade was in trouble.

She slid her hands under the serpent's coils, feeling muscles ripple beneath the warm, gilded skin, and shifted Addy to the bed beside her.

"No one should come after you here." Rue sounded indignant. "In your own quarters, you're out of the game."

Last night had been Spring's Eve. Tomorrow was Spring's Day. Between them lay a span of time unmarked on any calendar, separating the old year from the new. In Tai-tastigon, it was called the Feast of Fools, when the gods were mocked to their servants' content. Here at the randon college, authority suffered a similar fate. Possibly similar upsets occurred all over Rathillien.

"You are going to stay here, aren't you?" Rue demanded. "If not, I have to call up your ten-command to act as your bodyguard so that no one scalps you."

Jame smiled. Mindful of her lordan's dignity which Rue associated with her own, the cadet didn't want her pulled into any foolery. From what she had heard about Tentir's Day of Misrule, Jame didn't especially want to participate either. She had intended to wait until Rue left and then slip out the window to spend the day training with Death's-head. Now she had to find Shade. Damnation.

"I imagine that the Commandant is going to keep to his quarters."

"Certainly. Why would anyone want to play silly tricks on him, or he to spoil anyone's fun? Mind you, it did happen once, with Ardeth's war-leader Aden."

Jame remembered the haughty Highborn from his visit earlier that spring and from the last cull when he had served on the Randon Council. Nothing, not even redeeming the Shame of Tentir, made a Highborn girl worthy in his eyes to be a randon cadet. "What happened?"

"He was commandant here then and not at all popular. Didn't think that the randon were strict enough, that they coddled us all rotten, that nothing was as good as in his day. That sort of nonsense. Well, the cadets rounded up a troop of captured sargents to serenade him and when he stuck his nose out to complain about the noise, somebody grabbed his scarf. They made him serve everyone at the day's end feast out of his own hoard of delicacies. It got messy, a proper food fight as I hear tell. He's never forgiven the college."

Good enough reason, Jame thought, for the less popular officers to make themselves scarce. She had heard that others, better natured, often participated, assuming that roving bands of cadets caught them and managed to nab their scarves, thus ensuring their obedience. Sargents and master-tens would also be fair game for anyone below those ranks.

A light knock on the door heralded Brier's arrival with a sheaf of papers. Jame tossed the blanket over Addy and rose to dress.

"The duty roster for next week," said her acting master-ten when she was admitted, and handed it over.

Jame scanned it, noting dozens of spelling errors but not commenting on them. "This looks good."

The big Southron relaxed marginally.

"So what are your plans for the day, Brier?"

"I've more paperwork to do. Let the children play."

"Hey!" Rue protested. "I'm no child."

"Close enough." Jame could see that her servant was fretting to get away. "What mischief are you up to, Rue?"

The towhead grinned. "We've set a guard on the strategy instructor's quarters—you know, the one who always throws his wooden hand at us to keep our attention. If he comes out, let's see how he likes being on the receiving end."

"Don't hurt him," said Jame sharply.

"Of course not. That wouldn't be playing the game right. What we've gathered to throw is a lot softer than his hand but less sweet smelling."

"I thought you had a whiff of the stable about you."

She was about to send Rue on her way when the door burst open. Timmon plunged through and slammed it after him in the face of an Ardeth hunting party.

"They've got a list of chores as long as your arm," he gasped, leaning against the door. "All the household duties I've avoided since last summer. They've actually been keeping score! Can you believe it?"

"Easily," muttered Rue as Jame, laughing softly, pulled on her boots.

"Given that," she said, rising to stomp them home, "why are you here?"

He flopped onto her bed. "I was on my way down to breakfast, half asleep on my feet, and clean forgot what day it was. Before I knew it, they'd cut me off from my quarters. Eek!"

Addy had emerged and was crawling across his hand.

"Will it bite me?"

"I wouldn't be at all surprised. Just hold still. Rue, go and have fun. Brier, if you don't want to play, at least take the day off. Don't worry about me."

Rue grinned and slipped outside where she could be heard indignantly driving Timmon's pursuers out of the Knorth barracks. With a stiff nod to Jame, Brier followed her.

Meanwhile, the snake had achieved Timmon's lap and was

poking around there, curiously, to the Ardeth's rigid discomfort. Jame scooped Addy up and draped her around her neck.

"You can stay here if you want."

"Will you stay with me?" he asked hopefully.

"Sorry, no. I have something to do."

First, she went in search of Jorin and found him curled up on the chest in Greshan's quarters that contained the hibernating wyrm. The ounce seemed to be spending more and more time there, as if on watch. The last time Jame had opened the box to check, she had seen movement inside an increasingly transparent chrysalis. Soon it would hatch...into what? No one knew anything about the life cycle of a darkling crawler. Not for the first time, she questioned the wisdom of keeping such a thing around, but then in its caterpillar phase it *had* played with Jorin and purred. "Darkling," as she well knew, was a relative term.

Leaving the cat on sleepy guard, she went out the window and climbed to New Tentir's roof.

Even though crusts of snow still lingered under some of the denser evergreens, it was a fine, crisp day with spring in the air like the warm hint of wild clover. Early flowers freckled the training fields. Wispy clouds floated overhead, chasing their shadows northward up the Riverland's valley floor.

Noise below caught her attention.

In the square, a squad of sargents was being drilled and getting thoroughly mixed up as they tried to follow the contradictory orders shouted at them by gleeful cadets.

Meanwhile, one of the more unpopular ten-commanders thundered around the arcade in a punishment run.

And off to one side, a solitary randon officer wobbled as if drunk through a game of hopscotch, surrounded by a crowd of jeering cadets. One of them was Damson, from Jame's own ten-command. She remembered now that this particular randon had often made fun of Damson's weight and stocky build, just as Vant had done. That in turn reminded her of how Vant was said to have stumbled into the fire pit as if pushed. Glancing up, Damson caught her eye, flinched, and slid back into the crowd. Sometime soon, Jame thought, she needed to have a word with that cadet.

First, though, she had to find Shade.

Sliding a hand under the serpent's head, she looked at her eye to eye. "Where is your mistress?" The black tongue flicked the tip of her nose, but she got no other response.

Jame wasn't sure how smart the adder was—enough to find her, but not enough to lead her back to Shade? That was odd. Then again, while Jorin had alerted her barracks that she was in trouble when the Randir had kidnapped her and thrust her into Bear's den, the cat hadn't been able to convey anything but his distress. Of course, no one of the Falconer's class had been present, which might or might not have made a difference. Perhaps a dog would do better. That in turn reminded her of Gorbel's pook Twizzle. From here, she could see the tall, semiblind Caineron barracks. Well, why not ask?

Gorbel looked around as she swung in through his bedroom window. "Don't you ever use the door?"

"You know how I would be greeted below. Fash has a score to settle with me."

"Huh. Since the Council meeting, yes, not that he didn't deserve what he got."

The Caineron Lordan was setting his boar spears in order, his armor with its cuirass and skirt of braided leather nearby ready to be donned.

"I'm not about to waste a good hunting day playing silly buggers with a bunch of retarded brats," he said, seeing her glance at his gear. "Twizzle stays here, though. For one thing, it's too dangerous. For another, he makes tracking almost too easy."

"I was just about to ask if I could borrow him."

She explained.

Gorbel grunted. "So that's why you're wearing the Randir's snake like a damned torque. What, no note tied to her neck, or should that be to her tail?"

"I'm serious, Gorbel. Something is wrong."

"There always is, when you're around. All right. Take Twizzle. He can't follow a normal trail worth scat, but if you fix your mind on what you want, he should take you to it sooner or later."

He dumped the pook into her arms. She reversed him. Dog and snake regarded each other with what seemed like wary recognition.

On the way down, Jame made the mistake of taking the stairs. On the landing, she met Higbert.

"Just the person Fash wants to see," he said and made a grab for her scarf, only to recoil as Addy reared back to hiss at him.

"All right, all right, go! We'll catch up with you soon enough and that precious Brier of yours, too."

Jame wondered, on the way down, what the Caineron had in mind for her five-commander. Few escaped Caldane's clutches, but Brier had, to take service with her brother. Gorbel might not mind; clearly others did. However, Brier was also a seasoned warrior who had come up through the ranks. Surely she could take care of herself.

On the arcade, she was almost knocked over by the master-ten compelled to the punishment run and saw that it was Reef of the Randir.

"Run, *run*, RUN!" shouted her cadets.

Not popular, huh? thought Jame, watching her go. *Surprise, surprise.*

Two more approaching cadets made her hesitate, but they were only Gari of the Coman and Mouse of the Edirr, both students in the Falconer's class.

"We aren't after you," they assured her, "just out to see the fun. What are you doing with Addy? Where's Shade?"

"I don't know. In trouble somewhere. I've got to find her."

The two exchanged looks. "Then we'll round up the rest of the Falconeers to help."

"Here." Mouse detached one of the twin albino mice from her hair and handed it to Jame. "If you find Shade first, tell Mick and Mack will tell me. If we find her before you do, Mick will start squeaking. Just follow the direction in which he's loudest."

Jame accepted the mouse and let it nestle on the crown of her head, tiny pink paws nervously gripping her braids. A rap on the nose diverted Addy from what would normally have been her dinner.

Gari eyed the diminutive Twizzle. "Maybe he's a great tracker, maybe not. We'll see if we can find Tarn and Torvi."

They left.

Jame checked that Addy wasn't about to have Mick for a snack, put Twizzle down, and followed his flouncing progress along the arcade.

In the great hall, cadets had stretched a rope from one second-story balcony to the other and were making a captured randon cross it. Jame recognized Bran from her special weapons class. He wobbled wildly, causing her to catch her breath. Then he noted her in the shadows and winked, or seemed to—with only one good eye, it was hard to tell.

The pook led her down the stairs into the subterranean stable where she found the horse-master mucking out stalls.

"Some fool cadet thought it would be funny to set me at this work," he said, pausing to wipe his bald head with a sleeve. "As if I didn't do it every day anyway, assistants notwithstanding. Have I seen Shade? No. She comes here as little as possible; the horses don't like her pet—which I see that you've got. Also a mouse, also a pook. What is this, a field day at the zoo?"

"Sort of."

"Well, you're to go on down. One of your cadets passed by and asked that I send you on if you followed her."

Now what? wondered Jame, descending into the sullen light and steaming heat of the fire timber hall.

Damson stood near the edge of a fire pit. Jame came up beside her.

"This is where Vant fell?"

"Yes, lady."

"And that was your doing. How?"

"I can make small changes in people's heads. Make them dizzy. Make them stumble. Make them feel what it's like to be fat and clumsy."

"Now I remember. When Timmon, Gorbel and I were standing at attention in the snow, something made me fall over."

Damson shuffled, not meeting her eyes. "Vant kept whispering in my ear: 'Do it, do it, do it, you fat little sow.' And so I did."

Jame reflected that she had been lucky only to have lost her balance, and that into nothing worse than snow. A few small changes in the head . . . ! How much did it take to cause seizures or even death? Damson appeared to be a Shanir linked to That-Which-Destroys, her power an inversion of a healer's in that it allowed her to hurt without touching, apparently without even much thought. God's claws, how dangerous.

"Don't do it again," she told the cadet. "If you strike me, I may strike you back. Hard."

"Oh, I wouldn't hurt you. You're nothing like Vant. I like you. There. Do you see him?"

The hall with its smoldering timbers cast few shadows, but one seemed to stand against the charred bark of an ancient tree on the far side of the pit. Fire laced its flaking skin and its eyes glowed . . . or was that only a trick of the light?

Damson snickered. "How he glares! Where's his high and mighty pride now?"

By the smirk on the cadet's plump face, Jame suddenly realized that Damson didn't regret her deed. On the contrary, she had come back because the memory of it gave her pleasure.

"Now see here: you can't kill people just because they're unpleasant to you."

"No?" Damson seemed puzzled. "Why do I have this ability, if not to use it?"

Trinity. Was the girl ignorant or insane? Jame herself tended to take responsibility for things genuinely not her fault, like Vant, hence the Burning Ones and the Dark Judge who came sniffing after her—or was it Damson they were after? But this cadet seemed to have no sense of responsibility at all, and precious little conscience. Was she like a hole in the air to them? How did one judge such an anomaly as a Kencyr with no inborn sense of honor?

"Think," she said, a little desperately. "There has to be a balance. What Vant did to you was nasty, but was it worth his life?"

Damson pouted. "You almost killed him yourself after Anise died."

"But I didn't. The Commandant brought me to my senses in time. Do you trust his judgment? Yes? Then consider before you act: would he approve?"

"I'll...try." A bit resentfully she added, "You do make things hard."

Jame sighed. "They often are. The easy thing isn't always the right thing. We Shanir have to use the Old Blood responsibly or we risk becoming the monsters that some of the lords think us."

"You mean, like your brother."

"Tori does have that tendency, which is another reason not to abuse your gifts while in his service."

With that, Damson trudged off, looking thoughtful and somewhat huffy.

Jame scanned the dark across the pit, but no one was there. Perhaps there never had been.

"Why *are* so many of us monsters?" she asked no one in particular.

Receiving no answer, she followed Damson back into the cooler, upper air.

⟨⟨⟨ II ⟩⟩⟩

THE CADET HAD DISAPPEARED by the time Jame reached the upper hall, but Bran's tormenters were still there, cheering his successful passage across the rope. One of them saw Jame. In a moment, all had given chase. She dashed up the stairs and soon lost them in the dim hallways of Old Tentir, far from the outer walls. There, let them stay until they either stumbled out or someone heard their piteous cries for help.

Her feet had taken her near Bear's quarters as so often they did. She retrieved a candle stub from a niche and followed the rank, animal smell, thinking with a pang of her teacher shut up alone in his stinking den. The question of justice still bothered her. Where did it lie in what had happened to him? To begin with, nowhere, probably. He had been a warrior and had gotten his wounds fairly in battle—yes, fighting for her father in the White Hills, for a man who could not abide such a Shanir as Bear was and had been.

For that matter, Ganth's madness had infected the entire Host, and most held him responsible for that day's brutal outcome. Was he Shanir, to have had such power? She hadn't thought of that before, but it made sense. What irony, though, given how he had felt about those of the Old Blood, like herself.

But did everything have a reason? That was hard to believe without some overarching, all-powerful authority, which didn't seem like a description of the Kencyrath's Three-Faced God unless he/she/it was far more devious and cruel than Jame had ever supposed. After all, wasn't that why her people clung so desperately to their labyrinthine code of honor? Without it, what were they? With an absent god, what else held them to account and gave them worth? There *must* be limits, and personal responsibility.

Her thoughts circled back to Bear. Surely there was nothing just in his squalid confinement.

Or was there? Long ago, he had dismembered a cadet foolish enough to taunt him and Lord Caineron had given his brother Sheth a choice: confine his brother or kill him.

One could argue that Caldane was protecting the other cadets. Knowing the man, though, Jame believed that he was setting a test for his war-leader. If the Commandant killed his brother, he could claim that he was only following his lord's orders, even though he clearly didn't think that Bear deserved death. At the same time, Caldane believed that the guilt for this unjust act would not be his, because he personally hadn't carried it out. That was Honor's Paradox: did one's honor lie in oneself, or in following orders?

We are ultimately responsible for our actions, thought Jame, *or we are not.* That much, in a world of gray values, seemed black or white.

In this case, though, the result was endless, sordid imprisonment, to the torment of both brothers.

Perhaps somebody shared her dissatisfaction. Approaching Bear's door, she saw that someone had been at work on the outward swinging hinges. One pin had been pried half out of its socket and tools lay scattered about the hall floor. Whoever it was would need heavier instruments, though, and perhaps had gone to fetch them.

Then she heard it again, as she thought she had several times while traversing these dusty corridors: the sound of light, swift feet, following her.

With a rush, they were upon her and she was sent sprawling. Candle, serpent, and mouse arced away into the darkness. Twizzle yelped as she fell on him. Then a weight crashed down on them both and hot breath roared in her ear. Hands fumbled at her scarf, wrenched it free.

Jame stumbled to her feet. Turning, she faced Narsa. Oh no. Not again.

The Ardeth cadet had drawn back a step. She was a handsome Kendar, dark-haired and fine-featured, but by the flickering light of the dropped candle her visage was ghastly and twitching, her breath ragged.

"You've done it again," she panted, "taken him away from me! This was to be our special day. We were supposed to spend it together."

In bed, Jame assumed with a flare of exasperation, just as she assumed that the girl meant Timmon.

"That isn't my fault, or his. He was cut off from his own quarters and chased into mine."

"You claim that you don't want him. You could have sent him back."

Jame thought about that.

"I suppose I could have, with a guard. It didn't occur to me. I had something else on my chest at the time."

Where was Addy? Having a poisonous, short-tempered serpent loose somewhere underfoot didn't seem like a very good idea. For that matter, with Jame's scarf in one hand and a knife in the other, Narsa didn't look particularly safe either.

She tried again. "Timmon is stuck there now, twiddling his thumbs, no doubt missing us both. Join him, with my blessings."

The Kendar gave an angry sob. "Oh, so noble, so condescending. Would you throw me to him like a bone to a dog? What good would that do anyway? He prefers you. He always has. And now that I'm p...p...p..." She couldn't finish the word, but her hand dropped to cradle her stomach.

"Oh, Narsa, I really am sorry."

This was serious. Sexual relations at the college were discouraged, as they were in the field, but one recognized that youth will have youth. To become pregnant while at Tentir, however, was automatically to be expelled. Although Kendar could usually control conception among themselves, they had less luck with Highborn lovers.

"Does Timmon know?"

"Would it matter to him if he did? What have I ever been but a pastime to him until he could bed you?"

"If it's any comfort, he hasn't, and isn't likely to. Please, Narsa. Put away that knife and let's talk sensibly."

"I don't need sense. I have this." She brandished Jame's scarf in her face. "You have to do what I say." Abruptly she tossed Jame the blade. "And I say, 'Kill me.'"

Jame nearly fumbled the catch. "What? I can't!"

"Come on. It's easy. My honor is already dead. Should I give the world another bastard? The Ardeth are jealous of their oh-so-pure blood, more than any house except yours. Timmon should have thought about that when he spent his precious seed on me. You Highborn take us and you break us."

"Not on purpose. Not usually."

"Then let this be different."

She flung herself at Jame and cried out with sharp pain as they met breast to breast. Then the Kendar collapsed into the Highborn's arms sobbing. Jame dropped the knife and held her. Ancestors be praised that she had lowered the point in time. Narsa shuddered in her grip, so strong, so alive, so desperate.

We take them and we break them, who are so much better than
ourselves. What kind of a god gave us such unjust power?

"No!" Narsa thrust her away, turned, and ran.

 **III**

JAME DIDN'T FOLLOW HER. Instead, she knelt and listened at
the iron bars of Bear's feeding slot, surprised that the ruckus hadn't
drawn his attention. From inside came stentorian snores. Somehow,
he had slept through the whole thing.

A hiss near her hand made her look down. There was Addy, coiled,
angry. She and Narsa must have nearly trampled the serpent, and
the knife had come close to impaling her when Jame had dropped it.

"It's all right," she told the snake, carefully drawing her fallen
scarf out from under her.

Addy took some soothing before she consented to being picked
up again, and Jame felt more hesitant this time about draping those
restless coils around her neck. Highborn, especially the Randir, had
some immunity, but still a strike—especially to the throat—could
be dangerous. Adder's venom dissolved flesh, among other things.
Instead, she slipped the serpent inside her jacket to form a slowly
slithering belt against her skin.

Twizzle emerged cautiously from the shadows.

"Woof?" he said.

A trembling morsel of white tucked into a corner proved to
be Mick. With the mouse again tucked into her hair, Jame set
out after the pook.

IV

TWIZZLE'S CLAMOR DREW HER to one of the outer second-
story, west-facing classrooms. The chamber was full of cadets all
crowded against the window to peer down into the training square.
Rue separated herself from them and ran to grab Jame's arm.

"You've got to do something!" she cried, pulling her toward the windows where the others made room for them.

Below, Brier Iron-thorn staggered back and forth, buffeted by a dozen jeering Caineron, her clothes torn, her face streaked with blood.

"What in Perimal's name is going on?" Jame demanded.

"Higbert called her out as your acting master-ten. I mean, we all know that that's really your title, but she does most of the work."

"I know that. We split duties." She flinched as a Caineron hit Brier in the stomach and she fell. Several more landed kicks before the Southron could struggle stubbornly to her feet.

"Why isn't she defending herself?"

"She did at first. When Hig called her out, he was only backed by three Caineron. The rest ran out after she'd accepted his challenge. It wasn't long before they had her scarf. Then they ordered her not to fight back."

Two Caineron grabbed the Knorth's arms and held her while a third lashed out at her face. Blood sprayed. Brier spat out a tooth.

"This isn't right." Jame saw several randon including the Brandan Captain Hawthorn watching from the arcade rail. "Why don't they stop it?"

"First off, she told everyone not to interfere. Second, I don't think the randon can step in, not today."

This is a test too, Jame thought. *They want to see how we behave, left to ourselves. And Gorbel isn't here to call his hounds to heel.*

"Well," she said, "Brier didn't order me."

She clambered out onto the tin roof of the arcade, gave the rathorn battle cry at the top of her lungs, and jumped down onto the back of the nearest Caineron. An answering yell echoed from all sides as Knorth and their allies charged the square.

Among the uproar came the terrible bell of a Molocar. Tarn's Torvi rushed onto the scene, shouldering cadets aside left and right. He bowled Higbert over and ripped at his throat. The next moment, incredibly, the cadet was up and running with his cohorts on his heels. All plunged into the Caineron barracks and slammed the door after them.

"I can't leave you alone for a minute, can I?" said Jame, helping Brier to rise. The Southron glowered, then caught her breath sharply and wrapped arms around her bruised ribs.

Meanwhile, Tarn was prying something black out of Torvi's

jaws—two scarves, one with the Knorth crest embroidered on it, and other with the Caineron. Jame presented both to Brier.

"Do with them as you will."

"With pleasure," said the Southron grimly and limped after the fled enemy, tying her own sodden scarf around her neck as she went. Rue and the other Knorth rushed to support her.

"That was well done," said Hawthorn, coming up to Jame as the assault began on the Caineron barracks.

Jame glared at her. "Was it? These are mostly children. Would you give them rules and then not hold them to account?"

"Not entirely. Remember, they won't always be under our eyes. Nothing they do today will be held against them, short of a blatant breach of honor, but we watch and remember. We also note what their superiors do. What's that, around your waist?"

"Something held in trust." Jame flicked open her jacket to reveal Addy's triangular head questing upward between her breasts.

"And you've got a mouse sitting on your head. Let me guess: the Falconer's class."

Pink nose in the air, Mick started chittering.

"At last!" said Jame, adding to Twizzle, "Small thanks to you."

Under the randon's bemused gaze, she revolved to see in which direction the mouse squeaked the loudest, then set off at a run for the Randir barracks.

❧ V ❧

SHE FOUND MOST OF THE FALCONEERS in the Randir basement gathered around a gaping well mouth.

"She's down there?"

"So Mack says."

"And my trock," added Dure.

"And Torvi."

Addy slithered out of Jame's coat, disconcertingly like a short length of glistening, spilt bowel, and disappeared down the shaft.

"That settles it. Shade, can you hear me?"

Her voice echoed hollowly off stone walls, down dank depths, to fall flat on a stone ledge just visible by torchlight.

"Where's the water?" asked Tarn.

"Below the shelf, I think," said Mouse, leading perilously over the edge to peer down. Gari caught her by the belt. "This must be the Randirs' shallowest well, not always useable."

"It's raining in the mountains," said Drie.

Gari snorted. "And dark on the other side of the moon. So?"

"I think he means that the water level is about to rise." Jame stripped off her jacket, adding to forestall the others' protests, "It looks convoluted down there. Which of you is skinnier than I am? Someone, find a rope."

A nearby bucket supplied the latter. Anchored at the top, Jame swung over the rim and descended, touching the slimy walls as little as possible. Some twenty feet down she landed on the ledge. It looked as if in excavating this well, the Randir had run into a slab of rock too hard to be easily removed, so they had circumvented it. Running water sounded around its edge. Jame wriggled down a crack and dropped into a lower tunnel extending west to east. Water rushed by on one side in a channel down toward the Silver. On the other, under the overhang, lay a dark, trussed-up figure. Firelight reflecting off wet stone caught Addy's golden coils looped over it.

"I sent her to you for safekeeping," said Shade's voice out of the shadows.

"What, not to summon help?" Jame considered this as she probed the other's bindings: stout chain and rope tight enough to stop the blood. "Maybe that's also why Twizzle wouldn't lead me to you. D'you want to die?"

"Do you know who put me down here?"

"At a guess, Reef and her cronies."

"There you're wrong. Reef would have saved me as her lady's granddaughter if the others hadn't kept her busy all day. Some Randir would follow the rightful heir if they could. To them, I'm the Witch's freak."

Ouch. Shade would also serve Randiroc if she could, but who in her house would believe that? Both sides must see her as the very emblem of the enemy.

"So, if you escape, that proves you guilty, or so they think. Only death can assure your innocence. And, if they're lucky, the coming flood will wash your body down to the Silver. I hate double binds. These, on the other hand, you should be able to escape."

Shade's mulish silence was answer enough.

"All right. Here's something they didn't consider: you have friends."

"I do?"

"God's claws and small, furry fishes, of course you do. Who d'you think tracked you down here and is waiting on top to help pull you out? Half the Falconer's class, that's all."

Shade stirred for the first time. "I have friends," she repeated dubiously, with an undernote of wonder.

"And we have company."

The shadows rustled. Reflected light glinted off hundreds of beady eyes: wild trocks, scavengers capable of stripping flesh from bone in seconds. Then from up the tunnel came the approaching roar of water. The eyes blinked out and claws scuttled away.

Jame cut the ropes. To deal with the chains, she hoisted an outraged Addy by her tail and held her twisting over the metal. Venom dripped on iron, ate into it.

"Too slow. Shade, do something!"

The nascent changer grunted and flexed her hands. They became long and narrow enough to slip through the chains, likewise her bare feet, leaving scraped skin on the links.

"That hurts," she said through her teeth.

"Would you rather drown?"

The water beside them was rising, starting to fill the tunnel. Shade wriggled through the gap and started to climb the rope to urgent cries falling from above. Jame followed her. The rushing water nearly plucked her off the rope, but then she emerged from the cleft onto the ledge. From there, it was up the rope with the rising flood lapping at her heels.

VI

BY NOW, IT WAS NEARLY MIDDAY and cadets were returning to their barracks for a noon meal prepared by their ten-commanders. At the top of the stair, still well within the Randir precincts, the assorted cadets who made up the Falconeers encountered Reef. The master-ten Randir was gray with dust and fatigue after a morning-long punishment run, but not too tired to notice their presence within her domain. She stopped short, staring.

"What are you lot doing here?"

Then she noticed Shade, covered with well-slime.

"And what happened to you?"

A Randir ten-commander came up behind her. Jame noted Reef's scarf tied around her arm. She stopped, stony-eyed, when she saw Shade.

"So."

"Just so," Shade answered her.

Reef looked from one to the other. "What in Perimal's name is going on here?"

"A mistake," said Shade, eyes still locked with the commander's.

"We'll see about that. The rest of you, get out."

The cadets left, glad to have escaped the crossfire. Jame hesitated.

"Go," said Shade. "It's over for today."

"What was that all about?" asked Tarn as they gained the arcade boardwalk.

"House business," said Jame. "Just be glad it isn't yours."

Trinity, what a mess the Randir are, she thought, *and the Ardeth too. Ha. Let's not forget the Knorth. How many other houses are secretly coming apart at the seams?*

At the square, they parted, each to his or her own quarters, Mouse with Mick and Mack again settled in her hair.

"That just leaves you," said Jame to Twizzle.

The pook wriggled what was presumably his hind end and jumped up into her arms.

"All right," she told him as he licked her face. "At least until your master returns."

CHAPTER VIII
New Year's Eve

Between Winter 120 and Spring 1

I

"THERE YOU ARE!"

Jame found herself in the grip of Rue. "Come on. D'you *want* to be scalped?"

They made a dash back to the Knorth barracks. Brier Iron-thorn met them inside the front door. Her bruises were settling into two black eyes and a swollen lip. How the rest of her looked, Jame could only guess.

"Did you get into the Caineron barracks?"

"No. But I still have this." The Southron indicated Higbert's scarf bound around her upper arm.

"What will you do when you catch him?"

Brier smiled, revealing missing teeth. "Something appropriate."

Rue tugged at Jame, fussing. "Come upstairs and change. You're dripping with muck."

"Shouldn't I be helping in the kitchen?"

Brier waved her off, disgusted. "Go. We don't need green slime to garnish the soup."

Jame found Timmon still in her quarters.

"I saw Narsa," she said, kicking his booted feet off of her bed. "She's very upset."

"She'll get over it," he replied, unconcerned.

Should she tell the rest of it? No. That was Narsa's secret. However, his indifference grated on her.

"You're going back to your quarters," she told him. "Everyone should be at lunch by now. Take my ten-command if you're still shy about facing your own."

He went, reluctantly, and returned when she had just finished changing into dry clothes.

"Now what's the matter?" Then, with a change of tone, "Timmon, sit down. You look terrible. Here, drink this."

The Ardeth downed a cup of water with shaking hands, nearly choking on it. A dash of freckles stood out on his white face like flecks of dried blood. "She was there. Narsa. Hanging over my bed. Still warm."

Jame sank to her heels beside him, feeling as if someone had just punched her in the stomach. Suicide without even the dignity of the White Knife, solitary, desperate, and unexplained, except to the one whom Narsa had felt to be her mortal rival. To whom did her secret belong now?

"...and her leg," Timmon was saying. "Dangling there, all black and swollen. What could have happened to it?"

"Addy! She was underfoot. If Narsa trod on her..."

"You mean the Randir's snake could be to blame for Narsa's suicide?"

Jame was taken aback by his sudden eagerness. "It must have been hideously painful," she said cautiously, "perhaps even fatal without a healer's immediate care."

"That makes sense. Sort of. Narsa didn't like healers. Besides, we have none currently in residence. If the pain became unbearable... I mean, dammit, she wouldn't kill herself just because I didn't meet with her as we had planned, would she? Well, would she?"

"I don't know. But she's still dead."

"I realize that. What I mean is you don't think I'm to blame... do you?"

"Timmon, it was your bed she hanged herself over. That means something."

He was up now and pacing. "Why should it, except that she was angry at me? What cause she had for that, though, I don't know. We both had fun while it lasted."

"You're trying to slide out of responsibility again."

"For what, and if so, why not? My father took his pleasure where he pleased, and he was a great man."

"Sweet Trinity," said Jame, exasperated. "According to whom?"

Oh, where was that flash of steel that she had seen at Gothregor when Timmon had spoken up for his house and driven Fash back? Even now, she sensed that he was arguing with himself more than with her. Pereden would easily have shaken off Narsa's death, without bothering to find reasons for it. His son was having a harder time of it.

As if reminded by his reference to his father, Timmon had drawn out the packet that the Highlord had given him and was holding it gingerly.

"How do you suppose your brother got this?"

Now it was Jame's turn to feel uneasy. Somehow, she was sure that it hadn't been Torisen who had taken ring and finger from the pyre. She also still didn't know why her brother had killed Pereden in the first place, only that all Perimal would break out if anyone else learned that he had.

"I honestly don't know," she said, feeling herself turn cagey in turn. "Does it matter?"

"It might. Perhaps they came from the Southern Wastes, although why one of the Highlord's people found them when Grandfather couldn't is beyond me. That must be it, though. After all, everybody knows it was a changer at the Cataracts impersonating my father who led the Waster Horde."

He said this last with a note of defiance, but also unease. However much he might reassure himself, not everyone who had been there believed the changer story.

"One of these days," said Jame, "you're going to have to step out of your father's shadow. My advice is that you burn that finger, wear the ring, and be the man that Pereden should have been."

Timmon hesitated, uncertain, then slipped the relics back into his pocket.

"It's too soon," he said obliquely.

Jame sighed. He was so nearly worth saving. When it came down to it, though, she didn't entirely trust her own feelings. Perhaps, as when Lord Ardeth had used his Whinno-hir Brithany to test a young Torisen, it was time for a second opinion.

"Well, then, what now?" she said. "I have things to do. You can continue to skulk here, go back to your household chores, or come with me, but only if you swear on your honor never to tell anyone anything about what you may see or hear."

This clearly intrigued him.

"Keeping secrets, are we? All right. I'll swear and I'll come."

II

AGAIN, JAME VISITED HER UNCLE'S QUARTERS first to check on Jorin. When he heard her enter, the ounce yawned, jumped down from the chest, and stretched to seemingly impossible lengths.

"I thought even you would have slept enough by now," she told him, and opened the box.

The chrysalis lay cocooned in ruined finery like an egg in a gaudy nest. The shell had become entirely translucent. Within it, something stirred in an azure glow etched with shifting lines of gold.

"Any day now," said Jame, tracing a fine crack with her fingertip. "Then we'll see."

She, Timmon, Jorin, and the pook slipped out the front door of the barracks. Under cover of a rowdy game of blind-tag played between sargents and randon in the square, raucously coached by cadets, they gained the northern gate unnoticed and left Tentir.

Above the college was a random collection of boulders that had rolled down from the mountains above, some as small as a bald man buried up to the eyebrows, others twice a man's height. Death's-head charged around one of the latter, skidded to a halt, and brandished his scythelike twin horns in Jame's face.

"If I were the horse-master," she said, holding very still, "that would be my cue to bash him in the snout with this tool bag."

Timmon had scrambled backward halfway up a boulder. There he lost his grip and fell at the rathorn's feet. Death's-head pawed around him, then retreated with a snort.

"Given that you haven't been trampled to death," said Jame, "I think that means that he's accepted you."

Harmless, was the word that had formed in her mind. *Mostly.* What kind of a judgment was that?

Timmon scrabbled to his feet, staring. "What . . . how . . . t-this is the colt who ambushed us at the swimming hole, isn't it? The one that Gorbel hunted? Do you ride him?"

Jame made a face. "After a fashion."

"D'you think he would let me?"

The rathorn, advancing, knocked him over.

"I don't think so."

The colt wheeled on his hocks and disappeared around a

boulder with a taunting flick of his silken tail. Timmon followed him with Jame hard on his heels, hoping that she hadn't set him up for the slaughter. What followed amounted to a game of hide and seek. Timmon grabbed a creamy tail. Bel-tairi squealed and bolted. Back came the rathorn, roaring to her rescue, and Timmon scrambled up another rock, only to descend again when the colt and the Whinno-hir had calmed down and fallen to grazing.

"I didn't know that rathorns ate grass," he said, trying hard to breathe normally.

"So will a dog or a cat, if it suits them. He's omnivorous, as far as I can make out, although rocks disagree with him. Here." She handed Timmon a curry brush from a sack that she had brought from her room. "You take Bel."

She watched as he approached the mare, noting how he moved so as not to startle her. Either he knew about her blind side, or instinctively avoided it. Then too, she always grazed with it toward the rathorn. Her single dark eye rolled warily at his touch, but she soon quieted under it. That was good: mild as she was, few people could handle her after the torture that Greshan had inflicted on her. Fair enough for a second (or third?) opinion.

Both equines still had their winter coats, but were beginning to shed heavily. Jame dragged the bristles down the rathorn's shaggy neck, scraping a swatch clean. He leaned into the brush with a groan of pleasure and presented her with his neck to scratch, especially up under the ivory armor where a growth spurt had left tender, new, itchy skin.

"How in Perimal's name did you tame him?" asked Timmon, watching over the mare's back, fascinated.

"I didn't. I blood-bound him."

"Oh. What about the Whinno-hir?"

"Bel was entrusted to me. She goes her own way."

"And Gorbel doesn't try to hunt him anymore? This close to the college, you'd think he would be easy game."

"Gorbel owes Death's-head his life after the cave bear incident. He steers hunters away from this area. I'm counting on you to do the same, and to keep the secret."

"Of course. I swore that I would, didn't I? I'm not as feckless as you seem to think."

"Do I?" Jame murmured, putting her weight into her task.

"Well, maybe I was. Once. You would have hated me as a child.

I hate the thought of me then. Did you know that, in addition to being my half-brother, Drie used to be my whipping boy? Whenever I did anything wrong, he was punished for it. Father used to watch and laugh, but it annoyed him too, because Drie just seemed to drift away from the pain. He was poor sport, Father said, but it made me uncomfortable enough so that I would behave, at least for a while."

He bent to his task, grooming Bel's dappled flank, not meeting Jame's eyes.

"What we didn't know was that Drie had formed a bond with a huge, old carp in Omiroth's pond. Whenever he was beaten on my behalf, that's where he sent his mind, into the deep, murky water, out of touch, beyond pain. I don't know how Father found out. The next time I misbehaved, though, he made Drie catch that fish and eat it, raw. Drie wasn't the same after that. He wouldn't swim, although he had loved to before, and he would cry when whipped. Father was delighted. I was . . . ashamed."

"So you brought him with you to Tentir, to get him away."

"Yes. And he's been much better here, more like the happy, half-awake boy I used to know, at least since last summer."

When Fash and Higbert threw him into the Silver, Jame thought. Presumably he had met a new companion in the swift waters, carp or trout or catfish. However, the story left a harsh taste in her thoughts, as if someone had asked her to kill and eat Jorin. Or Bel.

Timmon was watching her askance. "I've shocked you," he said. "As uncomfortable as it made me, I don't think I ever realized the horror of it until I met you and the Falconeers. Now, the whole thing seems abominable. And Father *laughed*. Would a truly great man do that? I don't know. I'm confused. Tentir has made me question most of what I used to believe. So you tell me: am I responsible for Narsa's death?"

Jame bit her lip. Did her loyalty lie with the dead or with the living? To ask the question was to answer it.

"Narsa was carrying your child."

Timmon's face bleached behind its freckles. "Oh," he said. "Then I am responsible. I had better go and tend to the body."

He turned and wobbled off, leaving Jame with her mouth open. Sweet Trinity, had he simply left Narsa hanging? But he was gone before she could ask.

⊰◈⊱ III ⊰◈⊱

CURRYING THE TWO EQUINES took much of the afternoon, until Jame's arms ached with the continual downstrokes. Hair fell like snow, then like dust, until clean, spring coats shimmered under the brush. The effort and its result did her good, creating two less murky things in the world on the eve of a new year. The sun had set behind the Snowthorns when she finished. It was late afternoon, almost time for the feast.

Calling Jorin and the pook to heel, she went down to the college.

Trestle tables had been set out in the square and cadets sat at them according to house. The time for snatching scarves had apparently passed, although Brier still wore Higbert's tied around her arm and kept grim watch for him.

Timmon sat at his own table, with empty seats to either side. It would be some time before he made peace with his house or with himself. From the rigid set of his shoulders, Jame could tell that he understood and accepted that.

The randon provided the feast from anything left over from the winter, it being too early for the spring crop. Left to themselves, most houses would have been reduced to root vegetables, dried beans, and salted meat, but this was the eve of the new year and all leftover supplies had been consolidated. Jame saw delicacies and smelt spices alien to her house for months. Galantine pie with dried berries, almond fish stew, swan neck pudding, spiced wine and cider . . . Her mouth began to water.

As cadets settled to the feast, speculation ran rampant among them: who would be scarved the Commandant of Misrule? Perhaps so-and-so because she was funny; perhaps what's-his-name for the hideous expressions he could make; perhaps someone else because everyone liked him.

A stir arose at the door to Old Tentir. Out of it came Fash and Higbert, carrying chains. The links attached to a collar and the collar, under a dirty white scarf, was worn by Bear.

He stopped on the threshold, swaying, blinking bloodshot eyes.

Since he had emerged during the ambush in the stable, everyone had known at least by rumor that Bear was the legendary monster in the maze, rumored to eat cadets for lunch and supper, if not for breakfast. Even his past had come to light, with randon at last feeling free to describe his feats in happier days. Few, however, had seen him. His huge, shambling form and the obscene cleft in his skull awed them, while the wildness of his looks made many draw away. So did his rank smell, overlaid by the sharp tang of applejack.

They must have gotten him royally drunk to get that collar on him, Jame thought. No wonder he had slept through her clash with Narsa outside his door.

Fash and Higbert led him, stumbling, to the head table and induced him to sit.

Jame found that she had risen to her feet, as had every other cadet. They sat when he did, but on the edge of their benches, poised for Trinity knew what.

In the awkward silence that followed, Fash presented Bear first with a cup of ale, which he swigged down in a gulp, then with a roast haunch of venison. The big man looked at it suspiciously and licked his lips. A nervous laugh rippled through the Caineron as he suddenly snatched it up and tore at it like a wild beast.

This is wrong, Jame thought. *Wrong.*

Fash snatched the haunch away and held it up, making Bear paw for it. Then he thrust it under the table. Bear went after it. The table heaved. Despite themselves, more cadets started to giggle nervously. Others called at Fash to stop.

The table suddenly overturned as Bear rose. He gripped a chain and jerked Higbert within his terrible grasp.

Brier stood up, holding the cadet's scarf.

"I order you. Don't resist."

Higbert, terrified, went limp. Bear plucked at his limbs, making him dance like a puppet. Rue started to clap in time, followed by others, but Bear's movements were becoming more and more violent. He had torn a cadet apart before for teasing him.

A black coat swished past and there was Commandant Sheth Sharp-tongue by the high table. From his brother's grip, he carefully detached Higbert. Bear's mock scarf, slipping, revealed that the strap around his neck had spikes on it, turned inward. It was a punishment collar for unruly direhounds. Fash jerked on it, and Bear lashed out in pain at the nearest person—his brother. The Commandant fell.

"Get spears!" someone shouted, and weapons appeared in Caineron hands so quickly that they must have been hidden under the table.

This was all planned, thought Jame. She struggled to reach her Senethari's side, using her claws when cadets didn't move fast enough. Bear was ringed with steel, striking at any point that came too near. The Commandant lay at his feet.

"Kill him!" Fash was shouting. "Kill him!"

"What in Perimal's name is going on here?"

The new voice, while not a roar, carried such power that the struggling cadets stopped. Gorbel stood in the doorway to Old Tentir, his armor reeking with boar's blood, his attendants dimly seen behind him in the great hall carrying the prize of his hunt on a pole thrust through its hocks. As he stumped forward, cadets cleared a path. Jame took advantage of their distraction to slip within the steel ring and kneel beside the Commandant. He had been struck across the face, luckily with the back of Bear's hand, otherwise he would have had no face left to speak of. Already he was struggling to rise.

"Weapons up!" Sheth ordered the cadets and the handful of randon who had joined them.

Gorbel entered the ring and faced Bear. His hands came up and his head down in a cadet's salute to a senior randon. Others joined him one by one, until Bear was surrounded by a circle of silent respect. Jame removed the collar from his neck. Bear snuffled and slowly straightened. Awkwardly, as if he had almost forgotten how, he returned their salute.

The Commandant climbed to his feet, shrugging off the hands that reached out to steady him, and touched his brother's shoulder. Face to face, one saw the resemblance between them: beyond the elder's unkempt wildness and the younger's somewhat ruffled suavity, the same sharp features, the same set of jaw and hawk's eye. Then Sheth led Bear away, through the silent watchers, back to his noisome den.

 **IV**

IT WAS DUSK BY THE TIME the Commandant finally returned to his quarters which, like his office, opened off the Map Room. He stilled on the threshold, sensing movement by the balcony.

A figure advanced into the room, the hunched shoulders of the Snowthorns over its head, a nimbus of evening stars above that. No Kendar was so slight; no Kendar but Harn Grip-hard would have approached him at such a time, after such a day. But Harn was with the Southern Host by now. Odd, to miss his old rival so.

"I came to see if you and Bear are all right," said the Knorth Lordan.

Sheth sighed and unwrapped his official scarf. In fact, his face still throbbed and several teeth had been loosened, but it could have been so much worse.

"Bear is asleep," he said. "They must have saved up their rations of applejack for a long time to get him so drunk."

"Gorbel did well, though, didn't he?"

"Very well. His father errs in underestimating him."

"You do realize that Fash set you up to sanction Bear's execution."

"The thought had crossed my mind," he said dryly. "Also that he would have been unlikely to think up such a scheme on his own."

"Caldane is pushing. He wants to be sure of you."

"Of that, too, I am aware. Why else do you suppose that he demanded that you renew your lessons with Bear?"

She stepped forward, almost into the light of his candle, speaking urgently. "Ran, you mustn't give in. This is Honor's Paradox, pure and raw, and you are the honor of Tentir."

This amused him, or would have if he weren't so tired and his face didn't hurt so much.

"Child, what will you say next?"

"Only this: my first Senethari fell prey to the paradox, and to prove that I am serious, I will tell you who he was: Tirandys himself."

The room seemed to shift. He was acutely aware of all the battle maps painted on its wall from the Cataracts to the Fall, three thousand-odd years ago. So many victories, so many more tragic defeats. It was as if the fabled past had risen before him in the figure of one slim girl. The randon had long wondered who had first taught her the Senethar, and here was the answer, impossible as it seemed.

"Child, Tirandys was of the Master's generation, long, long ago."

"He was also a darkling changer, who learned too late that his honor couldn't be trusted to his lord. Time moves differently under shadows' eaves. You met him yourself at the Cataracts, when he was impersonating Prince Odalian of Karkinaroth."

Sheth remembered the prince—a poor, doomed fool who had wanted to emulate the Kencyr and had paid for it with his life, or all the time had they been dealing with one of the Master's chosen, the originator of the Senetha himself?

"Do such legends still walk under the sun?"

"You should know, for you are one of them. Senethari, please. I don't want to lose another teacher to Honor's accursed Paradox."

She took his breath away. Singers' lie and scrollsmen's fact, all of the Kencyrath's long, tortured history seemed to unroll before him. Was he truly set upon the same path? He was ambitious, yes, but this was too much. One did what one could, where one was. For him, it was here in Tentir's Map Room, faced with a shadow that embodied everything he had ever fought both for and against.

"You, a Knorth, tell a Caineron this?"

"Not a Caineron," came that voice out of the darkness of his own soul. "The Commandant of Tentir."

He fingered his scarf without thinking. "Then a Commandant has heard you."

He stepped forward to draw her within his candle's light and she resolved into a slim girl whose silver-gray eyes were too large for her thin face. He touched her scarred cheek.

"Ah, you Knorth, who make even your enemies love you. To bed, now, child. Tomorrow is a new year."

She withdrew, saluting him. "As you command, Senethari." And left.

V

BEFORE JAME RETIRED for the night, however, she checked the wyrm's chest one last time. Jorin crouched before it, quivering, tail a-twitch, like a cat waiting for its prey to break cover. The chest itself rattled on the floor in a nervous little dance.

Jame opened it.

The chrysalis was rocking back and forth in its tawdry bed. Cracks laced its shell, then shards fell away to reveal something within covered with a dark, wet caul.

A gasp sounded from the door. Rue stood there open-mouthed, with other cadets arriving to gawk behind her.

"Lady, be careful!"

"Stand back," said Jame, still unsure of what she was dealing with.

The struggles inside the chest stilled as if exhaustion had taken hold. Jame carefully hooked her claws in the membrane where it seemed the thinnest. It split at her touch. Something like a child lay within, curled in a fetal position, thumb in its mouth. Its body, however, was scarcely more than a tangible shadow and nearly as light when Jame picked it up. She saw that it had not one set of arms but three, the middle two rudimentary with hands folded over its stomach, the lower two almost but not quite legs.

The membrane fell in twin drapes from its shoulders, rustling and unfurling as golden light began to spread through its veins. From black to midnight blue to azure, the veil lightened as if with the sunrise into a pair of glowing wings.

Jame held them away from her body so as not to damage them. Jorin, sniffing, seemed inclined to bat until a quick word from her made him withdraw his paw.

The wings brushed the floor and spread to an arm's width each. They were already drying. The shadow child sighed, removed its thumb from its mouth, and opened its eyes. They too were golden.

Memory stirred.

Golden-eyed shadows crouched over her in Perimal Darkling, around the Master's bed. Long fingers like shadows in the coverlet's creases poked at her. Except for their eyes, their bodies seemed no more substantial than those shadows.

"Who *are* you?"

Forgotten us so soon? Shame, shame, shame! Our lord sent for us, called us from our dim world into his dim rooms, up from the depths of the House. Said, "Teach this child the Great Dance, as you taught the other one. One name will do for both." And so we taught you, the new Dream-weaver. Years, it's been, all to be consummated tonight. Now get up, up, up ... or shall we get into bed with you?

No!

Jame shuddered at the memory, but what she held, blinking at her, was innocence.

"I think I know your elders," Jame said to the shadow child.

"May you too achieve that last metamorphosis and teach others how to dance, but not as I almost did. Farewell, unfallen darkling; Beauty, farewell."

It smiled at her, flicked its wings, and rose from her arms. The others rushed in as it fluttered out the window and rose against a gibbous moon near the full. All watched it until it veered north and was soon out of sight.

"Legends indeed," said Jame, turning to her cadets. "And a happy new year to you all."

CHAPTER IX
Echoes of Kothifir

Spring 20–21

I

SPECKLED WITH DRYING BLOOD, the Coman scout panted up the ridge through leafless trees.

"Their headquarters are near Perimal's Cauldron," she reported. "They spotted us. Hurl got egged."

"The first cadet lost and it had to be one of mine," said the Coman master-ten-commander Clary. "Still, that's useful information. We can storm them while we still have full sacks."

Jame sighed, her breath a cloud on the crisp air. Clouds scudded overhead against a bright sky, and the occasional snowflake drifted down. Spring, ever fickle, had turned to glance back at winter.

The Coman was annoyingly eager to leap ahead with the exercise. Perhaps uncertainty unnerved him, or maybe he wanted somehow to make his half of the team look good at the expense of hers, which was stupid. Of all houses to be paired with on this rare, much-coveted double lesson, why couldn't it have been the Brandan or the Danior, her natural allies? Instead, she was set against both on the other side.

Anyway, hadn't she seen Clary talking with Fash before the class? Fash, as usual, had been jovial. Clary had looked uncomfortable. Everyone knew that the Coman lord couldn't make up his mind whether to support the Knorth or the Caineron who, after all, were his blood-kin. Awkward for him, unfair for his cadets, who couldn't decide where their loyalty lay.

Still, while at Tentir all were family, regardless of house politics. That, according to the Commandant.

Ha.

"Such an assault should only be out of desperation if we run out of time," she said, repeating the sargents' earlier advice. "As it is, we still have most of the day if we need it. No one has found the target yet, and that's the main objective."

"It would help if we knew what we were looking for," Clary grumbled.

He had a point, and made another one by not meeting her eyes, which also annoyed her. Surely she had gotten past that point at Tentir after two culls. Her ten-command stirred restively, picking up his tone and her discontent with it.

"The sargents say we'll know it when we see it," she said.

"'Ware, camp," called a sentry.

Someone crunched up the northern slope from Tentir through the detritus of last year's leaves. Color flared between white birch trunks, crimson shading into purple with swirls of turquoise. Who wore a court robe in the wilds? A thin, sallow face appeared, shiny with sweat under a thatch of lank, black hair.

"Graykin, what are you doing here, much less dressed like that?"

Her Southron servant drew himself up, trying for dignity's sake to catch his breath, and slid his hands lovingly over his fine, silken raiment.

"Beautiful, isn't it? I'm traveling with a caravan of merchants. One has to dress the part."

"At m'lady's expense, eh?" said Rue, coming up.

She had complained about how much of her allowance Jame had settled on her servant, not knowing how guilty Jame had felt about shortchanging him earlier. After all, before the Brandan settlement neither Jame nor Tori had had a bean to spare. Now either Tori had forgotten (again) or it was up to her to outfit all the Knorth cadets. So far, though, she hadn't had a chance.

"Aren't you supposed to be researching the Southern Wastes at the Scrollsmen's College?" she demanded of Graykin.

He glared down his nose at her and sniffed. "I've learned all that I'm likely to at Mount Alban, thank you very much. It's time to head out into the field, or rather south to Kothifir to prepare the way for you, Lordan."

Why should that title irk Jame so much, coming from him?

Probably because, as her self-appointed sneak, he equated his value with hers, and had what she considered to be delusions of grandeur.

Brier Iron-thorn loomed over them, the late-morning sun turning her cropped, dark red hair into a fire-tipped halo. She was frowning. "This caravan of yours, it came from the south but started peddling its wares at the Riverland's northern end? Is this a sanctioned expedition?"

"Sanctioned by whom?" demanded Rue. As a brat from a northern border keep, she had limited firsthand knowledge of the South, which clearly irked her.

Brier, a born Southron herself, took pity on her and, incidentally, on Jame.

"By King Krothen of Kothifir. All spoils of the Wastes pass through his fat hands so that he can claim taxes and whatever catches his fancy, hence the source of his vast, personal wealth and, by extension, the existence of the Southern Host. Merchants are always trying to get around him, but whatever he doesn't touch, wherever it goes, eventually crumbles to dust."

Graykin clutched at his treasured finery. "What, even this?"

"Probably. Perhaps that's why your new friends are trying to outrun their customers, but they'll have little luck: most Kencyr know Southron ways."

"Well, I don't," said Jame. "What's in the Southern Wastes except sand, dead cities, and an occasional inconvenient salt sea?"

"That's the mystery," Dar said, shamelessly eavesdropping with Mint at his elbow. "Seekers go into the desert, leading caravans, and come back with treasures. Sometimes Kencyr are hired as guards against clashes with Nekriens, Wasters, and Karnids, but they're sworn to secrecy. Lord Caldane would give half his wealth to know what's going on, which is why no one employs Caineron guards."

Rue had been shifting from foot to foot. "Maybe the merchants have something that won't crumble when you look at it. Lady, please! You need finer clothes than your forage jacket."

Poor Rue. Obviously she hadn't forgotten the disgrace, as she saw it, of Jame's appearance before the High Council.

Graykin handed Jame a sack of coins. "You have no idea what these are worth," he said. "I've taken enough for my needs. Squander the rest if you want."

My brother gave me this, Jame thought, balancing the bag's not inconsiderable weight on her palm. *He didn't have to. Maybe, on some level, he also misses the days when we shared everything, before Father came between us.*

She gave the sack to Rue. "Spend what you like, within reason. We won't lose for lack of one cadet—I hope," she added to the Coman ten-commander, who was looking restive.

"Can't you discuss all of this after the lesson?" he demanded.

"I may not be here when you're done," said Graykin, himself beginning to fidget. "The caravan is moving off as soon as its business here is finished . . ."

"Definitely unsanctioned," murmured Brier.

". . . and I don't want to be left behind."

Yet he stayed, fretting from foot to foot. There was clearly more on his mind.

"Gray, what aren't you telling me?"

He spoke in a low rush, leaning toward her. "You gave that knot letter to Kindrie and he's had it translated."

"What?" Jame felt a jolt of shock. She had entirely forgotten about Kinzi's scrap of linen.

"Did he steal it, then?"

"No. It must have been in the knapsack with . . . never mind. What did it say?"

"That damned haunt singer forbade me to tell you—me, your personal sneak! You'll have to ask your cousin."

Jame chewed her lip, trying to work out when she could take time off to visit Mount Alban.

"Camp!" came the sentry's urgent cry, closely followed by a volley of missiles.

Brier shoved Jame behind Graykin, who grunted and sat down, hard, almost on top of her. Cadets sped off in pursuit of the intruders, snatching slings from their belts and white ovoids from their pouches.

"Look what you've done to me!" Graykin gasped, clutching his chest. "I'm dead!"

Jame knelt beside him. "Oh, don't be silly. It was only an egg."

"This?" He threw wide his arms to expose red ruin.

"Well, an egg with the yolk blown out, refilled with whatever blood the butcher had on hand, and resealed with wax. Messy, I grant you, but hardly fatal."

"But my robe!" wailed poor Graykin.

"Rub it in salt and soak it in cold water before you wash it.

That's what the losers of this skirmish have to do with all the soiled clothing. It and they get thrown off Breakneck Rock into the Burley which, at this time of year, is no treat."

The Coman was nearly dancing with impatience. "We have to shift camp. Now."

"All right, all right. If I don't make it back to Tentir in time, Gray, I'll see you in Kothifir."

As Graykin wobbled off, Jame turned to the Coman. "I suggest that we move west toward the cloud-of-thorns. There are passageways beneath them if we have to scuttle. Niall, stay here and tell the scouts as they come in where we've gone."

They moved out.

No one spent much time in this area, and now Jame saw why. Close as it was to Tentir, and relatively small, it seemed to embody all the strangeness of the uncharted Riverland. Beyond sight of the college, they moved through areas ankle deep in snow where winter still ruled and others bright with spring flowers. The land rippled in moraines that ran mostly north to south, down to the snow-swollen Burley; but that tributary of the Silver seemed ridiculously far away—a rushing sound rather than a presence—and the now-veiled sun seemed to shift from one side of the sky to the other. Unseen birds called. Leaves rustled under the unwary foot.

Throughout, they kept watch not only for the other team but for the elusive "something" that was the prize of the entire exercise.

Eventually they arrived at the clumped cloud-of-thorn bushes with the river loud beyond them and Breakneck Rock beyond that.

"There are fifteen of us, eighteen when the last scouts and Niall arrive," Jame said. "We should be able to comb this dollop of wilderness from one side to the other."

"Separate? D'you think that's wise?"

She could almost see the Coman assessing the risks and trying to decide how to make her responsible for them. Fash must have been most persuasive. Even so, Clary looked uneasy. What had that wretched Caineron said to him anyway?

"We could, of course, huddle here until nightfall, leaving the wood to our scouts and the other side. Does that sound better to you?"

Clearly, it didn't.

"Form a line and spread out," she told the cadets of the two ten-commands. "Keep in sight of each other to either side. Somehow, I think it would be very easy to get lost in here today."

The cadets obeyed her, Clary continuing to grumble. To the right was Brier; to the left, Damson. The Coman, she noted, gravitated to the side closest to Tentir, pushing the Knorth toward the river. She gripped her sling and counted the intact shells nestled in moss in the sack hanging from her belt. Two dozen. Over the past fortnight they had all grown heartily sick of scrambled eggs. This had better be worth it. The signal rippled down the line, from the banks of the Burley to the shadow of Tentir.

Right, she thought, waving them forward. _We're off._

Brier stayed perhaps closer than she should have, as if determined to keep Jame under her eye.

Dammit, Jame thought, _am I that easily broken, nothing but a shell full of blood, sealed with wax? What's the worst that could happen to me here?_

What about an encounter with the Dark Judge? Little had been heard from that great cat since the onset of spring, but he was out there somewhere, and Jame still felt shy about straying too far from the college after dark. Sometimes she sensed his restless presence in her dreams, but something kept him at bay. Long might it last.

To her right, Damson disappeared behind a stand of budding lilacs. The bushes seemed to move with her, now cutting off Brier as well. New shoots erupted out of the ground ahead of the main stands, rasping against each other. It was, after all, the season for arboreal drift. Everything in the valley that could move probably was, toward sunnier slopes, toward water, away from predators with axes.

Was someone calling?

"Wha ... wha ... wha ..."

Jame stopped, the breath catching in her throat. She had considered the Dark Judge, but not the Burning Ones. Did they ever come this far south, especially without their master who had lain in the earth since the winter solstice? Lilac and raspberry canes rustled and rose, hedging her in. Sounds from beyond reached her muffled and distorted. Her own voice, when she called out, was swallowed by the burgeoning leaves.

A shadow fell across her. She squinted up against the low-slung sun at something black suspended over her head. It had an almost human shape—wide-flung arms, at least, and between them what seemed to be a hunched head. But no feet. It stirred, by no wind felt below. The sun flamed around its edges.

"Sssoooo. Forgotten about me, had you?"

She peered upward. "Vant? What in Perimal's name are you doing up there?"

"Ooohh, just hanging around, waiting for you. My new friends are here too, at least in spirit."

Was that really a voice or just the sloughing of the wind in the leaves? The day had turned dreamlike around her, cut off as she was in this pocket of strangeness. Why, after all, should her former five-commander haunt her, when she had had nothing to do with his death? But he had appeared to her, not to Damson, who must be at most a dozen yards away and wouldn't be shy about taking credit.

As if she had heard her name called, Damson appeared, fighting her way through the thicket. "There you are, Ten! Who are you talking to?"

Above, cloth ripped. The black shape plummeted toward Jame, blotting out the sun. She tried to fend it off, but it threw its dismembered arms around her neck and bore her down. She fought free with Damson's help to find that she had been wrestling with one of the Commandant's old, leather coats.

"This must be what we were sent to find," said Damson.

From outside the hollow came the muffled sound of shouting. The two teams must have clashed just beyond the grove's precincts. Damson plunged off to join the fray. Jame paused to whack the coat several times against a rock, just to make sure, then followed the cadet. Beyond the lilacs, white missiles laced the air, accompanied with yelps and jeers. There was Clary, setting an egg to his sling. He saw her, hesitated, switched eggs, and swung. Jame glanced behind her for his target, and her temple seemed to explode.

I owe Graykin an apology, she thought, on the slide down into darkness; *Being egged is more painful than I realized*. Then the coat was jerked out of her grasp and she fell.

A long time seemed to pass. The lilac break crept past and the shouts receded. She leaned back against a tree, silently cursing her throbbing head and the blood trickling down her face.

"Damn!" said someone almost in her ear, in her brother's voice. "That hurts."

He shifted against the other side of the tree, his coat rasping against its bark.

"Tori?"

"Jame?"

"What are you doing here?" both asked simultaneously, then, "Where is 'here'?"

"An hour north of Gothregor."

"Fifteen minutes south of Tentir. What happened to you?"

"Storm threw me. We were tracking a rogue golden willow and it charged us."

"You didn't fell it, did you?"

"That would require it to stand still first. Trinity, I hate arboreal drift. And you?"

"I'm not sure. Something hit me."

"Careless, careless..."

"No more so than you, run over by a tree."

"At least you're past the main threat."

"What?" she asked, confused. She heard him draw himself up.

"The Commandant told me that someone was sure to challenge you to combat before the end of the school year. That happened at the High Council meeting. Why else d'you think I allowed that bastard Fash to take you on? Even so, under all of our eyes, he went further than I expected."

"Oh, that wasn't an official challenge, just one of M'lord Caldane's little tricks to humiliate us both."

She sensed her brother's dismay, even as his voice began to fade.

"Then you've got to get out of there. Listen, Jame, I can't protect you. Not at Tentir. Much less so far away at Kothifir. I can't let you go."

"If the randon will it, you can't stop me."

"Who can't?" said a new voice, attached to a pair of large, surprisingly gentle hands. "What have you done to yourself this time?"

Jame blinked up at Brier. She needn't turn to know that Tori was gone.

"Clary came back to camp with the Commandant's coat, but without you. What happened?"

Jame almost giggled. "I think he hardboiled his eggs."

Brier's big hand was full of shell shards plucked from Jame's clothing. Among them lay a blood-stained rock.

"Not this hard," she said grimly. "And with the power of a sling behind it..."

"Never mind." Jame pushed her aside and wobbled to her feet, remembering the Coman's expression. "Fash had him confused."

Behind them they heard shouts, laughter, and splashes: the losers were paying their forfeit in the Burley's frigid waters. Jame wiped her forehead with her sleeve and decided not to bother. There was little enough blood. Besides, her team had won. Somehow, though, she didn't think that Clary would revel in that victory.

They walked back to Tentir where, it transpired, the merchants and Graykin had already left, having found few customers among the canny randon.

Rue had bought a length of shimmering white samite, however, which she presented almost defiantly to Jame.

"It was dead cheap," she said, "and I think I may know how to keep it from fading away."

"Good luck to you, then," said Jame, and thought no more of it.

On impulse, she went to Bear's den and sat down outside of it.

"How does one manage?" she asked him through the grate. "Brothers and sisters...how can Tori and I talk when to do so freely both of us have to be either asleep or concussed? How do you communicate with the Commandant with so few words in common? Yet I'll swear that he loves you, and you, him."

She considered Sheth's guilt. He had followed his lord's orders that Bear be either confined or killed. Who could have guessed, all those years ago, that the torment would go on so long?

Control: Caldane over Sheth, Sheth over Bear, Tori over her. Command aside, how did one let go when love was the bond?

"Tori will stop me if he can, for my own good. Ha. And yet he gave me this." She fingered the carven cat with its snapped-off hind leg, the maimed symbol of their past. "Did we ever really share everything?"

Mine, mine! No, mine!

"He trusts me, yet he doesn't. Do I trust him?"

Bear snuffled in the dark behind his door. Huge, ivory nails protruded through the grate, groping. On impulse, Jame gave him the carving. More snuffling, then a sharp snap: he had broken off the cat's other hind leg.

Jame sighed.

I will stop you.

Not if I can help it, she thought.

☙ II ❧

HOURS AGO, KINDRIE HAD SEEN the merchants pack up their wares and leave the training square, with Graykin in his gaudy finery rushing to join them at the last minute. The healer had meant to travel south with them from Tentir as far as Gothregor, but that clearly was not to be. The Southron had glanced up at the second-story common room window where he stood, then had flinched away. Kindrie wondered if Graykin had even told Jame that her cousin had arrived and was waiting for her in her quarters.

The barracks were deserted, everyone out attending class. Life hummed all around him, echoing in the empty rooms as if in a seashell's chambers. He had grown used to the constant stir of Mount Alban and his place in it. This reminded him of his isolation in the Priests' College at Wilden, where no one spoke to him except in abuse. The best he had hoped for there was to be left alone, free to retreat into the Moon Garden that was his soul-image, where no one could hurt him.

Why had he never met his mother there, except as a pattern of moss and lichen against a stone wall? That blurred face had watched silently over his childhood and he had never recognized it until it had come to claim him, a terrible thing of cords and hunger...

But life was different now. He had a family. He had friends.

So he told himself. At the moment, though, he felt alone, and cold, and hungry.

Who are you, that anyone should take notice of you? whispered the ghosts of his past.

Plates clattered in the dining hall two floors below and the smell of cooking rose. Cadets were returning from their lessons, talking, laughing. Footsteps sounded on the stair. A slim figure entered the apartment, speaking to someone over her shoulder. Then she turned and saw him.

"Kindrie! Have you been here all this time? That wretch Graykin, not to have told me!"

She advanced and took his hands, hers warm within their black gloves, his cold in her grasp, while her hunting ounce Jorin sniffed his legs.

"What happened to your face?"

She touched a darkening bruise and laughed. "The children here play rough, but they haven't yet driven me out."

No, thought Kindrie, they wouldn't. One of them at least must be a slow learner not to have realized that by now. He envied her cheerful toughness, so unexpected in one seemingly so fragile.

She turned and called down the stair. "Rue, bring food up here. Tonight I dine with my cousin. And set a fire. It's going to be a chilly evening."

The towheaded cadet brought up bowls of thick soup, fresh bread, and a pitcher of ale. While they ate, the ounce begging them impartially for scraps, Rue piled kindling under the large bronze basin and set it on fire. Slowly, the chill left Kindrie's bones and his spirit.

"It doubles as a bathtub," said Jame, referring to the basin, "but you know that from the last time you were here. Would you like it to be filled? No? Then what's this about Kinzi's letter being translated?"

Kindrie explained.

Jame swore, rose, and began to pace. Jorin scrambled out of her way.

"I should have paid more attention," she said. "After Lyra swallowed half of it, though, and I couldn't read what was left... Trishien's translation is certainly suggestive and in line with my own suspicions, but what can we do? Kirien is right: this isn't proof. I don't know what would be, short of a confession from Rawneth herself."

"Will she get away with it, then?" The thought closed Kindrie's throat. So many dead, all the women of his family except his mother and she left in lonely exile...

"The Bitch of Wilden has kept her secret for decades so far. And to use Kinzi's letter would be to betray the ladies' precious knot code."

"Does that matter?"

"Not much. The winter I spent in the gentle care of the Women's World was almost as bad as yours in the Priests' College at Wilden. I owe them nothing. But there are three of us now. One of us is bound to stop her, somehow."

"Probably you."

Jame smiled with a flash of white, bared teeth. "Oh, I would like that very much."

Kindrie regarded her as she paced. Her clenched hands drove nails into her palms and her eyes flashed silver in the firelight. A shiver passed through the soulscape. It occurred to him suddenly that she had just fought down an incipient berserker flare. Her control frightened him almost as much as her potential violence.

"You *are* dangerous, aren't you?"

"Sometimes, very much so. Others, I trip over my own feet. But you can tell Kirien this to add into the mix: the night of the fire when your contract was signed, the darkling changer Keral was there posing as Rawneth's servant."

Kindrie stared at her. "How do you know that?"

Jame made a face. "It's a bit hard to explain. Sometimes I see visions, as if various places are trying to show me things. Autumn's Eve in the death banner hall and in the Moon Garden, I glimpsed a lot that still confuses me. But Keral was definitely there. Moreover, I don't think Rawneth had any idea who or what he was. She isn't the sort to pay much attention to servants."

"So that would mean," said Kindrie slowly, working it out, "that Keral is probably Lord Randir's father."

"And Shade's grandfather, which is how she inherited her dose of darkling blood. What we don't know for sure is what face Keral showed Rawneth as they made love."

"Wouldn't it have been Greshan's?" Kindrie asked, confused.

"No. She thought he was Greshan at first, but then he changed, and not back into Keral. Kinzi said that Rawneth was pleased. I don't see her happy to have been tricked into congress with a lackey."

"Who, then? Gerraint?"

"No. At a guess, your own father, Gerridon."

"But the Master isn't a changer, is he?"

"No. My dear uncle Gerridon has had as little to do with the shadows as possible. Others pay for his seeming immortality. But Rawneth wouldn't know that. I always thought that M'lord Kenan reminded me of someone. Now I know whom: Keral."

"So Kenan is also a changer?"

"That I don't know. Maybe it skipped a generation, but as secretive as the Randir are, how would we know unless he loses control and betrays himself? Rawneth is or was watching Shade through her serpent Addy, presumably to see if she starts to show her bloodlines, which she has. Some cadets of her house are already after her, but not for that."

She told Kindrie about the attempt to drown Shade in the Randir basement during the Day of Misrule.

"This is very confusing," said Kindrie, running a hand through his white hair, leaving it in unruly cowlicks. "You say that the cadets who tried to kill Shade aren't bound to her grandmother? Then to whom?"

"Not to Randiroc, maybe not even to Kenan. You know the Randir better than I do. Who else is there?"

Kindrie thought back to his time at Wilden, most of which had been spent in the Priests' College. "Some Randir Highborn only serve Rawneth because they fear her. There are also Randir Shanir in the college, not all there willingly. Some of them may be able to bind."

"Huh. No wonder the Randir cadets are so confused, except for those bound directly to Rawneth. The whole thing is as murky as dirt soup. I'm obliged to you for bringing me news, however. Was that the only reason you dropped by Tentir?"

"No. I was on my way to Gothregor, to give Torisen this." He rummaged in his pack and brought forth a leather cylinder containing a roll of parchment. They spread it out on the floor where Jorin tried to sprawl on it, but was chased off. Names covered every inch of it, some with miniature ink portraits beside them, faces deftly caught in a few flicks of the brush.

"This is wonderful," said Jame, examining it. "Everyone bound to Tori must be here."

"Very nearly," Kindrie admitted, glad that the firelight hid his blush of pride. "I started with the names we collected last fall and went on from there. The Knorth scrollsmen were a great help."

"Tori will be very glad of this." Her voice warmed him. At last, he had done something of value for his newfound family— enough for his cousin to forgive him for being a Shanir? That remained to be seen.

"You'll have to wait to show it to him, though. Your merchant escort is gone, and I don't think anyone here is free to go south with you just now."

Kindrie's disappointment surprised him. After all, Torisen didn't immediately need the list, but he had so looked forward to giving it to him.

Still trying to prove yourself, aren't you? he thought with some scorn. *What, do you want so much for him to clasp you to his bosom?* Dammit, yes.

Rue cleared the dishes and brought out a sleeping mat for Kindrie. He settled onto the latter and drowsily watched his cousin strip for bed. Her fair skin seemed a patchwork of multicolored bruises, old and new—the common lot of any cadet, he supposed. From his last experience with her soul-image, he knew better than to offer his healing touch, not wanting to be knocked through the nearest wall. After all, she couldn't help what she was any more than he could. So near, so far, and yet family.

"G'night, cousin."

"Good night."

In the morning Kindrie rose with the cadets and shared their breakfast. Jame waved him off from the door of the great hall, then disappeared back into Old Tentir bound for her first class of the day.

Kindrie gained the New Road and hesitated. It would be far wiser to turn north, back to Mount Alban. His hand stole down to touch the leather canister. Oh, but he had so wanted to show his work to Torisen. How dangerous could it be, really, especially if he kept to the west bank? He could stop that night in the safety of Shadow Rock which, after all, was held by his bone cousin, Holly, Lord Danior. Would either Jame or Tori hesitate? No. That settled in his mind, he turned right and rode southward, toward Gothregor and all that lay in between.

CHAPTER X
Spring Equinox

Spring 37

THE VERNAL EQUINOX FELL on the thirty-seventh of spring, another example of the Kencyrath not quite getting things right on their new world, nor bothering to change it over the three millennia or so that they had been there.

It was also the free, seventh day of the week at Tentir, hence Jame felt no guilt about slipping out in the early morning to find and saddle Death's-head. Mindful of her late arrival on the solstice, she started before the college was stirring, also before Fash could taunt her about her frolics with the native "savages," as if they were anything of the sort.

As usual, she set her destination in mind and gave the rathorn his head. Much good it would have done her to try to guide him with a bitless bridle and his contrary attitude, even if she had known the way. Better to trust him and the folds in the land: the New Road would have taken much too long as it was a good one hundred miles north to Kithorn.

Besides, on it she would have risked overtaking the Commandant and Gorbel, who had both been summoned by their lord to Restormir.

"In the middle of a school year? What for?" she had asked Gorbel.

He had grunted. "My father is fussed. By his reckoning, you should long since have been sent packing from Tentir. What he means to do about it, though, I have no idea."

Neither did Jame, but supposed that she would find out.

As she and the rathorn traveled north and rose with the land, winter reasserted itself. Snow lingered under trees and blew down from the heights in sparkling veils, momentarily obscuring the landscape. Few birds sang and no trees drifted. When they came within sight of it, the Silver was a gray and white sheet of frozen water. Still, they set a good pace, arriving at Kithorn in the early afternoon.

This time, the keep courtyard was packed with Merikit, with more spilling out the gatehouse doors. Voices and laughter rose from within.

Curious but seeing no way to force an entrance, Jame circled the wall. Bright faces turned to look down at her from on top of it.

"Here, Earth Wife's Favorite! Up here!"

Jame stood in the saddle and worked her claws into the crumbling stonework. Death's-head promptly walked out from under her. She scrambled up to join the children.

"You're just in time," whispered Prid. "The Maid is about to reject her suitors."

Below, only the sacred square around the covered well remained relatively clear. Within its precincts a fantastic figure clad in the relics of a white court gown strutted and preened before the audience as if before a wall of mirrors.

"There was a maid, oh so beautiful, so proud," murmured Jame, remembering her previous venture into the Merikits' sacred space.

Swish, swish went the embroidered hem. Where had they gotten that dress?

Then Jame remembered: this had been Marc's home keep before the Merikit had slaughtered everyone in it. Someone must have pilfered this finery before the flames had claimed it. She reminded herself that the massacre had been over eighty years ago, the result of a misunderstanding, not malice, and that Marc had long since claimed the blood price for it. Still, she wondered what Highborn lady had last worn that tattered garment and what she would think to see it now.

Not, of course, that it currently clothed a female. Only shamans could mum before their gods. This one was masked to conceal the wizened features of Index's old friend, Tungit.

Other shamans decked out in decrepit finery of the same era approached the Maid and were dismissed by her with haughty gestures and personal insults that made the audience roar with laughter.

"No chief's son would do for her, oh no. Why this particular mummery, Prid?"

"The equinox is the Eaten One's festival. We need her permission to fish the Silver and she needs us to break open the ice. Listen!"

"I would rather be a war maid and track the wild game," declaimed the shaman, to a muted cheer from Prid. On her other side her cousin Hatch glanced at her wistfully.

The Maid's mother sidled up to reproach her. "Take a mate and become a proper wyf," she squeaked in a high voice. "I have a fine lodge. To whom should I leave it if not to you?"

"What want I with hearth or housebond? What is a lodge but an earthbound trap?"

The audience shuffled their feet. Some began to stomp until all had picked up the beat.

"Oh no!" cried the mother, wringing her hands. "The earth is shaking! The River Snake must be hungry. Who will save us?"

The Maid swayed her hips seductively, to more laughter from the crowd. "No need for a hero. I will deal with him, for who can resist my charms?"

As the mother withdrew, the Maid began to pantomime gingerly walking on ice. Flagstones shifted under her feet, limned by bright lines of sacred space. "Ooh! This is harder than I thought."

Into the square crept a shaman wearing the catfish-skin cape.

"Look behind you!" cried the children on the wall.

"Did I hear little birds twittering? Wakie, wakie, snakie, snakie!" She slipped. "Oops. I've fallen into the water. Oh no!"

The fish-man slithered over her.

"Munch, munch, munch."

"And he ate her all-l-l up!" came the triumphant chorus of the onlookers.

Then they all turned and began to stream out of the courtyard, leaving the square empty.

"Come on," said Prid. "Let's hurry back for the feast."

Jame went with her. She had no doubt that she had just witnessed one version of that unfortunate maiden's transformation from mortal into the immortal if eternally compromised Eaten One. At the same time, it had seemed to be ringed with other stories, other maids and other fates—something tragic, profound, and complex reduced to a farce. Pride falls, but what of bravery and rebellion against a fate not of one's choosing, brought to such an end? Did the audience laugh so as not to cry?

And she remembered Prid quoting from this mummery at the

winter solstice. No wonder Gran Cyd had warned her not to, given the Maid's fate.

They came to the rebuilt boys' and girls' lodges reserved for those like Prid too old to stay at home but too young to know which way to turn their lives.

"I've moved into the men's lodge," Hatch told her. "It's on the west side of the village next to the war maids."

"Now that you've come of age, what will you do?"

He gave her a crooked smile. "The same thing I've always done: wait for Prid."

Overall, thought Jame, he was lucky to live in a society that gave him the freedom to fit in where he wished, or to decline until he was ready. The men's and women's lodges seemed to be halfway options. Jame glanced at the tawny-haired girl skipping beside her and wondered if she would outgrow her desire to run wild with the war maids. It seemed to Jame that one had to pick one's discipline eventually or risk never growing up at all.

On the other hand, who was she to condemn the warrior life?

Here was the village on its palisaded hill, and inside the orderly mounds that marked each individual subterranean lodge. Ma, Da, and their twin girls greeted Jame from their threshold. Among the Merikit even two women could have such a family since the mother decided who had fathered her children. Other lodge-wyves waved. Most took it as a great joke that Jame was the Earth Wife's Favorite and Chingetai's heir, therefore officially male.

Gran Cyd waited outside her lodge, resplendent in crimson and gold with a rich fur cape draped over her bare shoulders. Her dark red hair, elaborately braided, shone against the white fur. She had the glow of a woman with child, but as yet showed little other sign of her pregnancy for which (to her embarrassment) Jame had been credited, along with that of half a dozen more among the lodge-wyves.

"Come," she greeted Jame. "We must make haste to the feasting ground by the Silver Steps."

Jame was somewhat chagrined. Sitting on the wall had chilled her and she had been looking forward to the warmth of the underground communal hall. The queen saw her shiver.

"Wait." Gran Cyd descended into her lodge, and returned with a black fur cloak almost as sumptuous as her own. "A present," she said, slinging it over Jame's shoulders despite her protests.

"What are the Silver Steps?" Jame asked as they departed the village, followed by a crowd mostly comprised of women and children.

"You will see."

They walked about a mile upstream over a path beaten through the snow by the men going before them. Here the Silver's ice showed deep fractures and dislodged chunks ground against each other as the current rushed under them.

By now it was midafternoon with the sun beginning its tumble down the sky toward the western mountain peaks. Jame regarded the lengthening shadows with unease. She hadn't been this far north since the winter solstice, much less with night coming on.

"What do the Burning Ones do while their master sleeps in the earth?" she asked Gran Cyd.

The queen raised an eyebrow. "Why do you ask?"

"I saw them at the solstice, with someone whom I didn't expect to see. A Kendar named Vant."

"So." She walked on for several strides, thinking. "Perhaps that explains it. Normally, from solstice to Summer's Eve the Burnt Man's hounds sleep. This winter, though, we had a kin-slayer in the men's lodge, one brother killing another. It sometimes happens, when the weather is bad and no one can go out. The walls close in. Tempers grow short. Nonetheless, we drove out the slayer, thinking that he would perish of the cold; instead, the Burning Ones came, led by one who did not burn except for his eyes. Perhaps that was your Kendar."

"Perhaps," said Jame, chilled. It still seemed strange that Vant should hunt with the Burnt Man's pack, but there was a rage in him that apparently had survived his death by fire. And he was Greshan's grandson, tenacious of life.

"I will have justice, or I will have revenge."

Against whom? Torisen? Damson? Herself?

"If so," said Gran Cyd, following her own thoughts, "he does his followers no good. They should have slept the cold time away, keeping their fires banked. What came for our slayer could barely shamble through the snow. If he had not fed them, I doubt that they would have survived winter."

That sounded like Vant, who had never learned that to lead is also to serve.

Moreover, it explained why he hadn't brought the Burning Ones south to hunt his true prey: they had been too weak.

Were they still? Should she fear them as she did that other seeker-out of guilt, the Dark Judge?

But the sun still shone and, really, what did she have to feel guilty about?

Don't answer that.

They passed several waterfalls, then a series of them rising in tiers to the lip of an escarpment overhung with ice. In the field below the men had set up trestle tables and were cooking in huge cauldrons suspended over pale, bright flames.

"Here are the Steps," said Gran Cyd. "Climb them and behold a wonder."

Jame found a twisting trail beside the river and scrambled up it, clinging to bare shrubs. At the top, she looked out over an ice-locked lake winding back between steep, dark mountains into premature dusk. Wintry sunlight gleamed blue off the nearer shore, deepening to cobalt under the streamers of snow that drifted over it. Sparkles here and there reflected back from ice rills as if the night sky had fallen into the ocean.

"Is this the headwater of the Silver?" Jame asked as she regained the queen's side.

"Yes. It stretches through a chain of lakes farther north, to the foot of a glacier, in the shadow of a greater darkness."

That sounded uncomfortably like the Barrier with Perimal Darkling on the other side. One tended to forget that it was there, just out of sight.

"That, they say, is where the blackheads breed. We have yet to see one. The northern tribes speak of a lampreylike fish native to those benighted waters that lays its eggs in other fish and seeks to migrate with them even as the eggs hatch within and devour their host. If they should ever find their way into the Silver..."

Chingetai laughed behind them, making Jame start. "A tale to frighten children. They even claim that the larvae can reanimate the dead. I ask you!"

Cyd turned to face him, hands on her hips. "You are a great hunter and raider, housebond, doubtless, but no fisherman upon the ice. The depths beneath terrify you."

The chief swelled in outrage. He really was a big man, thought Jame, looking up at him, seeing mostly chest and the underside of a jutting, bearded chin. Still, he wasn't quite up to Marc's stature, in any sense of that word.

"Nothing scares me!" he declared. "When my sick friend craved fresh salmon, did I not go out onto the ice and catch him one? He was so overjoyed that he devoured it raw and so regained his strength."

"Not noticeably," said the queen wryly.

She indicated a haggard man hovering near the cooking pots as if led there by his nose. His eyes were glassy and while otherwise thin, his belly swelled like that of a pregnant woman. The cooks shied away from him.

Chingetai harrumphed and stalked away.

"Fresh salmon, at this time of the year. I would think that he caught one of the mothers of the school who return more than once to spawn, except that this one was male. With eggs. Nonetheless," Gran Cyd lowered her voice and leaned to confide in Jame, "it *was* an act of courage for him to go out onto the ice. He fears deep water in all its forms and has ever since his sister was chosen when they were both children."

"Chosen for what?"

"Ah." The queen turned away from her. "Here is my sister Anku, leader of the war maids."

Anku might have been the queen's age or slightly older; with her weathered face and trim, hard body, it was difficult to tell. She smiled at Jame. "I hear that you have cast your glamour over my grandniece Prid. She talks of no one else."

"I don't deserve that."

"Ah, but who among the Kencyr is closer to being a war maid than you, and such a one as to have fought the River Snake and won! Prid envies what she sees as our free life."

"It's hardly that," said Jame, thinking of the trials of Tentir.

"So you and I know full well. But Prid remembers her mother, who died in child-bed. For her, the village lodges stink of duty and death. A pity for that nice boy Hatch, now that she is almost of an age to make her choice."

The crowd stirred. "Here comes the feast!" exclaimed many voices.

The men served them steaming bowls of fish stew—perch, pike, walleye, and blue gimp—all the fruits of winter fishing boiled up with the season's last root vegetables, washed down with tankards of strong ale. Noisy, almost hectic merriment spread. Unlike the previous time when Jame had feasted with them, rather than simply enjoying themselves, the Merikit seemed to be trying to get drunk as fast as possible.

One of the men tending the fire suddenly knelt, drew out a long, charred stick with a knob at each end, and brandished it on high with a shout of triumph. The Merikit cheered.

"A Burnt Man's bone," said Gran Cyd, pleased. "Probably a femur. They have been showing up in our fireplaces ever since the winter solstice. We have maybe half of them by now, set aside for the Summer's Eve bonefires."

At that time, Chingetai would use them to close the Merikits' borders; but if even one was missing, as had happened last year due to Jame's unintentional interference, the rite would fail. Such matters in the hills certainly were complicated.

"You seem very pleased," said Jame to the queen, speaking under the noisy chatter. "Has the Burnt Man's protection as a border guard entirely been withdrawn this past year?"

"Oh, but yes. Not that it isn't weakened every year between the burning of the effigy and the return of the bones on Summer's Eve. We risk something, sacrificing one of the Four and then waiting for his resurrection. Hence the importance of this ritual evoking the protection of the Eaten One."

"I'm still confused," Jame said. "You need special permission to fish the Silver, but not the Silverhead?"

"The lake falls under the protection of neither the River Snake nor the Eaten One. We take our chances with what swims there."

"Then, too, one of your stories says that the Maid was eaten by the River Snake, another that she stuck halfway down the gullet of a giant catfish."

Tungit paused in passing. "Lady, these are men's mysteries, not to be questioned."

"Then go away, old man," said the queen, not unkindly, "lest our foolish talk offend you."

The shaman shrugged and continued on to his place at table.

"I will be sorry someday to lose that old one. He has as much sense as his creed allows him and, I suspect, somewhat more. Look, Earth Wife's Favorite."

She drew a stone figurine out of the pouch that hung at her waist and gave it to Jame. It was roughly diamond-shaped, bulging toward the middle, tapering at the points. It took Jame a moment to make sense of the lines scratched on it. Two sagging breasts, a pendulous belly, no head, hands or feet to speak of... all the stress was on fertility, none on personality. "This is the Earth Wife?"

"A crude version of her, very, very old, from far, far away. Here is another." Cyd dipped her finger into her ale and traced three circles surrounded by a fourth on the tabletop.

Jame stared at it. Although it resembled a crude face, it could be an even cruder, rounded out version of the figurine. "That's an *imu!*"

"So it is. And both of these images were ancient long before Mother Ragga was even born."

Other maids, other fates, thought Jame.

The sense came back to her of layered truths blurring into each other with the ages. Once she had asked the Earth Wife who made up the rules that governed her somewhat erratic nature and she had replied, "Don't know. They just are."

If Jame had guessed right, the Four had come into their present forms some three thousand years ago with the arrival of her own people and their temples on Rathillien. But what if the templates that shaped them had already existed, as many as there were cultures to create them? That would explain why their roles were so multiform and often contradictory. No wonder the transformed Four were still trying to sort themselves out.

"Oh!" said Prid at a nearby table. She was staring at something in her hand that she had found in her stew. It was a small fish carved out of rock crystal.

Her friends drew back in a growing circle of silence.

"Oh, granddaughter," murmured the queen in obvious distress. "Not you."

The Merikit rose and quietly cleared away the feast. Bowls were emptied on the snow, their contents buried. Fires were doused, tables removed.

"The fish is caught," ran a murmur through the crowd. "The fish is caught."

"What's going on?" Jame demanded, but received no answer.

Prid stood alone, shivering.

Gran Cyd wrapped the girl in her white fur cloak.

"Be brave, child," she said. "You knew that one of the maidens' lodge would draw this fate."

Prid gulped and nodded, but couldn't stop shaking.

"There was a maid, so beautiful, so proud," she whispered, and the crowd answered:

"No chief's son would do for her, oh no."

To one side, Hatch struggled in the grip of his friends.

Jame opened her mouth to protest, then shut it again. She had seen what harm could come of meddling with Merikit ceremonies, but sweet Trinity...!

The river ice ground its crystal teeth. Something huge swam beneath it, much too large for such a shallow depth. River Snake or Eaten One? Prid gingerly stepped out onto the ice over its slushy margin, clutching the cape around her.

Her people took up the chant: "There was a maid, there was a maid..."

This was what they had been nerving themselves to face with all of that ale.

Prid slipped, up to her knee in slush. The ice around her was pockmarked and dull, and it crackled alarmingly underfoot.

"Oh," she quavered. "I've fallen into the water."

With agonizing slowness, she shifted her weight and pulled herself out, dragging her soaked leg as if it had fallen asleep. One could almost hear her teeth rattle together.

Jame could barely hold herself still. "What if she makes it safely to the other side?"

"Then the Eaten One has rejected her and we have lost her blessing."

The vast shape beneath the dark ice bumped against it and white cracks spread. Chunks lurked free. Prid staggered on among them.

A warning shout turned everyone's attention upstream. Chingetai's friend had staggered over to the open water at the Steps' foot and was vomiting into it. His lips peeled back, splitting to the hinges of his jaws, then to his ears, and still the black, writhing forms spewed out of his mouth into the river.

"Blackheads!" someone cried.

There was a rush to pull him away, but already he seemed to have disgorged half of his own weight and still the seething tide continued. By the time Chingetai reached him, he had sunk to his knees. His flesh melted away and he collapsed, nothing but loose bones in a sack of skin.

Dark, serpentine forms darted under the ice, converging on the river leviathan. It smashed up through the ice, broad, bewhiskered mouth agape, blackheads attached like streamers along its gray sides, and crashed down again. The entire ice floe was breaking up.

Prid tottered, shrieked, and fell in.

Hatch gave a shout of horror.

Jame swore and darted forward.

Gran Cyd clutched at her but only caught the black cape.

Jame's dash faltered as she felt the ice shift under her. It was unevenly pocked with rot where the rushing current had eaten it away underneath, and now the cracks were spreading. How did one tell good ice from bad? She had meant to dive in after Prid, but every nerve told her to stand very, very still.

Then the block on which she balanced began to tip. Down it she slid, into the frigid water, and the ice closed over her.

Jame's first thought was *I've gone deaf.* After the confusion above, the silence below clamped down on her like jaws. No, that was the water flooding into her clothes. Numb and heavy, she sank. The light above receded. Where was Prid? Where was the bottom? Shallow as the river must be here, she seemed to be descending into an abyss. In its depths in a great roiling, the Eaten One struggled against its attackers. One by one, they detached, uncoiled, and disintegrated like ribbons of shadow.

Something white caught the corner of Jame's eye. It was Prid's fur cloak, still wrapped around her, now saturated and dragging her down. Jame grabbed at its hem. Her fingers were so numb that she couldn't tell if she had caught it until it unfurled, spilling Prid out of it. Quick, let go of the fur and grab the girl. Prid's eyes were wide open and alive with terror.

We should both be unconscious, even dead, thought Jame.

Instead, they had apparently fallen into sacred space, where gods and monsters contend. It was even possible, with caution, to breathe, although the frigid water nearly stopped the heart.

The leviathan of a catfish rose to meet them, bristling mouth agape wide enough to swallow ships whole. In its maw like a pearl, a beautiful, pouting, pale green face turned upward toward them. The Eaten One spoke in a burst of rapidly expanding bubbles, silent until they enveloped the two swimmers and bore them rapidly toward the surface: MINE. SHE. IS. NOT.

The erupting bubbles shouldered aside the ice. Cold air hit bare skin like fire. Ah, such pain! Prid fainted. Jame clung to her with one arm and clawed at the ice with the other. They had fetched up near the shore, but considerably downstream, borne by its rapid current. Someone was shouting. Hatch. Hands gripped their sodden clothes and dragged them out. How could the cold burn so? Jame curled up on the bank, shaking, vomiting water and fish stew.

Gran Cyd stood over her.

"Oh, child," she said. "What have you done?"

CHAPTER XI

Rain

Spring 37–43

I

IT WAS SNOWING WHEN JAME LEFT the Merikit village the next morning. Snow turned to sleet on the ride south, and sleet to chill rain. By the time she reached Tentir late that night, she was soaked and shivering.

Rue ordered Greshan's huge, obscenely ornate bath filled for her. Jame lay in it slowly thawing out, listening to rain ping against the bronze hood and flinching as icy drops found their way down the smoke hole to tap on her bare shoulders.

The next morning rain still fell as cadets gathered in the muddy square for assembly. Most lessons were held inside, but that provided only partial relief. While not the winter chill, this was perhaps more piercing. No place in the college seemed warm more than a dozen paces from the nearest fire.

Jame's second class took place in the Map Room with the Coman master-ten Clary. It was the first time they had met since he had hit her with a rock during the egging exercise. She came up behind him as he bent over a scroll.

"Why did you do it?"

He flinched, but didn't turn to meet her eyes.

"Fash said . . ."

"Fash says many things. You shouldn't listen."

Clary hunched his shoulders as if against a blow. "I've been waiting for you to complain to the Commandant."

"Have I ever, about anything? It isn't likely to happen again, is it?"

143

The back of his neck turned dusky red. "No. It was a shoddy trick. I wish I hadn't done it."

"Good."

She passed on to Brier, who was studying a map of the Southern Wastes.

"Urakarn," said Brier, pointing to a mark on the western edge of the desert. "Here is the plain before it where my mother and your brother followed Genjar to defeat against the Karnids. Genjar came back. So many others didn't. They say that the ground there is still white with powdered bones. And this"—she swept her hand eastward—"is the dry salt sea over which they escaped. Is it true that my mother returned under the salt, under the sand, to save you?"

The previous spring, a weirdingstrom had carried the entire Scrollsmen's College all the way south taking Jame and Brier with it. Jame remembered the terror of sinking, of sand closing over her head, the salt on her lips turning wet, the ancient sea returning.

Then Rose Iron-thorn's hand had closed over her own and drawn her up to the air, to life. *For your brother's sake . . .*

"I think so."

Would they soon be revisiting those mysterious regions? Hot, dry, barren . . . Jame glanced out the window at the cold rain still descending in rods. How far away the Wastes seemed. Strange to think that someday, in some foreign desert, she might regret that it wasn't raining.

The downpour continued the next day, and the next. Nothing dried properly. The Silver rose, beginning to gnaw away its banks. Wells brimmed on the verge of overflowing. If the Eaten One indeed represented water, she was clearly showing her displeasure, but at what?

MINE. SHE. IS. NOT.

"She" undoubtedly referred to Prid, but why had the river goddess rejected her, with what consequences for her, her people, and all other dwellers of the Riverland? The solstice sacrifice usually went without a challenge from what Jame could learn. What happened to the sacrificed Favorite was more obscure.

And still the rain fell.

Oh, Gran Cyd, what have *we done?*

II

LATE ON THE FOURTH DAY, the college had visitors.

The ten-commands of Jame and Timmon were on the second-floor balcony of the great hall, putting out pots to catch drips before they could run down the lower walls and soak the house banners which already sagged under the weight of their dank stitches.

"If this keeps up," said Jame, emptying a sauce pan into a roasting pot, "wouldn't it be better to roll them up and store them somewhere dry?"

Timmon grunted. "If such a place exists."

The outer door ground open, swollen wood scraping on flagstones. Riders entered clad in oiled coats on dripping horses. Following them, a rose-colored canopy squeezed through the door. Something pale glimmered under it.

"It can't be," said Timmon, staring. "Sweet Trinity, it is. My mother."

Lady Distan extended her gloved hand to a white-haired randon who helped her to dismount.

"And that's Ran Aden. What in Perimal's name are they doing here?"

"You'd better go down to greet them."

Timmon chewed his lower lip. "Will you come with me?"

"Given how they both feel about me? Just go."

Reluctantly, Timmon went. His mother offered him her pink-gloved hand to kiss and allowed herself to be escorted out of the hall.

The horses and riders descended into the subterranean stable.

Aden was left surveying the hall. From his expression, nothing he saw pleased him.

A randon of his house, hastily summoned, stepped forward to welcome him. The Highborn looked down his nose at him.

"What, not Sheth Sharp-tongue?"

"The Commandant has been summoned home for an urgent consultation, Ran."

"Really. How irregular. In his absence, I am the senior officer here. Until Sheth deigns to resume his post, Tentir is under my command. Now, show me to the Commandant's quarters."

"Well," said Brier at Jame's shoulder as the two randon left.

Jame made a face. "That remains to be seen."

III

"CAN HE REALLY TAKE OVER TENTIR, just like that?" asked Dar over dinner. "I've never heard of such a thing before."

Everything on the table was cold, the well having overflowed in the basement and put out the kitchen fire. Trocks and newts had taken refuge on all available tabletops, while salamanders smoldered under the surface, emitting sullen bubbles.

"Ran Hawthorn was left in charge, and she seems to have accepted it," Mint remarked. "Ran Aden is just too senior to argue with."

"The Commandant will be back soon," said Erim. "She may not feel that it's worth a fuss."

Still, thought Jame, gnawing a slightly soggy heel of bread, she wished that Harn Grip-hard were here instead of with the Southern Host. If nothing else, as the Highlord's war-leader he outranked his Ardeth counterpart. As Erim said, though, Aden's tenure couldn't last for long. Already the Commandant's return was long overdue.

She also wondered about Lady Distan, Timmon's mother. Granted, it wouldn't have been raining when she set off with her escort from Omiroth, but what need had kept her stubbornly on the road in such inclement weather? A postprandial visit seemed in order.

When Jame arrived at the Ardeth barracks, however, everyone was still at table. She slipped up to Timmon's quarters to wait for him there, not reckoning that his mother would come with him. There was her voice on the stair, though, and the swish of her damask robe. Too late to run. Where to hide? Ah, under Timmon's bed, where she had taken cover once before, accidentally on top of the wolver. She could almost hear his amused, gravelly voice: *Under other circumstances, this would be fun.*

Under these circumstances, definitely not.

"At last," said the lady, entering the room. "Privacy."

"Mother, guest quarters have been prepared for you. After such a long ride, aren't you tired?"

"Now, would you hustle me off so fast after I have ridden so far to see you?"

Timmon's bed was covered with a lace counterpane. Jame watched their feet through it—Timmon's in fine-grained but sensible boots, his mother's in rose-colored slippers. For such a dainty woman, she had large feet, proud in the up step. One could imagine them mincing over armies of the fallen.

"Very well." Timmon sounded resigned. "I'm pleased to see you, of course, but why are you here?" Then his tone sharpened. "Has something happened to Grandfather?"

"One might say so. My dear, I know that you didn't mean to cause trouble at the High Council, but you must see what a problem you created by letting Adric think that you were Pereden."

Timmon's feet shuffled. "I didn't tell him. He told me."

"And you didn't correct him. About everything else he seems rational—so far—but this quest for the relics of his beloved, fallen son has partly unhinged him. When he refers to you as Pereden, he is content. When he calls you Timmon, as he does more and more frequently, he grows fretful."

Jame wondered what Timmon had done with the finger and ring of his father. For that matter, blood and bone, he was a sort of relic in himself.

"I'm sorry about that."

"So are we all. You do see, though, if he names you his heir as Pereden, Dari will have good cause to question both his judgment and your claim."

"Mother, you assume that I want to become Lord Ardeth."

"Of course you do. Haven't you enjoyed being his lordan?"

Timmon began to pace restlessly. "Here and now, yes. It gives me status at the college. I never thought that it would last, or wanted that responsibility."

She stopped him. They must be standing face to face. "Foolish boy. If not lordan or lord, what will you be? Just another Highborn subject to the will of others. Oh yes, your randon collar will give you some authority, but still you must follow orders rather than give them. Did I raise you for such a fate?"

He stepped back. "No, Mother. You raised me to be like my father."

She pursued. Jame would imagine her gloved hands smoothing his coat, possessively patting it. "And what better model could I give you? Pereden was the perfect man, the perfect mate. I could never have given myself to any one else, and have to no one since. You owe your existence to my choice and judgment. Oh, what a lord he would have made!"

The door opened.

"Drie." Timmon's voice echoed with his relief at this interruption, then sharpened. "What's the matter?"

"Water has gotten into the fire timber hall, into the fire pits."

"Sweet Trinity, the stables. Mother, accompany Drie to your quarters. I need to help with the horses before the steam scalds them."

He rushed out.

Jame forcibly restrained herself. Bel was in the subterranean stable, sheltering from the rain.

Drie and the lady faced each other.

"You," she said, with such patent loathing that it made Jame's skin crawl. "He should have left you behind long ago. What does a lordan need with a whipping boy?"

"Lady, Pereden was my father too, by a Kendar mother. Would you dishonor his choice of mates?"

"Oh!" Her riding whip whistled down with a crack across his shoulders and he cowered, submissive, before her. "Stand still, you. This is what you were born for."

Jame wriggled out from under the bed. The lady's back was to her, the whip raised again. She caught the other's arm, drew back, and swept her feet out from under her. Distan went down in a billow of rose chiffon.

"Run," Jame hissed at Drie who, after a wide-eyed stare, did so. Jame followed him—fast enough, she hoped, to avoid recognition.

Tentir seethed. Below, horses were screaming. A stream of them, freed, rushed up the ramp and out the front door of the great hall. Bay, chestnut, sorrel, black... Jame didn't see Bel's creamy, dappled hide among them. She edged down the ramp by the wall against the upward stampede, flinching away from heaving shoulders, rolling eyes, and pounding hooves. Here was the horse-master, slapping haunches.

"I haven't seen her," he gasped. "Likely she's behind, guiding the others."

Steam exploded between the floorboards, blowing some clean out of their beds. The water couldn't begin to extinguish well-seasoned ironwood, but its clash with fire filled the air with hot, searing jets. Jame staggered among them, feeling sweat prickle out all over her body. The escaped horses thinned out. Here came one like a phantom out of the mist. She grabbed a white mane and swung onto a dappled back. Up the ramp, into the hall, out the front door. Mud slithered underfoot. Bel nearly fell. Cold rain dinned on heads and shoulders. Tentir's training fields spread out before them beneath a sheet of water, under a full moon shredded by flying clouds.

⟨⟨⟨ IV ⟩⟩⟩

THE NEXT MORNING, Aden addressed the assembled cadets from the shelter of the Commandant's balcony while they stood below in their ranks, in the pouring rain, getting wetter and wetter.

"You are all sloppy and lazy," he told them, down his long nose, "disgraces to your houses and scarves. My time here may be short, but I intend to teach you what discipline is. To begin with, you will run—I say *run*—to your classes in formation, in cadence, stopping only to salute any randon whom you may pass. Randon, return those salutes. I will be visiting your classes. If I find any inadequacy, you will repeat them in your free time, all night long if necessary. Punishment runs will increase in number and duration. Expect nothing but field rations and inspections. That, I think, is enough to start with."

There was a sodden pause.

"Salute!" roared the duty sargent, and they did—to every officer in sight, in no particular order.

A scramble followed as the ten-commands fell in and sprinted off, many headfirst into each other. For the Commandant, they would have done it perfectly. By unspoken agreement, for Aden Smooth-face they turned the maneuver into a shambles.

"That was fun," Jame remarked to Brier, limping slightly from a kicked shin. "Still, I expect we'll pay for it."

Throughout the day, Aden descended on class after class, finding fault with most of them, assigning punishment duties. Feet began to pound around and around the muddy square. The field rations turned out to be shot through with chartreuse mold. And still the rain fell. Under the steady downpour, amusement turned to dour obedience.

That evening Timmon dined with the Commandant Pro Tem and his mother on provisions that the former had brought with him, without which he apparently never traveled.

"He thinks we're all plotting against him," he reported to Jame afterward. "Well, in a way we are, but he also mentioned a Day of Misrule when he was truly Commandant here and some trick or other was played on him."

Jame remembered what she had heard. "He was lured out of his quarters by a racket and tagged. The cadets made him share his stash of delicacies at the feast."

"Something so trivial?"

"Obviously not to him."

"He doesn't like the Shanir either. You and Drie in particular drive both him and my mother wild."

"Drie had better stay out of her way. Now that you've begun to slip out of her grip, she's setting him up as your whipping boy again."

"Oh no!"

"Oh yes, as if beating him can still make you behave."

She watched Timmon consider this. His mother might be right.

"I also think," she added, "that she hates him personally for being your father's son. About Aden, is it possible that he gave your father the idea to make Drie eat his bound-carp?"

Timmon stared at her. "It is and he did. Over dinner, he bragged about that almost as much as he complained about his lost treats. Something about all Shanir really bothers him."

"He isn't one himself, is he?"

"That may be the problem. He seems to think that we have an unfair advantage over him. In my house, that could be true. Ability aside—and it's no small thing to climb so high in the randon ranks—Aden owes his internal house rank largely to being Grandfather's younger brother. Watch out for him."

"Oh, I will. And you watch out for Drie."

Timmon leaned against the rail. Here under the tin roof they were sheltered, but in danger of being trampled by punishment runs. One went past, the boardwalk booming under their feet.

"Brandan," remarked Timmon. "At least he isn't playing favorites."

"You think not?" Jame wondered if Aden knew that Lord Brandan's sister Brenwyr was a Shanir maledight.

Timmon picked at the moss encrusting the wooden rail. "It's

funny how knowing about my father and Drie has changed the way I feel about both of them. That is, I always knew about the carp, but I never realized what it meant to Drie. Mother and Great-uncle Aden are really getting on my nerves, the way they keep praising my father and comparing me to him. I know, I know: not so long ago I would have been delighted. Maybe, though, he was simply human, not the paragon I was raised to believe in."

He glanced at Jame almost shyly under a fringe of damp hair. "How did you feel about your father?"

Jame considered this.

"I always thought that he was a monster. He was so bitter, so frustrated, with no time for Tori or me as children except to shout at us. Everything revolved around his passion for our mother, who was lost to him forever."

She paused, remembering how once he had found her in the hall of the Haunted Lands keep and for a moment had thought that she was her mother returned. Then with recognition the softness had run out of his expression like melting wax.

"You."

She remembered being slammed against the wall and pinned there.

"You changeling, you impostor, how dare you be so much like her? How dare you! And yet, and yet, you are . . . so like . . ."

And he had kissed her, hard, on the mouth.

"My lord!" Her Kendar nurse Winter stood in the hall doorway. He drew back with a gasp.

"No. No! *I am* not *my brother!"*

And he had smashed his fist into the stone wall, next to her head, spattering her with his blood.

"What?" asked Timmon, watching her.

Jame shook herself. "There was so much I didn't understand then. What child sees adults clearly? When I turned seven and sprouted these"—she flexed her claws and grooved the mossy rail with them—"he called me a filthy Shanir and drove me out of the house into the Haunted Lands."

Timmon's eyes widened. "He did?"

She laughed, without mirth. "That's how Tori and I were first separated. Your granduncle isn't the only one who can't abide those of the Old Blood. It's a funny thing, though; the more I find out about Ganth—say, what happened to him here at the college or how his own father treated him, not to mention that foul beast I have to call uncle—the more human he seems. Do any of us really know our parents? They seem so big at first, and then they shrink."

"My father didn't live long enough for that. He's still the golden boy to all who knew him. And yet . . . and yet . . . there's something wrong. Why did he call your brother a liar?"

Jame flinched at the dream memory of Pereden's neck breaking under her brother's hands and of Harn's comforting rumble: *All right, Blackie, all right. Don't fret. He wasn't worth it.*

She still didn't know what that meant.

Timmon left soon afterward, grumbling about no dry linen to be found in the entire college. How nice for that to be one's primary concern, although somehow she doubted that it truly was Timmon's.

THAT NIGHT JAME DREAMED that she walked the Gray Lands where the unburnt dead drift. It was no surprise that she should find herself here, given her conversation with Timmon; however, she wondered if this was the dreamscape, the shared soulscape, some errant fragment of her own disordered mind, or a bit of all three.

Here, at least, were those familiar, sickly hills rolling under a leaden sky which leaned over them with almost palpable weight.

Whip grass twined and whined at her feet, seeking to take root in her boots: . . . *stay with us, stay . . .*

The air was sticky with warm drizzle, the hollows full of stagnant water under a scum of ash, sluggishly aroil as if disembodied drowning men struggled there. At the margins all was melting, life and death dissolving into water.

In the way of dreams, it didn't surprise her to find Ashe at her side. The haunt singer leaned on her staff, pallid and slack of visage but still iron-willed, as must be anyone who walks the world's edge. Her voice as usual was rough and halting.

"Water ultimately . . . dissolves everything. It can . . . unmake the universe."

"Is that what will happen if the Eaten One doesn't relent? To find her work here is . . . disturbing, to say the least. Have our worlds become so intertwined? But truly, Ashe, I don't know what she wants."

"The question is not asked of you . . . for once. Nor is that . . . the answer you seek here."

Someone splashed through the mucky sedge below.

"Father!" Timmon called. "Father!"

On the opposite slope, a swirl of wind fretted the grass. Blades rose and wove themselves around a flaw in the air, plaiting themselves from the legs up into the semblance of a human figure. Something like a head turned. Dry grass whipped about it like sere hair.

". . . I . . . I . . . I . . ," keened a thin, high voice like a breath blown over a blade of grass.

Timmon floundered up the slope toward it, holding the seared finger that was all that remained of Pereden Proud-prance, and which trapped him here in the Gray Lands, if just barely. Pereden took it in a stem-woven hand and settled the missing finger in place as if assuming a mislaid glove. A quiver ran through him as grass became underlaid with wicker. He drew himself up, creaking. Some hint of his former appearance returned, although rustling fitfully around the edges.

"I . . . I . . . I was my father's favorite. I . . . I deserved to be. I deserved everything, b-b-but he took it all away."

"Who did? Father, look at me! Talk to me!"

Blank sockets instead of eyes swept past him, seeing what? Through them, one saw the inside of his empty, plaited head. "He spied on me. He told Father, 'Peri is weak, Peri isn't to be trusted.' He was jealous, so he lied. Father didn't believe him, oh no, but the others did."

He coughed ash and spat twigs like so many tiny bones. Some tangled in the dry grass around his mouth and bobbed there. He gnashed on them petulantly.

"I knew I could turn the Waster Horde. The Host would have done it for their beloved Blackie, but they failed me. Everyone fails me. Poor me. Oh, but the Wasters, they knew my value. Yes, they did. 'Beat Blackie. Take his place,' they told me. So I led them against the Kencyr Host. I would have won too, if Father hadn't betrayed me as well. Why should he meddle and stop the fight when I was so close to winning? It was my battle—mine!—against

Blackie and all his lies. I told him that I would tell Father all that
I had done, and why. Oh, that scared him, lick-ass that he is.

"'It will kill him,' says Blackie. 'And I promised to protect his
interests. I keep my promises, Peri.'"

"Ah, his hands on my neck! Why is that all I remember? Where
am I now? Someone has cheated me. You." He clawed fumble-
fingered at Timmon, who retreated before him back into the water.
"Return it to me, all of it. I...I...I...was my father's favorite.
I...I...deserved to be. I deserved everything...."

Timmon flailed in the water. The hungry dead rose up around
him.

"Now," said Ashe, and Jame plunged down the slope.

The water was viscous and rank, full of clutching currents. She
grabbed Timmon. How hard it was to lift him, how treacherous
the water.

"I...I...I..." he muttered, echoing his father's reedy, needy voice.

"Not you, not yours," she shouted at the thing unraveling on
the slope with her full Shanir power. "I condemn you, I deny
you, I break you!"

Timmon suddenly came free in her grasp. They lay tangled
together in her bed, both fully clothed, both weeping water. Timmon leaned over and vomited. Then he began to cry.

"There, now," she said, cradling him in her arms, brushing wet
hair from his clammy brow. "There, there. He wasn't a monster.
He was only weak. It happens. Now sleep."

And Timmon did.

❧ VI ❧

THE FOLLOWING DAY was wet, muddy, and miserable.

It started with a fight between Timmon and his mother in
his quarters. No one heard the exact words, but they caught the
tone. Soon after, Lady Distan rode off with her escort, despite the
pounding rain and warnings of possible flash floods.

Aden Smooth-face stayed behind.

He appeared at Jame's second lesson of the morning, which
happened to be the Senethar.

She had expected to see him before this, given how he felt about her. It surprised her that he had chosen to visit her strongest class. He knew that it was, too: she remembered him observing her coldly in his gray mask during the second cull, the one for which he had voted to fail her.

Today they were practicing fire-leaping, as if in defiance of the weather. Kick, strike, pivot, sweep...the kantir continued, twenty cadets trying to move as one yet somehow not quite matched in time. Everything seemed soggy. Joints creaked. Limbs swam rather than catching fire.

We are dissolving into one uncoordinated mass, thought Jame. *Water melts everything.*

Its beat was in her ears as it hit the tin roof below. Its weight dragged her down. Was this what it meant to be lethargic? Never in her life had she felt so dull or slow.

Aden clapped his hands. "This is unacceptable," he said in his voice of raw-edged silk. "Are these to be the next generation of randon, who can't even pick up their feet? You, instructor, choose your best and let me instruct."

The officer in charge was the Brandan Hawthorn. Her glaze swept the class, resting on no one.

"You," said Aden. "Knorth. Dare you meet me?"

Every instinct said "Don't," but what else could she do?

They saluted each other, he from superior to inferior, she non-committal, and took their positions.

He struck at her face in a blur and advanced, hands weaving. It was hard to remember that, although younger than his brother Adric, he was still a centenarian. She didn't want to hurt him. Jame retreated. This wasn't fire-leaping as she knew it. She blocked a strike, and felt a line of fire across her arm. Fabric parted, blood flowed. What in Perimal's name...? He struck again at her face. Again she blocked, forearm to forearm.

Retreat again. Now attack.

The heel of her hand snapped his head back and sent his white hair flying. There was blood on his chin; he had bitten his tongue.

Follow with a heart strike. Close and sweep.

He staggered, but kept his feet. Agile old man. His face remained as smooth as his movements, but Trinity, what a basilisk stare. One of his eyelids drooped. Here he came again. Her balance was off. His return sweep reaped her leg out from under her and she fell, he on top of her, his knee in the pit of her stomach driving out breath. His fists smashed into the floor on either side of her head. Strapped to his wrists, twin blades poised an inch over her eyes.

"Submit," he hissed. "Leave Tentir today or I will blind you."

With difficulty, Jame focused not on the knife points but on his eyes. The drooping one began to twitch.

"Blind me and answer to..."

"Your brother?" It was a sneer.

"No. To the Randon Council."

He drew back and the blades retracted into his sleeves. He ran his hands through his white hair to straighten it.

"And this was your best student," he said to Hawthorn. "You teach poorly, and Sheth Sharp-tongue made you his duty officer. To the square with you and run until I tell you to stop." With that he stalked out.

CHAPTER XII
A New Favorite

Spring 43

I

AT NOON, JAME HEARD that Timmon was in the infirmary and went there, past Hawthorn running laps around the square.

She found the Ardeth Lordan soaking a scalded hand in cool water while the apothecary prepared an alkanet lotion for his red-blotched face.

"What have you done to yourself this time?"

His grimace deepened as it pulled at scorched skin.

"I was down in the fire timber hall. The only really hot flames are there, but so are steam jets and boiling water. You wouldn't want to see my legs."

"But why...oh, I understand."

Timmon gave her a sidelong look. "I woke up in your bed. It wasn't exactly what I expected."

"I know. To begin with, I wasn't there."

"But you were, when it mattered."

The apothecary smeared the lotion on Timmon's face and covered it with a light dressing. Then, discreetly, he left.

"You burned your father's finger, didn't you?"

"Yes. By wedging it into the cracks of a fire timber. It was time. This morning Mother saw that I was wearing his ring." He held up his other hand with Pereden's moon opal signet on it. "When I wouldn't tell her where I got it, she threw a fit and stormed out."

"It was good of you not to betray my brother, not that I have any idea how he came by it either." She regarded him curiously.

"Do you remember the Gray Lands, and what your father said that he had done?"

Timmon gulped, looking sick. "It wasn't just a dream, was it? I thought not. We were on the edge of the soulscape, where I have no control. Sweet Trinity, how could he? To join the Waster Horde against his own people, just for spite, and then to threaten to tell Grandfather all about it...He hated your brother because he couldn't live up to him. I see that now. How...petty."

"That's one word for it. So now you understand that Tori didn't lie about him?"

Timmon laughed, with a crack to his voice. "I expect that your brother didn't say half as much as he could have. To do more would have been to destroy Grandfather."

"'And I promised to protect his interests,'" Jame quoted softly. "'I keep my promises, Peri.'"

"'Ah, his hands on my neck! Why is that all I remember?' He killed my father, didn't he? There at the Cataracts, he broke his neck."

"I think so. Will you tell Lord Ardeth?"

Timmon gulped. "I could. I should. But now can I? Torisen was right: it would kill Grandfather, and certainly cause a blood feud between our two houses if not a civil war within the Kencyrath. And...and besides, Pereden wasn't worth it."

Jame took his unburnt hand and kissed the cracked ring. "I agree."

Timmon flushed. "I'm not used to being taken seriously," he said. "So far, life has just been fun and games. But it was never that, was it? Behind the Wasters were darkling changers, pushing. This entire world could have fallen because of my father. Right there. Right then."

"Yes, but it didn't."

"No, but it still could. Not even my grandfather really believes in the threat, at least within his lifetime. How long have we waited for Perimal Darkling to attack? Generations. Millennia. But how far away from us is it really?"

"Sometimes," says Jame wryly, "right behind us."

His attention sharpened. "Your sleeve is bloody."

"Your dear great-uncle brought knives to a fist fight and threatened to put out my eyes. There's something wrong with that man."

Timmon shivered. "So you feel it too. D'you think he's going... soft?"

"Like your grandfather?" Jame had laughed at the idea that

senility was contagious. Was it really so different, though, from Caldane sharing his hangover with his Kendar or her father infecting the entire Host with his madness in the White Hills? Clearly what happened to one's lord had repercussions among those bond to him. Did that extend in particular to his close relations?

"I don't know," she said, "but he's dangerous."

II

"I COULD DO WITHOUT THE RAIN," Jame remarked to Shade, "or without Ran Aden, or preferably without both. How long d'you suppose Caldane means to keep the Commandant at Restormir?"

Shade shrugged. It was a foolish question anyway: how was anyone to know?

They were in the Falconer's class, as usual sitting along the wall, this time without their animal companions. The exercise was that each of the latter was to seek a particular object of its master's choosing somewhere within the college.

Rain rattled on the tin roof outside. The fireplace sputtered fitfully. Jame had noticed that no flame burned properly, even with dry tinder, of which there was little. Meanwhile, leather mildewed, cloth rotted, and food spoiled. The whole world seemed to be melting.

"H'ist." Shade touched her arm.

Aden had entered the mews.

The cadets rose, saluted, then sank back, warily, to their lesson. Jame watched him pace before them.

Over the past few days some of his smoothness had rubbed off. His white hair, while slicked back, seemed frayed at the ends and his eyebrows were ruffled. Lines were now more obvious on his face and his eyelid twitched almost in a flutter. What was it like for him to return to a place where his touchy pride had received such a blow? Did he even see the cadets before him or those of some forty years ago? Did he hear snickering where there was only cautious silence?

"You." He turned suddenly to Shade. "To what creature are you bound?"

"A gilded swamp adder, Ran."

"Low enough, certainly. And you."

The Edirr cadet jumped. "T-to a scurry of mice, Ran."

"As low or lower. You."

Gari met those angry, hooded eyes with more confidence than he would have before seeing much worse things on the long ride to Gothregor. "To any swarm of insects you care to name, Ran."

"Snakes, rats—"

"Mice," squeaked Mouse, around a fist stuffed in her mouth.

"—and fleas. What great Shanir you all are, to be sure. Much good your precious Old Blood does you. Old man, how dare you waste precious class time with such frivolities? What good can such 'skills' do anyone?"

The merlin on the Falconer's shoulder bated and panted angrily, but his blind master only smiled.

"Laugh at me, will you? Shortly we will see who finds this amusing. And you"—he stopped before Drie—"A fish, isn't it? Some fat old carp in the keep pond. You smile. I know that look. Nothing can reach you while you are with it, isn't that correct? Oh, I think that we can arrange something that will shake even you, boy. Pereden's bastard, come to Tentir. Amazing. Insufferable."

Jame had risen to her feet, the hair at the nape of her neck prickling. Where did the old randon think he was, Tentir or Omiroth, and when?

"Ran," she began, but was interrupted by the bounding return of Jorin.

"Waugh," said the ounce, and dropped a coin at her feet where it spun, flashing gold, then rolled toward a crack in the floor with the cat in wild pursuit.

Aden was glaring after him when the Molocar Torvi knocked him over to bring a food bowl to his master—his idea or Tarn's? Jame wondered. Before Aden could regain his feet, the rest arrived: Addy with a ribbon, two mice hauling a scarf, and a chittering swarm of three-inch-long water beetles bearing nothing but their own busy selves. The randon flailed at each beetle in turn as it rushed over him. Some of the beetles got sidetracked into his clothing, causing him to slap furiously at himself.

"You think this is funny?" he panted, although no one had dared to laugh. "We'll see. Oh, yes, we will." And he stormed out.

"What," asked Shade, "was all of that about?"

"Nothing, I hope," said Jame, but she regarded an unperturbed Drie uneasily.

III

THE REST OF THE DAY PASSED without incident, except that Captain Hawthorn continued to run around the square, having received no order to stop. She had settled into the steady, loping stride of a veteran and seemed prepared to continue all night if necessary, but her regular passing by their lit windows began to unnerve the cadets.

"Does he mean to run her to death?" asked Mint. "*Can* he?"

"Eventually." Jame threw down her Gen cards, unable to concentrate on the game. "Damn."

Erim came in, shaking off his wet coat. "Ran Aden's lights are out. He's gone to bed."

"Sweet Trinity." Jame rose abruptly. "I'm going to stretch my legs."

The others stared at her, at first barely comprehending such a breach of protocol. Then Dar leaped to his feet.

"Me too," he said.

"And me." "And me." "And me."

They waited until Hawthorn passed once again and fell into step behind her. Other cadets emerged from other barracks as they passed, more and more. They ran in cadence, and the boardwalk shuddered under their booted feet. When the walk could hold no more of them, the rest of the student body began to stomp in time to the runners' beat within their barracks.

Boom...BOOM...*BOOM!*

Even the rain was drowned out.

A light glimmered on the Commandant's balcony, a candle held high by a wild-haired figure swathed in a silken dressing gown.

"Stop it! I said, all of you *stop!*"

The runners halted in place. Faces upturned, they waited, hair straggling wetly over their faces, their breath hanging on the dank air.

"You insubordinate, worthless brats, I'll settle with you later. For now, just...just go to bed. All of you. Now!"

And so they did.

⫷⟡⫸ **IV** ⫷⟡⫸

AS NIGHT DESCENDED, THE STORM BUILT to a crescendo, the beat of the rain now punctuated by distant, approaching thunder. The rumble of it growled down the valley from the north like a giant clearing his throat while glimmers of lightning played within the clouds.

Jorin had crawled under the blankets and was huddled as close to Jame as he could get, in danger of pushing her off her pallet. He hated the cold and damp, but thunder worst of all.

Trinity knew how the rathorn colt was doing out in the wet. She would have to check his coat for rain rot as soon as it was practical.

Bel at least had taken shelter in the great hall of Old Tentir with as many of the herd as would fit. The horse-master was in for a long night.

What would happen if the rain never stopped? "Water ultimately dissolves everything," Ashe had said. "It can unmake the universe."

A world of water . . .

And that awful man, Aden. Had he really gone soft, as Timmon feared? She had heard that when senility struck, all one's true characteristics came spilling out without check. What a terrifying thought. Surely the Ardeth randon hadn't always been as he was now.

Still, the Commandant must return to the college soon. Why had Lord Caineron summoned him in the first place, let alone Gorbel? Such a thing had never happened before during her stay at Tentir. She gathered, listening to the randon, that it was unusual at the best of times. Even a war-leader like Sheth held an independent command when he was responsible for the college. Trust Caldane to meddle.

And so Jame's thoughts rolled, tumbling over each other, in and out of fitful sleep.

Gradually she became aware of an insistent, four-part beat. Water fell into a pan: drip-drip-drip-drip. . . . Rain hit the shutters: splat-pat-pat-pat. . . . Thunder echoed: BOOM-room-room-room. . . . And under it all ran words, a half chanted, bubbling refrain:

. . . *mine-she-is-not, mine-she-is-not, mine-she-is-not, mine-he-is* . . .

Jame woke with a start. What?

Prey to a sudden, half-realized fear, she scrambled into her clothes and, leaving Jorin under the covers, ran down the stair, out into the storm. There on the boardwalk she collided with Timmon.

"He's followed Drie to the river," he gasped, but stopped her as she started east toward the Silver. "No, to the Burley."

Which was just as well considering that the lower fields were underwater.

Otherwise, no need to ask who "he" was. "Why" was another matter.

"I had supper with him again," panted Timmon, wiping streaming hair out of his eyes as they floundered through the downpour, "or would have if all his provisions hadn't gone moldy. Such colors, you wouldn't believe. I wonder if he laced them with poison instead of spice, the way Grandfather does."

"I bet Lord Ardeth tried poisons on him when they were boys, just to see how he would react."

"Trinity. D'you think? Anyway, this time he blamed the cadets for the spoilage, not Grandfather or the weather. Then, after I'd left, you stopped Hawthorn's run."

"That wasn't just me."

"Oh, depend on it, he noticed. And he was so pleased to be punishing the Commandant's duty officer. Through her he meant to pay back the whole school for its laxity and insolence, or so he said."

He checked her with a hand on her arm, looking troubled and more than a little scared. "I think he's gone mad. His eyelid was twitching so much that he sealed it with candle wax, and he kept calling me Pereden."

"But why Drie, and why now?"

"You woke Granduncle up with your stampede. The next thing I knew, he was in my quarters brandishing a whip, saying that he meant to know where I had gotten Father's ring or he would have the hide off of Drie. A few lashes and, well, I couldn't stop myself. I wrestled the whip away from him and broke it. He was to deal with me, dammit, not with my half-brother. While we were shouting at each other, Drie slipped away. As soon as he noticed, Granduncle went after him. I couldn't stop them, so I went after them."

Stopping first to collect her, Jame noted; but still he *had* prevented Aden from beating Drie.

They fought their way through lashing cloud-of-thorn bushes toward the swimming hole.

Lightning outlined two figures on Breakneck Rock. One gripped the other by the collar and carried something silvery. By the after-image, Jame recognized the latter as a fish spear.

"Pereden, Distan, welcome. Have you come to see Tentir purified?"

Rain plastered his white hair over his face, over the eye sealed with wax that still continued to twitch under its lid. That side of his face had gone slack and the corner of his mouth drooped.

" 'I suppose that we will lose your valuable company tomorrow,' he said. 'Meanwhile, keep my quarters since you have claimed them.' Damned half-breed. When they rise that high in the service, there's no putting them in their place. Why can't anyone realize that I've been doing my best to save Tentir?"

"What is he talking about?" Timmon asked Jame, raising his voice over the thrashing wind and rain.

Jame shook her head, although she had a suspicion. Ancestors please that she was right.

The swollen, surging Burley had risen halfway up the face of Breakneck Rock. Behind Aden, unseen by him, a broad, leathery back surfaced in the river. Lightning glimmered off its wet skin. Then it submerged again.

Timmon clutched Jame. "It's huge! How can something so big be in our swimming hole?"

Jame remembered the chasm beyond the underwater ledge that gave the rock its name, from which huge eyes had once watched her. She also remembered the shallow Silver Steps and what had lurked there.

The wind changed direction, blowing from the west down the gullet of the canyon that fed into the hole. Stinging rain whipped sideways. With it came an approaching roar more felt than heard. It must be raining even more heavily in the mountains than here.

Drie leaned eagerly toward the rock's edge against the short leash of the Highborn's arm.

"Get back!" Jame called to him, Timmon's voice joining her own: "Ran, let him go!"

Aden made a face at them like a dolorous clown. "Could it be that you don't understand either? No, no. Peri, remember the first time we caught this freak at his piscine perversions? He wouldn't cry when we beat him, because he was with that damn carp. What right had the bastard to defy us or to try to escape? What right have such creatures even to exist? You never should have sired one, Peri.

Distan, you laughed too. So many abominations at Tentir: Shanir, half-breeds, even the Highlord's unnatural sister, ancestors preserve us. Well, I can free the college of one freak at least."

He shook Drie. "Call it, boy, call your filthy familiar."

As if in response, a vast head reared up and slammed down thunderously on the rock. Its eyes were the size of ships' wheels; its bristling whiskers, spars. The cavernous oval of its mouth gaped. Something like a pallid tongue flopped out to scrabble with over-grown nails on stone. The Eaten One existed only from the thighs up, the rest stuck down the catfish's gigantic maw. Her skin glimmered pale green; her hair draped like seaweed on a low-tide shore. But the face that she turned upward was of transcendental beauty, even with its lambent eyes and needle teeth bared in a smile.

Drie broke loose and threw his arms around her as hers closed around him.

"GLUP," went the catfish, and swallowed them both.

Aden belatedly raised his spear to thrust it into one of the creature's eyes, but it slid back into the water, out of reach. Water slopped over the cliff top.

The wind was roaring now, and a wall of debris like jagged jaws swept toward them down the Burley. Hands jerked Jame and Timmon back from behind. A tangle of branches, tree trunks, and boulders flayed the rock face, taking Aden with it. Then a wall of water hit stone in an explosion of spray. The flash flood swept on carrying all before it. Aden could be seen for a moment on the crest of the tide before it lifted him over the lip of Perimal's Cauldron and bore him down.

"I was wrong," said the Commandant. "We have seen the last of M'lord Aden before morning."

Jame turned and threw her arms around him. "Ran, you're back!"

"Er...yes," he said, disengaging from her hug. "It would seem that I was missed. Poor Aden. He was beginning to be a prob-lem, as I discovered tonight when I returned not only to find him trying to run my duty officer to death but also settled in my quarters. I fear, though, that you have also lost a friend and you, Lordan, a half-brother."

"Lost perhaps," said Jame, looking down river thoughtfully, "but I imagine Drie is finally where he always wanted to be, and the Eaten One has the Favorite of her choice. Look. It's stopped raining."

CHAPTER XIII
Secrets

Spring 44

I

THE GREAT RAIN HAD STOPPED but a gray sky still pressed down heavily over the Riverland. Low, hurrying clouds shrouded the mountaintops, occasionally spitting on the sodden earth beneath as if as an afterthought.

"Remember," each drop seemed to say. "What I did before, I can do again."

Torisen stood in the midst of his ruined crops, surveying the damage. While Gothregor itself stood on a high bluff and so had escaped the waters, the fields downstream around the curve of the Silver had been ravaged. The dikes of the water meadow where the hay grew were gone. The grain terraces above existed only in strips, broken by the smear of landslides. The winter wheat and rye had been stripped to the stalk and then beaten into the ground. Spring seed, so recently planted with such hopes, had washed away. Due to the late, cold spring, barley and flax hadn't yet been sown, but couldn't now be until the terraces were repaired.

"So in time we'll have barley bread, beer, and enough rope to hang ourselves with," said Torisen sourly.

His steward Rowan shot him a sideways look. Her face, as usual, was expressionless, frozen in place by the scars across her forehead spelling out the name of the Karnid god. "We can still turn the inner ward into a vegetable garden, once the livestock return to the fields."

Torisen laughed despite himself. "I can just imagine Caldane when he hears that I'm growing cabbages on my doorstep."

"Very nourishing, cabbages. Also carrots, onions, parsnips, and beets."

"So we can eventually make vegetable soup. What about the next hay crop?"

"The roots are still there, under all of that mud and silt. They should recover. Anyway, now you have the funds to buy new seeds."

"Hmmm," said Torisen, unhappily.

He turned to squish back to their horses and Yce, all waiting for them on higher ground. Rowan limped after him. Both Kencyr wore thigh high boots and were glad of them as the clinging mud oozed halfway up to their knees.

Squelch, plop, squelch, plop . . .

True, he did have Aerulan's dowry, as much as he hated drawing on that (in his opinion) tainted source. His father Ganth had demanded an obscene amount for the girl's contract in perpetuity and Lord Brandan had insisted on paying it for her death banner. Torisen had wanted simply to give it to him. To profit from old pain felt wrong. However, both the Jaran Matriarch Trishien and Jame had told him that to refuse the price was to do even more harm, not that he quite saw why.

It also confused him somewhat that Aerulan had turned out to be the beloved not of Brant but of his maledight sister Brenwyr, she who had cursed Torisen's underwear into ribbons and suffered the backlash in her own shredded garments. There was obviously much about the Women's World that he still didn't understand, nor was he likely to unless he worked up the nerve to ask his sister about her winter within its halls.

Coward, said his father's voice behind the locked door in his soul. *Then again, what do you need with such trivial knowledge?*

He wanted to snap back, *Trying to have it both ways, Father?* but keeping still worked better with that hectoring, inner voice.

His people must come before his pride. That was his responsibility, his dearest honor. He had already used the dowry to buy this year's seeds, the previous harvest having been destroyed by the hail and ash engendered by last year's volcanic eruption farther north. He would draw on Aerulan's bounty again if he must.

And go on bended knee to ask your sister what she knows about the Women's World?

That too, if necessary. Odd, how the once unthinkable slowly became possible—almost. Nothing dramatic had happened; he had only had some time blessedly free from nightmares to think. Now his innate good sense warned him that there was much he needed to know about Jame's mysterious past before that ignorance harmed them both.

Responsibility. How many forms it took.

That morning the Kendar Cron had come to see him.

"Lord, you know that this past winter my young son Ghill died."

Torisen remembered it—how could he not? The boy had tried to ride one of the new-dropped calves brought in to shelter from the storms and an unlucky fall had broken his neck. Worse, the accident hadn't killed him outright. When the parents had seen that he was paralyzed, they had requested the White Knife. Torisen had never before brought death to one so young or so brave.

Cron had held himself very straight, but his eyes had shone with anxiety. "I and my mate would like to have another child. Not that anything can replace what we've lost, but the room is so quiet without him."

To sanction the birth of an infant was to guarantee it a place in one's house. Sweet Trinity, one more name to remember...

True, he hadn't forgotten any since the death of Mullen, but still it was as if he gave a piece of his soul to each Kencyr whom he bound, and there was only so much of him to give.

Then there had been that petition from the Randir Corvine, who turned out to be a former Knorth Oath-breaker. He hadn't known that there were Knorth in Wilden. A worrying thought, that, but also an intriguing one. What an opportunity to learn about the Randir from the inside. He didn't blame any Knorth who had had the good sense not to follow his father into exile. Still, it bothered him that their need had driven them to such a haven. There was also the remote possibility that to invite any of them back might be to welcome a Randir spy into his house. After all, some might see Ganth's madness as a betrayal, as Torisen did himself.

So, two claimants, one position. To which did he owe allegiance, the past or the future?

Rowan gave a stifled exclamation. Torisen turned to find her sunk thigh-deep and floundering.

"Don't come near, my lord," she said hastily as he moved to assist her. "Perimal be damned...I've blundered into a shwupp pit."

"A what?"

"That's right," she said, as much to herself as to him. "You usually aren't here in the spring, nor has it ever been this wet before. Fetch me a pole and I'll be fine. Oops."

With that she sank again, up to her waist. The mud made obscene sucking noises, like a tongue exploring a rotten tooth. She lay back on the quavering bog to spread her weight and tried to wriggle free her legs.

That might work with sinksand. Torisen wasn't so sure about the present case. Expressionless she might be, but Rowan was taking her current predicament a bit too calmly.

"You might go for help," she suggested.

"And leave you here in your mud bath?"

He circled her, stepping carefully. The mud around the Kendar, agitated by her efforts to escape, was clearly more liquid than the surrounding earth. By now, water must be pouring into her boots. How deep was this pit anyway?

"I think you just want to get rid of me," he said.

"Should you stay to laugh? Bad enough what they will say in the barracks tonight. Of all the stupid accidents..."

"What aren't you telling me?"

He risked a step forward, bent, and gripped her under the arms. It quickly became clear, however, that to pull her clear through sheer strength was out of the question; while the earth retained its grip, he was more likely to dislocate both of his arms if not to rip her in two. Still, if he could stop her sinking any further until her natural buoyancy came to her rescue...

"What, for example, is a shwupp?"

Bloop.

Bubbles rose in a series of small, wet explosions, approaching.

"My lord. Blackie. Just go."

Bloop, bloop. Here came more trails, from every direction.

Yce splashed toward them. Lighter than they, on huge paws, she ran as if through melting snow although spattered brown to the eyebrows. Then she paused, ears pricked, head cocked.

Bloop, bloop, bloop...

At the end of a trail of bubbles, she pounced and dug furiously. A slick head, eyeless and seemingly all teeth, burst out of the ground. Webbed claws churned the mud. It screamed as the pup's jaws closed on its neck. Then she was on to another trail and another, but there were too many of them, all converging on the hidden pit.

Rowan's legs came free, her boots shredded. The watery pit seethed with muddy bodies like some obscene eel stew. Tori dragged her clear and helped her up.

"Yce, come!"

The two Kencyr staggered back to their horses with the wolver pup mounting a furious rear-guard defense. Torisen gave Rowan a leg up into her saddle and swung into his own. Yce grinned up at him, white teeth, lolling red tongue, and blue eyes in a mask of mud.

"Good girl."

 **II**

IT WAS LATE AFTERNOON before they regained the fortress. Torisen paused within the guardhouse, regarding the penned-up livestock that had well nigh destroyed the inner sward. After the ravages of cows, goats, sheep, and pigs, one might as well plow up what was left for Rowan's vegetable garden. Ancestors knew, it was already well manured.

Around the ward were his garrison's domestic offices and lodgings; across it, the old keep; beyond that, the Women's Halls, and then an acre of desolation—all within the walls of the greater fortress. If only his soul-image were as large as Gothregor with its thousands of empty rooms, he need deny no one shelter there. The thought struck him that, thanks to the locked door in his soul, he only had access to about a third of it.

What, truly, was behind that door?

His last conversation with Trishien nagged at him. Something had happened, something he hadn't been able to remember at the time but which kept coming back as if slowly rising out of the well of sleep.

"Just a drop of blood on his knife's tip, not strong enough to bind for more than an hour or two, just long enough to make the game interesting. 'Dear little Gangrene,' he called me..."

That had been his father talking about his foul uncle Greshan, talking through him. Greshan had temporarily blood-bound Ganth—how many times, and what obscene game had he played with him?

There had been more, too.

He remembered Trishien standing with her hands pressed to her lips, speaking not to him but to his father: "Ganth. You didn't want your son to leave you, to go against your will. Don't tell me that you . . . you . . ."

Torisen shivered. Enough for now. To ashes with the dead and with the past.

He turned to Rowan. "Find Cron, if you please. Tell him that he has my blessing."

III

MARC PAUSED IN MIXING the raw ingredients of a new batch of glass as Torisen wearily mounted the stairs to the High Council chamber.

"You look a proper mess, lad."

"So do the fields."

Torisen sank into his chair. More brown with mud than white, Yce trotted into the High Council chamber after him and took refuge under the ebony table.

"I should be glad that they didn't wash away altogether. Most of the ash did. We can't even think about planting again until things dry out some."

"There's time yet," said Marc soothingly. "Anyway, you have funds now to tide us over if the summer harvest fails."

"So everyone keeps reminding me."

To distract himself from that unpleasant thought, he looked up at the map. Marc had fitted the gaping, stone embrasure with a gridwork of horizontal iron bars. Slotted into the uppermost was as much of the Riverland as he had so far been able to assemble. Shot incongruously with ruby to indicate gold dust, the Silver looped downward with luminous glass clusters on either side to indicate most of the Riverland keeps. Each section was made out of materials native to that particular region plus cullet from the old window to augment it. Oddly, glass fragments representing contiguous geological areas easily fused together without heat, seam, or the need of lead jointure. The result so far looked like a twisting vine shooting off lumpy fruit in a dozen glowing hues at more or less regular intervals.

"That melded glass is surprisingly strong," said Marc, contemplating his handiwork. "I think I could hammer a nail with it. Perhaps, when the map is complete, it won't need a brace at all."

"D'you think it ever will be—complete, that is?"

The big Kendar shrugged and cast a discontented look at the vacant Western Lands. The Eastern were nearly as bare, with many gaps in between. "There's a lot of space left to fill with these little pieces, much of it country which we Kencyr have never seen. Mother Ragga has supplied materials for some of it and your agents bring more home every day from wherever our reach extends." He laughed. "It's become quite a common effort, almost a competition. Not all the bits fit together so far, though."

He indicated the ebony table on which a crude map was drawn in chalk. Small sacks and fragments of cast glass dotted it like random pieces of a puzzle not yet attached to the whole.

"I suppose," he said, scratching his bristly chin, "that I could fill in the blanks solely with recast cullet from the original window and with local material, all held together with lead strips. That would be the normal way of things."

However, Torisen heard the reluctance in his voice, a master craftsman hesitant to compromise.

"No," Tori said, "go on with whatever comes in, mixed with old glass to stretch it out as you've been doing. This may be the work of several lifetimes, but it's a good start."

Marc shot Torisen a look under his shaggy, singed eyebrows. "Something else I've noticed. Travelers report that the recent floods have changed the course of the Silver yet again, especially between Shadow Rock and Wilden. See here: there used to be several meander-loops in the river, but now water has cut across the neck of the largest."

"Well, I'll be damned. So that was what Holly was talking about. I got a letter from him this morning complaining that the Randir were encroaching on his land where the river boundary had changed. Of course he would be upset: that loop contains the richest bottomland in his domain."

Holly tended to scrawl when excited. The map made clear what his hasty words had failed to convey.

"I take it that the Randir have claimed everything on their side of the river," said Marc. "Is that going to cause trouble?"

"How could it not? The Randir squeeze in wherever they can, and the Danior are too small to fight back properly. I'll need to see to this"—*and hope that I have authority enough to make them listen.* "But look here," he continued, puzzled. "These changes just took place. How did you know to include them in the map?"

Marc shrugged. "I didn't. They just appeared."

"You mean that the finished glass flowed again? How is that possible?"

"Blessed if I know. There's something magical about the whole project, if you ask me. I mean, how does one go from a handful of sand, soda, and lime even to simple glass, much less to something like this?" He indicated the growing expanse of glass, subtly aglow in the afterlight of dusk. "There may be possibilities here that we've never dreamt of. Have you tried yet to scry with it?"

Torisen shook his head, exasperated. "All it gives me are bad dreams. I look at the Southern Host's camp and what do I see? Harn, wearing a pink dress. I ask you!"

"Hoy, Tori!"

The cry came up the stairwell, closely followed by the hairy, grinning face of the wolver Grimly. From under the table came a rumbling growl. Yce shot out to tackle the newcomer at the head of the steps. Both tumbled back down with a yelp.

Torisen plunged after them.

Below in the death banner hall, gray and white fur rolled about the flagstones, snarling and snapping. Grimly retained half his human form to hold the young fury at arms' length. The pup seemed to have grown rudimentary hands of her own with which she tried to grab and pull him into her powerful jaws.

"I come all the way from the Holt and this is how you greet me? Ouch!"

"Yce, stop it!" Torisen circled them, unsure how to break up the battle.

"One side, lad." It was Marc with a bucket of cold water which he dashed over the combatants.

They broke apart, sputtering. Tori wrapped his arms around the pup and lugged her back. Liquefied mud made her slippery, as did her furious squirming. She snapped at him, ripping his sleeves but not his skin. Her yammering had the cadence, almost the form, of swear words.

"I said, *stop!*"

All of his force went into the command, and the pup subsided in his grasp, panting.

"Sorry," he said. "I don't know what got into her."

Grimly rose and shook himself, one limb at a time as if to make sure that all were still attached. "I do, in part. That's a common greeting between Deep Weald wolvers, to establish dominance. We of the Holt pick our leaders for their singing. Our wild cousins trust only strength. And did you see those hands? She's starting to change. With adolescence she'll be able to shift more and more into human form. Given her attraction to you, Tori, I'd watch out."

The keep door opened and Burr walked in, bearing a covered tray. He stopped, regarded the assembled company, and thrust his burden into Marc's hands.

"I'll bring more food."

Soon afterward Torisen and Grimly were established in the High Council chamber at the empty end of the table with bowls of venison stew, fresh bread, and tart cider. At their urging, Marc joined them while Burr remained in obdurate attendance. Yce retreated under the boards to gnaw on marrow bones.

"Burr thinks I won't eat if he doesn't watch me," remarked Torisen, spearing a baked apple.

The wolver eyed his friend's thin face. "There's something in that. You Knorth. So hard to keep alive, yet so much harder to kill. What's put you off your feed this time?"

"Nothing. Don't fret me, Grimly."

"Like that, is it? All right, all right. Marc, here are some odds and ends from the edge of the Deep Weald to add to your masterpiece."

The Kendar accepted the offered leather sack with thanks. "Any chance of material from farther in?" he asked rather wistfully.

"Perhaps. We Holt dwellers don't mix much with the Weald, as you know. I did hear a curious story when I was collecting this lot, though. The King of the Wood has sent out scouts for news of an offspring missing since last summer. White with blue eyes, they say. A rare combination."

Under the table, Yce cracked a bone.

"D'you think our pup is the stray?"

"Not that exactly. If she left her pack, she had good reason."

"Maybe she got curious and set out to explore," suggested Marc. "The way you did from the Holt to King Kruin's court in Kothifir."

"I was older, though, and had an invitation. Anyway, she wasn't satisfied with my pack. Maybe I wasn't wolf enough for her."

"So she latched onto me? Don't be silly."

"I'm not. I told you: Deep Weald wolvers are attracted primarily to strength. That's you."

Torisen laughed, but Marc only smiled.

"So, should I send her back to her father?"

"Only if you want her to be killed. That's the other reason why she may have run. The rest of her litter were slaughtered, and all the ones before it. The Wood King doesn't want any rivals. So it's been ever since he came to power. Before that, he passed for human in Kothifir. I wasn't the first wolver to accept King Kruin's invitation."

Torisen put down his knife, a cold chill running up his spine. "Grimly, are you talking about the Gnasher?"

"I think so. Until his scouts contacted me, I had no idea that he'd returned to the Weald, much less that he'd become king there. I'm here now in part to warn you, for the pup's sake. He's bound, sooner or later, to find out where she is. Whether or not he'll come after her is another matter."

"If I might ask," said Marc, "who is this Gnasher?"

Torisen remembered that hulking presence and those cold, blue eyes, a big man with the shadow and teeth of a wolf.

"When King Kruin was ill, he employed the Gnasher as an executioner and an assassin, to thin the herd of his own potential heirs."

Grimly snorted. "Thin? He was out to exterminate the lot of them. Kruin seemed to think that if no one was left to inherit, he would live forever."

"But Krothen survived," said Marc.

"Yes, with some help."

Torisen looked up at the map, remembering those desperate days. There was the chaotic swirl of glass that represented Kothifir, and below it in more orderly array, the Southern Host's permanent camp, a small city in its own right.

Torisen suddenly chuckled. "I just recalled my attempt to scry and that dream of Harn in a pink dress."

The wolver and Burr exchanged quick glances. They weren't used to Torisen speaking casually about even his most trivial dreams, given how he had once half killed himself trying to avoid them.

"What," said Grimly cautiously, testing his ground, "like the one you made your sister wear after the Cataracts?"

"I'd forgotten about that."

"If so," said Grimly dryly, "you're the only one who has. Not for a moment do I see Harn Grip-hard tarted up like a Hurlen whore—unless I've seriously misjudged the man. I wonder, though: is it possible that, bound to you as he is, you accidentally scryed one of his nightmares?"

Torisen sought to brush this away, even as he remembered dreams stranger yet that he had shared with his sister, not that he was about to share any of those. "Even if I did, why should he dream something so absurd?"

"Well, when your sister passes Tentir, she's likely to join his command. For that matter, isn't the Knorth Lordan usually the commandant of the Southern Host?"

"Not Jame," said Torisen firmly. "She doesn't have the experience."

"Neither did Pereden. His was purely a political assignment, to please his father."

"And a fine mess he made of it."

"True, but think what revenge Harn might unconsciously fear your sister would take for her treatment back then."

"Harn had nothing to do with it. She'd be more likely to stuff me into pink flounces."

"Now that," said the wolver, "I'd like to see."

Torisen's laughter died. "You said 'when she passes Tentir.' Perhaps that should be 'if.' Sheth has warned me that as the Knorth Lordan she will face a final, potentially lethal challenge. I thought we were past that after the High Council meeting, but apparently not. Greshan died during his."

"The lass has faced challenges before," said Marc gently. "No one has gotten the better of her yet."

There it was again, the subtle reminder that the big Kendar knew more about his sister's past than he did. He could ask Marc now, or wait until they were alone. No. They were Jame's secrets, to tell or not. He would ask her if she passed her challenge, if he allowed her to face it at all.

Torisen looked up at the map of the Riverland, at the piece

marked with the glow of his own blood in the cast that represented Tentir.

And if you interfere at this late date, will she ever forgive you? Will the randon? Yet alive is better than dead... isn't it?

So Torisen's thoughts revolved, twisting this way and that. When the others fell silent, watching him, he didn't notice.

CHAPTER XIV
In Sodden Fields

Spring 45–47

1

THE NEXT MORNING BROUGHT another letter from Holly, Lord Danior, almost illegible in his agitation.

"Either his fields are overrun with frogs wearing light armor," said Torisen to Burr, scanning the note by the slanting rays of a rising sun, "or the Randir have invaded. He's begging for the Highlord's immediate intercession. This is going to be messy. Tell Rowan to assemble a war-guard and provision it for a week at least."

While the garrison scrambled to obey, Torisen knocked politely on the door to the Women's Halls to request an interview with the Jaran Matriarch. To his amusement, the guards insisted on blindfolding him, as if he didn't know the way by heart, although usually his path led over the rooftops.

Trishien, greeting him and Yce in her airy study, also laughed. "At least this time you came through the door, not the window." She swept him a deep bow, the lenses in her mask flashing. "To what do I owe this unexpected pleasure?"

He told her about Holly's summons. She frowned behind her mask.

"I don't know much about the rules governing borders in the Riverland, except that the Silver usually establishes them. Then again, the river has shifted several times in recent memory, if never before directly between keeps. Consequently, there should be some established precedence."

"So I had hoped. Would you please write to your grandniece to ask if any scrollsman at the college is an expert in such matters? If so, I would like to meet him or her between the Danior and Randir keeps two days from now."

Trishien tapped her pen with long, ink-stained fingers, mildly amused. "So. You deign to resort to our Shanir skills."

Torisen fidgeted. "I would send a post rider, but that might be too slow, and this is important."

"Not just a woman's trifle, you mean."

"Lady, I didn't mean to belittle your skills. They just...make me uncomfortable."

"You may be grateful for them yet."

He regarded her curiously. "Has something happened? What have you heard from Kirien?"

"News that you should rather hear from your sister or cousin as it concerns your house. My own involvement was a breach of faith with my sisters."

Torisen saw that she was deeply embarrassed, which confused him even more. How could women's secrets involve him?

"You do know, I suppose, that this dispute will be seen as a test of your leadership."

If she wished to change the subject, so be it, although he found this new topic no more comfortable.

"I do seem to rule by fits and starts," he admitted wryly. "In this case, I really do need expert advice, hence my request to you."

"Which will of course be honored."

"But not my curiosity satisfied."

"I repeat: ask Jameth or Kindrie."

With that he had to be content.

By early that afternoon Torisen set off with a hastily assembled war-guard, Yce and Grimly trotting on either side of him. It was some fifty miles to the disputed territory, a two-day ride over the broken River Road. When the pup tired, she crouched and sprang up onto Storm's flanks behind the saddle, nearly causing the stallion to bolt. Torisen found a pair of stubby hands gripping his waist. Sharp nails bit into him until Storm settled down with a snort and a toss of his head, as if in disparagement of the company whom his master chose to keep.

Near Falkirr they passed another party traveling south across the Silver on the New Road.

"Who's that on the white horse being chased by a pink canopy?" asked the wolver, craning to look. "At that pace, she'll be lucky not to break her neck."

"I think it's Adric's daughter, Lady Distan, probably come from visiting her son Timmon at Tentir. Why the haste, I have no idea."

They camped off the road for a short night and arrived between Wilden and Shadow Rock by noon the next day.

Of the scrollsman expert, there was as yet no sign.

Holly, on the other hand, was overjoyed at their arrival.

"You see how it is."

He gestured to the contested ground. Formerly, it had been a large, flat region surrounded by a meander-loop of the Silver. Enfolding it on either side were a pair of pincerlike bluffs claimed by the Randir, studded with rotting stumps. However, the tip of the northern bluff had given way in a landslide into the river, diverting it across the loop's hundred-foot-wide neck. The Danior held the western bank of the new cut while the Randir hovered across the old riverbed, now fed only by runoff from Wilden's moat and bidding fair to become an oxbow lake. Between the old course and the new lay a deep meadow currently overwhelmed with silt, but already showing green shoots of lush grass.

"The field is too muddy for fighting," Holly added, "or we would have been at each other's throats by now."

"Grimly, go take a look upriver," Torisen told the wolver. "Yce, you can let go now. Holly, can you spare me enough planks to build a platform for a tent?"

Thus the Highlord set up his camp between the two forces in the middle of the muddy field, precariously, on quaking, oozing ground reached by plank pathways.

"No sign of a shwupp infestation, at least," he remarked to Rowan. "I suppose the grass roots are too tough for them to chew through."

"Perhaps. These are creatures that can gnaw through solid bone, though. Just stay off the marsh."

Lord Danior and a representative from Lord Kenan met in the tent's reception chamber at dusk, but not hospitably over dinner as Torisen had hoped. He was also disappointed that Lord Randir himself didn't attend. His spokesman was a sleek Highborn named Wither with a gold ring in one ear and the filed eyeteeth that signaled his joint allegiance to Lady Rawneth. Torisen had heard that politics among the Randir were complicated and unconventional, but also that mother and son usually spoke as one. He wondered again about the Knorth oath-breakers like Sargent Corvine who had taken shelter in Wilden after Ganth's fall. To whom among the Randir did they owe their allegiance?

Wither sipped his wine. "A fine vintage, my lord. From your own vineyards?"

"Hardly, since I have none. This comes from the Southern Lands."

"Ah. We had heard that Brandan funds have allowed you to improve your cellar."

Torisen's smile tightened. Trust the Randir to rub his nose in his debt to the Brandan—or rather in theirs to him.

"Personally," he said, "I prefer cider."

"As does Lord Brandan. Shall we proceed? The issue seems simple enough to us. The Silver has always served as the border between keeps, so the border changes with the river. As you see." He indicated the rushing cut with a wave of his hand. "Your objection, my lord?"

Holly put down his cup. "This bottomland has been ours for generations. We developed it into the rich source of hay that it is now."

"Yet the flood has washed away your dikes."

"As it has many times before. We always rebuild."

"Has the river shifted this much before?" asked Torisen.

"Never. The northern bluff has always diverted it and then the swoop of the land has carried it eastward, as you see from the old bed, until it bends back westward around the southern bluff. If the Randir hadn't logged those hillocks bare, they wouldn't be crumbling now."

Wither examined his nails. "Do you blame us, then?"

Holly only glared. Although he had dealt with the Randir all of his life, he couldn't match them in polish or wiles.

Soon after, Wither left, with the understanding that they would wait for the expert's opinion.

Holly stared out over the moonlit ground, gleaming silver under a sheen of water. "We get most of our hay from that field," he said bleakly. "I don't know if we can survive the winter without it. You think it's hopeless, don't you?"

"I don't immediately see what I can do," said Torisen. "The Randir have a good argument. They want it ratified, though, and respected by the rest of the High Council. Maybe Trishien's scholar can give us an edge."

"If not, it won't look good for you either, will it? I'm your bone cousin. You should be able to defend my interests."

"I will if I can." Torisen sighed. "Perhaps a lord like Caldane can ride roughshod over his neighbors—in truth, he doesn't seem to know how to ride any other way—but in a Highlord it would be seen as a sign of weakness."

This time Holly sighed. "Yes, of course I know that. You do realize, I hope, that your overthrow or death would plunge the entire Kencyrath into chaos."

Torisen paused to consider that. He supposed it was true, given that the only other pure-bred Knorth in the Kencyrath was his sister Jame. If he fell, would anyone propose her as Highlady? It seemed unlikely, unless the randon stood behind her. A quiver of jealousy ran through him. They might...as they had supported him? Not quite. She was nearly one of them now, as he had never been.

His warning given, Holly retreated to Shadow Rock.

Torisen stood for some time regarding the sparkling lights of the two keeps on either side of him, each up its own slot valley, then went to bed.

II

SOMETHING WOKE HIM IN THE SMALL HOURS of the night: a splash, a muffled cry. Under the cot, the wolver growled and Yce sat up at its foot, ears pricked.

Torisen rose, knife in hand. At the outer flap he found Burr, Rowan, and most of his escort, the rest presumably guarding the tent's far side.

"What?" he breathed in Rowan's ear.

The Kendar shook her head, still listening intently. The moon had either set or been overwhelmed with clouds, for it was very dark. Neither Wilden nor Shadow Rock showed more than a star-dusting of dim lights, barely enough to distinguish the bulk of each fortress from its enclosing valley. A faint breeze stirred the tent's canvas.

...*bloop*...*bloop, bloop*...

The listeners stirred. More plopping sounds came from every part of the meadow.

"It seems that I spoke too soon about the lack of shwupp," said Torisen.

"But what are they after?" asked a young guard nervously.

"We'll find out in the morning," said Rowan, "or not. Shwupp don't leave much. In the meantime no one is to leave the platform. My lord, you should go back to bed. Tomorrow will be a long day."

Torisen acquiesced, but didn't sleep. He could hear the guards speaking softly to each other all around the perimeter of the tent and their feet shuffling on the wood. From beyond them, out in the sodden meadow, came a stealthy sound as if of some great pot boiling.

. . . bloop, bloop, bloop . . .

Near dawn it at last fell silent.

Torisen emerged to find Holly already on the platform, bearing panniers of breakfast. Together they stared out over a field now blotched in half a dozen places with spreading circles of blood.

"It's pretty clear to me what happened," said Holly. "The Randir sent assassins after you last night. Some of them stumbled into shwupp pits. The rest fled. I wasn't fooling yesterday when I said what your death would mean to the Kencyrath. Here in particular, the Randir are only waiting to gobble us up. How we few Danior have lasted so long against them is beyond me, but this is sure: you aren't safe out here. Come back to Shadow Rock with me and conduct your negotiations from there."

"I appreciate the offer, but you must see that I can't. It would be taken as a sign of weakness and of favoritism. Besides, I seem to be well guarded as long as we take up the plank walks at night."

"Yes, and as long as nothing claws its way up through your floor."

"I doubt that they'll try with Grimly under the bed and Yce on top of it."

Holly grinned. "Have you finally gotten the pup to cuddle with you?"

"Hardly. Every time I stretch out my legs, she snaps at my toes."

Yce, at his feet, wrinkled a black lip as if in amusement.

Grimly emerged from the tent, sniffing the fragrance of new-baked muffins and hot, honeyed ham.

"What did you see upriver?" Torisen asked him.

"About what you expected." Grimly flipped open a basket and scrounged down through the contents to the meat pies. "You were right, Lord Hollens. Without roots to hold earth and rock, that northern bluff is rotten, even worse on the far side to the east than here where it's already slid."

Torisen was about to pursue this when movement caught his eye. A company of riders was passing rapidly northward along the New Road, one an elderly, white-haired man on a foam-flecked gray mare.

"That's Lord Ardeth, isn't it?" said Holly, staring. "He must have met his daughter on the road. What's going on at Tentir, that people should be rushing back and forth from it?"

"Assuming that he's Tentir-bound," said Torisen, although in his mind he had no doubt.

Dammit, Jame, what are you up to now?

III

"CAREFUL WITH THAT BUCKET," said Jame. "There's a salamander in it."

Damson paused to glare at Dar, who had handed her the vessel in question as part of a bucket brigade hauling mud out of the flood-damaged Knorth kitchen. The muck inside the bucket seethed and stank. An incandescent, spotted back surfaced, then disappeared again in a petulant gout of steam.

"Too hot for you to handle?" Dar inquired innocently.

His expression turned to a worried frown and he swayed as if about to pitch face-forward into the slimy mud that coated the floor ankle-deep.

"Damson!"

The cadet made a face at Jame's sharp tone, but Dar stopped wobbling. Then he started to belch.

Mint slipped a steadying arm around him as the paroxysms continued, bending him double. "Permission to get some fresh air, Ten?"

"Go. And you, behave," Jame said sternly to Damson. "See if you can get that beastie into the fireplace," she added, indicating the raised, reasonably dry hearth. "If it settles in properly, we'll never lack for a kitchen spark again."

She watched as the cadet gingerly prodded the lizard into a nest of kindling, which promptly ignited. The salamander curled up in the flames, steaming and purring like a kettle.

"Ha!" said Damson, with a glance after her would-be tormenter.

She and Dar had been sparring for weeks but, to Jame's relief, Damson hadn't pursued it to extremes. Was she finally growing a conscience, or was it only because she felt Jame's eye constantly on her? Now a third possibility occurred to her: Damson might actually be enjoying herself.

"You missed a spot," said Timmon from his perch above the mess on a countertop.

"I'm missing the entire floor, but it's down there somewhere. Why aren't you helping to clean up your own barracks?"

"I'd much rather watch you work. I've been good . . . mostly. Doesn't that buy me the right to indulge myself once in a while?"

"You're starting to slide out of things again."

"Truly, only out of some. But I wanted to ask you: have you spoken to Gorbel since he came back from Restormir?"

"I've tried. He doesn't answer."

"Huh. Something's afoot there. Fash and Higbert have been smirking all over the college, and we haven't seen much of the Commandant either."

Voices sounded above, one of them urgent.

Timmon froze in dismay. "It can't be."

But it was.

Lord Ardeth descended the stair and stepped into the mud without seeming to notice it.

"My dear boy!"

Timmon scrambled to his feet. "Grandfather!"

"I was on my way to visit you when I met your dear mother on the road. Is it true? Do you have Pereden's lost ring? Where did you find it?"

The sight of the gaping cadets who surrounded this tableau spurred Jame to action.

"Up. Out," she said to them. They sidled around the edges of the room and fled up the stair. "Timmon, why don't you take m'lord to your quarters for some refreshments?"

Anything to get him out of this stinking hole, to make him

forget that wretched ring, not that that was likely with it in bold display on Timmon's finger.

"My lord," she said, raising her voice, "I'm sorry about the death of your brother, Ran Aden. It was a terrible accident."

Ardeth waved this away, as if of little interest. "Dear Aden was growing a bit difficult. It happens to some Highborn at a certain age. No doubt I would soon have had to replace him as war-leader anyway. Now, Pereden—"

Timmon interrupted desperately, with his most charming smile. The kitchen in all of its disarray seemed a brighter place for it. "Yes, do come with me, Grandfather. You must be weary after your long ride."

He led Adric up the stairs past Jame, who flattened herself against the noisome wall to let them pass.

Ancestors preserve us, she thought as she hurried after them, then broke away at the barracks door, bound for Old Tentir. Adric's cream-colored riding leathers had been stained not only with sweat but also with flecks of blood.

She ran down the ramp to the subterranean stable, there to find the horse-master grimly examining Brithany by torchlight. The gray Whinno-hir drooped in her stall, her sister Bel-tairi at her side anxiously nuzzling her neck.

"Look," said the horse-master, almost speechless with indignation. "Just look! He's put spurs to her sides and near whipped her flanks raw. How *could* he?"

"The man is ridden by demons of his own. He probably didn't realize what he was doing."

"What he'll do, if he takes this mare out again tonight, is kill her."

"He's in the Ardeth barracks now. I'll see that he doesn't leave until tomorrow."

How to do that, though?

So Jame wondered, standing at the rail looking up at Timmon's lit windows. Dusk was falling. Soon it would be time for the cold supper on which they had all subsisted since the flood. Surely Adric wouldn't leave before then, but after?

Unless he could completely befuddle the man, Timmon was bound to tell Adric where he had gotten the ring. Holding out on his mother was one thing, on his sovereign lord, quite another. She had been a fool not to realize that the burning of Pereden's finger would affect his father, although Adric still seemed to be somewhat confused between his son and grandson. Torisen had to be warned about this latest development, but how?

Along the southern rail, the Jaran master-ten was smoking a pipe and blowing rings into the cooling air. Jame approached her.

"I've a favor to ask. Someone in your barracks is in far-writing communications with the Scrollsmen's College. May I speak with him or her?"

"Whom at Mount Alban do you wish to contact?"

"Kirien, the Jaran Lordan."

The master-ten puffed contemplatively. "We value our Shanir in this house, and we protect them. You will only cause pain."

"Sweet Trinity, d'you think I would deliberately hurt any of the Old Blood, being one myself?"

"Deliberately, no, but in this case it's inevitable. Wait here."

She entered the barracks and shortly returned with a thin, pale boy. So this was the cadet who had strewn Index's messages over her sleeping body. Jame remembered seeing him at Senetha practice. She had wondered at the time why he was here and not at Mount Alban as some scrollsman's apprentice, but it seemed that he wanted to be a randon.

"Can you help me?" she asked.

The cadet pulled a rolled, blank parchment out of one sleeve and a steel-tipped quill out of the other. Jame noted that his right hand was bound in linen. He loosened the bandage and pocketed it. His palm was scored with seeping cuts.

"What do you want to ask?" he said, bracing the parchment on the rail and digging the quill into his raw flesh.

You can only hurt.

Jame gulped. If this weren't so important...

"To Kirien: please pass this message along to Trishien and ask her to tell my brother. Adric knows about the ring. He is coming to ask you where you got it."

The cadet wrote her message in sputtering block letters on the parchment, returning several times to dip the quill into his own welling blood.

Then they waited.

"She may not be in her study," said Jame.

"It shouldn't matter. The itch to write will take her."

His hand jerked into spiky script. "M'lady Kirien acknowledges the message, but reports that the Highlord had gone to Wilden to settle a border dispute. She also asks when Kindrie means to return to Mount Alban."

Jame felt a chill. "He isn't there now?"

The cadet's scrip rounded as Trishien joined the conversation: "'He isn't at Gothregor either.'"

"Trinity," breathed Jame. "Not here, nor at Mount Alban, nor at Gothregor."

She remembered saying good-bye to her cousin and his discontented expression. He hadn't been pleased not to take his pretty chart directly to Torisen on her mere say-so. After she had left, could he possibly have turned south rather than north on the New Road? If so, where had he been the past twenty-odd days? On the road, he should have been safe, but there were always wild animals and, these days, roving Noyat hillmen. Besides, Wilden lay between Tentir and Gothregor.

Oh lord, what if he had fallen into Randir hands?

CHAPTER XV
Wilden

Spring 48

1

IN THE COOL OF EARLY MORNING, Kindrie walked in the Moon Garden of his soul-image. Regardless of their season, herbs bloomed all around him: comfrey and yarrow, anemone and colt's-tail, masterwort and hoarhound, all white but all ragged and dispirited as if after a long drought. The stream at the garden's southern end ran low with brackish water. Kindrie cupped some in his hands, his fingers scraping the woven bed. It was as if a death banner underlay the whole garden, undercutting life.

No.

This was still his sanctuary and he would tend it. Most of the water spilled before he could carry it to a drooping patch of white heartsease. He shook his long, pale fingers above the blooms and they momentarily revived.

Drops of water, drops of hope.

As he turned away, the flowers withered again and petals fell.

Across the stream, a thing of tangled cords fumbled at the wall. Here in the soulscape, the flood had failed to wash away Tieri's remains completely. Those that remained had woven themselves into a flaccid travesty that moped about the garden idly tearing flowers apart. Mostly, however, they either followed him or clung to the wall from which her banner had hung, beyond which Perimal Darkling had once gaped.

"Mother, no." Kindrie tried to draw her away.

Sodden loops of cord fell over his hands, clammy to the touch.

My son, come to me, come...

If he pulled on them, she would unravel. He let go.

Kindrie suspected that she—no, it—was animated by Rawneth. From the first, he had felt her fumbling about his soul, seeking some chink by which to enter. Once the Witch of Wilden and her pet priest Ishtier had shut him out of his soul-image altogether. He shuddered, remembering that terrible time when he could heal no one, not even himself. Ah, the bitter taste of mortality! Moreover, he had been denied his only source of comfort and peace, without which life was a cold, ragged thing and he little better. What his cousin Jame must have thought of him then. No wonder she had treated him with so little respect, for surely he had deserved none.

He was stronger now, he told himself, able to walk his soul even as he regarded the blight on it that days in Randir captivity had brought. He could even unravel the sorry threads of this mock mother, but then he would be truly alone. Let her be.

A cord fumbled around his ankle.

My son...

Not strong. Weak, when even such a cold, slimy touch brought comfort. More cords twined up his body.

My son, lean on me. Who else have you?

He remembered riding down the New Road in the dark, nearing Shadow Rock, so glad to see its lights over the shoulder of a hill. Cousin Holly had emerged from the evening mist to meet him. How his heart had leaped, and then fallen at the other's cold smile.

"Come to me, have you? Fool. Bastards have no family."

And he had delivered Kindrie to the Randir patrol that followed him.

Something was wrong there. What? Oh, he was stupid, unable to think straight. Had this memory come to him once or over and over, night after night? How often had he felt this clammy touch, dreamed this dark dream.

Lord Danior be damned. Surely Jame, Tori, Kirien or even Ashe would come to look for him.

Fool. Bastards have no friends.

A lifetime of experience told him that. He had been an idiot to believe otherwise.

The cords climbed higher, threading in and out of his skin. Soon they would reach his throat.

Something stuck his shoulder, and the garden blurred.

"Up, you slugabeds, or break your teeth on the charred scrapings of the pot!"

Kindrie groaned and opened his eyes. He lay on a narrow, lumpy cot in the subterranean Priests' College at Wilden. Before him on the luminous moss that covered the wall were twenty-five thin scratches. He added a twenty-sixth. It seemed to him that he had been a prisoner much longer than that, since childhood even, friends and family only a desperate dream.

Beyond detaining him, however, the Randir seemed to have no other immediate use for him than to throw him back into the routine of the Priests' College. He had been theirs once; now he was again. Of course, if they had known that he was a purebred, legitimate Knorth, he would have had value as a pawn or a hostage. As it was, he accepted their seeming indifference gladly. Far better that than M'lady Rawneth's special attention.

He drew his hairy brown robe over thin shoulders. There had been muscle there once—well, a little. Here, however, there was no exercise but the Great Dance and no sustaining food except for that allotted to the high priests, and he was only an acolyte.

Outside his door, he joined the brown-and-gray-clad mob as it shuffled down the spiral corridor past dormitories and classrooms. The subterranean college was built in a spindle shape, narrow at the top and bottom, wide in the middle. Above, the novices and acolytes lived in squalor; below, in unguessed at luxury, the priests, minor and high. In between was the communal dining hall.

Other acolytes shoved and pinched him.

"Thinks he's too good for us." "Yah, runagate!" "Are you happy to be home?"

Breakfast was thin gruel, watery milk, and stale bread already spotted with blue mold. All around him, pinched faces bent to their meal, many under the ragged mops of white hair that betrayed those of the despised Old Blood.

One novice, younger and plumper than the others, pushed back his bowl.

"This is awful," he whined. "I want my mother!"

A Coman, Kindrie thought, about six years old. From the traces of brown dye in his hair, he had been hidden away at home until his Shanir nature had betrayed itself.

"Mommy's boy, mommy's boy!" the others chanted at him. Most, like Kindrie, had been delivered to the college as babies. It had been mother and father to them, a lean breast and a hard hand.

The newcomer buried his face in his arms and burst out sobbing.

"Up, you motley rats, up!" cried the stewards, passing among them, thwacking with rods. "To class with you all!"

Kindrie touched the boy's shoulder in passing and found himself for an instant in the other's soul-image: a small, bright chamber with childish drawings on the wall and a woman's voice speaking in the next room.

"Mother!"

The boy leaped up, but his face crumpled when he saw the dank stone that surrounded him. Throwing off Kindrie's hand, he blundered after the others.

Had it been kind to remind him? Kindrie wondered, following. Already shadows were gathering in that childhood nursery and the beloved voice was fading. It took the strength of innocence to cling to such an image, and there was little of that in this dark place. Was he himself still innocent? In an odd way, yes. Under the circumstances of his childhood, he had never really grown up. Here and now, that was the only strength that he had.

He filed into his first class, where those of pronounced Shanir power met in a claustrophobic room lit only by garish lichen murals of unpleasant designs.

"Who is our lord?" demanded their instructor, a minor priest disparagingly behind his back called a priestling.

"No one!" chorused back the assembled acolytes from the circle that they made around him.

"Who is our patron?"

"Lady Rawneth."

"Whom do we serve?"

"The high priests."

"Who is our family?"

"Each other."

"On whom do we spit?"

"On our cruel god"—each except Kindrie turned to mime spitting over his shoulder—"who has forsaken us."

The catechism over, the instructor turned to his class. "Remind me. What can each of you do?"

"I can make dogs howl, master."

"I can start fires with a touch," said a boy with a hideously scarred face.

"I can shake the earth," said another who himself couldn't stop trembling.

"I can madden birds."

"I can make snakes dance."

"I can carve stone images that move—all right," the acolyte added, to the jeers of the others, "very slowly."

"And you?" the instructor said to Kindrie.

"I heal."

"No. You can manipulate soul-images and walk the soulscape, as our Lady Rawneth does. Are you greater or lesser than she?"

"That isn't for me to say."

"Then I will. You are lesser because you can only heal, not destroy or create. Now, show us your power. Hinde, stand forth."

The twitching cadet nervously crossed the circle to face the Knorth.

"Well? Touch him."

Reluctantly, Kindrie did.

In his soulscape and in the room itself, not the acolyte but his entire surroundings began to quake, to the startled protests of the other students. Dust rattled down from the ceiling. Stones groaned. Standing still in the midst of growing chaos, Kindrie focused. In his soul-image, someone huge was shaking the boy, now a mere infant.

"Oh, you little Shanir bastard..."

Kindrie gripped those enormous, tormenting hands.

"You're killing him," he said. "One more seizure and he will die. You are nothing but a memory, to torment him so. Go away."

Then they were back in the classroom, the boy quiet and bewildered in his grasp, the stones settling around them. Angry shouts came from neighboring rooms.

"What did you do?" demanded the instructor.

"I sent away a baleful influence."

"You destroyed it!"

"No. Only he can do that. See. It has him in its grip again."

The boy broke Kindrie's hold and backed off, shaking, sneering. His thoughts echoed in the Knorth's mind:

"I deserve it, I deserve it, I deserve it..."

"Try me," said the fire-boy, suddenly before him, gripping Kindrie's sleeves.

Kindrie felt heat. The dank wool smoked and stank. His hands in turn gripped the other's wrists. He was falling toward fire. No. The one falling was a child on a hearth, ignored by his parents as they argued about his fate. That had been decided long ago but still he fell, only to be thrust away by Kindrie's will.

The acolyte looked at his hands, aghast. His ruined face crumpled on the side not fixed with scar tissue. "I can't," he said, almost in tears. "What have you done to me, you bastard?"

Nothing that would last, thought Kindrie sadly as the other, blundering, withdrew. Not without his consent. That was one of the bitter lessons he had learned over the past three weeks: those here below in the Priests' College had been made to embrace their wretchedness. Earth shaker and fire-touch both might have turned their talents to more constructive ends, but not under the college's direction.

For the rest of the lesson, the instructor ignored him while the burnt boy wept scalding tears and the trembling boy complacently jittered in place, occasionally gulping back foam.

The next class was wind-blowing Senetha as practiced for the Great Dance. Ah, the freedom to move, almost to fly, but here one also felt a touch of the power that the dance was meant to channel. It streamed in at the top of the college from the Kencyrath's wide-flung temples and spiraled down through it, bound for the catch pool below, the cloaca of divinity. From whence did it come? Different currents had different scents—the musk of Tai-tastigon, the jungle sweat of Tai-than, the spice of Kothifir, the dust and ashes of Karkinaroth—and there were other flavors there too, including one very strong like simmering brimstone. Kindrie was gingerly trying to backtrack this last when the class ended.

Next (without any intervening lunch) was elementary runes, taught by a former randon whose eyes kept straying to Kindrie.

"Not like that. Here. Look." He bent over Kindrie's wax tablet and drew on it. Kindrie noticed that the back of the priest's neck was scarred, but not heavily enough to disguise the swooping lines of the rathorn sigil. On Kindrie's pad he had written, "Wake up! She has her nails in you."

She ... who?

The cords, climbing higher and higher, obscenely burrowing in and out of flesh ...

For a moment he knew what was happening to him, and then it was gone. The priest had scraped clean the slate.

Last came potions and powders.

"Today we will compound a dust to stop an enemy's breath," announced the instructor, "something so simple that even our esteemed Knorth Bastard should be able to master it."

The other students tittered and shot him sidelong glances, but Kindrie had his doubts. Nothing that he tried in this class ever came out as planned, perhaps because most of it was meant to harm.

Throttle-weed, ash-berry, powdered bilge-beetle ...

The instructor was right: what could be simpler—assuming that he really did want someone to choke.

The priestling gingerly sniffed at Kindrie's concoction, the antidote clutched ready in one fist. His breath caught and his eyes bulged.

Trinity, thought Kindrie, dismayed, *did I really do it right?*

Then the man drew a whooping gasp and began convulsively to sneeze. His explosive breath scattered the powder throughout the room. Some bent double helplessly as if about to blow their brains out. Others keeled over chairs and table, sending their own ingredients flying to add to the confusion. Kindrie stood back in alarm, holding his breath.

Someone tapped him on the shoulder. He turned to face a senior priest holding a cloth to his face. "Of course, it would be you," he said in a tone of muffled exasperation. "Come along. Someone wants to see you."

Kindrie went with him, but not before surreptitiously sweeping what little was left of his experiment into a pocket.

His guide led him up the spiral ramp to the foot of a stair, then up into the stone building, hardly more than a shed, that masked the college's entrance. Outside was Wilden's high, windy terrace looking down over the fortress' many barred family compounds full of steep, narrow buildings like so many pinched, inward-turning faces. The shadow of the Witch's Tower fell across the flagstones, turning puddles to ice where it touched.

Kindrie hesitated on the tower's threshold, loath to enter, and looked out over the clean world denied to him. Beyond the sweep of buildings, down on the river flats, he saw a large tent flying a black flag with white tracery on it, too distant to make out.

"Who is that?" he asked his escort.

The priest laughed. "The Highlord, come to settle our little border dispute, or so he thinks."

Torisen, so close . . .

Clean air seemed to blow through him for the first time in weeks, but the priest's hand closed on his arm as he took an involuntary step toward the terrace's edge.

"Do you think that we don't know?" the man breathed in his ear. "You could call him 'cousin,' but wait: bastards have no kin, do they, even so high-blooded a one as you. Aren't you glad that we took you in? This way."

He pushed Kindrie into the Witch's Tower.

"Now climb."

The shadows struck him cold as he mounted the twisting stair and his breath smoked. Kindrie remembered the first time, as a child, that he had come this way, not knowing what awaited him.

"Let me see you, infant." Oh, that chill, caressing voice. *"Come close. Closer. Close enough. They say that no one can do you lasting harm. How . . . intriguing. Shall we see?"*

Another more recent memory: *"What a pretty chart. Here are all the Highlord's dependents lined up so neatly. Does he really need such an aid to memory? Dear me. The written word is so easily destroyed, though, isn't it?"*

And she had thrust the scroll into the fire.

Witch. Bitch.

At least he still had the rough notes in his room at Mount Alban.

Rawneth lived in the upper stories of the tower, but the doors to the lower of these were closed. Only the way to the top level stood open. Kindrie paused at the head of the stair. Open windows all around let in the wind to swirl sheer curtains of dusky purple and deep blue, spangled with stars like the night sky but turned by the afternoon sun into glowing twilight. Through shifting veils he saw movement, heard muffled voices. The Lady had company in her tower.

"My dear," she was saying, "now is not the right time. I told you so two nights ago. If you succeed today, might not we be blamed too?"

"Nonsense," said a familiar, confident voice. "I'm too clever for that. Look."

A dark figure loomed behind the drapes and swept them aside. Sudden sunlight momentarily blinded Kindrie, but he heard the smile in the other's voice:

"I even have the perfect witness."

Kindrie caught his breath as his sight returned, haloed around the edges. That curly brown hair, that smooth, young face so full of seeming innocence...

Rawneth's guest was Holly, Lord Hollens of Danior.

II

IT WAS THE SECOND, long, restless day for Torisen, spent waiting for the scrollsman expert to arrive who hopefully could settle this land squabble without a pitched battle. Holly's people prowled on one side of the contested ground. On the other, the envoy Wither had pitched a pavilion and could be seen in it placidly reading as he waited. His lack of guards was almost an insult. Holly himself, having heard that Randir were already on his side of the river, poaching, had ridden off to hunt them. Torisen wasn't sorry to see him go. Lord Danior made a very unquiet companion when frustrated.

The sun beat down, unusually hot for the time of year. Gnats rose in swirling clouds from the marshy land. They didn't bother Torisen—stinging insects never did—but he could hear his guards slapping at themselves and swearing. Either he had brought too many of them or too few—not enough to protect him in case of an assault, too many to make this seem like a casual affair. He had let the Randir maneuver him into placing his prestige behind the dispute. If he couldn't protect Holly's interests, his allies would look at him askance. If he did so by breaking law or custom, however, friends and foes alike would have good cause to question his judgment.

Across the plain, Wither looked up from his book and gravely saluted him. Torisen gave him a nod and debated retiring into his own tent for a nap, but that was something he seldom did, as everyone well knew.

He didn't even have Grimly to bicker with. That morning, there had been a slight tremor and he had sent the wolver to scout the lands north of the keeps with strict instructions to stay in human form so as to give the Randir bowmen no excuse to shoot at him.

Midafternoon brought a warning cry from his guards.

Torisen emerged from his tent to see Adric, Lord Ardeth, splashing toward him over the marshy ground on an exhausted gray mare.

"Really, Adric!" Torisen touched the Whinno-hir's shoulder, stained nearly black with sweat. "Someone, rub her down and find some firm ground to walk her on until she's cool. And now, my lord..."

He led Adric into the tent and induced him to sit. When he offered the old man wine, Adric took it but absentmindedly, without tasting it. He continued to fidget through the ceremony of welcome, and Torisen's heart sank.

"Now," he said finally, "what brings you from Omiroth to randon college to my humble tent in such a lather?"

Adric put down his cup and leaned forward. "I would have been here earlier, but someone slipped nightshade into my evening tipple and I overslept. I've talked to my grandson Timmon. He tells me that you gave him Pereden's ring. Where did you get it?"

Torisen sipped his own wine, mentally bracing himself. He had known ever since he gave the ring and finger to Timmon that this moment was coming.

"My lords, I hope I don't interrupt."

A wizened Jaran scrollsman stood at the tent flap, nearsightedly peering inside. "I was at the High Keep examining some rare manuscripts when your summons reached me. Then I had to consult Mount Alban's library and certain of my colleagues. Sorry if I'm late. Wine? I wouldn't say no. A hot day, is it not?"

Burr entered and served him while Torisen scrambled to make sense of his sudden appearance. Of course. This was the expert for whom they had all been waiting. As if in confirmation, Wither appeared at the flap.

Adric plucked at Torisen's sleeve. "About the ring..."

"I hope," the Randir was saying courteously to the scrollsman, "that you come bearing the solution to our little dilemma."

"It isn't quite as straightforward as it seems. Some of the older scrolls refer not to the riverbed but to the River Snake's back, which is said to run all the way from the Silver Steps to the mouth of the river bordering on Nekrien."

Wither waved this away. "Mere primitive superstitions. What do the charters between Bashti and Hathir say?"

Grimly entered. "Tori, you should see the shape of the land to the north. Oh, and here's Holly."

The young Danior lord paused on the threshold of the already crowded tent, his face in shadow. In his coat of blue velvet laced with silver, he was surprisingly well dressed for someone who had spent the day tracking poachers. Apparently he had caught one, for he led a brown-robed figure by a tether around his neck. Torisen met a pair of anxious, pale blue eyes over a white gag.

"Kindrie?"

Holly twitched the lead, making his prisoner stumble forward. "It's just a runaway acolyte from the Priests' College. I was about to send him back."

"That, be damned. He's my cousin!"

"He's a bastard, kin to no one."

Torisen flicked a throwing knife out of his collar, spun Kindrie around, and cut the rope that bound his wrists. The Shanir scrabbled free of the gag.

"Tori," he croaked, "I saw Lord Danior with Rawneth!"

As Torisen turned, incredulous, toward Holly, he saw the knife in the other's hand. It darted toward him. His lighter knife turned the other's blade, but only so far before snapping. As he twisted aside, he heard cloth rip and felt a line of fire across his ribs. Burr swore and lunged to the rescue, only to crash into Wither. Holly yelped. Grimly had bitten him on the leg. He slashed at the wolver, clipping off the tip of one furry ear, then stumbled as Yce barged between his legs. Torisen grabbed his knife hand at the wrist, bent it, and sent him crashing into the table. Wine flew in a crimson arc across Ardeth's face.

"Oh, I say," protested the scrollsman, snatching up his own cup.

In the moment that Holly was down, Kindrie threw the remains of experimental powder in his face. His features convulsed.

"Ah-*choo!*"

Dust flew everywhere, wrecking havoc. Bodies lurched about in paroxysms of sneezing, falling over furniture and each other. The canvas walls bulged and jittered as if the tent were also suffering a fit. Guards outside cried out in alarm. Those who reached the door first, however, also doubled over, coughing and half-blinded with tears.

Inside, only Torisen and Kindrie had had the wits to hold their breaths.

The figure that Torisen pinned writhed under his hands, distorting fantastically. It gasped, sneezed again, and seemed nearly to blow off its own face. An elbow weirdly bent caught Torisen in the chin, knocking him back. Before he could recover, his opponent had lurched out of the tent through the incapacitated guards with the two wolvers in close pursuit.

Torisen also started after him, but stopped when Kindrie fell to his knees, choking.

"...cords..." wheezed the Shanir, clutching at his throat. "In my...soul-image."

Torisen only saw the rope tether still around Kindrie's neck, but it had tightened and was digging into the healer's flesh. When he worked his fingers under it, he found himself grappling with an entire network of tough threads that bound the Shanir from head to foot. A woven mockery of a head like an inflated sack rose behind Kindrie and hissed at Torisen. Then Kindrie found a loose thread and jerked at it. The cords unraveled with a sigh, leaving Torisen with the original rope in his hands. He dropped it as if it were a dead snake.

"Are you all right?"

Kindrie nodded weakly, still clutching his bruised throat.

"I-I didn't know...I didn't realize...all this time, sh-she had me..."

Before Torisen could ask what he meant, Holly burst back into the tent with a wolver gripping either arm of his leather hunting jacket.

"What in Perimal's name..." he began, then took in the chaos only beginning to sort itself out inside the tent as various shaken Highborn extricated themselves from the furniture and each other.

Rowan pushed past him and moved quickly to her lord's side.

"Blackie, you're bleeding."

"I know."

Burr opened Torisen's coat and shirt to examine the slash across his ribs.

"As usual, m'lord, you're luckier than you should be," he said, and handed Torisen a table linen to hold against the seeping wound.

Holly lifted the arm to which Yce was attached and regarded her dangling from it, growling around her mouthful of leather.

"Will someone please tell me what's going on?"

"Release him, Yce, Grimly. D'you think it likely that my own cousin would try to skewer me, much less that he could change from a dress coat to hunting clothes in seconds?"

Grimly rose, assuming a less hairy, somewhat chagrined aspect. "We did lose sight of him in the confusion," he admitted, "and neither of us could track worth scat with a snout full of that wretched powder. So when we saw M'lord Holly here coming up the plank walk, bold as you please, we just grabbed him."

"Oh, that's as clear as mud soup," said Holly. "I take it that you thought I was an assassin. I also take it by the carving on your precious hide that there *was* a would-be assassin who looked like me. So, who and how?"

"I think I can explain," said Kindrie hoarsely, still sitting hunched on the floor, his face as white as his hair.

Torisen gave him a hard look. "One thing among many that I don't understand," he said, abruptly changing the topic, "is why you're here at all."

"He...the other one...brought me as a witness to Lord Danior's presumed perfidy. Beyond that, I've been a prisoner in the Priests' College these past twenty-six days."

"Did you know about this?" Torisen demanded of the Randir envoy.

Wither shrugged. "I may have heard some rumor, but really, the priests go their own way under my lady's protection. Besides, the man is a bastard."

"If anyone says that one more time, I shall wax violent and ruin more perfectly good napkins."

"Is there anyone here," asked the scrollsman piteously, "who wants to hear the results of my research?"

"I do at least," said Wither, with a courteous inclination of his head.

"Well, all complications aside, it comes down to this: the river establishes the boundary between keeps."

"Thank you."

Torisen sighed. "That's it, then. I'm sorry, Holly."

The earth trembled again, shaking them where they stood, making the planks chatter like teeth under them.

"That was a strong one," Holly remarked.

The wolver had darted out the door. Now he returned. "Tori, everyone, come look!"

Torisen, on his way out, hesitated at the abstracted, pained look on Kindrie's face.

"I said the next seizure would kill him," whispered the healer. "These are that wretched boy's death throes."

Outside, a cloud of dust rose over the shoulder of the northern bluff. The far side seemed to have suffered a considerable landslide, and the eastern end had crumbled altogether. Water and debris boiled through the new cut as the Silver raced to regain its old bed, slicing off a chunk of former Randir land for good measure. They watched as the river, fanged with debris and gilded with the sunset, surged around them. Then Torisen turned to Wither.

"Well," he said, "that's it."

Wither made a face. "As you say. This time. Fare you well, my lord."

On his departure, Adric emerged from the shadows where he had retreated to avoid being trampled in the uproar and to mop off his wine-soaked clothes. "About Pereden's ring…" he said.

Holly shot Torisen a look, then drew himself up with a gulp. "I gave it to the Highlord," he said. "It was on the finger of a corpse being burned on the common pyre at the Cataracts along with the renegade changers."

Adric breathed a sigh of relief. "My boy, why didn't you say so in the first place? Obviously it was worn by the changer who impersonated my dear son. Tori, you should have given it directly to me."

Torisen meekly agreed.

"If you will come with me, m'lord," said Holly, scrambling to recover himself, "I would be honored to host you for the night. Tori?"

"I'll join you later."

Left alone with Kindrie, Torisen searched for and found a bottle with enough wine left in it for two small cups. His side wrenched at him as he bent to pick it up and the stain on the linen grew.

Kindrie moved as if to help him, but Torisen waved him off.

"It's only a cut. Let's not push our luck. The question remains: what in Perimal's name just happened?"

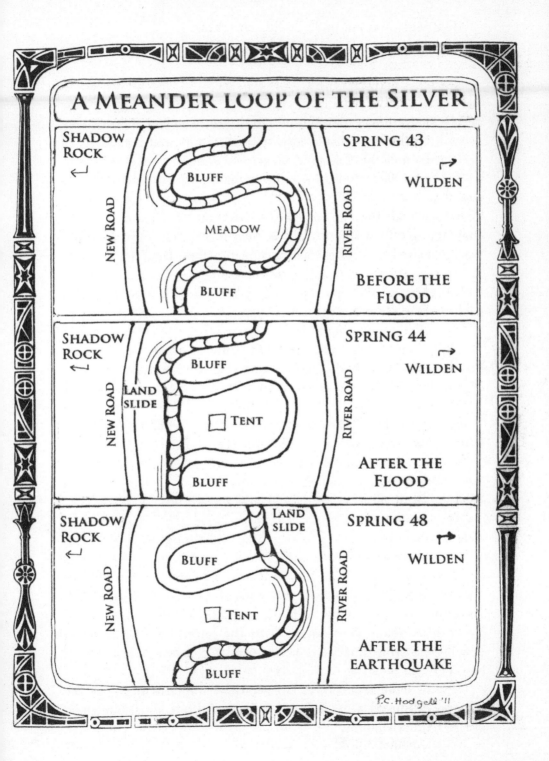

A MEANDER LOOP OF THE SILVER

SHADOW ROCK ←
BLUFF
MEADOW
BLUFF
NEW ROAD
RIVER ROAD
SPRING 43
→ WILDEN
BEFORE THE FLOOD

SHADOW ROCK ←
LAND SLIDE
BLUFF
☐ TENT
BLUFF
NEW ROAD
RIVER ROAD
SPRING 44
→ WILDEN
AFTER THE FLOOD

SHADOW ROCK ←
LAND SLIDE
BLUFF
☐ TENT
BLUFF
NEW ROAD
RIVER ROAD
SPRING 48
→ WILDEN
AFTER THE EARTHQUAKE

P.C. Hodgell '11

⟨⟨⟨ III ⟩⟩⟩

KINDRIE DREW A DEEP BREATH. He was still shaken by how deeply Rawneth had tricked him into despair. She had almost stolen everything that he valued most: friends, family, self-respect... all the things that the Priests' College also sought to destroy.

She could have broken me, he thought. *She almost did. But not quite.*

He accepted the cup of wine, waited until his hands stopped shaking, and then drank from it. Warmth spread outward from his empty stomach. Breakfast had been a long time ago.

"To begin with," he said, "you were attacked by a changer."

Torisen snorted. "That much I guessed. I have come up against such creatures before, you know."

"Yes, of course. I should have started further back. My lord... m-my cousin, our great-grandmother Kinzi stitched a letter on the night that she died. A copy came into the hands of the Jaran Matriarch and she translated it for us."

"Who, pray tell, is 'us'?"

Kindrie heard the warning in his voice like steel half unsheathed. Who knew what, and why hadn't he been told?

"Kirien, Ashe, I, and... and your sister's sneak Graykin. I told Jame myself what we had learned and was going to tell you when I got to Gothregor. As you see, I never made it."

"Then tell me now."

Kindrie gulped, tried to organize his thoughts, and began again, adding as many details as he knew. When he was done, he anxiously regarded the Highlord who sat before him frowning.

"Let's see if I understand this correctly," said Torisen. "Kinzi writes, no, stitches a letter to her lover Adiraina but is interrupted by Bashtiri shadow assassins. Both the letter and the contract proving your legitimacy are sewn onto the back of Tieri's death banner."

He shot Kindrie an unreadable look. "Congratulations, by the way, on not being a bastard and welcome to our small but interestingly inbred family."

"Thank you. I think."

"Condolences on your paternity, though.

"To continue, the banner disintegrates, dropping its secret into Jame's hands. She turns both the fragmentary letter and the contract over to you, and you seek a translation of the former from Lady Trishien. She reports as follows: Kinzi saw Rawneth and Greshan together in the Moon Garden several days after the latter's death. They made love, in the midst of which Greshan's face changed, presumably into Gerridon's. Jame now reveals that last Autumn's Eve she had a series of visions of that night in which she recognized Rawneth's 'servant' as the infamous and apparently immortal changer Keral. She assumes, therefore, that Keral was Rawneth's lover and the father of Kenan. When Kinzi summoned Randir mother and son to Gothregor for Adiraina to test the bloodlines of the latter, Rawneth forestalled her by taking out a contract with the shadow assassins on all the Knorth women. Hence the Massacre. But it doesn't end there. To bring us up to date, I have just been attacked in the vicinity of Wilden by a changer. According to the above reasoning, Lord Randir has changer blood. Therefore, I have been attacked by Lord Randir, who has since run away."

Kindrie sagged in his chair, feeling the emptiness of defeat.

This time when he had first come into Torisen's presence, he had felt a subtle change in the other's attitude toward him—not quite acceptance, but something close, and he had wondered: could the Highlord really be changing his attitude toward the Shanir? To know for sure, he would have to touch Torisen's soul-image, but he had specifically been warned not to do that. Perhaps that harsh voice behind the locked door only waited like a snake in a hole for the provocation to strike. He thought, now, that he heard it stir.

"You don't believe me," he said numbly.

"On the contrary," said Torisen, dropping his sarcastic tone, "I do. But will anyone else?"

"Your sister does. So do Kirien, Ashe, and Trishien."

"Three at least of whom are sensible women. However, I have to deal with the High Council, and that will require solid proof."

"Jame said the same thing."

"Four sensible women, then. The attack on me is nothing. A farce, as it turned out, thanks to whatever it was that you blew into that changer's face. The slaughter of the Knorth women, though . . ."

Torisen ran a hand through his hair, ruffling white streaks in the black. "We seem to have fallen into an old song:

> "Formidable foes (female or male)
> Bought the Bashtiri, blades for hire,
> To kill the Knorth. Unanswered questions
> Haunt the wide halls of the High Lord's home:
> Who kens old quarrels that cost us Kinzi?
> Who now will whisper a name to the wind?

"Do we really now have the answers to those questions and, more dangerous still, a name? If so, what do we do with them? What happened here today is confusing at best. Someone who appeared to be Holly tried to stick a knife in me. No one but you and I saw his contortions after you spread that powder. It's a long reach from there back to the slaughter of the Knorth ladies. Even with proof, we're talking about one of the most powerful houses in the Kencyrath, an ally of the Caineron. To challenge it could lead to civil war."

"So all of those blood prices will go unpaid?"

"I didn't say that. My instinct is that today's assassination attempt and the previous one were clumsy crimes of opportunity, instigated by Kenan, with Rawneth no more prepared to follow them up than I am to pursue her. The time isn't ripe."

"And when it is?"

"Oh, then we'll see." Torisen's expression made Kindrie shiver. "Sooner or later, there will be a reckoning."

CHAPTER XVI

Tests

Spring 48–54

I

THE HORSE EYED JAME WARILY, no less so than she did him. He was a chestnut gelding with a white star and white legs, tall enough so that she could hardly see over his withers. As she saddled him, he shifted restlessly in the crossties. When she slipped off his halter and attempted to bridle him, he backed up in the box stall and raised his head out of her reach.

"Here." The horse-master entered, clouted the horse on the jaw to settle him, then forced the bit between his clenched teeth.

"This one had a wildcat land on his back once. See the scars? Mind you, it didn't exactly attack, more like fell out of a tree on top of him. Try telling a horse that there's a difference, though. He's hardly a mount that I would have chosen for you."

"It was the instructor's idea." Jame glowered at the Caineron randon watching from outside the stall.

"Huh," said the officer and moved on, shouting, "Get a move on, you bed of slugs!"

The horse-master tightened the chestnut's girth.

"Remember," he said under his breath, "you may be able to ride a rathorn and a Whinno-hir, but to the average horse you're a predator, to be gotten away from as fast as possible. If you're scared—and I can see that you are—try not to show it."

Fine for him to say, thought Jame as she led the horse up the ramp with her ten-command and their Caineron counterparts clopping around her. The rathorn Death's-head obeyed her, if unwillingly, but she was only able to ride him because the bond between them allowed her to feel his shifts an instant before he made them. As for Bel-tairi, anyone could ride that sweet-tempered mare if they had her consent, never mind that only Jame did. All other horses to her were large, powerful, unpredictable creatures—and to them she was a thing with claws.

Outside the northern gate, the cadets swung into the saddle. They were paired this time with Gorbel's ten-command. Gorbel himself sat on his dun gelding to one side, not meeting Jame's eyes. He still hadn't spoken to her since his return from Restormir nor attended the Falconer's class. She wondered what his father had said to him.

"To begin with, once around the college," said the instructor. "Walk, trot, canter, gallop. Keep in formation. Off you go."

The others walked off. Jame's mount backed up, shaking his head.

The randon slapped it on the haunch and it bolted to catch up, barging between Fash and Higbert at the far end of the line from her own ten. Their horses snapped at hers. Fash, laughing, gave her a not-so-playful shove.

The instructor caught up on the far right next to Brier.

They rounded the front of Old Tentir and began to trot. Jame could sense the pent-up energy in her mount, or was it his terror? Whichever, it felt like bestriding something on the verge of explosion. She tried to relax. The chestnut lurched sideways into its neighbor and began to buck, throwing Jame forward on his neck. She rapped it on the head. Instead of quieting, it bolted ahead of the line to a shouted curse from the instructor. Her own ten picked up the canter to keep pace.

They swung around Old Tentir to its southern side. The right flank hugged its wall, the left veered into the wild moraine area where the egging exercise had taken place. Jame's horse dodged trees and leaped over rocks. An outcrop of the latter separated her and her stirrup mates from the others.

Fash rammed the chestnut, lifting it half off its feet. On the other side Higbert lashed at her with his whip. Suddenly she was in a running battle through undergrowth, over treacherous ground. What in Perimal's name...? The other horses crowded in on her. Fash grabbed her jacket and jerked. Already off balance, she fell between his mount and her own, down among the pounding hooves.

They thundered over her head.

Jame lay very still for a long moment, waiting for the stab of pain. In its place came a dull ache across the shoulders and down the back. All of her limbs still seemed to work, her brain as well (or ill) as usual. Only when she sat up did she remember the phantom touch of a tree trunk at the back of her neck . If she had fallen a moment later, it would surely have broken her neck.

"Hoom."

Jame looked up at the sound of someone nearby clearing his throat, but no one was there.

Before her lay a steeply ridged, wooded landscape sprinkled with spring flowers, patches of vivid green, and a few pockets of late snow in the deep kettles. In the distance, Perimal's Cauldron fumed and muttered.

"a-HOOM."

Pebbles and dirt clods rattled down the nearest slope, expelled from a hole under a stone ledge. Boulders on either side gave the impression of puffed up cheeks. Shifting her position, Jame could make out two deep nooks above that might almost have been sunken eyes.

"Mother Ragga?"

"Hack, ack . . . ack . . . pu-toom!"

A family of hedgehogs, unceremoniously expelled, tumbled down the slope, unrolled at the bottom, and hastily shuffled off single file.

"So, this is the sort of game you cadets play."

The Earth Wife's voice came from the back of the hole, muffled, as if it spoke within close-set walls.

"Not usually," said Jame. She started to rise, but realized that with her change of perspective the earthen face had disappeared. When she subsided, it was back.

"Humph." More debris spat out. "I have a warning for you, missy: don't forget Summer's Eve in the hills."

"That's only twelve days away. What's so important this time?"

"Remember last Summer's Eve? That idiot Chingetai tried to claim the entire Riverland by laying bonefires up its length instead of using 'em to close the boundaries of his own land."

"Surely he's not going to try that trick again."

The hillside rumbled. Stones rattled down it. "I should hope not. This time he's got to do it right or stay open to more raids from both north and south. But the Noyat are already on Merikit ground, waiting. He's going to need help."

"Will he accept it from me?" For that matter, Jame thought, given past experience, was it wise to ask her for anything short of an apocalypse?

"He's a fool if he doesn't take all the help he can get."

Of course, they both knew that Chingetai *was* a fool; how big a one remained to be seen.

Voices called her name through the trees. Jame rose to answer them. In so doing she lost sight of the Earth Wife although a subterranean mutter pursued her:

"Remember Summer's Eve."

Brier and Rue rode toward her leading her horse, in a high lather with wild eyes and a limp. Rather than mount him again, Jame swung up behind Rue. The randon instructor was waiting for them by the north gate where they had started their chaotic run.

"So there you are," he said to Jame while the other Caineron snickered.

Fash and Higbert looked at Gorbel as if expecting him to speak, but he continued to glower into space, jaws clamped shut.

"I think you Knorth have had enough excitement for one day," said the randon. "Here. You've earned this."

Jame stared at the black pebble that he had dropped into her hand.

"What was that all about?" she asked as they led their horses back down the ramp to the stable.

Brier regarded the stone with lowered brows. "So. The final testing has begun."

Seeing that Jame was still confused, Rue rushed to explain. "The first time we competed against each other, remember?"

"Oh yes. Vividly. I barely earned enough points to enter the college."

The horse-master shook his bald head at the state of her mount and felt his hock, but didn't comment. She led the horse into his stall and began to rub him down. He still quivered whenever she touched him.

"Then the Randon Council cast the stones," continued Rue, busy in the next stall.

Another near miss, thought Jame. If she hadn't redeemed the Shame of Tentir in the person of Bel-tairi, even the Commandant had been prepared to throw her out.

The chestnut continued to fret. Losing patience, Jame slapped him on his sweat-slickened barrel. "Behave!" He bounced nervously and settled down somewhat.

"Then there was the Winter War."

"But that didn't count, did it?"

"Not officially. It should be good for something, though, shouldn't it?"

Rue called to the other cadets for confirmation. No one knew for sure, but it only seemed just: after all, the Knorth team had won, if through a series of maneuvers on Jame's part that still perplexed most of her house.

"So," said Rue, finally getting to the point, "this time the instructors have most of the say."

"Each senior randon is given six pebbles," cut in Dar from across the aisle. Trust him not to be able to keep quiet. "Three white and three black, for the best and worst performances in their classes. They can give them out all at once, but more likely one at a time. The Commandant has a set too."

"Randon aren't supposed to give white tokens to their own house," Mint added from her other side, "but they can give black."

"Anyway," said Rue, "how many white you get by Summer's Day determines where you go on graduation."

"If you graduate," muttered Damson.

"True, some don't," Erim agreed. "Next worst is to have to repeat your first year here at the college."

Which Tori would never let her do, Jame thought.

"Kothifir is for the best," said Mint. "Next best is some other foreign post. Then there are the cadets who are sent home to join their house garrisons."

"How many white pebbles qualify you for Kothifir?" asked Jame.

"It varies from year to year. Usually one white will do it, or one black for failure. There are some twenty randon with six tokens each. Most of us never get one at all, which means that we get sent wherever we're needed. That could be good or bad. Ten-commands may also get broken up as in the second cull, say, if the commander gets a black, or a commander's white might pull through his or her entire ten-squad intact. Then too, black cancels white and vice versa, so you're already one behind, Ten."

"Lovely," muttered Jame.

It wasn't until she and the others were on their way to the

next lesson that it struck her: if she was going up into the hills for Summer's Eve, she would miss the last day of classes with its potential tests. Well, never mind, she thought, setting her jaw; she would just have to earn enough white tokens before then.

⟪ **II** ⟫

FROM THEN ON, EACH LESSON taught by a randon became a test of nerves, if nothing else. Would the instructor award a pebble or not? Which color, and to whom? Some handed out all six immediately, based as much on past as present performance. Others seemed to be waiting until the last minute. A few with particularly strict standards had the reputation for only distributing as many as they truly believed to be earned, black or white.

The Falconer's class eyed each other, wondering. Tarn and Torvi seemed clear winners, and so they proved, to some good-natured grumbling from the others. After all, one expected a dog to obey. Gari and his various insect hordes also received a white. So did Shade and Addy.

Jame sighed and ruffled Jorin's fur. Her link with the ounce had improved, but not as much as she and (clearly) her instructor would have liked. Trust a cat to go its own way.

The Falconer only handed out one black and that, in absentia, to Gorbel, who since his return from Restormir had never reappeared in the mews.

"Pleased?" Jame asked Shade as the latter fingered her white stone.

"Moderately. I see through Addy's eyes now but so, I suspect, does my grandmother Rawneth."

Jame had noted that Shade had been restraining her changer tendencies ever since her own house had put her down the well. Perhaps that was safest, but it seemed like throttling a natural talent.

Kindrie had stopped by on his way back to Mount Alban and told her about Kenan's presumed impersonation of Holly at Wilden. What a horrible time her poor cousin had had. Really, the three of them had to take better care of each other.

However, there was no longer any question in Jame's mind where Shade had gotten her changer blood, and little where Kenan had gotten his. Did darkness come with it? Not intrinsically when innocently got, as far as Jame could tell. She was closer to the shadows herself due to her past behavior but also closer to their despised god thanks to her basic nature. On the whole, she felt herself to be more compromised than an innocent victim like Shade. The Randir, however, still seemed to have doubts.

Shade looked up. "Gari. When do the crown jewel-jaws migrate north?"

"Any day now. Why?"

The Randir only shrugged, but Jame could guess. Migrating with the "jaws" would be the Randir Heir Randiroc, whom Rawneth had been trying to assassinate for years. The Randir at the college loyal to the Witch would be watching for him. So, apparently, was Shade.

Classes continued. Jame got another black in swordsmanship, not unexpectedly, even though it came from a Jaran instructor. Then she and Brier both got whites after fighting each other to a draw at the Senethar in a match that took the entire class period and left both barely able to stand. Another white came into Jame's hands for her skill with the scythe-arm. That made two of each, already a surprising number for any cadet but not an advantage in that they cancelled each other out.

Among her ten-command, Erim received a white for archery, no one apparently having yet realized that he could only hit inanimate objects. Niall also scored for field surgery after Killy pinned a randon to the ground with a lance through the leg, thus earning a black for himself. Jame suspected that Damson had rigged the accident since the plump cadet liked neither Killy nor that particular instructor. Moreover, she was fond of shy Niall, whose battlefield experience at the Cataracts was well known.

"How about you?" Jame asked Timmon when they crossed paths between lessons.

"A white for diplomacy," he said proudly.

She laughed. As practiced at Tentir, diplomacy and debate were closely linked, with the hitch that one truly had to convince one's opponent. "You're a charmer. What could be easier?"

"Well, there is that. I hope to get another white for the Senetha, though. Shade has."

Jame wasn't surprised, given what she had seen of the Randir's skills. She hoped she would also score in that discipline, but so far the class hadn't appeared on her daily roster.

"And Gorbel?"

"A white for strategy, of all things."

That didn't surprise Jame either; people always underestimated the brain behind that bulging brow and sullen expression.

"Too bad they don't test for hunting skills," she said.

Timmon looked at her askance. "You want him to pass, don't you?"

"Well, yes. I'm annoyed that he keeps avoiding me, but otherwise, for a Caineron, he isn't half bad."

"And me, for an Ardeth?"

"You're shaping up into something interesting; and no, I don't mean sexually."

"Damn."

The next time Jame's ten was paired with Gorbel's, it was for a race, starting at the swimming hole, ending on top of a cliff across the Burley.

"How you get there is up to you," said the Coman randon in change.

The cadets looked at the cliff, which rose a good one hundred feet above the water. Some gulped and turned pale. Most turned and trotted downstream toward the bridge, meaning to cross and approach their goal the long way around, from its more accessible far side.

Jame eyed the cliff face. It was rife with slanting crevices and had an inviting ledge two-thirds of the way up.

"Well?" she said to Brier, who had stayed by her side as if waiting to see which way the cat jumped.

The Southron squinted up against the afternoon sun. Like most Kendar cadets, she suffered from height-sickness, but had nearly mastered it.

"I'm game if you are, Ten."

"See here." It was Gorbel who also, unnoticed, had stayed behind. "I need to talk to you."

"Oh, do you, at long last? Then follow."

Jame circled the swimming hole, darted out onto the spit that separated it from the Burley's next level, and jumped from rock to rock across the rapids to the opposite bank. From this narrow, gravelly margin, she leaned back to judge her ascent, then unsheathed her claws.

The cliff face was most accommodating, offering many grips for hands and feet. It was a pleasure to climb. Halfway up she glanced down at Brier who was making steady if not quite as rapid progress.

"All right?"

The dark features turned up toward her, rigid with determination. "Just don't fall on me."

They reached the ledge and pulled themselves up onto it for a brief rest. The wind was sweet on their sweating faces, the cliff's shadow cool. Swift water chuckled below. Downstream Perimal's Cauldron rumbled deep in its throat. Across treetops and New Tentir's outer wall, they could see the roof of their barracks.

"Nice place for a picnic," Jame said.

Brier grunted and closed her eyes.

They opened again at a rattle of stones below. A pallid, sweaty face scowling with concentration glared up at them. Gorbel had climbed halfway to the ledge and was fumbling for a new grip.

"He really must want to talk to you," said Brier.

"Go on when you're ready. I'll wait for him."

After a moment, Brier rose to her feet and resumed her ascent. Jame leaned over the edge.

"To your right. Now reach up. Good. Not so good."

Gorbel had stepped on loose shale and for a moment hung by his fingertips, feet scrabbling at the rock face. All the Caineron Jame had ever met were deathly afraid of heights.

"Come on. A few more feet. Now, reach for my hand."

His weight nearly pulled her off the ledge, but after a fierce struggle she managed to haul him up.

"Now," she said, panting, "what's so urgent...that you had to follow me...up a sheer cliff?"

"Please." He gulped and leaned back, looking sick. As if with a life of their own, his hands still clung white-knuckled to the rock slab on which he sat. "There's no privacy at the college, and I was running out of time."

"Ancestors preserve us. For what?"

"To warn you. If I don't challenge you to armed combat before the end of the school year, my father is going to disown me."

"Oh," said Jame. This was bad, much worse than simply being

replaced as Caineron Lordan. "Would the randon let you graduate without a house?"

"I'm not inclined to find out."

"So we fight. Huh. Maybe I should have let you fall."

"That wouldn't help: Fash would be glad to take my place. By the way, the challenge includes all the Tentir Highborn cadets of both houses."

Jame counted on her fingers. "That's one against . . . five?"

"Eight. My command doesn't include all the Caineron Highborn. Speaking of the randon, if you pass, Father has also threatened to demote the Commandant and reassign him so far into the hinterlands that it will take him a month's hard ride just to get there."

"The randon would allow that?"

"In house, they have no say. Worst of all, though, Father can strike at Sheth's nephews and nieces in the service, some of them Bear's children."

"All this to stop me from graduating Tentir? Thal's balls, I won't even be a fully collared randon until I've spent two years in the field."

Gorbel snorted. "Father has finally grasped that you aren't easy to stop. The same may have occurred to your brother."

"Still, to threaten innocents . . ."

"I know. It won't make Father popular with the Randon Council, but then he never has been."

They both contemplated Caldane's little tests by which he established the loyalty and ambition of his officers, pushing hard against the bounds of Honor's Paradox.

"Hey!" the randon officer called over the cliff's grassy edge, from a cautious distance. "Are you two setting up house down there?"

Gorbel groaned and rose. "What did I say. No privacy. There is this, though: I can challenge you however I like. Well, it's to mounted combat with your choice of weapon. Think about it."

Jame did as she followed his agonizingly slow ascent the rest of the way to the top. Hmmm.

They found the two ten-commands waiting for them.

"Last up," said the randon, and dropped a black pebble into Jame's hand. She looked at it.

"Well?" the Coman demanded, with a note of challenge in his voice.

It was unfair. He was waiting for her to say so.

"Nothing, Ran." She pocketed it.

⧓ III ⧓

THAT EVENING, THOUGH, AFTER SUPPER, Jame lined the black pebble up with its mates on the dining hall table and regarded them. Two white river rocks and three dark gray ones, all about an inch long and half an inch thick, all smoothed to perfect ovals. They might have been markers in a game of Gen; perhaps some had been. The game she played now, however, was much more serious.

"You should complain to the Commandant," said Rue, scowling at them.

"Have I ever, about anything?"

The towheaded cadet wriggled, uncomfortable. "Well, no. And yet..."

"And yet I shouldn't have to." Jame tapped the latest black stone with a fingertip, saw that she had extended a claw, and retracted it. "The Coman knew that I held back to make sure Gorbel didn't fall. He can't have thought I deserved this. So where is honor here?"

Brier deposited three mugs of cider on the table and swung a long leg over the bench to join them.

"We aren't tested for one lesson alone but for all," she said, "and for each randon's opinion as to our general fitness. Did you think, lady, that you'd won all of them over?"

"Well, no. Given who they are and what I am, that would be impossible, but still..."

"But still you hoped that you had."

Jame considered this. Maybe she was naïve. Where honor was concerned, did she see it as black and white as these pebbles on the table before her? But then they were actually natural shades of gray. Wasn't she herself similarly shaded, caught between Perimal Darkling and her own Three-Faced God? Yes and no. If her own honor were compromised, surely she would know it. Thanks to Tori, she hadn't yet personally faced Honor's Paradox. Perhaps neither had the Coman randon. If he didn't think she was fit to be an officer, it was his duty to say so; and he had, however unfair the pretext.

"You think it's all politics," she said to Brier.

The Southron shrugged and drank. As a former Caineron, ancestors knew she had seen more than her share of unfair dealings between Highborn and Kendar.

"Yes," said Rue, "but would the Commandant see it that way?" Black stone, white stone, touchstone.

Jame considered Rue's faith. Did she share it even as Sheth confronted his own crisis of Honor's Paradox with his brother?

Even then, she thought, regarding Brier Iron-thorn's stoic, teak-dark face and Rue's flushed, rebellious one. *Especially then.*

IV

DURING THESE LAST DAYS, Jame had her last lesson with Bear.

As usual, she was pulled aside after assembly and instructed, almost furtively, to report to the Pit. Surely secrecy was no longer required, she thought as she made her way deep into Old Tentir. The other cadets were already aware that she took lessons from the former monster of the maze, and everyone knew about her claws.

It seemed like a lifetime ago that she had considered them such dreadful secrets. Jame extended her nails through the slit tips of her gloves and flexed them. Click, click, click. Ah, how good that felt.

But don't get too comfortable, she told herself. *Whenever you use them, especially in anger, you draw closer to the Third Face of God.*

So the Arrin-ken had warned her, and she felt it to be true. The last time she had nearly flayed Vant alive, something of which she was far from proud. But to use them rationally, naturally, in self-defense—that ought to be different.

Here was the Pit, as desolate as ever with its splintered walls and lingering aura of spilt blood. A shadow passed before the torches in the observation room above. So. The Commandant had once again come to watch her train with his brother.

The opposite door opened and Bear shambled in, prodded from behind. He wheeled to confront his keepers, but they shut the door in his face. He wedged his massive claws into the crack, gouging out new splinters but failing to wrench it open, then turned to scan the room. Jame donned the mesh helmet and saluted. He ignored her. Firelight flared on the crevasse in his skull through the tumble of gray hair. Had it closed further? Jame couldn't tell. His clothes were more unkempt than ever, his aspect both more aware and more desperate. He saw his brother in the balcony and mouthed at him. One word broke through the babble of sound: "Why?"

Jame dropped her salute and, after a moment, removed the helmet. She touched his arm. He swung around, gigantic in the flickering light, looming over her.

"Why what?" she asked him.

He struggled with articulation, mangling words, then thrust her aside in frustration. She fell back against the wall, rapping her head sharply against the panels.

Bear raised his fists, not against her but against the silent, still figure above.

"Why? Why? Why?"

His voice cracked, then broke into a roar. In answer, the lower door opened and sargents swarmed in to subdue him. He flung them about as if their padded armor were tenantless until Jame got in his way again. She put her hands on his broad chest, ignoring the frightful sweep of his claws as they slashed the air around her head. Though he surged back and forth, he didn't again strike her and she managed to stay with him as if in some uncouth dance, her agile feet against his lumbering ones. At last he stopped, panting, leaning into her until her knees nearly buckled.

"Why?" he asked his brother again, almost plaintively.

Why am I a captive? Why doesn't my mind work properly? Why have you done this to me?

Sheth didn't answer. What could he say?

Bear's shoulders slumped. He allowed himself to be herded out of the room without a backward glance.

Jame and the Commandant were left regarding each other. After a moment, Jame tendered him a sober salute which he acknowledged with a slight nod. Then she left the Pit by the opposite door.

V

IT HAD BEEN A DISTURBING INCIDENT and Jame thought a great deal about it, without reaching any solution. It especially bothered her that she was about to leave Tentir, one way or another, while Bear remained a prisoner within it. Still, what could she do?

In a dream that night, she found herself arguing with her brother.

"Where is honor in all of this?" she demanded of him or rather of his back as he paced, long black coat swishing, hands clasped behind him. "Bear was a great randon before he fell in battle. His condition isn't his fault."

"You've seen how dangerous he can be," said Torisen over his shoulder. "We owe our cadets, our people, protection."

"Of course he's dangerous," she answered, exasperated, also beginning in her agitation to pace. "He always has been. With those claws, he's clearly aligned to That-Which-Destroys. Would you lock away all such Kencyr?"

"Such Kencyr are Shanir."

"So are those who create and preserve," said Kindrie, passing them with his white-thatched head bowed in deep thought. "Should they also be cast aside, as I was?"

"I can't answer for them," Torisen snapped. "Don't you see? I can barely answer for myself."

"And who are you?"

"Highlord of the Kencyrath, guardian of a flawed society."

"Then let me smash the flaws out of it."

"What else might you destroy, eh?"

"I won't know until you trust me to try."

"Yet there is good," mused Kindrie. "Honor's Paradox can break us, or make us stronger while honor itself is our strength. And we are strong, despite everything."

So they argued back and forth as their paths crossed and recrossed, never quite bringing them face to face.

Jame woke with some unanswerable retort on the tip of her tongue, and lost it to returning consciousness.

Her quarters were dark and quiet except for Jorin's gentle snore on the pallet beside her.

Where is honor? she thought again.

All this fretting had made her thirsty. As she rose to fetch a cup of water, however, her bare foot brushed something coiled on the floor that hissed in warning.

"Addy?"

She reached down and carefully picked up the swamp adder. Phantom light seeping down the smoke hole gleamed on restless, gilded scales.

"Were you sent to me for protection again?" she asked the snake. "What is Shade up to this time?"

No answer, as usual, except for a flickering black tongue and a mad, orange glare.

She settled Addy a safe distance from Jorin in the warm depression left by her body, dressed, and slipped out of her chambers. One floor down, the cadets slept in their canvas-partitioned quarters. Below, the common hall lay empty and silent. Out onto the boardwalk...

Jame shrank back. Against the northern side of New Tentir, the Randir barracks were stealthily astir where a number of cadets waited in the shadow of the arcade's tin roof. The moon in its last quarter caught Master-Ten Reef's sharp features as she turned toward a figure darting across the square. Whispers followed, and a hand pointing southward. The waiting Randir streamed out of the shadows like a pack of direhounds running mute on the trail.

Jame followed them out the southern gate. There to her relief they turned east toward the river instead of into the treacherous moraines. Downstream lay a bridge and across it to the south a woodland backed up against the toes of the Snowthorns. If the cadets hadn't been so intent on their prey, they might have heard her following them for the wood was dark and full of snares for the hasty foot, but no one looked back. When Jame caught up with them, they were crouched behind a rank of bushes under a spreading maple newly leafed out. Jame climbed the tree and edged out onto a bough over their heads. The limb creaked under her weight. One Randir glanced up, but didn't see her among the broad leaves. The others' attention was fixed on the glen before them.

Moon and starlight glimmered on two figures there—a hooded man astride a pale horse and a dark, slim girl, one hand on his bridle, earnestly speaking to him. A breeze rustled through the clearing and the rider's outline seemed to flutter. The mare's ears pricked toward the bushes. She shook her head and mouthed her bit.

The branch creaked again and slightly gave way.

The Randir drew their bows.

"'Ware arrows!" Jame cried, a moment before the bough broke, dumping her and its leafy weight on top of the Randir.

Many were knocked flat. Some, however, let fly. Most of their arrows went wildly astray; others, however, streaked across the glen.

The mounted figure seemed to disintegrate into a swirling cloud of jewel-jaws, moon- and shadow-hued. A sword flashed, cutting all but one of the missiles out of the air. The remaining shaft ripped through the hood between head and shoulder, snatching it away from Randiroc's pale features and white, shaggy hair. He had swung Mirah to cover Shade. The mare danced in place for a moment, then sprang away before the Randir could nock another flight. Whatever happened, Randiroc would not fight the children of his house.

As Jame struggled out of the tangle of limbs, human and arboreal, she thought she saw the Randir Heir still standing there across the clearing. Then he turned and fled. Some Randir fought free to pursue him. They had barely sped away when a second wave of cadets barreled into those still on the ground. Rawneth's supporters and her opponents fought fiercely, in silence, while Jame wriggled free, only to find herself in the grip of the ten-commander who had put Shade down the well.

"They're after him," she gasped.

The commander released her. "Then go."

Jame ran through the trees toward the sound of fighting, to find the supposed Randir Heir in the hands of his enemies. Jame dropped two cadets with fire-leaping kicks and a third with earth-moving before they realized they were under attack. The other three turned, blades in their hands. Their prey, released, crumpled to the ground.

"This is no business of yours, Knorth," said Reef.

Jame maneuvered for position, noting their stance and weapons as they spread out to surround her.

"You've struck down a fellow randon in unequal combat after an ambush," she said. "That should concern everyone at the college."

"Would you tell, then? Go away, little Highborn. Quickly. Before we deal with you as we have with this renegade traitor."

The one behind her lunged at her back. Jame slid aside in a wind-blowing move, caught the other's wrist as it shot past, and broke it. The attacker's momentum sent her stumbling into her mate. Both went down as other Randir began to stagger to their feet. Reef feinted, then slashed, ripping Jame's jacket as she leaped backward.

Voices called out behind them. Reef backed off, turned, and fled, followed by her companions.

Jame rushed to the fallen "lordan." Not to her surprise, the latter's features were in painful flux back to Shade's. The changer clasped her stomach, trying to hold back a tide of blood. Her hands and the ground beneath her glistened darkly in the moonlight. Jame held her.

"You should be changer enough to close this wound."

"What does it matter?" Shade spoke through clenched teeth, and gasped as a spasm of pain shook her. "Ah! I would have bound myself to him, but he refused."

"He didn't refuse because you're tainted. I've told you: you aren't."

"Why, then?"

Trinity, much more of this foolishness and the Randir would bleed to death through sheer stubbornness. Jame scrambled after her wits.

"Think about it," she said urgently. "The way he lives, in hiding, always on the run—how could he accept a follower?"

"I could serve him at the college, in the field, anywhere."

"He would still be responsible for you, and he can't be. Look at all the trouble I've had supporting Graykin, and we've been under the same roof all winter."

Shade stared at her. "That scruffy little Southron is bound to you?"

"Yes, but for Perimal's sake don't tell anyone. It was an accident. You said once that you didn't need to be bound to anyone any more than I do, but you can still serve him without that. Look how useful your skills were to him tonight, and may be again in the future. Some day he and Rawneth will clash. Then he'll need all the allies he can get. Will you consider that, and please stop bleeding?"

Shade was still for a moment. "All right," she finally said. Her face contorted with effort. Then she sighed and removed her hands from the former wound.

Jame looked up to find that they were surrounded by a circle of silent, watchful Randir.

Two of them stepped forward and helped Shade to rise. Weak from blood loss, she sagged in their steadying grip.

"This is our business now," said the ten-commander, "and our sister. We will care for her."

They left, bearing Shade with them.

"I'll send Addy home," Jame called after them. "Shade?" But they were gone.

Jame sat back on her heels and considered her torn, blood-soaked clothes. More work for Rue, if she could even save the slowly rotting fabric. Perhaps the changer's blood wasn't corrosive enough yet to dissolve steel, but it had certainly ruined yet another bit of Jame's limited wardrobe.

But oh, what had she said? Now the Randir knew that Graykin was bound to her, and no lady was supposed to bind anyone, never mind that Rawneth did. That settled it: whether he wanted to hear or not, she had to tell her brother before someone else did.

VI

THE NEXT MORNING AT ASSEMBLY, a wan Shade appeared, in company with many battered faces and some broken bones. However, it seemed that no one wanted to report the night's events to their house. That, thought Jame, was just as well, given their lady's reaction the last time an assassination attempt on the Randir Heir had failed.

CHAPTER XVII
Out of the Pit

Spring 57–58

I

THE DAYS TO SUMMER'S EVE melted away.

It was full spring now, the wind-combed grass on the hills a vivid green speckled with bluebells and dancing golden campion, the apple orchard a drift of sweet blossoms. Birds sang and bees throbbed drunkenly through the air, sometimes bouncing off inauspiciously placed tree trunks. After classes on the afternoon of the fifty-seventh, Jame walked through a high meadow beyond the northern wall, idly gathering wild flowers and watching butterflies for Jorin to chase.

With three black tokens and two white, she was failing Tentir. Only one day of potential tests remained—tomorrow—if she meant to ride north to the hills on the fifty-ninth of Spring in time for Summer's Eve.

Moreover, she hadn't yet been tested in the Senetha or the Sene, the two related disciplines besides the Senethar where she could hope to excel. What if they came on the last day, the most important of her college career, when she was gone?

Should she go at all? Where did her responsibility lie, in the hall or in the hills?

On the face of it, the answer was simple. Tori had placed her here against all advice, against even his own common sense, with the sole requirement that she not make fools of them both. If she failed, would anyone care why? They would say that she was and always had been unfit, also that Torisen was a fool to have proposed her in the first place. If a fight with the Randir was coming, even possibly a civil war, did she dare weaken his position in any way? She wasn't just any Kencyr, either, as Ashe had once pointed out, but a potential Nemesis. Someday one third of the Kencyrath's destiny might depend on her.

She considered what would happen if she did indeed fail Tentir.

The Women's World certainly wouldn't take her back, nor did she want to go.

Nonetheless, lords would fight for her contract, the Ardeth and Caineron hardest of all. Dari with his rotting teeth and breath of a rotten eel, Caldane himself, perhaps . . .

G'ah, think of something else.

The cool wind, the sun hot on her face, a froth of white bells at her feet, and Jorin crouching behind a tuft of grass insufficient to hide him, ears pricked to the drowsy drone of a bumblebee. His hindquarters wriggled, one paw came up, and he pounced, barely missing.

"You wouldn't have liked the taste anyway," she told the ounce as he plumped himself down and began to wash as if nothing had happened.

Tori could still take you as his consort. How would you like the taste of that?

Jame felt her cheeks flush.

Yes, she loved her brother, but in that way? Scraps of dreams returned to her, the sort that Timmon favored but could never control, the sort that left her abashed but tingling.

Is it so bad, after all, to be a woman?

Perhaps not, but in the context of property? For a Highborn lady, there was no other way.

Then there was Rathillien.

Ultimately, the Kencyrath's fate might depend as much on its relationship with this world as on the coming of the Tyr-ridan. The Four had started out hostile to her people, with good reason given that they saw the Kencyrath as invaders. The Eaten One might be content with her Kencyr consort for a season, but the Burnt Man favored no one except perhaps the Dark Judge, and Mother Ragga still had doubts. Nothing would turn her against the Three People faster than Jame's failure to attend Summer's Eve, not to mention the consequences if Chingetai failed again to close his borders against the Noyat and other tribes farther north under the Shadows' sway.

Maybe there had been some way for Jame to escape her northern entanglements, but if so, she hadn't found it.

Face it, she told herself glumly. *Your loyalties are divided, and you have no one to blame for that but yourself.*

On top of all that, she also had to meet Gorbel's challenge on Summer's Day. That morning at assembly the Caineron Lordan had formally issued it before the entire cadet body while the Commandant had looked down expressionless from his balcony.

"Run away," Fash had advised with a grin while Higbert snickered behind him. "Now." Both obviously expected an easy fight. "D'you think you stand a chance against even one of us on horseback, much less eight?"

Jame had ignored him.

Her own house had been harder to snub. Reactions there ranged from horrified shock to a gallant if somewhat desperate defense from her own ten: the lordan had pulled off miracles before; now—somehow—she would do so again.

Brier had given her an appraising look. "Is this fight to the death?"

"Not so far as I know"—with a passing thought to her uncle Greshan's fate. "More likely to the shame, which is quite bad enough."

In the end, though, their anxious chatter had driven her away into the high meadows, to be alone and to gather her thoughts, so far without success.

...run away...

What if she went to the hills and failed to return in time to meet Gorbel's challenge?

Fash would laugh and Gorbel would be disappointed in her. So would her own people and all the unlikely friends she had made during her sojourn at Tentir, the Commandant not least. Would even her brother's honor survive such a blow? He had tacitly supported her by letting her stay at Tentir for the past year. She owed him for that...

And was about to fail him unless she earned at least one more white token. If she didn't win one tomorrow, despite everything, maybe she should try again the day after and let Chingetai enjoy whatever mess he was sure to make of things.

She wished she could ask the Commandant for advice. Once before, he had made it clear that her duty lay with the Merikit, but this time he had said nothing, and much more hung in the balance.

A thought struck her: was this her personal Honor's Paradox? True, Torisen hadn't ordered her to do anything dishonorable, nor was he likely to unless through ignorance of her true situation. However, she was being called on to exercise personal responsibility, and what was the paradox if not a test of that?

So her thoughts rolled, back and forth, between the hills and the hall, one last time for each.

"Huh," said Jame, squinting up under a hand at a sun now in decline. Her face felt tight and hot from so long in its rays. Night creature that she had been before, she should have remembered how easily she burned by day, especially at this altitude.

She whistled up Jorin, who was happily engaged in batting an ants' nest to pieces, and they went down to the college for supper. On the way, Jame detoured through Old Tentir and left the bouquet of flowers outside Bear's door. She could hear him snuffling at them through the bars as she retreated.

THE NEXT MORNING JAME WAS ROUSED early by the college stirring.

"What's happened?" she asked Rue, who brought her a mug of ginger water in a state of high excitement.

"They say that Bear has escaped. Search parties are forming."

Everyone scrambled into his or her clothes and down into the square where dawn set aglow the eastern sky, and breath smoked on the crisp air.

The Commandant walked before them, his long coat swishing at his heels, his hands clasped tightly behind him.

"You have all heard the news. This is our business, we of Tentir. Here it started, here it ends. One of our own is lost. He must be found."

The cadets were sent by squad to search the school, focusing on Old Tentir. Ten-commands inched into the labyrinth bearing torches, keeping within sight of one another. Some tied themselves together with strings that all too often snapped. Others marked the walls with chalk. Soon the plaintive cries of the lost began to echo hollowly.

"What if he's turned savage?" whispered Rue, creeping on Jame's heels, giving voice to a fear that haunted them all. "I mean, who could blame him? But we're the first people he's likely to run into."

Jame didn't answer. It seemed to her altogether possible that Rue was right, that the man had again become a monster, but oh lord, what then?

Her ten was assigned to a spot not far from Bear's quarters, deep within the old college. They passed his door; it had been smashed open from within, its shattered boards spattered with the blood of broken knuckles. Shredded flowers lay strewn across the threshold.

Beyond, the walls closed in around them, innocent but empty, lined with doors. Most were unlocked, yielding to rooms vacant except for dead spiders trapped in their own webs and white, scurrying things that shunned the light.

"Watch the floor," said Jame.

They were farther in than most went and the boards beneath them were furred with dust.

"Here," said Brier.

They saw the prints of large, bare feet and fallen petals leading up to a wall, disappearing into it.

"Now what?" said Brier.

Jame fumbled around the skirting, looking for the catch. A panel gave, a hidden door opened.

Graykin had only revealed a few of Tentir's secret ways to her, of which this was one. Bear presumably knew them all from his time here as commandant, so long ago. The cadets gingerly descended the narrow, dark stair, batting at cobwebs, and found themselves in the public corridor that led between Old and New Tentir to the north gate. Here the footprints disappeared, but surely there was only one direction in which they could have gone.

"You can return to your quarters now and get some breakfast," Jame told her command. "Don't tell anyone."

Brier loomed over her, frowning.

"Are you sure about this?"

"I had better be, hadn't I? Bear is Shanir, aligned with That-Which-Destroys. So am I. If we can't deal together, who can? Besides, he's my senethari."

Brier grunted. "So be it. Good luck to you." She led away the rest of her puzzled squad.

Jame slipped out the side door and crossed the training fields. Beyond was the wall and the apple orchard, adrift in white blossoms. Above was the meadow where she had gathered the wild flowers.

She didn't see Bear at first because he was kneeling in the deep grass, but a wisp of silvery gray caught her eye and below it she discerned his craggy profile. When she cautiously approached, she saw that his lap was full of early daisies. Clumsily, with blood-scabbed knuckles and his great claws clicking inches from his fingertips, he was trying to make a daisy chain. She knelt before him.

"Here. Let me try."

Jame had never woven flowers before, but she quickly caught the knack of it. One braided the stems, so, with the petal-fringed faces outward, then added another and another. When the chain was long enough, she twisted its ends together into a frail crown and placed it on Bear's head. He sat back on his heels with a grunt. She had never before seen him look so serene and almost noble, the cleft in his skull hidden, gray hair and white petals tumbling together over his brow in the warming breeze.

Then he lifted his head and sniffed the air. Following his gaze, Jame saw the Commandant sitting still on his great warhorse Cloud at the meadow's lower edge. He wore gray hunting leathers. Sunlight glinted off the head of a long-shafted boar spear.

His lord had only given him two choices: to imprison his brother or to kill him. Here was Honor's Paradox at its most stark.

Bear rose to his feet. The two randon regarded each other across the waving grass. The wind blew. Bluebells nodded. Jame held her breath.

Sheth inclined his head in a salute. After a moment, Bear returned it as if the gesture had stirred a long-buried memory. The daisy garland slipped down rakishly over one eye. He removed it and absently dropped it over Jame's head where it first caught on an ear and then settled onto her shoulders. He turned to go, then paused and swung back. In his palm was something small that he gave to her, folding her hands over it. Then he turned again and shambled off toward the distant tree line.

Jame watched him go.

Then she looked at what he had given her. It was the wooden cat, recarved so that its broken hind legs curled under it as if in a crouch. She could trace claw marks like chisel strikes, clumsy but still with a mind behind them.

The Commandant watched his brother's departure without moving until Bear disappeared into the trees. Then he rode up to her and lifted the garland with the tip of his spear as if for inspection, incidentally presenting the blade to Jame's throat.

"Huh," he said, flicked off the daisy chain, sheathed the spear, and offered Jame his hand, She accepted it and swung up onto Cloud behind him. They rode back to Tentir without exchanging a word.

 **III**

EVENING CAME AT LAST, at the end of a long day. Thanks to the Bear hunt, everyone had missed their first two classes. Then Jameth had scored another black in writing.

Rue thought the last grossly unfair. No one wrote better or faster than her lady, nor with a finer hand, but the instructor in this case had been a Randir, and the Knorth could expect little justice from that house.

As she mulled a cup of cider for her mistress, Rue glanced over her shoulder at her.

Jameth sat on her sleeping pad with crossed legs, elbows on knees, chin on her clasped hands, frowning into the fire under the bronze basin. Having proved for the umpteenth time that he couldn't fit into her lap, the ounce Jorin curled up beside her with his chin on her thigh. Flickering light picked out the shadows on her fine-drawn face, the curve of her body. She had unbound her hair but had laid the comb aside after a few absentminded sweeps. Rue handed her the cup, picked up the comb, and knelt behind her.

Surely Jameth had proved herself over and over again during this last year, the cadet thought, running the tines through a swathe of heavy, ebon silk. The time was long past when Rue saw anything strange in the presence of a Highborn lady at Tentir. Most cadets felt the same way. It was the randon—some of them, at least—who couldn't see past bloodlines to genuine if rather strange ability.

True, one day of tests remained, but Jameth would need at least two whites just to break even, and what hope was there of that? Rue herself had as yet earned neither white nor black, but that was common among the average Kendar. If it occurred to her that the future of her ten might depend on their commander's fate, she pushed it to the back of her mind.

Jameth stiffened.

"Sorry," muttered Rue, struggling with a snarl.

"There, in the fire. Rue, fish that cinder out for me. No, that one."

It was hard to see which she meant, so Rue raked half of them out onto the hearth. Jameth picked one up.

"Damn," she said. "Mother Ragga just won't let me forget."

Rue peered at the small, black knob veined in red that Jameth juggled from one gloved hand to the other.

"What is it, lady?"

Jameth's smile was lopsided. "For once, not a finger bone. It's a Burnt Man's knuckle. That settles that."

"What, lady?" But Rue received no answer.

Soon after they rolled up in their blankets to sleep. When Rue woke in the morning with Jorin curled up beside her, Jameth was already gone.

CHAPTER XVIII

Summer's Eve

Spring 60

I

ONCE AGAIN, AS AT THE WINTER SOLSTICE, Jame regarded Kithorn's inner courtyard through its outer gates. This time, not snow but wild flowers blew between the flagstones, and she was mounted on Bel-tairi, having left Death's-head at the college in reserve against future need.

Otherwise, the inner square was again full of bustle and gaudy figures: the Earth Wife flouncing about with her bright, full skirts; the Falling Man rustling with black feathers; and the Eaten One squatting under his catfish cape, glowering out through gaping piscine jaws. Only the Burnt Man was absent, although the bonefire heaped in his northern corner dwarfed the Earth Wife's miniature clay lodge, the Eaten One's basin, and the Falling Man's wicker cage. Other Merikit scurried around them purifying the square and setting up torches.

It was also much like the previous Summer's Eve when she had been tricked by Hatch into fighting to become the Earth Wife's Favorite. There was the serpentine molding around the well mouth that led straight down the River Snake's throat; there, the indentation where the Snake had claimed the previous Favorite, except for his sheared-off feet. The whole, now as then, was lit by a blazing sunset that tinged all beneath with crimson shadows.

The shaman wearing the Earth Wife's skirts saw Jame and trotted out to greet her. Under a straw wig and rouged cheeks, she recognized Tungit's wizened features.

"It's about time," he said, making a grab for Bel's bridle as if to prevent her from escaping, but the Whinno-hir shied away from him. "Did you bring it?"

Jame handed him the knobby, blackened knuckle.

Tungit sighed with relief. "The last Burnt Man's bone. It was only a guess that it had come to you, though the Earth Wife did say that she had done something to bring you running." He called over a boy and gave it to him. "Quick, put this in the bonfire set beside the hanging man."

"Where is Chingetai?" Jame asked as the boy ran off.

"Placing the other two hundred and five gathered bones to change the bonfires into bonefires."

"What, all in one night?"

"Set the fires beforehand, didn't he? A week's work he made of it, all the time avoiding Noyat scouts. Well, tonight he has to run the whole circuit again, putting a bone in each fireplace, still dodging the Noyat. They'll be out in force tonight, thick as jewel-jaws on a fresh kill."

Jame remembered that once the fires were primed, each with its own cinder bone, Chingetai would play the Burnt Man and ignite them all simultaneously by jumping over the first—presumably hidden in that mound of kindling in the square's northern corner. Still, that was a lot to do in one night. She said as much again to Tungit, hoping for more information.

"Ah." He shoved back the straw wig and wiped a sweaty, wrinkled forehead with the back of his hand. "Take your questions to Gran Cyd's lodge. Maybe she has time to explain."

Jame rode on, thinking that this time both the village and Kithorn's square seemed to have their roles in tonight's ritual. Perhaps it had been the same last Summer's Eve, but if so she had never heard of it. Generally speaking, Kithorn was men's business and the village, women's.

Here was the Merikit homestead on its palisaded hill under a smoldering sky. The gates opened before her and closed behind, manned by girls from the maidens' lodge.

"Ride on, Favorite, ride on!" they called. "Gran expects you."

The wooden walk echoed hollowly under Bel's hooves. Lodge-wyves popped out of their sunken houses amid billows of savory smoke to wave as she rode by. If all went well tonight, the village would feast. If not, they might find themselves fighting for their lives.

The courtyard outside Gran Cyd's lodge was crowded with armed men and women who cleared a path for Jame, Anku calling out a greeting, echoed by her war maids. Dismounting, Jame descended into the lodge. A fire burned on a raised hearth at its northern end, illuminating bright tapestries and a wealth of rich furs melting into the shadows. Otherwise, the lodge seemed to be empty. Muffled voices came from behind a hanging in back of the Cyd's gilded judgment chair. Behind the tapestry was another short flight of stairs. Again Jame descended and ducked under a low lintel deeply carved with *imus* into the loamy shadows of the Earth Wife's lodge.

"About time," said Mother Ragga, sitting back on her haunches in a flounce of skirts. An irregular ring of small stones surrounded her in the middle of her lodge's dirt floor. Outside it stood Gran Cyd in a green gown shot with gold thread, her dark red hair spilling over white shoulders. The gentle swell of her belly made her more statuesque than usual, her presence enhanced by imminent motherhood.

"You can't go," she was saying patiently to Prid, as if she had said it too often already. "This is work for your elders."

The girl shook her tawny mane in frustration. "I'm old enough to be a war maid. Almost. Besides, Hatch is out with the men hunting the wood. Please, Gran!"

"Your cousin is older than you, however closely the two of you have been raised. Stand back, my love."

Then they saw Jame. Prid rushed to her across the stone circle, drawing a growl of warning from the Earth Wife.

"My granddam won't let me stand by my sisters. Will you?"

How like a child she was, refused by her mother, turning to her father. Jame touched the girl's bare shoulder. It felt surprisingly thin and her face, upturned, was full of something close to desperation. Something had changed since the spring equinox, but what?

"It isn't for me to say whether you go or stay," she said gently. "Prid, what's the matter?"

But the girl turned away, biting her lip, without answering. Meeting Jame's eyes, Cyd make a slight, helpless gesture.

The ground shivered. Glowing cracks opened in the floor, spelling out the Four's sigils. The square was probably similarly marked by now. Heat warped the air over each fissure. Jame slipped off the scythe-arms sheathed across her back, then her jacket, taking care where she dropped them.

"What's going on?" she asked.

The Earth Wife indicated the circle with a sweep of her plump, grubby hand. "These stones come from each of the preset bonfires. When one flips over—see, like that one!—we know that Chingetai has placed a cinder bone there and turned over the stone's mate in the firebed. Thus we track his progress."

Jame observed that the Merikit chief had already completed a third of his circuit, fast work indeed.

"How far out are the fires placed?"

"About three miles, centered on the village. A closer circle would have been more secure, but our noble leader must needs use the folds in the land to grab all he can."

"As when he tried to seize the entire Riverland."

The Earth Wife snorted. "That would never have worked, not with the fires in a line like that. He got carried away by more than the weirdingstrom. As it is, this"—here she indicated the map—"may work, unless he gets caught. The set fires are hard to find, just a few dry twigs and a pinch of kindling. Unless the Noyat actually see him place one, they aren't likely to stumble across it. And the Merikit are doing their best to harry them through the woods." She shook her starling's nest of a head, dislodging twigs and a confused caterpillar. "Still, they're spread pretty damn thin."

Another stone, the next in the progression, stirred, then tipped over.

"So the danger," said Jame, working it out, "isn't so much with the sites ahead as with the primed sites behind: the Noyat only have to snatch the bone out of one of them and run off with it."

Much the way she had done, she reflected, before the previous Summer's Eve, without being aware of the consequences.

"Snatch it and keep it," Mother Ragga agreed. "If a stone turns out of sequence, chances are that the Noyat have disturbed the site. Then we send Merikit to check. Hence that mob at the door."

It still sounded chancy to Jame. "Why aren't they all out guarding the set bonefires?"

"Think. How better to say, 'Here it is'? Besides, we haven't enough warriors to guard each and every site properly."

"Why aren't the Noyat busy with their own bonefires?"

Ragga glowered at her. "Ask a lot of questions, don't you, missy?

I've noticed that before. It's very annoying. In answer, the Noyat don't set 'em. Put their trust in the Shadows, haven't they? We Four are nothing to them unless the Burnt Man catches one of 'em over a border that he's sealed. Even then, he doesn't catch 'em all."

Jame considered the Earth Wife's stricture on her curiosity and dismissed it: how else was she to learn?

"You know, I've never really understood what it means to close the hills. I thought it just meant that you didn't welcome intruders, and that the watch-weirdlings warned you if anyone crossed into Merikit territory with iron. To come without, presumably, would mean to come in peace, as my brother did last winter. But what if the Noyat were to arrive with bows and flint-tipped arrows?"

The Earth Wife gave a snort of laughter that made the rocks shiver. "So they did last Winter's Eve. This entire past year, thanks to you and Chingetai, they could have marched across with an entire smithy strapped to their backs. When the hills are properly sealed, though, the folds in the land confuse intruders. They may cross into Merikit land, but their chances of finding its heart, the village, are slight. Meanwhile, we can hunt 'em down at our pleasure."

Jame was a little disappointed at this. She had hoped that no one could enter Merikit territory at all and so by extension penetrate through it into the Riverland. Still, she could see how a proper sealing decreased the odds of the latter.

"Look!" said Gran Cyd, pointing. A stone, flipped over once, had turned again, then another and another.

Mother Ragga swore. "They've found three bonefires. Prid..."

But the girl was already on her way up the stairs.

Gran Cyd watched her go, and sighed. "Things have not been easy for my grandchild since the spring equinox, when she failed as the Ice Maid."

"That was hardly her fault."

"Perhaps not. To my mind, she did all that was asked of her, but the refusal of the Eaten One to accept her has raised questions, not least about her chastity. Why was she found unworthy? The other girls made her so miserable that she left their lodge—which was flooding at the time anyway—and the war maids are of two minds whether to accept her into theirs. Ever. Only Hatch and Anku have been unfailingly kind."

Jame had wondered how the thwarted rite might affect her young friend. The war maids might take what lovers they pleased but apparently not so their younger sisters, if that was the problem. It would do no good to protest that the Eaten One had preferred a different Favorite, and that a Kencyr; the Merikit would still ask, "Why?" And they, like the Riverland, had suffered the consequences.

"Where has she been living?"

"With me. My daughter left her a lodge of her own, but she would be alone there and very unhappy. I don't believe that she has been back to it since her mother died in childbirth."

A moment later Prid returned with two Merikit men and Anku.

"Here, here, and here." With a stubby finger, the Earth Wife indicated sites on the map. "Go."

They left quickly. Prid looked after Anku longingly.

"Gran..."

"No."

Meanwhile, Chingetai was halfway through his circuit, presumably unaware of the disturbance behind him.

"My housebond is clever at woodcraft," said Gran Cyd, hugging herself. Jame had never before seen her show uncertainty, and found it alarming now. "Dressed in nothing but his tattoos and Burnt Man's ash, he should be hard to catch."

"Yet they must have at least seen him," said the Earth Wife. "That's three parties gone on the hunt, all of our reserve."

They waited anxiously. The fissures on the floor widened and the air above them danced with heat. Runners returned to announce that they had retrieved two of the missing three bones.

"Actually," one man admitted, "the Burning Ones got to them first. We only had to sort out the right bones."

"Where's Prid?" Jame asked suddenly.

As one, they realized that they hadn't seen the girl since her great-aunt's party had set out.

"Damnation," said Jame, grabbing her jacket and weapons.

"Be careful!" the queen called after her.

She slung on clothes and arms as she rushed up the two short flights of stairs and out into the deepening night. The space before the lodge was empty except for the very young and the very old.

"Prid?" she asked them.

"Gone with the war maids," came the answer, as if she had needed to hear it.

A child, perhaps four years old, held Bel with the mare's patient consent. Jame seized the reins and mounted.

"Run," she told the Whinno-hir, and turned her toward the outer gate. The girls there barely opened it in time to prevent horse and rider from piling into it nose first.

Outside, Bel stumbled on the steep descent, then gathered herself and leaped forward. They had only to follow the Silver, as Jame had done at the spring equinox. The Silver Steps were about a mile from the village. She hoped to catch up with Prid, but doubted that she would given the other's head start. By now it was full dark, the red faded in livid gashes from the sky, the way lit by intermittent shafts of moonlight piercing a patchwork of clouds.

Bel emerged at the meadow where on the equinox the Merikit had feasted in honor of the Eaten One. Ahead, a circle of figures at the foot of the falls played a slight form back and forth between them to bursts of stifled laughter. Cloth ripped. White skin shone.

Bel shied at a body half hidden in the deep grass. For a moment, Jame looked down into the still face of the war maid Anku, an arrow through her throat. Other bodies dimpled the meadow. They must have walked into an ambush.

By now the intruders had seen her and their circle split open. Some drew bows but their leader stopped them. Even from here, Jame could see the scar-twisted lip of the Noyat chief Nidling who had led the horse raid against Tentir and killed her cadet Anise. He held Prid with an arm twisted up behind her back, then thrust her contemptuously away to fall in a small heap at his feet.

"Well, well, well." His voice carried clearly across the meadow. "Have you come to play, little girl?"

Jame swung down from Bel. As she walked toward him, she tugged free the scythe-arms at her back and slid her hands into their leather grips. Black rage built in her, giving a tiger's lope to her stride. Here was her prey, too long denied, here her claws, two and three feet long respectively with deadly spurs behind. Cool night breathed in her face, spiked with the sharp scent of blood. Lithe and loose-limbed, she moved into her element.

The Noyat were spreading out, moving to encircle her with drawn knives. Good. She wanted them within reach. A flicker behind her. She spun and parried a thrust. Her blade slithered up her attacker's arm, splitting cloth and skin. A backhanded slash opened a second mouth below his chin and he fell away in a spray of blood, suddenly speechless. Two came at her from either side. She slid out from between them with a wind-blowing move. As they crashed together, she swept in low, hamstringing them both.

The others were drawing back. Whatever they had expected, it wasn't this cold, silent savagery.

"Well?" demanded their leader. "Get her!"

She had reached Prid and stood over her.

"All right, child?"

"Y-yes..."

Two more took their chances and fell, gutted, to her spurs. That still left seven including Nidling. Jame smiled at them. "Next?"

Six turned and fled. Dark figures tracked them through the grass, leaving smoldering trails as the Burning Ones took up their master's hunt.

Jame faced the chief, still smiling. "Alone at last," she said, hearing the purr roughening her voice, relishing it. This, after all, was what she had been born for. Damson had been right to say, "Why do I have this ability, if not to use it?"

He had a short sword, perhaps stolen in some southern raid, but he handled it clumsily, gripping the hilt with both hands. Jame might have sympathized; however, she was having too much fun. Thrust and parry, slash and retreat, steel rang. Oh, how she loved her twin blades. One needn't even get one's hands dirty.

She was backing the Noyat up toward the Silver. Behind him, water cascaded over the stepped falls, fretted now with the tumbling dark whips of blackheads. The borders were down, the infestation spreading. She slashed at his chest, opening his felt coat. Tucked into his belt, a black stick protruded like a rib sprung free. Jame snatched it.

"Prid, quick."

The girl seized the cinder bone and scrambled up the path beside the Steps. At their top, on the edge of the dark lake, she thrust her prize into a tangle of branches. Barely had she fallen back when the bonefire ignited. Above it, for a instant, in midleap, Chingetai appeared, his braids wildly swinging, his face screwed up in determination. Then he was gone. Behind him, the fire continued to flare. Out of it, limb by limb, rose the Burnt Man. His skin crackled with fiery fissures. His charred eyepits scanned the meadow.

"YOU."

Jame fought to stand still, repelled as she was by his hot, stinking breath. Prid shrank back against her as her own anger sputtered and died. Such rage hardly seemed a match for the figure now drawing itself up out of the flames. Obviously, he remembered her role in the holocaust of the winter solstice.

Then his head turned, creaking, toward the Noyat who was backing away with open mouth and goggling eyes. The northern tribe didn't believe in the Four. Had their chief thought that such a creature was a tale fit only to scare children?

"Ha-ROOM," said the Burnt Man, spraying him with flaming cinders. Some nestled in the folds of his clothing and began to smoke against his bare skin.

He didn't know where to turn. The Merikit land had closed, leaving him adrift and tottering on the riverbank. Behind him, the water seethed obscenely with blackheads. His foot slipped, and he fell in. Serpentine forms swarmed over him, nuzzling, biting, burrowing. His clothes shredded under the assault. Round holes appeared in his pale skin and leaked red around the thrashing black bodies as they bore into him.

Prid gagged. Jame held her, the girl's face against her shoulder, but she herself watched steadily as the blackheads claimed Anise's blood-price.

The roiling water surged backward up the falls. A great, gray, bewhiskered head had surfaced at their foot.

"BLOOP," said the monster catfish.

In its gaping, oval mouth behind the serrated teeth lay two figures, blissfully entwined, paying no attention to anything but each other.

"Drie!" Jame called. "Drive them back!"

The giant mouth closed, fringed with shredded blackheads, and the fish surged forward. Blackheads fled it, squirming up the Steps, taking with them the tattered remains of the Noyat. To the last, until they dumped him over the upper lip of the falls into the seething lake, his eyes were fixed in horror on Jame.

The Eaten One sank in a swirl of clear water.

"Hoom-ha," said the Burnt Man, folding himself into the dying fire, and squatting there with his knees jutting high over his charred lump of a head.

Looking past Jame, Prid gave a little shriek.

Jame turned, and there was Vant, smiling down at her. His

clothes fluttered in blackened scraps. The skin on his face seemed to come and go, charring in patches, eaten down to the bone in others, re-forming over all in an ever-changing map of devastation.

"What are you doing here?" Jame asked him, resisting the urge to back away.

His smile widened. Incandescence rimmed the edges of his teeth from the banked fire deep in his throat. She had forgotten that he was so tall and broad.

"You asked me that before, in the lilac grove." He driveled fire and impatiently wiped his mouth as if plagued with spittle. "Where else should I be, when we have unfinished business?"

"I mean, why here, with the Burning Ones?"

"Ah. In the pit at Tentir where you left me, I sensed that there were others like myself, so I went to them and they accepted me as their leader."

He seemed pleased with himself. Finally, someone had recognized his qualities.

Jame became aware of the Noyat plunging about the meadow, unable to tell from moment to moment in which direction they went as the closing of the hills played havoc with them. On their trails crept the Burning Ones, leaving behind smoldering tracks. Some hillmen doubled back and were caught. Their screams and the sizzle of their flesh rose above thrashing screens of grass. Others would probably escape, for their hunters crawled painfully on the stubs of limbs attached to wasted torsos. Gran Cyd had said that they needed the winter to sleep, but Vant hadn't allowed that. Driven by his own need, he still hadn't learned that to lead was also to be responsible for one's followers as well as for their actions. Honor's Paradox, it seemed, had many facets, all of them sharp-edged.

Jame was also very aware—more so, apparently, than her former five-commander—of the Burnt Man crouching on the ridge above them. Vant had arrived at the solstice just as the master of fire had laid himself in the earth for the winter. A vacuum had formed and Vant had stepped into it. He no more believed in the Four than had Nidling of the Noyat, nor did he see what lurked over him with head cocked as if puzzling over this miniature usurper.

Clutching Jame's shoulder, Prid whispered in her ear.

"What does the little savage say?" Vant asked.

"That you're dead."

He laughed, which set him to a harsh, racking cough. "Now, is that likely? I walk, I talk, I think."

"So do some haunts. Look at your hands."

As with his face, flesh came and went there over a lattice of white bones. He regarded the phenomenon, and dismissed it.

"True, I was badly burned after you threw me into the fire."

"Vant, I wasn't there."

His face contorted. Skin ripped and sloughed off over taut muscles. "It was your fault. Deny that if you dare."

"I do."

As she spoke, Jame realized that she truly didn't feel guilt anymore, that she never should have in the first place. What had happened to Vant wasn't fair, but it also wasn't her fault.

He jerked back with a hiss like raw meat on a hot grill. "You will admit it. Someone is to blame. If not you, then who? I will have justice, or I will have vengeance."

The night growled back at him. *"All things end, light, hope, and life. Come to judgment. Come!"*

Something huge prowled the meadow's edge, a great darkness shot with fiery fissures that opened and closed as it moved. The earth trembled under its paws and the bones of fallen Noyat crunched.

Jame freed herself from Prid's clutch.

"Stay here," she told the girl, and moved to face the blind Arrin-ken. Who better to support her cause, but sweet Trinity, how dangerous even to ask.

"Lord, a judgment!" Vant cried behind her.

She and the Dark Judge circled each other. He moved out into the moonlight, seemingly as vast as the mountain range that he claimed as his domain. Heat rolled off his body. Loose strands of her hair rose, crinkled, and stank in the draft.

"Ah," he muttered and cleared his throat like boulders grinding together. *"I would gladly judge you, little nemesis, as I have so many others of your kind. What are you to us but grief and disappointment?"*

Jame gulped, her mouth dry. She had dealt with the Dark Judge before, and barely escaped with her skin. All that had saved her was his obsession with the truth.

"I could be the way to Master Gerridon and to the changer Keral who blinded you."

"So they might all have claimed."

"But this time there are three of us, all potential Tyr-ridan. Do you dare take the risk?"

"If you should prove unworthy, if..." He raked his face with lethal claws as if to wipe it clean. *"Argh, where is the stench of guilt? You should reek of it."*

"Sorry," said Jame. "Not this time."

"You!" The great head swung toward Vant. *"Judgment you have demanded. Receive it you shall. Who threw you into the fire?"*

"She did!"

"Liar."

Jame backed away as the Blind Judge prowled past her, closer to Vant. Prid gripped her arm. The Burning Ones crept past toward the hunched figure on the ridge.

The Arrin-ken indicated Jame with a sideways sweep of his massive head. *"I know this one. If she could take the blame, she would. That has confused me before. Someday I will judge her, but not for this. You, however, tried to pull your lord into the flames with you and now you have lied, yet I smell no sense of guilt on you for that."*

"It was his own fault! A lord shouldn't humiliate his followers as he did by subjecting me to that...that freak, his sister!"

"Look to your own winter's servants. See how they crawl, mewling, back to their true master, how he gathers them up one by one. Is honor only honor when it serves your purpose?"

Vant sputtered with outrage. "How dare you judge me? I am a lord's grandson, and I *will* have revenge."

He started for Jame.

The Dark Judge reared up behind him, blotting out the stars and, with one mighty blow, batted off his head. It rolled, gibbering, to Jame's feet. By reflex, she kicked it into the river where the heat within, meeting the ice-melt water, exploded the skull.

"Bloop," said the lurking catfish, and swallowed it. "Burp."

Vant's body remained on hands and knees, swaying.

"Yours," said the Arrin-ken to the Burnt Man, who nodded and gathered up one more smoldering corpse to run, silent, at his heels.

"And you."

The blind, blunt face swung toward Jame, who tried not to recoil from its fetid stench.

"Our time will come. And for the cadet Damson perhaps sooner. Be careful how you call me."

"And you, beware how you answer." The words came from deep within her Shanir nature, and she shuddered to utter them.

"Huh." The gust of his breath singed her lashes and made her eyes sting. *"You have grown, little nemesis."*

When she blinked away involuntary tears, he, the Burnt Man, and the Burning Ones were gone. A cricket sang tentatively, then another and another while the Silver Steps chuckled beside them.

"Come on," said Jame to Prid in a shaken voice. "Let's go home."

⧉ II ⧉

BEL CARRIED THEM to the Merikit village where Gran Cyd waited to enfold her half-naked granddaughter in rich sable.

Jame rode on to Kithorn. There she found the square containing sacred space nearly filled with blue smoke to the height of the torches. Vast shapes moved within the murk, shifting preposterously: the walls of the Earth Wife's lodge; the Falling Man perpetually plummeting within his wicker cage; the catfish's gigantic bewhiskered mouth out of which the Eaten One and Drie smiled at her. Largest of all, however, a bonefire blazed in the square's northern corner. Smoke billowed from it, filling the square, tinged cobalt by the torches.

Bel whickered and minced uneasily as Jame rode her slowly around the square. Where was everyone? There was the smithy in which she had been held captive the previous Summer's Eve; there, the steps up to the ruined stub of Kithorn's tower.

"Hello?" she called, if only to break the silence.

Around the southwest corner of the square, she encountered Hatch, clad in green, fiddling with something behind his back. Jame dismounted, keeping her distance.

"Prid is safe," she said. "The hills are closed. And this is entirely too much like last Summer's Eve."

A torch burst into flames beside her, one of a sequence closing the square. Bel retreated, snorting.

"Chingetai is trying to advance the midsummer rite, isn't he?"

she said to Hatch. "You and I are supposed to fight to become the Earth Wife's new Favorite, but you don't want that role and neither do I. Can you slip out of it again?"

He lunged at her, an ivy crown in his hand, and tried to plant it on her head. She blocked him with water-flowing, almost causing him to stumble into the square.

"You don't understand," he panted, collecting himself. "Who will protect Prid now?"

She feinted again, then caught him in an earth-moving maneuver that sent him sprawling. "Protect her from what?"

"She failed as the Ice Maid of the Merikit. You ruined her reputation. You owe her recognition. I could give that to her as her housebond, but I can't if I become the new Favorite."

So, although valued for their sexual potency, Favorites weren't allowed to take life-mates during their tenure. Somehow, no one had thought to tell her that.

"Would she accept you?"

"What choice does she have? The maidens have cast her out. The war maids have refused her admittance. She can't hide in her granddam's lodge forever."

Damnation. Had she saved Prid only to make her an outcast? Should everyone have to fight as hard as she herself had for a role in her own society? But wait. What place? Wasn't she about to fail Tentir?

Hatch had escaped his fate once by clapping the ivy crown on her head and once by throwing himself at his opponent's feet, just before the latter had been crushed by a lava bomb hurtled by the Burnt Man from an erupting volcano. Hatch couldn't count on such a coincidence to save him again. He probably would have thrown the fight before now if he hadn't felt compelled to explain.

"Listen," she said, maneuvering to keep out of his reach. "Whatever happens next at Tentir, I have to give up the Favorite's role. Events in the hills can't depend on me anymore. D'you really want the Burnt Man breathing down your neck?"

"Just take the crown," he urged, lunging at her again.

"Dammit," said Jame, and flung herself under it at his feet.

Chingetai, on the steps of Kithorn's stair, burst into applause.

Hatch threw the crown on the ground beside Jame and stomped on it. "She cheated!"

"Boy, you have no right to complain."

Chingetai descended and thrust over a torch, which hit the next in line and the next. Smoke billowed out of the collapsing square, causing eyes to water and lungs to seize up. Briefly, one glimpsed the expanse of sacred space within, figured with the burning sigils of the Four like so many incandescent, heat-warped crevasses. Then all blurred. Out of the haze shuffled the Earth Wife.

Shamans passed behind her, dragging a goat. At the well's lip, they hoisted it up and over. The animal's terrified bleat echoed up the shaft all the way down. Then, briefly, the earth quivered. No need this time for any other scapegoat to feed the Snake.

"Dear son," Ragga said, grabbing Hatch by the arm. He tried to wrench free, but could as easily have shifted Rathillien on its axis. "I present you to your father."

This was called "fooling death." The Burnt Man was supposed to accept his mate's new lover and favorite as his son, which didn't say much about his powers of perception.

"My son," he echoed in an earth-shaking rumble. Both he and a looming black figure shot with red stood there, overlapping.

Their heads turned toward Jame. *"My fool."*

"All right," she said, coughing. "You needn't rub it in."

Chingetai shook himself, shedding a black cloud of ash.

"Ah, what was I saying? My grandson-in-law."

Jame felt her mouth drop open. "What?"

"Now that your duty to the Earth Wife has ended, it's time that you settled down, and I have just the right lodge-wyf for you."

The Earth Wife seized Jame and hustled her through the dispersing haze with Chingetai on their heels. On the other side, they found themselves in the village before the communal underground hall. Chingetai seized an astonished Prid and thrust her forward.

"Granddaughter, behold your new housebond!"

A great shout welcomed their appearence within the lodge. Row upon descending concentric row of faces turned up toward them, mead cups raised. All were women. At the door men fought, not very hard, to rescue the groom, but were driven back with showers of food on which to make their dinner. Jame and Prid were seated side by side, half stunned by the noise, with no idea what to say to each other.

"Bitter honey and sweet!" cried the women, raising their mugs. "Roast rabbit for a fruitful union!"

"No need to worry about that." One of the women carrying

Jame's putative children stood up, sporting her round belly, followed by the rest. All looked well pleased with themselves as the hall rang with shouts of approval.

One hand on her own stomach, Gran Cyd saluted Jame. "To the Favorite's success!"

"What?" asked Prid, seeing Jame's expression.

"I'm not ready to be a father."

Cyd gestured for her to rise and, when she did, rapped her smartly with a stick once on each shoulder, then sharply on the head.

"Ouch," said Jame, as the crowd roared congratulations. "What was that for?"

"To seal the contract and to remind you that your new wyf is allowed to beat you only three times, with no larger a stick than this. If she does more than that, or if you complain to me more than thrice, the marriage is void."

Jame caught Prid's glance. They both looked hastily away, blushing. Jame drank deep, for something to do. She had once sworn never again to get drunk, but surely this was an exception. Her head began to swim.

At last the feast came to an end and they were led, with much discordant song and shouted advice, to the mouth of a lodge, down which they were thrust. Jame lost her footing on the stair and sprawled, cursing, at its foot. Finally, the racket above withdrew.

Jame looked about her, her ears still ringing. A fire had been set on the raised hearth and candles surrounded the better furnished of the two sleeping ledges. Otherwise, the lodge appeared to be long deserted, with dust thick around its edges and the musty smell of old tapestries. At the far end of the chamber hulked the spidery ruins of a large loom.

"Your mother's?" she asked Prid.

"Yes." The girl was shivering despite the warmth, thin arms wrapped around her. "I used to sit under it and watch the shuttle fly back and forth. My mother was the best weaver in the village. Gran's walls are hung with her work. I haven't been here since she died. It smells like, it smells..."

Her teeth chattered together.

"That was a long time ago," said Jame, shaking her head to clear it. "I smell only history."

Prid, roused, glared at her. "You don't understand. That was where she lay. Alive. Dead. There was so much blood. I touched my baby brother's fingers. So perfect. So still."

"Clean deaths, then. Natural. My mother..."

"Yes?"

"She imploded, rather than touch me. I think she meant it for the best."

"Oh."

Jame gave her a wolf's feral grin, all teeth. "You see, there are worse things, and more outlandish. Beware, if you take me as a model."

Prid gulped. "I wanted to be a war maid like great-aunt Anku, but her way has also led to death."

"In the end, all things do. Better to ask how to live. What will you do now, Prid?"

The girl gave a shaky laugh. "Keep lodge for you, apparently, and weave, if I can remember how, and try to be happy."

"I'm not going to be here often. You could divorce me. Here's a log, if you'd like to beat me over the head. I promise to complain loud and long."

Prid shook her tawny mane. "I have no place else to go, except back to Gran Cyd, and I'm too old now for that. Married to you, I at least have the status of a lodge-wyf. Oh, but to live here alone...!"

Clinkers rattled down the smoke hole, followed by Hatch, who narrowly missed landing in the fire.

"You could have used the door," said Jame.

The next moment he had barreled into her. She fell backward between the hearth and the bed, barely able in that confined space to raise her arms against his flailing fists. One caught her agonizingly in the eye. She countered with an elbow to his mouth that split his lip. Prid was shouting at them. Jame got a foot into Hatch's groin and hoisted him sideways. He rolled into the fireplace on his back amid a fountain of sparks, some of which settled in his clothes and began to smolder there. Oblivious, he scrambled free and threw himself at her again. Candles flew.

Prid dumped a bucket of water over them both.

They separated, panting, to opposite sides of the lodge.

"What in Perimal's name..." gasped Jame.

"You monster!" he spat at her.

"Both of you, shut up!"

They looked at Prid in surprise. She let the bucket fall and burst into tears.

"All right," said Jame, dropping onto the opposite ledge. Hatch hadn't put out her eye, she decided, fingering it gingerly, but given how her head throbbed it was hard to tell. "I assume there's some reason why you just tried to kill me."

Hatch had gathered Prid in his arms and glared at Jame over the girl's bent head.

"Earth Wife's Favorite, father of Gran's unborn child, I don't care what sort of a freak you are. You shan't have her!"

"You," said Jame profoundly, "are confused—not that it isn't a confusing situation. Housebond I may be, but I'm not about to do anything to Prid that she doesn't want...or maybe that she does. G'ah, I hate being drunk!"

He glared at her. "Well then, what are we going to do?"

"I don't bloody know." She tried to rise and fell back with a reeling head. "Tonight, or rather tomorrow, I have to ride back to Tentir. In the meantime, the two of you figure it out."

With that, she rolled herself up in the musty blanket and fell asleep.

CHAPTER XIX
Challenge

Summer 1

I

JAME WOKE LATE, with a vicious hangover.

Someone was bustling about the lodge, singing. A billow of dust made Jame sneeze. She rolled over, blurry-eyed, to observe Prid bundling up old tapestries, assisted by Hatch. They had already made fair inroads on the dwelling's dank clutter, most of which they apparently had disposed of by shoving it up the stair into the open. Cheerful voices above indicated that they had help.

"Oh, you're awake!" Prid exclaimed, seeing her move.

"Not so loud. G'ah, what did they put into that wretched mead anyway?"

"Everything left over from the winter, probably. Beer, ale, burnt water, fermented fish piss . . . People have been stopping by all morning to say what fun they had, as good as when Ma married Da, from all accounts. Here."

She handed Jame a beaker of water, which the latter gratefully drained, splashing the last of it on her flushed face. She had been dreaming. There was someplace she was supposed to be, some duty she had neglected to fulfill. A nightmare sense of failure rose like bile in her throat, unless that *was* bile.

She observed Hatch by the loom, carefully removing rotten threads and setting its wooden limbs to rights.

"We decided," Prid announced. "Hatch may have new duties in the village as the Earth Wife's Favorite, but he's going to stay here with me. Now that I'm a lodge-wyf, no one will object—unless you do."

It seemed like a sensible arrangement to Jame, and she said so. Prid would have company and Hatch, when she was ready, would have Prid.

Then she remembered what she had forgotten: Gorbel's challenge. "I have to go."

The blanket had twisted around her legs. When she tried to rise, she fell headfirst between the sleeping ledge and the raised hearth. Prid and Hatch disentangled her. She gave them each a distracted kiss, grabbed her gear, and scrambled up into a bright morning.

Merikit women were sorting the offerings of the lodge—what to keep, what to discard, and what to burn immediately. Their good-natured greetings followed Jame down the boardwalk, mixed with bawdy jibes from the men about the supposed pleasures of her wedding night. Hopefully no one understood the answers that she snarled back at them in High Kens, a language rich in courtly invective.

Bel waited for her outside the gate. She had brought the mare in part because the Whinno-hir was easier to ride but mostly because she knew the Riverland better than the rathorn did. Still, the sun marched steadily across the sky as they traveled southward by the folds in the land until at last they arrived in the rocks west of Tentir.

"It's about time," the horse-master said, rising from his seat on a low boulder that might have doubled for his bald head. "Gorbel and his friends have been waiting for you in the training square since just after breakfast, in full armor, getting crosser by the minute. The Commandant has given you until sunset to appear."

Both looked up at the descending sun, now less than half an hour above the western peaks.

Death's-head ambled up wearing his usual riding tack as Jame scrambled into her light leather armor. For arms, she took a buckler and, reluctantly, a short sword, scythe-arms being a risky proposition in mounted combat if one didn't want inadvertently to lop off ears or tails.

The horse-master surveyed her as she straightened her oversized helmet. Really, when she had time (if she had time), she needed to commission something better fitting.

"Ready?"

"As I'll ever be."

He gave her a leg up onto the rathorn's back and stood clear.

Picking up on her nerves, if not on her mood, the colt capered in place, slashing with his horns. Then he plunged forward with Jame hanging on for dear life.

Their grand dash faltered at the hall door. The portals to the great hall stood open, but Death's-head hesitated to enter where he had never been before, nor yet perhaps under any manmade roof. Jame coaxed him over the threshold.

The dark hall echoed like a seashell with the clamor of the cadets outside. A few voices picked up a chant, then more and more:

"...30, 29, 28, 27..."

They were timing the sun's descent.

The rathorn's ears twitched, but not at the ringing count. Darkness moved and became the Commandant, standing between them and the farther door.

"Well, Lordan."

"Well, Ran."

Would he stop her? What would be the point of that, though, when all he need do was cause a delay?

"...21, 20, 19, 18..."

Anyway, she had already solved his problem by failing to earn enough white pebbles to graduate from the college. Could he also mean to humiliate her by denying her this challenge? Certainly, his lord would love him for it.

"I thought you would come up with something, but this"—he indicated the rathorn—"rather exceeds my expectations. Can you control him?"

"After a fashion, Ran."

"...10, 9, 8..."

"Well then, let's see how you fare."

He turned and pulled open the door. A shaft of brilliant sunlight, the day's last, lanced through into the hall. Jame nudged the rathorn forward as if into the mouth of a furnace, out the door, into the square.

"...4, 3, 2..."

The voices petered out. Struck blind, Jame could see nothing. Then the sun set. Blinking dazzled eyes, at first she saw only black and crimson, then bit by bit what appeared to be the entire college lining the rail and the windows above, staring back at her. The eight armed Caineron riders waiting in the square seemed almost incidental.

The rathorn's jaw dropped. Overwhelmed, he tried to back up, but the Commandant had closed the door behind him. His rump hit it with a hollow boom and he lunged forward, snorting, startled.

"It's just a white horse in armor," someone protested, uncertainly.

"Are you daft? Look at all that ivory!"

"It can't be."

"It is!"

Someone else cheered. It sounded like Rue.

The noise spread, thunderous, and Death's-head brandished his horns at it. His defiant scream soared about the tumult, cutting it short.

In the startled silence that followed, Gorbel began to clap, slowly, in the heavy, measured way with which he had greeted her win at the Senethar so many months ago. The crowd picked up the beat.

The colt shook his head and moved forward along the rail. His hooves struck hard earth in time to the clapping. It picked up and he began to prance. The riders turned with him, their horses' eyes rolling white as they caught the rathorn's scent. Cadets fell back from the rail as he passed in a shimmer of white silk and ivory.

"Show-off," Jame muttered at him.

They regained their original position in front of the hall door and swung about to face their opponents.

Silence fell again, except for Death's-head pawing the ground.

"Have you words for me?" Jame asked Gorbel, following the formal pattern.

"I challenge you as the Knorth Lordan to prove your worthiness of that title."

"I accept your challenge."

Death's-head snorted. *Enough.* He laid back his ears and charged, nearly leaving Jame astride thin air.

One of the horses, a piebald, turned and bolted with a squeal, the rathorn roaring on his heels. Confronted with the rail, he vaulted over it into the packed ranks of cadets, there shedding his rider. Then, confused, he plunged through the front door into the Caineron barracks. Cadets who had lined the windows to watch jumped out of them. Crashes and shouts came from within.

The colt was already swerving away. Jame swayed perilously off balance in the saddle, nearly over the rail herself with all her weight on the outer stirrup, before regaining her seat.

They were charging back toward the riders still clustered in the middle of the square. This time three broke ranks and ran, screaming, before them. Death's-head thundered in pursuit. The Caineron cadets sawed on their reins, turning their mounts' foaming muzzles to the sky, but nothing would stop them. So many would smash the entire rail flat, never mind the cadets who lined it.

"Hall, there. Hall!" Jame shouted, echoed by Gorbel.

The door opened. Two horses bolted through, carrying their hapless riders with them, but the third was shouldered aside and crashed through the barrier near the Brandan quarters, into the passageway that led to the southern door. His rider, scraped off against the wall, lay blinking at his departure.

It had taken the rathorn less than two minutes to clear the square of his most skittish opponents. That left Gorbel himself, his five-commander Obidin, Higbert, and Fash.

At a hoarse cry from their leader, the four charged. Death's-head leaped to meet them, swerving at the last moment to pass between Fash and Higbert. On her left, Fash dealt Jame's buckler a blow that drove it back to her shoulder. On her right, Higbert hacked at her sword and sent it flying. Simultaneously, the colt slashed at Higbert's girth. Then they were past. Higbert slowly toppled over, saddle and all. Fash screened him as he dashed to the rail and dived over it. His horse plunged out of the square through the hall door.

That ended the second round, Jame thought, as the rathorn trotted around the perimeter, seeking his next prey. So far, their sheer number had prevented Gorbel or Obidin from striking a blow. Nonetheless, the loss of her sword was almost a relief as it allowed her to grip the colt's roached-up mane for balance. She had already grasped that her only chance for survival was to stay on the rathorn, and that she could do precious little to direct him now that his blood was up.

They would try to catch her between them again—or would they?

Here came Fash, gashing his mount's sides with his spurs, riding high in the saddle with sword upraised. The raw hate in his face struck her like a physical blow. She didn't like the man, but neither did she loathe him as much as he apparently did her.

Vant's features flashed before her, just before the Dark Judge had ripped off his head. He too had seen her as an abomination and as a personal insult. What about her inspired such malice? Everything she did seemed to slap someone in the face.

Philosophize later, she thought, gripping the colt's mane.

Fash's sword rang on her buckler, numbing her arm to the shoulder. Their mounts wheeled, head to tail, as he battered down her defense. Just before it fell, the rathorn rammed his nasal tusk into the horse's belly and wrenched up, disemboweling him. The animal squealed, stumbled over the descending loops of his own intestines, and went down. Fash sprang clear. Death's-head knocked him off his feet, then went after him as he rolled on the ground as if after a snake, pounce and strike, pounce and strike.

The crowd roared.

There was blood in the rathorn's mouth. Jame could taste it and the savagery that it unleashed in his veins, in her own. Ah, the intoxication of one's strength, of one's ability to kill and kill and kill...

Beast of madness, here is your heart.

In that jolting ride, Jame had bitten her own tongue, her blood mixing with the phantom taste of his. She fought to free her mind of that red haze, of that raging blood lust.

Obidin unintentionally aided her by riding up behind. Death's-head kicked the five-commander's mount in the face, dropping him. Fash used the momentary distraction to gather himself and leap, trying to pull her out of the saddle. She dealt him a stunning blow with her buckler, He fell away and rolled under the rail to safety.

That left only Gorbel.

Forewarned, the Caineron had chosen a steady gray charger well used to combat, but the smell of blood had roused him too. Both stallions reared up, striking out with their fore hooves. The gray's iron-shod foot opened a gash on the rathorn's unarmored shoulder. Gorbel clouted his mount on the head to bring him down. The beasts circled each other, ears back, snapping, while Gorbel smashed at Jame shield to shield. He got the edge of his buckler hooked under hers and wrenched it away. For a moment she stared into his glowering, sweat-streaked face, seeing his raised sword out of the corner of her eye.

In the audience, Damson leaned forward over the rail.

"Damson, *no!*"

The gray horse shied away from the power in Jame's voice, throwing Gorbel off balance.

The colt's head snaked out and he sank his fangs into the gray's throat. The gray squealed and tried to tear free, but he was caught as in a lion's grip and his blood poured out. The rathorn jammed his shoulder into the horse, driving him first to his knees, then to the ground. Gorbel went down with him and was pinned.

The horse rolled frantically, as if trying to escape its own death. Gorbel gave a grunt that, for anyone else, would have been a scream. His leg audibly snapped. The dying horse continued to thrash.

Jame swung down from Death's-head and darted to the Caineron's side.

"Help me!" she called over her shoulder as she tried to pull him free.

"I think not," said Fash, putting his knife to her throat. Then he stiffened and crumpled as a sword's pommel clipped him over the ear.

"I think so," said Obidin, sheathing his blade.

Between them, they dragged Gorbel clear, trailing his mangled leg. Ragged bone had ripped through his trousers at the thigh. Blood spurted. Obidin wrenched off his scarf to use as a tourniquet. It was too short. Jame gave him her own.

"Here, now."

The college surgeon pushed them aside and applied pressure to the torn femoral artery.

Death's-head was watching them curiously, his blood lust forgotten. The horse-master gripped his bridle and tugged him away. They left by the hall door, the rathorn still craning to look back over his shoulder.

Gorbel was carried out and so was the still-unconscious Fash.

Jame turned to find herself looking up into the Commandant's dark face.

"I lost my weapon, Ran," she said, stupidly.

He smiled. "No, you didn't, although one can hardly say that you kept it very well under control."

He looked around at the dead horses and at Obidin's, which was staggering to its feet with what appeared to be a broken jaw, at the shattered rail and at the Caineron quarters which still rang with shouts and frantic hooves. The piebald had apparently achieved the second floor and was refusing to come down.

"The college reduced to rubble..." murmured the Commandant.

"And me standing in the middle of it, looking apologetic. I know. Sorry, Ran."

He brushed this off. "It could be worse. At least the buildings are intact. Mostly. Ah, quite a day it's been. I have something for you, Lordan."

He dipped long fingers into a leather sack and drew out a white pebble.

"This is for Bear."

And another. "This is for the Winter War."

And another. "This is for not utterly destroying Tentir, although you did try your best."

Jame stared at the three white stones in her cupped hands. That made it five to four. She had passed the college.

"Commandant, senethari, are you sure?"

"If you mean, how will my lord like it, let me worry about that. Now, wave to your friends like a good child."

Jame gave a whoop of laughter and brandished the pebbles in her fist over her head. The Knorth cadets realized first what they were and what they meant. In the front row, Rue bounced up and down cheering. Timmon started off the Ardeth, Obidin the Caineron, followed by the other houses one by one including even a weak chorus from the Randir until the square rang with jubilant cries.

II

WHILE THE SQUARE WAS BEING CLEARED, cleaned, and prepared for the evening's feast, the Commandant visited the infirmary to make sure that his lord's heir would recover.

"Yes," the surgeon reported, "although only thanks to the quick action of bystanders."

Then he retired to his quarters.

Someone stood in the shadows by the balcony of the Map Room, looking down. A white shape at his feet raised its head and greeted the Commandant with the brief wave of a tail.

"You saw, my lord?"

"The whole bloody shambles."

"Granted, it got messy, but at eight to one the lordan needed an edge."

The other gave a sharp laugh. "How many edges does a rathorn have? Where did she get that creature and why wasn't I told about it?"

"No one knew, or perhaps only a few. I see that I must speak to my horse-master. Gorbel also didn't seem surprised."

"She would tell a Caineron but not me?"

"They have the Tentir bond, which is not a bad thing. I am pleased with most of my cadets this season. You should be too."

The Highlord moved out of the shadows. "I still mean to do it, Sheth. For my own peace of mind. Do you advise me not to?"

"I would say that it is unnecessary for her, but perhaps vital for you. She is your heir. You must learn to trust her."

"This, from a Caineron?"

"This, from the Commandant of Tentir."

He watched Torisen pace restlessly. Truly, he had the dark, Knorth glamour that made him a presence even in the room's growing dusk. Sometimes it was hard to remember that, despite the white in his hair, he was still a very young man—for the long-lived Highborn, not much older than the cadets setting up tables in the square below. Ah, if only Tentir had had his training, not that the randon of the Southern Host had done badly with him. But there was no bond.

"As far as the randon are concerned, she has proved herself. If you challenge her again, openly, it will seem that you trust neither her nor us."

Torisen ran a scarred hand through his hair. "It isn't that, exactly. Before today, I had only seen her fight once, at the High Council presentation, and that was as odd a combat in its way as this one. Kothifir is dangerous, especially now. Should I risk half of my surviving blood-kin there?"

The Commandant frowned. Half?

"Very well," he said, after a pause. "Test her you shall. Before dinner. Give her at least until then to enjoy her victory."

III

THE KNORTH BARRACKS WERE CHAOS. Only now did Jame realize how much her absence the previous day had disconcerted everyone. Some really must have thought that her nerve had failed and that she had run away.

"You see?" crowed Dar. "You *see?*"

Jame met Brier Iron-thorn's jade green eyes over the throng. The Kendar gave her a small, stiff nod. Perhaps, finally, she had proved herself to the critic whose opinion she valued the most, short of the Commandant's.

Short even of Torisen's?

How would her brother react to this success for which he had never planned?

Ah, but it was sweet to accept the congratulations of her peers, to know that they accepted her at last. She had never before had a real home. Now they were welcoming her into one bound not by walls but by fellowship. However, it was still hers to lose. Next came Kothifir the Cruel, an unknown entity, but she shoved aside this doubt. Whatever happened, they would face it together, united in their strength as much as in their ignorance.

She saw Damson standing quietly nearby with a little smirk on her round face.

"You were going to make the gray stumble," Jame said, in sudden enlightenment.

Damson shrugged. "I couldn't get into the Caineron's mind for some reason, but his horse...Was that wrong?"

How could Jame say "No" when that moment off balance had probably saved her life? Still, "In the hills, the Dark Judge mentioned you by name. He knows what you did to Vant and will be watching you now. Be careful."

"Oh," said Damson, for the first time looking alarmed.

"I should hope so," said Jame.

Rue pushed through the crowd carrying something. White cloth shimmered in her arms, every inch of it patterned with swirls of cream-colored embroidery. It was a coat, a beautiful coat.

"See?" said Rue. "Treasure from the Wastes it may be, but I figured that enough stitches would anchor it in this world. Everyone added their own with silk thread unraveled from one of your uncle's shirts. Trust me: we washed it half to pieces first. It's like our house banner, but special to our class."

Jame hesitated to don it; her clothes were splashed with the blood of both Gorbel and his charger.

"Take 'em off," Rue urged impatiently.

She stripped off her jacket and shirt. The coat slid over her bare skin like cool water and molded itself to her body.

"Oh . . . !" breathed the cadets.

"To the Lordan of Ivory!" someone called from the back of the crowd, and all cried, "Hurrah, hurrah!"

It was too much.

Jame broke free and fled to her quarters where Jorin flopped over to greet her with sleepy affection.

"Look, just look!"

She ran her hands over the glimmering sleeves, feeling the texture of silken stitches under her fingertips. Did the Kendar also use knot codes? She felt instinctively that they did, and that they had worked their own subtle magic into this cloth. So much work, done by so many, all on the sly. She hadn't even thought about the fabric that Rue had bought from the Southron traders since the day of the egging. Memory rose of the previous Lordan's Coat, so gorgeous but so foul, infused with Greshan's black soul. This was the heirloom now, and she the last lordan, bearing the record of her school days on her back for all to read who could.

Nothing could have pleased her more.

Calmer now, she slipped out of the precious coat and carefully folded it on her pallet. Rue had laid out clean clothes. She put them on, crept down the stair and, avoiding the still-packed common room, made for the infirmary in Old Tentir.

Gorbel lay on one of the cots, his leg heavily bandaged and splinted. He was very pale with a dark bristle of beard and black strands of hair straggling over his bulbous forehead. Jame remembered that he had waited for her all day in the hot square. Now he waited still, moving restlessly, his chapped lips parting with an audible smack. She offered him water in a ceramic cup. He drank avidly.

"Good," he muttered, his eyes still closed.

"More?"

He blinked at her. "Yes."

She poured him another cupful and supported his head as he drank. His hair was greasy with sweat. He squinted at her over the cup's rim.

"I knew you'd bring that monster," he said, "and that we would be lucky to escape from it alive."

"You had a good horse."

"The best. Old Gray-leggings will be hard to replace."

"Sorry."

"Don't be. It was to the death, whatever you were told. I just never counted on horse before rider."

"You'd rather it was the other way around?"

"I could have spared that idiot Fash."

"So could we all. Now rest. You left enough blood in the square to launch a small fleet."

At the door, his voice stopped her. "I nearly killed you."

"I know. Never mind. And cheer up: here comes Timmon with a nice bunch of flowers."

The water cup shattered on the lintel over her head.

"Now, was that called for?" asked Timmon, approaching with an arm full of white daisies, some pulled up by the roots and dribbling dry soil.

Jame closed the infirmary door. "He really isn't up to teasing."

"Would I do that?"

"In a heartbeat."

"Then you take these." He thrust the flowers at her. "In token of your victory. Besides, I look silly carting them around."

"And I don't?"

"They complement your eyes. Also, the Commandant asked me to tell you to meet him in the great hall."

"Why?"

"I have no idea. And congratulations," he called after her. "That was quite a show, if rather hard on the livestock."

IV

THE COMMANDANT PACED before the empty fireplace in the great hall. Dusk filtering through high windows supplied the only light, the only sound his heels clicking and a murmur from the square outside. He had locked the doors. The hall was as secure as he could make it.

Keeping him company were the looming banners of all nine major houses. He glanced up at his lord's against the northern wall, a great, swollen collection of stitches that all but obscured its design with more to be added that evening. What would Caldane say about today's events? His heir's near death would mean far less to him than the Knorth Lordan's success. Would he carry out his threats? Sheth accepted philosophically that Caldane might, and that his own active career as a randon might end as soon as word of today's events reached Restormir. If so, then so. He had emerged from the paradox with his honor intact, a thing which, in itself, would make Lord Caineron smash anything within his reach.

The Commandant looked up at the rathorn banner hanging over the fireplace and shook his head. Oh, the Knorth. He had thought before, more than once, that they put everyone to the test whether they meant to or not. So it had proved again.

Footsteps sounded on the stair. Jameth descended, carrying a sheaf of bedraggled flowers.

"You sent for me, Ran?"

He flicked a drooping daisy with a fingertip. "Very becoming. Not I. Him."

Puzzled, she turned in the direction that he indicated, down the hall. A pale face crowned with silver-shot hair seemed to materialize out of the growing gloom, approaching.

"Tori!" she cried, first joyful, then perplexed. Sheth saw her gulp. She faced the Highlord, straightening, as if against a force of nature.

"Have you words for me, brother?"

"Sister, I challenge you as the Knorth Lordan to prove your worthiness of that title."

"Truly, Tori?"

"Truly."

"Then I accept your challenge."

She handed the flowers to the Commandant, who received them with a raised eyebrow, and started down the hall toward the Highlord. They approached like images in a mirror, lithe, loose of limb, and black clad, their house and kinship proclaimed by the fine bones of their faces and by their silver-gray eyes. Three paces apart they stopped and saluted each other, equal to equal. Then they began to circle.

At first their moves were tentative as they felt out each other's skill. Torisen flicked a fire-leaping blow at Jameth which she deflected with water-flowing. He struck again, harder and faster. She blocked and snapped back with a response that grazed his cheek. With that, the fight settled into a serious match. Her style was classic and smoothly cadenced, his rougher but no less effective, though neither as yet had landed a telling blow. Fire-leaping met water-flowing, wind-blowing channeled aside earth-moving.

Their shadows moved with them, larger than they, and the banners rippled against the walls at their touch. Each gesture extended beyond itself to sweep dust from the floor and fan the Commandant's coattails. He felt the hair prickle on the back of his neck. His Shanir sense told him that here was power, barely aroused, barely controlled. Torisen reversed suddenly with a move from Kothifir street-fighting. Jameth blocked awkwardly and stumbled back against a pillar. She only brushed the stone, but it groaned and dust shifted down from the rafters. She came back with a Kothifir counterblow that knocked the Highlord off his feet.

The Commandant watched with interest: he had heard that the Southron Brier was training the lordan, but hadn't guessed that her lessons had proceeded so far.

He was also concerned. The hall seemed to swell with the force that it contained and his ears popped. Clearly, these two should never fight each other. He put down the flowers and drew a wooden flute out of his sleeve. At what seemed like a propitious moment, he began to play.

Jameth instantly shifted to the Senetha. Torisen, not so quick to adjust, carried through with his attack and kicked her in the head. She staggered. It had been a potentially killing blow, but she didn't fall. After a moment's pause, the Commandant continued to play.

They were dancing now. Jameth stumbled through the opening moves, kept on her feet as if by some external force that defied gravity. Torisen swayed to support her, but never quite had to. They glided through the forms again mirroring each other, swoop and turn, dip and rise. Hands slid past hands, arched bodies nearly touched, flesh tingled, to pass so close. Power was building up again, this time thick and erotic. The Commandant could feel it rippling up and down his spine but still he played as if unable to stop. The floor on which they danced was dark green shot with glowing verdigris veins, the banners multiplied, now with faces that watched and smiled, lop-sided, hungry. If he could have turned, what would have been on the hearth behind him?

Squeee, squeee, squeeeee . . .

Claws flexed on stone. The shapes of long-dead Arrin-ken rose at the edge of his vision to loom over him.

"You see how they are drawn together," whispered a mocking voice in his ear. "Ah, my dark lord's sweet blood-kin. What if they should touch? Who of us would survive the union of creation and destruction? Schoolmaster, should you forbid them, or wait to see what follows?"

The Commandant wrenched the flute from his lips, tasting blood as flesh sundered from wood.

Jameth stumbled and fell. As Torisen bent over her, she spat out a tooth and groaned. "Not the same one."

"I'm sorry. I couldn't stop in time."

"'S all right. It will grow back."

The Commandant slipped the flute up his sleeve. "Highlord, are you satisfied?"

"Trinity, yes. I was a fool to doubt you, wasn't I?"

Which of them he meant wasn't clear, but one would do for both.

The Commandant wondered, though, if Torisen's fears were unjustified after all. Jameth would make a good randon, no doubt, but Kothifir would be lucky to survive her. Might not the same be said about the entire Kencyrath? What, after all, had he been nurturing in his nest at Tentir?

Child of darkness, breathed the shadows. *Lordan of light.*

But those were thoughts for a different time. Outside the hall door, he heard the cadets bringing the feast to the table amidst laughter and cheers. They had earned this day. So had Jameth. He thrust the door open and gestured them through.

"Before you leave for Kothifir," he heard the Highlord say, "we have to talk."

She threw back her head with a crow of triumphant laughter. "Finally!"

The Commandant followed them up to the high table and there presented them to the assembled cadets.

"I give you Torisen Black Lord and his sister Jameth!"

The latter stood up. "For the last time," she said in a clear, high voice, eyes locked on her brother's, "my name is not Jameth. It's Jame, short for Jamethiel. Jamethiel Priest's-bane of Knorth."

⁓⁓⁓ LEXICON ⁓⁓⁓

Addy—Shade's gilded swamp adder

Aden Smooth-face—a senior randon and Lord Ardeth's younger brother

Adiraina—the Ardeth Matriarch, beloved of Kinzi

Adric—Lord Ardeth

Anise—one of Jame's ten-command, killed by the Noyat

Anku—leader of the Merikit war maids, older sister of Gran Cyd

Argentiel—That-Which-Preserves

Arrin-ken—the third of the Three People of the Kencyrath; huge, catlike beings who act as judges

Arrin-thar—use of claws or clawed gloves in combat

Ashe—a haunt singer

Bashti—one of the ancient kingdoms of the Central Lands

Bashtiri shadow assassins—assassins who, thanks to special tattooing, are invisible and can cast their shadows

Bear—Sheth's brain-damaged elder brother, a former randon and Jame's teacher in the Arrin-thar

Beauty—a darkling wyrm

Bel-tairi—a Whinno-hir, formerly Kinzi's, now Jame's

blackheads—parasitical fish from the Silverhead

Blackie—a nickname for Torisen

Boden—Lord Brandan's heir and nephew

bonefire—a bonfire containing a Burnt Man's bone

Bran—a Brandan randon who teaches obscure weaponry

Brant—Lord Brandan of Falkirr

Brenwyr—Lord Brandan's maledight sister

Brier Iron-thorn—once a Caineron, now second in charge of Jame's ten-command

Brithany—Ardeth's gray Whinno-hir mare

Burley—the small stream that runs down beside Tentir to join the Silver River

Burning Ones—servants of the Burning Man, mostly kin-slayers

Burnt Man, the—the one of the Four who represents fire

Burr—Torisen's Kendar servant

Caldane—Lord Caineron

Cataracts, the—where the Kencyr Host and the Waster Horde met in battle

Chain of Creation—a series of parallel universes connected through threshold worlds like Rathillien

changer—one of the Master's servants, who can assume any shape

Chingetai—chief of the Merikit

Clary—a Coman ten-commander

Cloud—Sheth's warhorse

Commandant—title of the head of the randon college

Corvine—a former Knorth Oath-breaker who has become a Randir sargent

Cron—a Knorth Kendar

d'hen—a Tai-tastigon knife-fighter's coat

Da—a Merikit woman who acts as a man; housebond of Ma

Damson—one of Jame's ten-command

Dar—one of Jame's ten-command

Dari—Ardeth's son and would-be heir

Dark Judge—blind Arrin-ken obsessed with justice

Death's-head—a rathorn

Director—title of the head of Mount Alban, the current one a blind Kendar

direhounds—gaze-hounds used to run down prey

Distan—Ardeth's daughter, Pereden's consort, Timmon's mother

dreamscape—the collective dream world of the Kencyrath

Drie—an Ardeth cadet; Timmon's half-brother and former whipping boy

Dure—a Caineron cadet bound to a trock

dwar—a deep, healing sleep

Earth Wife, the—the one of the Four who represents the earth

Eaten One, the—the one of the Four who represents water

Erim—one of Jame's ten-command

Essiar—Lord Edirr, twin of Essien

Essien—Lord Edirr, twin of Essiar

Falconeer—any member of the Falconer's class

Falconer—blind teacher of those Shanir with bonds to animals

Falkirr—Lord Brandan's keep

Fall, the—when Gerridon betrayed the Kencyrath to Perimal Darkling

Falling Man, the—the one of the Four who represents air

Fash—one of Gorbel's ten-command

Four, the—Rathillien's elemental powers

Ganth Gray Lord—Jame and Torisen's father

Gari—a Coman cadet with an affinity to insects

Gen—a board game

Gerraint—Ganth's father

Gerridon, Master of Knorth—the Knorth Highlord who betrayed his people to Perimal Darkling

Ghill—Cron's young son

Ghost Walks, the—apartments where the Knorth lived at Gothregor before the Massacre

Glendar—Gerridon's younger brother, who became Highlord after the Fall

Gnasher—wolver King of the Woods

Gorbel—Caldane's son and heir

Gothregor—the Knorth keep

Gran Cyd—queen of the Merikit

Graykin—Jame's Southron, half-breed servant

Gray Lands—where the souls of the unburnt dead walk

Gray-leggings—Gorbel's warhorse

Greshan Greed-heart—Ganth's older brother; Jame and Tori's uncle

Grimly—Torisen's friend, a wolver poet

Hathir—one of the ancient kingdoms of the Central Lands

Hatch—a young Merikit

haunt—anything that has been tainted by the Haunted Lands and is therefore neither quite dead nor quite alive; usually mindless, but not in the case of Ashe

Haunted Lands, the—lands to the northwest of Rathillien undercut by Perimal Darkling

Hawthorn—a Brandan captain

Higbert—one of Gorbel's ten-command

Highborn—the first of the Three People; ruling class of the Kencyrath

Hinde—a Randir acolyte who can cause earthquakes

Holly—Hollens, Lord Danior

Holt, the—where Grimly and his wolvers live

Honor's Paradox—Where does honor lie, in obedience to one's lord or to oneself?

housebond—Merikit term for a husband

Hurl—a Coman cadet

Ice Maid—a Merikit girl offered to the Eaten One as his/her Favorite

imu—primitive image associated with the Earth Wife

Index—a scrollsman who specializes in the Merikit and on locating information

Ivory Knife, the—one of the three objects of power, whose least scratch means death

Jame—our heroine

Jameth—a nickname which she hates

Jamethiel Dream-weaver—Jame and Torisen's mother, consort of the Master

Jedrak—former Lord Jaran

Jorin—Jame's blind hunting ounce

Karnid—a resident of Urakarn

Kedan—temporary lord of the Jaran

Kenan—Lord Randir

Kencyr—generic term for any member of the Kencyrath

Kencyr Houses—[see chart]

Kencyrath—the Three People; chosen by the Three-Faced God to stop Perimal Darkling

Kendar—the second of the Three People; usually bound to a Highborn

Keral—a darkling changer

Killy—one of Jame's ten-command

Kindrie Soul-walker—a healer, cousin to Jame and Torisen

King of the Wood—the wolver who leads the wolvers of the Deep Weald

Kinzi Keen-eyed—Jame and Tori's great-grandmother

Kirien—the Jaran Lordan

Kothifir—a great city on the edge of the Southern Wastes

Krothen—current king of Kothifir

Kruin—Krothen's father

Lawful Lie, the—the singer's prerogative to stretch the truth

lodge-wyf—a Merikit woman who owns a lodge and therefore can have housebonds

lordan—a lord's heir

Ma—a Merikit lodge-wyf

Macarn—Jame's elderly Kendar friend

Mack—a mouse

maledight—a Shanir who can kill with a curse

MAJOR KENCYR HOUSES

House	Lord	Matriarch	Lordan	Keeps	Emblem
Knorth	Torisen		Jame	Gothregor	Rathorn
Caineron	Caldane	Cattila	Gorbel	Restormir	Serpent devouring its young
Ardeth	Adric	Adiraina	Timmon	Omiroth	Full moon
Jaran	Jedrak	Trishien	Kirien	Valantir	Stricker tree
Danior	Hollens	Dianthe	?	Shadow Rock	Wolf's mask, snarling
Brandan	Brant	Brenwyr	?	Falkirr	Leaping flames
Coman	Korey	Karidia	?	Kraggen	Double-edged sword
Randir	Kenan	Rawneth	?	Wilden	Fist grasping the sun
Edirr	Essien and Essiar	Yolinda	?	Kestrie	Stooping hawk

Marc—a Kendar friend of Jameth

Massacre, the—some thirty years ago, shadow assassins killed all the Knorth ladies except for Tieri; no one knows why

Master, the—Gerridon

master-ten—the cadet in charge of a barracks

Merikit—a northern hill tribe

Mick—a mouse

Mint—one of Jame's ten-command

Molocar—a type of massive, powerful hound

Mother Ragga—the Earth Wife

Mount Alban—the Scrollsmen's College

Mouse—an Edirr cadet and Falconeer

Moyden—a scrollsman who knows about the prehistory of the Southern Wastes

Mullen—a Knorth Kendar whose name Torisen forgot

Narsa—an Ardeth cadet; Timmon's lover

Nemesis—the incarnation of That-Which-Destroys

Niall—one of Jame's ten-command

Nidling—chief of the Noyat

Noyat—a northern hill tribe under the influence of Perimal Darkling

Nusair—Caldane's son, killed by a changer

Oath-breaker—a Knorth who refused to follow Ganth into exile

Obidin—Gorbel's five-commander

Odalian—a prince of Karkinaroth

Old Blood—a Shanir

Old Tentir—the fortress part of Tentir, as distinct from the cadets' barracks

ounce—a hunting cat the size of a serval

Pereden Proud-prance—Ardeth's favorite son

Perimal Darkling—an entity eating its way down the Chain of Creation from threshold world to world

pook—a strange little dog capable of tracking across the folds in the land

Prid—a Merikit girl

Quill—one of Jame's ten-command

Ran—term of respect for a randon officer

Randiroc—the exiled Randir Lordan

randon—officer class

Randon Council—nine senior randon, one from each house, who alternate as Commandant of Tentir

rathorn—an ivory-clad, horned beast rather like a cross between a horse and a dragon

Rawneth—the Randir Matriarch

Reef—Randir master-ten

Regonereth—That-Which-Destroys, the Third Face of God

River Snake—the chaos serpent which extends down the length of the River Silver's bed

Rowan—Torisen's steward

Rue—Jame's servant; one of her ten-command

Sar—title of respect for a randon sargent

scrollsman—a scholar or singer

scythe-arms—a weapon composed of two double-pointed blades of unequal length

Sene—a combination of the Senetha and the Senethar

Senetha—dance form of the Senethar

Senethar—unarmed combat composed of earth-moving, fire-leaping, wind-blowing and water-flowing

Senethari—a master or teacher

Shade—a Randir cadet, Kendar daughter of Lord Randir

Shanir—Kencyr with special powers or traits; all have at least some Highborn blood

Sheth Sharp-tongue—Caineron war-leader and current commandant of Tentir

shwupp—a subterranean scavenger that traps its prey in muddy pits

Silver Steps, the—the series of falls between the Silverhead and the River Silver

Silverhead, the—the headwater of the Silver

singer—a scrollsman or scrollswoman entitled to use the Lawful Lie

soul-image—the image that embodies each person's soul

soulscape—the collective space where all Kencyr soul-images overlap

Southern Host, the—the largest standing Kencyr army, employed by King Krothen of Kothifir

Storm—Torisen's warhorse

Tarn—a Danior cadet and Falconeer

Tentir—the randon college

Thal—a Tastigon god

Those-who-returned—Kencyr who tried to follow Ganth Gray Lord into exile, whom he drove back

Three-Faced God, the—the god of the Kencyrath, composed of
  Creation, Preservation, and Destruction
Timmon—the Ardeth Lordan
Tirandys—a darkling changer; also Jame's Senethari or teacher
Torisen Black Lord—Lord Knorth, Highlord of the Kencyrath;
  Jame's twin brother
Torvi—Tarn's Molocar
Trishien—the Jaran Matriarch
trock—an omnivorous creature that looks like a rock
Tungit—a Merikit shaman
Twizzle—Gorbel's pook
Tyr-ridan—three individuals who represent the Three Faces of God
Urakarn—a city on the eastern edge of the Southern Wastes
Vant—Jame's former five-commander and master-ten
war maid—a Merikit woman who chooses to fight and hunt like
  a man
Waster Horde—a cannibalistic mass of people who endlessly circle
  the Southern Wastes
watch wierdling—a leather-encased Merikit corpse that acts as
  a watchman
Weald, the—the greater forest, of which the Holt is part
Whinno-hir—near immortal equines, allies of the Kencyrath
White Hills, the—where Ganth battled the Seven Kings and lost
White Knife, the—the agent of an honorable death, modeled on
  the Ivory Knife
Willow—Marc's little sister
Winter War—an annual military exercise carried out within Tentir
Witch of Wilden—Rawneth
Wither—Spokesman for Kenan
wolver—werewolves or wolfmen who change at will
Women's World, the—most Highborn women belong to this
  largely secret society
wyrm—a darkling crawler, or very large creepy-crawly with a
  poisonous bite
yackcarn—big, ugly beasts; a cross between wooly mammoths
  and warthogs
Yce—Torisen's wolver pup
yondri-gon—threshold-dwellers; Kendar without a lord who take
  on temporary service with a house